Uneasily, I held the pi... light. It had been scarcely ... stones from the old leather p....., in which they had resided since they were given to me, and sent them to the local jeweler to have them set in a brooch. It had cost a pretty sum, but it seemed worth it: At night of late, when the high wind raced down from the hills into the castle, whipping about the battlements and through the window, my belongings would shake on their perches and shelves and places of storage. On those nights, I could swear I heard the opals click together in the darkness, as though they were trying to speak.

As though on cue, again the wind rose suddenly. The candle sputtered and went out.

"I have heard of drafty castles," I muttered, "but this . . ."

I could not complete the feeble sentiment, for a cold mist followed in the wake of the wind, smelling of old water and ice and cavernous gloom. Somehow it carried upon it a terrible loneliness and sadness, so that as the mist passed over me, I wanted to cry out, to moan and blubber for no reason I could name or understand.

The whole chamber tensed, as though it awaited some monstrous change.

It was then that the shapes appeared. . . .

HEROES SERIES

THE LEGEND OF HUMA
Richard A. Knaak

STORMBLADE
Nancy Varian Berberick

WEASEL'S LUCK
Michael Williams

KAZ THE MINOTAUR
Richard A. Knaak

THE GATES OF THORBARDIN
Dan Parkinson

GALEN BEKNIGHTED
Michael Williams

DragonLance® HEROES
Volume Six

GALEN BEKNIGHTED

Michael Williams

Galen Beknighted

©1990 TSR, Inc.
©2004 Wizards of the Coast, Inc.

Distributed in the United States by Holtzbrinck Publishing. Distributed in Canada by Fenn Ltd.

Distributed to the hobby, toy, and comic trade in the United States and Canada by regional distributors.

Distributed worldwide by Wizards of the Coast, Inc. and regional distributors.

Printed in the U.S.A.

Cover art by Duane O. Myers
First Printing: December 1990
Library of Congress Catalog Card Number: 2004106794

9 8 7 6 5 4 3 2 1

US ISBN: 0-7869-3400-X
UK ISBN: 0-7869-3401-8
620-96601-001-EN

U.S., CANADA,
ASIA, PACIFIC, & LATIN AMERICA
Wizards of the Coast, Inc.
P.O. Box 707
Renton, WA 98057-0707
+1-800-324-6496

EUROPEAN HEADQUARTERS
Wizards of the Coast, Belgium
T Hofveld 6d
1702 Groot-Bijgaarden
Belgium
+322 467 3360

Visit our web site at **www.wizards.com**

For my mother and father

PROLOGUE

"THERE WERE SIX OF THEM," the NAMER began, leaning to scratch the sleeping dog at his feet. Seated around him beside a hundred campfires, the People looked up expectantly. His voice floated over them, clear at even the farthest fires, drawing the listeners deep into his story.

* * * * *

There were six of them, moving silently amid the wind-tilted shades of the vallenwoods.

Even the most vigilant and experienced scouts would have been surprised to find a band of Plainsmen this far north. They were wanderers, capable of great endurance and greater journeys, but Abanasinia was their home, months south of Solamnia and the Vingaard Mountains.

In the rising night, their shoulders were slumped and their steps shuffling and slow. Above them, high to the west amid the Vingaard Mountains, dark clouds settled like ravens and lightning flickered between the peaks. Wearily the Plainsmen wrapped blankets and furs more tightly about their shoulders, as if in their bones and memories they already felt the approaching rain.

One of them, a man almost unnaturally tall, his black hair braided and dappled in shadows, motioned silently at a clearing among the trees. In unison, with a sigh scarcely audible above the rustle of wind through the leaves, the rest of the Plainsmen sat, knelt, fell over—most of them in the very spot over which they had been walking or standing.

With his comrades lying still and silent around him, the big man crouched in the center of the clearing, his hands busy at some hidden task. Suddenly light burst from between his long, slender fingers, and, setting his hands to the ground in front of him, he sat back on his heels and watched the fire, smokeless and fueled by nothing more than the air.

Its red flames rose higher, and the light spread to illumine the faces of all the company. In unison, as though they had practiced it for years, they rose with the creak of leather and rattle of beads, arranging themselves in a semicircle behind their leader, their eyes on the scarlet fire.

They inhaled, and the light rose. Exhaled, and it sank. Attuned to their breathing, the firelight pulsed and wavered, and the leader reached high upon his left arm, upon the arm that steadies the bow, where a leather band that was adorned with five black stones rested.

"Now," the big man proclaimed expectantly as the red light bathed the crags and wrinkles of his face, glittered on the beads knotted into his hair, and glowed on the dark paint encircling his eyes.

Those eyes were green. They were odd, sometimes even ominous to a brown-eyed people, but no accident of nature. To a Plainsman, there are no accidents. Those eyes had marked him from birth as a vision catcher.

"Now is the time for the going inward, for the weaving of water and wind," he continued, drawing the leather band from his arm. His company breathed a measured breath, and the red fire pulsed like a heart beating. "For the wind and the water have risen, here in these mountains, and soon the Sundered Peoples will be joined once again, as legend and prophecy swore to their joining."

"Then this is the time, Longwalker? The time we have looked for?" piped a voice from the encircling tribesmen. It was the voice of a young girl, quickly stifled by a hiss from an older man beside her. About her, the others stared at the fire, breathing in and out together.

The leader, the one they called Longwalker, nodded, the faintest hint of a smile passing over his weathered, ugly face. "This is the time, Marmot," he answered, for the girl's naming night was yet to come, and the company called her by pet names and endearments. "Or the next, or the time after that. Until the time that we look for. The Telling is nigh, scarcely a year away. The old gods will not allow the sorrow of the last Telling, when the stories were broken and the tribes unhoused."

He spread the armband on the ground in front of him, its black stones staring up into the cloudy Solamnic night. Something glimmered in the centermost stone, faint like a watchfire at a distance on a pitch-black night. Steadily, calmly, the breathing of his companions as regular as a steady, single heartbeat behind him, Longwalker looked deep into the stone, his green eyes searching.

For a moment, he saw nothing—nothing but light and dark interwoven. Then the light resolved itself into shapes, into movement. . . .

Into three pale men, moving through a rocky landscape, bearing a heavy sack.

Longwalker squinted intently into the stone for some bend in a tree branch, an odd formation of rock—for landmarks, anything to tell him where the men were headed. He knew, however, that nothing—not even the stones in the belt in front of him—would show the dark opening into which they would pass and go under. The vision of the Namer's Passage would be denied him: He had known that much for years.

The sack turned and coiled in the hands of its porters.

Something was alive in there, was wrestling against canvas and rope and the burly arms that carried it.

It was as Longwalker expected. He looked up and turned toward his companions, his eyes glittering exultantly like flames in their paint-blackened sockets.

"Yes, Marmot. This is the time."

The Plainsmen stared at their leader hopefully, intently. In an instinct as old as their wanderings, the hands of the men went toward the knives at their belts, those of the women toward their amulets and talismans.

"But there is more," Longwalker added, shifting his weight, turning back to the stones and the fire. "More we need to know."

Again the stones shimmered and deepened, until it seemed to Longwalker that they had opened and swallowed the sky. The stars and the scudding clouds raced over the smooth black surface of the gems until one of them—the smallest, at the leftmost fringe of the setting, took on fire and form as another vision rose from the heart of the stone.

A room. Neither tent nor winter lodge—no, these walls were stone, and the fire in the stone was from a fireplace.

A castle, it was. A mountainous northern building.

Longwalker thought of the walls of that room. He waited for the vision to move, to show him more.

Shields. Three of them.

The Plainsman squinted, concentrating on what the stone showed him.

Shields. On one, a red flower of light on a white cloud on a blue field. On another, a red sword against a burning yellow sun. The third was . . . unclear, the standard lost in the shadows of the room and the shadows of the stones.

Longwalker nodded in resignation. Such was the nature of the scattered stones. This time they would show him no faces. He knew that the one he looked for was male, was you: .g, was on the brink of what the northerners called the Order.

That something in that young warrior had nothing to do with order. *He* was still stirring, was deeply unsettled.

The big Plainsman lowered himself from his crouch to a seat on the hard, rocky ground. The rain around him began as a fine mist, falling more heavily as he closed his eyes and thought of the hot sun on the Plains of Dust, dry memories balancing the cold and the wetness around him.

He had yet to see the one he looked for. But now he knew that the looking had not been fruitless. He smiled and opened his eyes, watching the rain as it picked up intensity and rushed out of the foothills on the back of the wind, gathering speed as it swept west over the light-spangled plains of Solamnia, its destination as unsure as prophecy.

Chapter I

It was an evening of torches and gems in Castle di Caela.

Outside, the sentries bundled against the night wind. They stood at the walls, looking north and west toward the Vingaard Mountains, where the brush fires had started in the foothills again, as they had last night and the night before.

The fires were burning brightly, like signals of a deep unrest.

The sentries clutched the top of the walls tightly in their vigils, for the wind was rising. The maples at the foot of the walls turned silver, then dark green, then silver again as the wind rushed through them, capsizing their leaves.

But it was no ordinary summer wind, blowing balmy

and warm in the sunlight, rising cool at dusk, and settling for good as the night drew on. For the day before, in the dark of the morning, a powerful storm rushed down and east from the foothills, billowing dust and dried grass and the faint smell of night in its path, gathering speed until it reached the castle, where it lifted a guardsman neatly from his post on the battlements and hurled him into the courtyard below.

A castle charwoman, by chance looking up to the battlements, had seen the man tumble, his cloak rippling through the air like an enormous black streamer. She said that for a moment when he passed overhead, he blocked out the moonlight, and she believed that her eyes had deceived her—that he was a passing cloud and nothing more.

They found him sprawled in the red light of the moon, his open eyes as vacant as the sky above him.

None of the men there, not even the oldest, had ever seen the likes of it.

So the sentries on the battlements clutched the crenels, carried stones for ballast in the lacings of their armor, tied themselves one to another, like rock climbers.

Behind and below them, sheltered by the walls, the courtyard and the Great Hall of di Caela glittered with a safer light. Pennants and canopies rippled softly, wagons and booths lay empty until the next morning, when trade would begin again on the grounds of the bailey. Tonight was set aside for ceremony, and from the heart of the light, the music of horn and drum was rising. The closest of the sentries, at the safest posts in the shadowy courtyard of the castle, no doubt caught the sweet attar of roses on the wind as it mingled with summer spices and the deep, inviting scent of wood smoke.

All of this—spice and attar, music and light—was unusual in Castle di Caela. The new master, Sir Bayard Brightblade, Solamnic Knight of the Sword, was strict to the Measure and a former knight-errant, used to the hardships of the road. He had little love of luxury.

Nonetheless, this evening was bright, festive, and ornate, despite the dangers of the morning, the high winds, and the austere lord of the castle.

Bayard permitted these ceremonies, because not often did a new Knight join the Order.

* * * * *

A cause for celebration. Expensive though it may be, Sir Bayard Brightblade thought, as he descended by candlelight from the master chambers of the castle. Around him, a hundred metal birds sat silently on their metal perches as if they awaited a signal—an outcry, perhaps, or a change of weather—to arise into the air and migrate.

Bayard scarcely noticed them, scarcely noticed where he stepped. The young page, Raphael Juventus, a lad of singular promise and talent, slipped gracefully in front of the master, scooting aside a chair that threatened to entangle him. Bayard's mind was on the ceremony about to begin.

From below, a trumpet swelled. Bayard leaned against the marble banister, stirring dust with his gloved hand. Raphael sneezed, and a dog lying asleep on the landing below started awake at the sound. It rumbled, the fur on its back rising, and slinked back into the dusty darkness of a doorway off the landing.

Distracting, this ceremony, Bayard thought. More home foolishness, when there's mayhem abroad. There's no telling what those fires bode up in the Vingaards, much less this terrible wind. Enough of wind and fire—it's rain we need now, more than music and spices.

Drought in the second year of my governance, he thought, fitting the ceremonial gauntlets on his large hands. He resumed his descent, passing still another silenced mechanical bird, staring stupidly at him from its perch on the landing, a spring dangling from beneath its left wing.

Now Bayard stood for a moment on the white marble platform overlooking the corridor, where the last of the knights straggled into the loud and fragrant room. Raphael, elegant despite his allergies, leaned against an empty bronze perch, sniffling from his vigilance against obstacles.

Unrest on top of the drought, Bayard mused, these fires and winds at sunset. And now a change of squires. I suppose that's what I get for saving the damsel and lifting the curse.

This and nothing to do.

He continued toward the doorway, smiling. The sentries at the great double doors noticed him on the stairway and snapped to attention. One of them lost a helmet in the process. It clattered to the floor, and from its crown toppled a pair of twelve-sided Calantine dice that fell to the floor and rolled to "King's Ransom," the charmed double nines that were the winning toss in the palace's most popular game of chance.

The guard stooped, dropped his pike, and picked up the dice. Then, reaching for his weapon, he dropped the dice again.

King's Ransom once more.

The other guard, the one with the helmet and scruples, eyed his fumbling companion suspiciously as Bayard and Raphael passed.

The doors to the dining room opened. Bayard saw the glimmer of candles on the dark mahogany in the great hall. An elvish cello began an intricate southern melody, laced with ice and elegance and mourning.

Nonetheless, Sir Bayard whispered, almost aloud, it is a gaudy night. No matter the wind or the fire, the danger or the rumors of chaos in the mountains. No matter the dust and disorder and the loaded dice of sentries. Whatever happens, this night is set aside. The Lady Enid will see to the festivity.

* * * * *

Despite the rising wind at sunset and the cold wet air that rustled through the windows into the Great Hall, lifting tapestries and occasionally gutting candles, the ceremonies began as Bayard knew they would: without incident, delay, or error.

It was the better judgment of the Lady Enid, seated at the head of the table, that despite the fire and the grumbling in the countryside, there should be a time to celebrate traditions.

As her husband Bayard fretted over things he could not control, stewed over far-flung mysteries and nearby little chaoses, Enid had arranged the banquet at hand and its invitations, arranged the comfort of guests, the lighting of rooms, the polishing of the mahogany tables in the Great Hall.

Finally she had arranged herself, her long blonde hair tumbling onto her shoulders, her great-grandmother's century-old gown shimmering with unimaginable jewels—a gown the Lady Enid thought was far too showy for everyday use and, to be honest, even for ceremonial nights.

Great-Grandmother Evania's taste, she reflected, had always been atrocious.

Nonetheless, Enid was expected to wear the dress.

And the pendant. Always the pendant, because people wanted to see it.

Pleasing the people who wanted to see her finery had not come easily to Enid. Nor, for that matter, had her delight in hospitality. Bayard, unaccustomed to his role as lord of the castle, continued to behave like a knight-errant. He surrounded himself with the exotic and slightly notorious characters he had met in his traveling years. Already Enid had played hostess to three bands of dwarves, a flock of kender, who departed merrily with the di Caela family silver, and close-mouthed Que-Shu Plainsmen, who sat on the floor instead of in the chairs.

She had even hosted a centaur or two—a gray-bearded character named Archala who drank too much, somehow found his way upstairs, and, owing to a hangover and the structure of his knees, could not descend the steps in the morning. They had to lower him from the landing by ropes and pulleys, or, she feared, he might have been there forever.

Then again, even the boy to be knighted this very evening had been no model of good manners, Enid thought. Despite his somber front and his protests, his "by the gods, Bayard, I'll do better," the lad's past behavior flirted with felony, and Lady Enid believed that the straight face she saw in the halls of Castle di Caela knew far more than it was telling.

The boy's guest list was a checkered one—interesting, to be sure, but not entirely respectable. Some of them Enid knew only by legend. Most, however, she knew firsthand

and well. In some cases, all too well.

There was Sir Andrew Pathwarden, the boy's father, for starters, drowsing over there at the table, long red beard spread like a fan across the mahogany. The old fellow was fatigued and well wined after his long ride from Coastlund, still in his muddy traveling armor. A mastiff curled and snored at his feet, and though Enid did not believe that such loud and canine presence was necessary, she said nothing, unsure of how etiquette up in Coastlund might be disposed to dogs. She believed, however, that the old man, though famous for his courage, was not all that used to delicate behavior.

Alfric Pathwarden, Sir Andrew's eldest son, slouched in an equally muddy heap beside his father, red and lumpish in the candlelight. The boy scowled and rubbed his sleeve. Though by now he should be well into a knighthood of his own, Alfric had only this month become his father's squire.

It was a situation, Enid noted, very much like having your brother escort you to a dance for the simple reason that nobody else has asked you.

How old was Alfric now? Twenty-four? Twenty-five? She could not remember, but it was far beyond graceful age for squirehood. To look at the way he kept his father's armor, it would yet be a while before someone arranged a ceremony like this for the oldest Pathwarden boy.

All the more reason to send a page to Sir Andrew's quarters. Best make sure the old man was comfortable, since he had been left to his eldest son's sorry devices.

Enid's own father, Sir Robert di Caela, sat to her left. Impeccably dressed, placed tactfully away from the other guests, he swirled his wine idly in the bottom of his pewter cup. Since he had handed the governance of Castle di Caela to his son-in-law in order to "free himself for the manly pursuits" of hunting and writing his memoirs, Sir Robert no longer paid attention to much of anything that went on about him. His mornings were slept away, his afternoons were taken with grooming himself, insulting the guests, and the practice of falconry. Of an evening, most embarrassingly, he ranged forth in full dress armor, pursuing the younger and prettier of the castle maids until he would drop over from exhaustion in the hall and be carried to bed by stout courtiers who had lost at the evening's gaming.

Enid had seen the memoirs in question and could quote them in their entirety: "I was born in the house of my fathers," they went.

Meanwhile, the quills, ink, and papers, purchased in monumental volume six months before when the old man handed over control of the castle, were stacked head high on his desk, gathering webs and dust.

At least he was seldom embarrassing before sunset.

Rumor had it around the castle—and even Bayard had come to believe this—that the streak of "distraction" that ran in the di Caela family had run after Sir Robert and caught him brilliantly.

"Sooner or later, Enid," Bayard claimed of late, "your father will fancy he is some sort of reptile or amphibian. The next thing we know, we shall be calling him down from sunning on the battlements or murking around in the moat."

Enid replied that all her father was really missing was a sense of something to do—a place at the heart of the castle.

To which Bayard answered, " 'Something to do' is not always there for the taking." He would sigh or grumble then and throw his supper to the very fat dogs.

Enid fingered the pendant at her throat. Once a thing of dangerous magic in the hands of the Scorpion, now an artifact of the old di Caela curse, it had been rescued from the collapsing Scorpion's Nest high in the Pass of Chaktamir. Rescued by her father, on the gods knew what kind of impulse—perhaps as a trophy, perhaps as an heirloom, perhaps to remind him how his days were once occupied.

Gold and large and pentagonal, it had a corner for each of the ancient elements: earth, air, fire, water, and memory. The elements that the learned now tell us are no more *elemental* than grass or light or the bulging dogs under the tables.

The pendant almost killed her once, which was another story. Now, drained of its magic, it was ornamental, ceremonial, bearing no power but the power of remembrance.

Already some were forgetting that it had been magic to begin with.

Some of the Knights Enid knew by reputation only. Sir Brandon Rus was a distant cousin, a young man of twenty-two or -three. He was traveling alone on his first quest, far from his mother's encampments in the Virkhus Hills. Throughout Solamnia, Brandon had won a reputation as a hunter. If the stories were true, his arrows were said to have missed only twice in the last seven years. Once (or so it goes) the wild shot missed the deer at which the lad had aimed, only to pass neatly through an assassin lurking in the bushes behind the animal.

The other time was much earlier. Indeed, according to some stories, it never happened. Brandon himself maintained he had missed only once. Nonetheless, some stories said twice.

Looking at Sir Brandon, Enid conceded that, given her father and her distant cousin, she was hardly the one to accuse the Pathwardens of quirky family ties. Though there was nothing objectional about Sir Brandon, he seemed just a little too taken with lore. There was nothing all *that* wrong with insisting on "thees" and "thous" in the old forms of address, or on the complex series of salutes with which Solamnic Knights of old greeted one another. Nothing, that is, except that none of the other Knights saw the point in going through the whole entangled ritual, and most of the younger knights had quite forgotten when to bow, if they ever really knew in the first place.

Brandon, on the other hand, lived for the history and ceremony of the Order. In the first night of his stay at Castle di Caela, he had buried them all in amenities and protocols. The morning was not much better.

Indeed, the boy must have known every legend about every Knight, for he told Enid half of them over a long, mortally boring breakfast, droning on about Huma and Vinas Solamnus while Enid's cousin Dannelle stood behind him, poured tea, and made faces at her over his shoulder.

So he continued, bludgeoning the guests with his talk, until even Bayard was ducking into dark corridors to avoid him.

Sir Robert had finally quieted the boy by asking him if he were the new dance instructor.

It was good that her father had done this before the other guests arrived. Sir Andrew would have thrashed the boy for his simple "damned eastern prissiness."

Now Brandon sat subdued at the main table, sober and bleak despite his conversation and bright tunic and polished breastplate.

He was like a castle chaplain without religion.

He was removed as far as possible from Sir Robert di Caela (who, it was rumored, had whispered threats against the young man's life). Brandon amused himself in a long discussion of lore with Gileandos, the Pathwarden tutor— Gileandos, whom Sir Robert once called "the most thoroughly educated fool on the planet." Enid tried not to listen to what they were saying, but Gileandos had lost much of his hearing in an accident the year before, when an alembic in his room exploded too near his left ear. Both he and Brandon were rather loud. Their discussion was obscure, almost gnomish, ranging over the little-known achievements of great Solamnic Knights in the past, over the magical properties of the weapons they carried, the armor they wore, the orbs and staves and wands they found on their way.

Brandon, it seemed, had to reach back a thousand years to find a magic he believed in.

And yet the young Knight was all too ready to give credence to the fooleries of Gileandos, who had already made sizable progress with the carafe of wine placed at his right hand. Gileandos, it was said, had explained away the high winds out of the Vingaards as "a quite natural atmospheric inclemency, the release of heat into upper regions where, reacting against the icy air above the timber line, it produces the . . . urgencies that confront us now."

Enid had paid no attention to her own childhood science instruction, but she remembered enough about weather prediction—learned from the simple act of arranging her father's hunts—to know that Gileandos was an imbecile.

For it took an imbecile to try to pluck the heart from the mystery in the mountains, as though some kind of explanation, no matter how foolish it was, could shield us from unexplainable danger.

Enid knew the old story that magic is inherited—that a child is born with insight, with an ear for the language of plants or a touch that can boil water or draw down a bird from the air. She wondered if this inherited magic thinned out from one generation to the next. It would explain a lot, she thought, if each family were given a measure of enchantment that watered down or grew scarce as it passed on from father to son, uncle to nephew. Unto a time when it ceased, when it dried up, and the young no longer had visions.

Yet there was also the young man to be knighted this evening, and he promised much despite his turn toward waywardness and contrivance. There *is* vision now and then, though most of it occurs in unexpected places, sometimes among those whom the tradition-bound Solamnic Order thought it could better do without.

Of all the sober company spread about the hall, only one was not restless, only one not unraveled by time and idleness.

Or so Enid believed.

To the left of Sir Brandon sat Sir Ramiro of the Maw, Enid's beloved "Uncle" Ramiro, busy with port and pheasant and paying court to Enid's cousin Dannelle di Caela, who had other things on *her* mind, Enid was sure. For the young man whose knighthood commenced tonight had led Cousin Dannelle a terrible chase. Just when it appeared that she had his eye, his attention, his . . . fonder instincts . . . then the stories would arise again from downstairs. The scullery maid, the baker's daughter, every other female crying foul.

"Everyone" included that most distant cousin, Marigold Celeste. The youngest daughter of Sir Jarden of Kayolin, she had cut a wide and scandalous swath through her father's mountain holdings until the old man, beside himself with outrage and as generally unfit to father a daughter as any Solamnic Knight, had given her the choice of "instruction among the lowland brothers" or the swift edge of a sword.

Marigold was dissolute but not stupid. Her father's decree put her on the road to Castle di Caela at once, her bags stuffed with cosmetics and cheeses and her hair sculpted and lacquered in the form of a gable to keep off the rain. The sympathetic reception she received from the ladies of the court began to cool when she entangled herself with the first available guardsman, then ranged heroically from guard to dueling instructor to seneschal, exhausting them one by one and finally settling on a lad sturdy enough to bear the full weight of her intentions—the very lad that stood to be knighted this evening.

She sat over there, at the farthest point in the hall from the Lady Dannelle. Her yellow hair, the various arrangements of which had made her notorious throughout Solamnia, was braided tightly, knotted in a surprisingly modest bun atop her head as though she were carrying bread to market. And there was something bucolic about Marigold—the heftiness, the shoulders as broad as a man's, and yet the strange allure she had for any hapless male who floated into her undertow.

Marigold smiled and batted her eyes foolishly. By now most of the castle knew the stories. If only one of them was true, Enid maintained, then the young man had a lot of answering to do—not to mention a lot of energy and stamina.

Meantime, her poor cousin Dannelle waited.

Undaunted by the difference in their ages and by Dannelle's most obvious lack of interest, Sir Ramiro leaned his three hundred pounds flirtatiously toward the trim redheaded girl, who smiled and nodded . . .

. . . and ignored him entirely, her eyes on the double doors across the room.

So all of them are assembled, Enid thought, leaning back in her chair, her brown eyes scanning the room wearily.

All except for Brithelm, Sir Andrew's second son, who was north and west somewhere, lost in the mountains and in meditation, no doubt.

Enid remembered his dazed countenance—the shock of mousy hair scattered as though he had been struck by lightning, the red robe often worn backward, sometimes inside out.

She hoped he was above the brush fires. And below the lightning.

He probably was, knowing Brithelm. For all the wrong

reasons, and through no design of his own. Still, his absence was unfortunate. Some of his graciousness was needed here, his humor and kindness and even his foolishness.

In its idleness, the world was downright gloomy and worrisome.

Enid smiled as Bayard entered the room, as the other Knights stood in respect to the lord of Castle di Caela, as the trumpets joined the sad melody of the viola.

That is why the music and the standing and the gestures and the fine dress, she thought. To charm the world out of worry for a night.

To remind us of our purposes.

Her husband approached, sat to her right, and removed his left gauntlet to take her hand under the table. It was times like these in which she forgave the broken crockery, the dog runs in the Great Hall, the drunken dwarf she found asleep in her bathtub, his stubby arms wrapped around an enormous smoked ham.

She looked at Bayard, whose stumbling and rough manners and moments of swordplay in the midst of his visitors only proved he was right: "Something to do" is not always there for the taking.

But tonight there was something to do. It was time for the crown of the ceremony, for the boy's entrance. If all had gone according to plan and ritual, Galen Pathwarden Brightblade would be waiting outside the double doors for the sound of the drum. He would be standing there, on the threshold of manhood.

The drum began, and all heads turned to the doorway. The drum continued.

And continued.

Bayard cast a troubled look at his wife, who betrayed a hint of a smile and shook her head.

"*Now* where is he?" Bayard whispered.

"A lesson for both of us, dearest," Enid whispered back. "You cannot control the drought or the fires in the mountains. Galen is cut from the same stuff. A natural phenomenon. There is no plan or ceremony . . ."

". . . can bring him to the right place at the right time," Bayard snapped, a little loudly.

Gileandos turned toward the head of the table, his face stern with disapproval until he saw that it was the lord of the manor snapping.

A sentry's head appeared in the doorway, frowned, and shook. Something rattled loudly in his helmet.

"Almost a Solamnic Knight, but at heart and at best still a damned weasel," Bayard muttered, setting down his cup. He rose to his feet, trying his best to look perturbed, but he smiled faintly as he walked toward the still double doors. All of which Enid noticed. She stifled a laugh and signaled to the page to begin a search through the castle.

She hoped Galen would be found soon. Not for the ceremony or the Order, necessarily. Certainly not so that one more posturing and privileged young man could bluster about in new armor.

But because Galen Pathwarden rode with the promise of unruliness. "Something to do" was always the strong suit of the Weasel.

Chapter II

"AND NOW THE LAD," THE NAMER CONTINUED, TURNING
*the strand of glittering metal in his hand. "The young man
on the edge of knighthood. Around him the whole story
turns, and in him the shards and fragments of the other tales
are brought together, reassembled, and made whole. Now I
can hear him, saying . . ."*

* * * * *

They didn't have to search all that far.

Bayard found me up in my chambers, the obvious and
most sensible place to look. Tonight, after all, was the Night
of Reflections: the final, solitary soul-searching that a
Knight must undergo before they lay on the hands and give

him the sword and gauntlets of the Order.

Just three years ago, I would have used this as a chance to escape all the rites and responsibilities. I would have tunneled from sight, become absent in the unfathomed dark of the castle before Bayard lit the torch to guide him down the corridor from the Great Hall.

That was three years ago, when I was the Weasel.

Now, by the gods, I was keen set on passing for Sir Galen Pathwarden, for joining the lot of them—Father, Bayard, Sir Robert di Caela, and the others. But it must have seemed as though my natural bent and the soft life of Castle di Caela had betrayed me at the last moment.

For Bayard found me sprawled on the chamber floor beside a damaged table, surrounded by my belongings. The wind, not as fierce as it had been the night before but stormy and strong nonetheless, dove under the shuttered window and raised tapestry, blanket, and cape around me in billows, until it must have looked as though I had set sail once more on the currents of cowardice.

I swear that was not the story at all. After all, there is a long history of even the bravest men swooning and fainting and losing their balance when the visions come upon them.

I must have cut a striking figure—a young man of almost twenty years, facedown on a shattered dressing table, basin and towels and accessories littering the floor around me. Dressed only in a green tunic and a Solamnic breastplate, I am sure that I looked like some awkward creature such as a sow bug or a grub—some crusty thing whose business lay deep underground.

*　*　*　*　*

I had embarked on the Night of Reflections in all good faith. That very morning I had hastened to the di Caela treasury—the room from which old Sir Robert still mismanaged the funds of estate and holdings—and there, accompanied by two stern old geezers seated at the counting table, who must have seen the Cataclysm firsthand, I willingly gave over my earthly valuables.

"Gladly I give for the good of the Order," I began, fighting every impulse that my past could muster. "For the good of the Order, gladly I give."

I could imagine the Weasel—myself three short years ago—looking over my shoulder and gaping, his faculties lost at the prospect of surrendering all cash and all ornament.

But I was a new man, all genuine and Solamnic and noble. Three years of instruction under Bayard Brightblade had seen to that. For despite your better judgment, despite your firm convictions that your skin is there to be saved at all costs, the constant discipline of riding until you cannot sit at table, and swordsmanship until your forearms shiver when you pick up a ladle—not to mention reading nearly twenty ponderous volumes on the Solamnic Measure—tends to thin your discretion to the point that honor and duty sound good to you.

The thought occurred to me that I had passed beyond recall when I set my coins, my naming ring, and a dozen other items of value onto the table between the distinguished Sir Elazar and the equally distinguished Sir Fernando. The old knights looked at my offering skeptically. No doubt they were unaware that Bayard had been there before them, ordering me two years ago to give all but my essential belongings to the peasants in the surrounding holdings.

I was sure that Fernando, who kept almost all of his youthful bulk (though he kept it somewhat lower now), was prepared to turn me upside down and rattle me for whatever valuables I might have hidden on my person.

"This . . . this is *all?*" he asked, his gray, bushy eyebrows bunching together like mating squirrels.

"All indeed, sir, except for one trophy of squirehood and my armor," I answered. As it had for the last six months or so, the truth felt surpassingly good in my voice.

Evidently it was less comfortable in Fernando's ears.

" 'Tis just as Sir Robert warned us," he said to Sir Elazar as the two old fellows launched into discussion, as unconcerned by my presence as if I were a footstool or a slight change in the outside weather. "The Weasel here would hold back whole estates from the Order, given a place to hide them and a nodding treasurer."

"I beg your pardon, sirs, but—"

"Nobody asked you to speak, lad," Sir Elazar interrupted, calmly but sternly, sifting through my belongings with a gloved hand. "And what, pray tell, is this 'squirehood trophy' of which you speak so . . . reluctantly?"

"I had not noticed my . . . *reluctance*, as you call it, sir. The trophy is a simple brooch, set with glain opals given to me by the Scorpion himself as payment for betraying Bayard Brightblade, lord of this castle and the Knight I have served with some dignity, I believe, in the past several years."

"If such is the case, Weas—Galen, why then do you choose to keep these stones?" Elazar probed, his blue eyes flickering as they scanned my face for lies.

I knew it well, that flicker and scan. At one time or another, I had seen it on every face from my father's to the lovely Dannelle's. On Bayard himself, many times I had seen the look of mistrust. It had come with the territory, and those who complained of my bad swordsmanship and my paltry skills with the lance tended to forget that every time I had taken up weapons in the last year, I had fought both my opponent in the lists and old Weasel—the boy I was three years ago, a mixture of deceit and cowardice, and just the fellow everyone expected to see at each stage of my squirehood.

The truth was, I had become tired of their expectations.

"I keep the stones," I explained coolly, leaning against the back of a tall mahogany chair, "only for the Night of Reflections. They remind me of my suspicious past, and yet they also serve to remind me of the first time I stood my ground and did not give in to graft. I shall donate them to the Order following my knighthood ceremony.

"If the two of you, in your experience and wisdom, have decided that I am withholding yet more treasure from the Solamnic coffers, you are free to inspect my person for it, from the inside of my mouth down to my nether parts."

Of all the vows of knighthood, that of respecting one's elders has always been the hardest for me to swallow. And after my short-tempered words there in the di Caela treasury, Sir Elazar and Sir Fernando were finding the swallowing hard themselves. They both rose to their feet with the clank of metal and the rub of leather, beneath which, if you listened attentively, you could hear old knees popping. Glowering like raptors, they stared down on the squire in front of them.

I glowered back, and I wish I could say my honesty and spunk won over the two old fellows that summer morning. But that is a tale from the old romances, where the virtue of a lad shines through his humble surroundings. This, on the other hand, was Castle di Caela.

Fernando braced himself against the counting table and hissed at me, his eyes narrowed.

"We didn't want you in the Order to begin with."

I nodded, but my critics were by no means through.

"No, we didn't want you," Elazar agreed. "You'd be astounded to know how many favors Sir Bayard has called in to win you your spurs."

Actually, I was far from astounded.

That evening, left alone for the Night of Reflections, my sword and armor and knightly belongings arrayed in front of me, I mused that indeed Bayard must have called in every favor owed him, not to mention every loan or bet.

I picked up the heavy broadsword. The blade glittered as I turned it in my hand.

Bayard had certainly risked enough on my account. Risked it from the outset, when he took it upon himself to prove that the third son of a threadbare Coastlund family, more accustomed to mischief than to the Measure, could be molded into a presentable Knight. I must admit, the long-ago adventures that followed that decision seemed to prove Bayard right—the adventure in the Vingaard Mountains and up into the pass at Chaktamir, where we hunted down the Scorpion and lifted the curse from Castle di Caela.

The problem was that once adventuring was over and daily instruction begun, Bayard was dismayed to discover that most of my resources came out under sudden stress. It seemed that I had no talent for all those things a squire was supposed to do.

How often I remember that nightmare year of training . . .

"Don't hold your sword like a feather duster, Galen . . ."

"That is a shield at your arm, not a tent, Galen . . ."

"Here is what happened in the rest of the tournament, Galen, after you fell from your horse and were knocked unconscious . . ."

So it had progressed, through a series of mishaps and head injuries, until, scarcely a month ago, Bayard had taken me aside, grasped me firmly by the shoulders, and expressed his confidence that at last I would attain the knighthood I had so devoutly come to pursue.

"I don't know what to do with you, Galen," he said. "The Order of the Sword is beyond you, as you prove every time you take up arms or sit a horse. And the Order of the Rose, with its dedication to wisdom and justice, well . . ."

I nodded, wise enough at least to understand what Bayard was too polite to say.

"But there is the Order of the Crown," he pronounced, "whose primary duties are those of loyalty and obedience. Obedience is . . . the hardest thing for you. But by the gods, you are loyal to me and to the Lady Enid, to your own family, and to the *idea* of becoming a Knight, which has put you through embarrassments and humiliations the likes of which no lad should undergo."

I tried to smile bravely and cheerily. Bayard stared at me for a long, reflective moment, then shook me vigorously until my dented, oversized helmet dropped smartly on the bridge of my nose.

"Loyal you are, Weasel, and three years ago I'd not have thought you capable of it. And if someday you achieve half of what I think you're incapable of, you'll be an excellent Knight."

I blinked at the compliment.

"So keep quiet and do *nothing*," Bayard concluded, "even if you think it will improve your chances for knighthood, for the odds are that whatever you do will misfire. Leave the rest to me, and afterward to your own loyalty."

* * * * *

So I had done, and now it was the Night of Reflections. Setting the sword aside, I had picked up my helmet. Dented and pockmarked it was, but the best I had under the circumstances. It was not the appearance that bothered me now; it was how I might marshal the tactics to adorn it.

Setting a helmet is a tricky thing, you see, especially among the Solamnic Orders, caught up as they are with chivalry and pomp and show and kindness to women. On ceremonious occasions, a Knight is expected to wear a favor on his helmet—an item of his lady's clothing, whether it be glove or scarf or, in some absurd cases, a slipper. This is meant to signify a special attachment between said Knight and said lady—a sentiment in keeping with courtliness and romance and general goodwill.

I practically had to pry a glove from Dannelle di Caela's clenched fist—I had developed an uncomfortable and delightful interest in her of late. On my knees yesterday at the foot of the great marble staircase, the hall around me loud with arriving Knights and the rustle of nosy servants and the occasional shrill of a mechanical cuckoo, brashly I dared her to embarrass me before all present, to refuse me the token in public because I *knew* she would in private.

Flushed, a little angry, she had stopped at the top of the stairs. I had shouted my request full voice in the corridor, and Father and Alfric, awaiting me by the entrance to the Great Hall, gaped up at the lovely red-haired girl who stared daggers down at me. Everyone was breathless at my breach of etiquette.

"I . . . I have heard tales about you, Master Galen," Dannelle replied in a rigid, formal voice that let me know I had already won.

"It would please me were you not to repeat ill-founded rumors in front of my esteemed father," I shouted merrily, gesturing at the old fart by the entrance, "so as not to spoil his enjoyment of seeing a dear son knighted in the twilight of his life."

Dannelle glared angrily at me, caught in the strictures of decorum. She spun about, the hem of her gray dress rising like a cyclone, and stomped away toward her quarters upstairs, stopping only for the briefest of moments to hurl a glove suitorward.

A knot of silk and sequins, it struck the step above me

with a commanding *thwack*. I took it as a sign of her increasing interest.

Dannelle's, however, was not the only token available. On the table in front of me also lay an item of more intimate apparel, supplied by one Marigold Celeste, one of the Lady Enid's distant cousins and a formidable sort to reckon with.

I vowed, as I had vowed often before, not to think of Marigold. I turned my thoughts from that black lace item, not even speculating as to how or why in the world one would wear such a thing.

* * * * *

Slowly, pensively, I had picked up my glain opal brooch from where it lay amidst other, less marketable things—a dog whistle and a pair of old sun-hardened leather gloves. In its humble surroundings, the brooch stood out like the opals against the silver circle in which they were set.

Long ago the stones had fallen into my possession, a bribe from a treacherous enemy. Now, set in a silver circle, they seemed more respectable—almost *tamed*, as though their shadowy beginning had nothing to do with this time and with the lad who held them.

Uneasily, I held the piece of jewelry up to candlelight. It had been scarcely a week since I had taken the stones from the old leather pouch, in which they had resided since they were given to me, and sent them to the local jeweler to have them set in a brooch. It had cost a pretty sum, but it seemed worth it: At night of late, when the high wind raced down from the hills unto the castle, whipping about the battlements and through the window, my belongings would shake on their perches and shelves and places of storage. On those nights, I could swear I heard the opals click together in the darkness, as though they were trying to speak.

As though on cue, again the wind rose suddenly. The candle sputtered and went out.

"I have heard of drafty castles," I muttered, "but this . . ."

I could not complete the feeble sentiment, for a cold mist followed in the wake of the wind, smelling of old water and ice and cavernous gloom. Somehow it carried upon it a terrible loneliness and sadness, so that as the mist passed over me, I wanted to cry out, to moan and blubber for no reason I could name or understand.

The whole chamber tensed, as though it awaited some monstrous change.

It was then that the shapes appeared. They took form out of the heart of the opals and the smoke from the extinguished candle. At first it seemed like a trick of reflected light—that a vapor had fallen from the night air, out of the confusion of wind and weather, and rested in the centermost opal. But the darkness hung all about the brooch, a greater dark inside of the dark, turning and boiling and adopting a solid shape.

Then the stones seemed to open in front of me, and Plainsmen appeared in the jeweled blackness. They moved silently, smoothly, with a motion born in the grasslands, where they ran with the deer and the leopard. Still too surprised to be frightened, I squinted to see them more clearly in the tricky light.

There were six figures, gaunt and dusty and tall, wrapped in furs and wearing old ornaments of beads and claws and leather thongs. Beneath the folds of mist—or was it fur?—draped over them, I could see their skin, weathered and tough, as though a century of winds and rain had descended upon them.

Their leader was the oldest, the tallest. On his head he wore the skull of an antelope, his graying forelocks streaming through its vacant eyes, its tall, thin rack of antlers lending him height and a fearsome otherworldliness, as though he were no Plainsman at all, but a thing out of nature or beyond it.

He scanned the landscape in front of him slowly, intently, as though he had forgotten something, had left something behind here. Then his gaze pierced the surface of the stone and rested upon me, and for a moment, his eyes flickered like a distant display of fireworks, green and beyond sound and at the faintest edge of sight.

I swallowed hard and gripped the arms of my chair. If I was expected to say something, I was confounded if I knew what it was. I started to hail the spectral figures in front of me, to offer them greetings or salute but most of all to find out who they were and what they wanted. I opened my mouth, but the leader cut me short, raising a lean hand and staring at me without malice or venom, or even all that much attention. He seemed to be looking somewhere beyond me, though he looked straight at me at the same time.

Slowly and dramatically, he beckoned. He motioned me to follow him into the center of the stone.

"Not on your life," I muttered, my right hand moving quickly from the chair to the sword on the table in front of me. Suddenly, in the black center of the topmost stone, the Great Hall of di Caela appeared. I blinked and looked again.

As if focusing my gaze, the scene in the opal shifted from wall to wall, resting finally on the high, curtained balcony from which in a nightmare time several years behind me, I had watched the Scorpion announce his evil presence in a hall dark with solemnity and night.

There, amidst the story of Huma carved in the marble frieze that covered the balcony ledge, my brother Brithelm's shape had joined the Knights and the dragons and the obscure tendrils of marble greenery.

As I watched, the stone shape turned and looked at me.

Brithelm's eyes were empty and obscure, his hair and skin dull, as though I watched him through a veil of webbing and mist. Slowly, emerging from the frieze like a cobra rising to strike, a pale hand, a knife in its grip, took shape from the stone and the smoke. Turning toward my brother, it set blade to his throat.

The white of the marble split in a dark red line. And surely enough, all light and sound seemed to retreat, and I seemed to see my brother at the end of a gray and swirling tunnel.

I cried out. Brithelm's eyes rested on me.

Then, as though he had heard me, he shrank back into the dark of the jewel, passing soundlessly into mist and rock, the sides of the opal converging above him like water converges to cover a sinking stone. The Plainsmen vanished along with him, as though they followed him into the dark. One of them carried a torch that glowed with a green, muted flame that cast its light only on the receding figures themselves, as though they drew in its radiance and absorbed it, leaving the rest of the room in shadows. I stumbled to my feet, reeling, as the Plainsmen drifted into the darkness of the thing in my hand.

From where I stood, they looked like pillars of light as they faded away. That light was the last thing I remembered until Bayard stood above me, shaking and waking me.

Chapter III

First of all, visions were never my strength.

They smack of magic, which for the most part, I do not credit.

For I have seen the illusionists early and late, dressed in the glittering robes embroidered with moons and stars and pentagons and strange planetary designs, sitting on horseback at the edge of the mist-covered drawbridge outside my boyhood home in Coastlund, camped in their eerie, geometrical tents on the plains outside Castle di Caela.

Everywhere that I have seen the magicians, they are trying to get indoors.

Once inside, once they are warm and fed and paid and provided for, I grant you that their tricks can be something to behold. I saw one elderly man set his apprentice on fire.

The boy moved through my father's hall, stepping gracefully around broken crockery, snoring dogs, and capsized
tables. All the while his hair and fingers were aflame, and
yet no heat touched him.

Once I saw a great glittering stone brought forth from the
folds of a dramatic red robe. The bearer of that stone spoke
some brief, inaudible words above it, and the crystal
clouded. Out of the light and mist at its heart, I saw a room
of eggs and bizarre, grotesque creatures hatching from
them—half man, but also half lizard or eft or dragon or
something. And then, before the vision faded, I saw the
stone, or one like it, glowing green and amber, embedded in
the chest of a young man.

That was a wondrous night's entertainment, for it was a
vision beyond my most fanciful imaginings.

Yet there is always hypnosis. There are mirrors that a
clever man can set at just the right angle to reflect the firelight.
There are strings and pulleys, secret pockets and panels.

I have always been prone to explain anything by its tricks
and its hidden machinery. Indeed, though my own adventures had taught me that there was genuine magic in the
world, sometimes at my very doorstep, I was inclined to
forget that in my search for reasonable explanations.

So it was as I lay safely on my own bed, puzzling over the
cryptic vision of the Plainsman. All the candles were lit in
the room, the logs in the fireplace burning as brightly as
poor Bayard could manage at a moment's notice. He had
discovered and wakened me, and now he was fuming about
the room, gathering my belongings, his impatience rising as,
caught up in my thoughts, I let him and the page he had
brought with him do all the preparations.

"I want things light around me," I said. "I want things visible."

Almost by reflex, the boy lit yet another candle.

"This is no time for dramatics, Galen," Bayard observed
quietly. "If for no other reason, you will become a Knight
out of simple good manners."

He was downright intimidating in full Solamnic armor.
He stood above me like a king from the old stories instead of
the man I had seen bedraggled by rain, thrown from his

horse in the mountains, or dozing by countless campfires in our long and difficult travels together.

It was as if the armor enlarged him, made him more than what he was, or at least more than he was while he snored or endured bedragglement. Right now he was formidable, banishing the memory of my six spectral visitors almost entirely.

I sat up.

Bayard folded his arms.

"Put on the armor, Galen," he declared flatly. "You realize, don't you, how dishonorable it is to doze on the Night of Reflections?"

"I beg your pardon? 'Doze,' did you say?"

With a rough shove, Bayard pushed me back down onto the bed. Sensing a confrontation, the page scurried to the opposite end of the room.

"Dozed. Drifted away. Nodded off. How long have you been asleep?" Bayard asked curtly.

I sat up, this time more hesitantly. "But I wasn't asleep, Bayard!" I shouted. "I was—"

He shoved me back onto the bed again.

"I thought I had seen it all from you," he declared, his gray eyes glittering, his teeth clenched. For a moment, I understood what it meant to be at the receiving end of his sword, and I blamed neither goblin nor ogre nor enemy Knight for turning and running away.

Unfortunately, I had no such options. I stood—or rather sat—my ground, and the chambers grew dreadfully silent except for the crackle of the fire and the sound of the page's rag squeaking diligently across embossed metal. By the time the boy was done with being unnoticed in my corner, the shield would shine like Solinari.

Bayard stood completely still, in that unforgiving silence of those who are, when all is said and done, better than you. The light from the candles seemed to sink and gutter.

"All of it!" he continued quietly, though his voice began to rise in irritation. "Mishap in the lists and chaos in the saddle, the unwelcome opinion of every veteran Solamnic who maintained you should be passed over and sent back to Coastlund. Put up with it all, I did, because something in me believed that you had the stomach for Knighthood—that out in the swamp and the mountains and up in the pass at Chaktamir, something had taught you a lesson, that you had come away from adventure more honest and wise and eager.

"So much for what I believed," he spat angrily. "You couldn't even watch through the night."

He raised his hand again, and before he could strike me, I had slipped off the bed and onto the floor. I crouched and glared at him, fists doubled. Bayard's eyes widened in surprise, and I heard a shuffling sound as the page dove under the shield he was polishing.

Now the silence downstairs erupted into a swift Palanthan dance, then faded into disarray as the musicians realized they knew different versions of the song. From the far end of my hallway, a mechanical bird trilled an off-key melody and then lay silent.

At that sound, and at long last, Bayard smiled.

"It seems as though Enid has forgotten one," he said, softly but audibly.

"Forgotten, Bayard?"

"The bird at the end of the hall."

"Survivor of the Great Dismantling of Two Twenty Eight," I proclaimed, and we both laughed.

"Most of them gone the way of dwarf spirits and dog runs," Bayard added, "since the Lady Enid took over the care of the castle from her father."

He looked down at me and frowned.

"If not sleep, then just what was it, Weasel?"

"Galen," I corrected, picking up the greaves. Slowly the boy approached me, holding the shield in front of him like . . . well, like a shield. 'Sir Galen,' it's about to be, and I'd like to go by 'Galen' henceforth, unless you're taking the advice of your elders and burying me in the provinces."

"Then 'Galen' it will be. Damn it, Galen, help the boy!" Bayard snapped, after the page spent a useless moment fumbling with strings on my person.

It was my answer, such as it was.

I sighed deeply as the boy attached the breastplate more snugly, then took the old, outsized greaves from my hands.

Bayard paced to the door and looked down the hall impatiently. "Assemble *yourself!*" he snapped. "It wasn't a week ago that you were my squire. . . ."

"And a good one I was, sir," I lied, casting a sidelong glance at the poor boy, who was beginning to sweat and tremble, his fingers fumbling at the laces.

"Well, buckle some buckle, or tie something yourself."

"Armor was always my weakness, sir," I stalled, picking up the ceremonial helmet as though it belonged to someone else, tugging the greave laces from the page's hands in the process. The boy whimpered and fell onto his stomach.

"I recall others," Bayard declared, "along with some you probably do not remember. Be consoled that at least the years have taken away no genuine talent in much of anything squirely. Raphael!"

Bayard tossed a key to the page.

"Get to my quarters and bring me a sword—any sword except the Nerakan disemboweler I took as a trophy from the pass at Chaktamir."

"Which would be a little fanciful," I observed sourly, and Bayard turned back to me.

"As I said, Raphael," he continued, his eyes on me, "virtually any sword will do, as long as the blade and the handle are . . . recognizably different."

* * * * *

The horns and drums resumed in the Great Hall below us. They struck up a dance tune from Coastlund, usually played by the peasants when a cow calved. The musicians were straining, kept so long that they had nearly run out of music. As Raphael went out the door, Bayard turned to me, setting himself to the task of assembling a version of a Knight for the evening.

"It is time to make you a Knight," he declared, "dozing or not. Before the Great Hall descends to dog races or swordplay."

We glanced toward my belongings, scattered over and under the table.

"Not exactly a knightly inventory," I pronounced.

"Oh, I don't know," Bayard said politely, even kindly. "A

dagger. A pair of stained, heavy gloves. Half a dozen glain opals and a tarnished dog whistle. Each has been good company to you, in its way, if I recall."

I nodded.

"Castle di Caela seems smaller, Bayard."

"Smaller? Suck in that stomach so I can tighten this breastplate. Maybe that's because you don't fit through the doorways like you used to, Galen. Soft living is demanding payment from your waistline, boy. If you're showing weight at nineteen, when you're my age you'll be—"

"Another Ramiro of the Maw, sprawled over two chairs in the dining room, drooling on the kinswomen?"

"Don't be so desolate, boy. Or so disrespectful. And do suck in that stomach."

"You don't understand, Bayard. Ever since the curse on Castle di Caela was lifted . . . well, things *are* better, I'll grant you that. But now this is just another old building on the plains—stone and mortar, wood and hair and iron, and maybe a legend or two to give it some color for visitors."

"What would you have, Galen? Ghosts in the dungeon? Spectral family members dangling from ropes?" asked Bayard, bending over to pick up one of my boots.

I remembered the face of the Plainsman chieftain and shuddered.

"By the way," Bayard continued impatiently, "it's high time you decided on a squire, boy. By tomorrow at the latest.

"Nonetheless, I do understand. I know what you mean," he conceded. "It's as though a sense of order has settled about things, putting them all in a proper place and banishing intruders and disrupters."

"Banishing the dwarf spirits, too," I offered distractedly.

Bayard nodded. "And the dog runs."

He stepped away from me for a moment, and walked toward the closet. "I just can't believe it, Galen," he said, the irritation from a moment before returning. With a sudden, flickering movement, he tossed one of my boots to me. It struck the floor by my bed with a firm slap, raising dust.

"I just can't believe it. That with your knighthood ahead of you, and the one thing holding you to the Code and Mea

---

sure your simple desire to go through with this . . . how you could risk it all for an hour's sleep!"

"Risk it?"

"Well," Bayard said, reaching for the other boot. "According to the Measure, the Night of Reflections must be spent 'in watching and in long thought, from sunset again unto sunset, for even the light of day is dark when the memory ranges.' "

"But it *was* watching, Bayard!" I protested. "Watching and the longest thoughts of all. As I was trying to tell you, Bayard, it was not sleep. It was . . . it was a vision!"

Bayard looked at me skeptically. Slowly the faintest hint of a smile spread across his face, widening and widening until he could contain his amusement no longer. My protector began to laugh, and the further I explained, the deeper and more uncontrolled his amusement became. He leaned against the closet, struggling for breath and balance, shaking his head in wonderment as I concluded my account of the Plainsmen, of Brithelm, and of the strange visitation.

"So . . . so they wanted you to follow them *into the brooch?*" he gasped.

Sullenly I nodded.

"Oh, this smacks of the old days!" he exclaimed. "One dodge after another, to avoid duty and danger and chores and—"

"Very well, then!" I exclaimed angrily, taking an aggressive step toward Bayard before my better judgment reminded me he was stronger, quicker, and wiser in the ways of combat. "Call it sleep and be done with it! Done with *me*, for that matter!"

"And what am I supposed to think?" Bayard answered, his laughter fading. He took up the laces on my greaves once more.

From the bed, the black eyes of the brooch stared up at me.

"That I must be losing my mind, sir?" I asked mournfully.

In the brief silence that followed, I gathered the whistle and the brooch into my hand and clicked them together for noise—any noise.

My old companion smiled once again, though this time

his eyes were troubled. He tugged at the laces of the breast-plate. The air rushed out of me, and I reeled for a moment, my hand on the bedpost.

I turned and faced the window. Outside, the banners cracked and fluttered on the parapets, catching the last red shower of sunlight as the day went down behind the mountains. I suddenly felt silly. No matter what I said, my past was the translator. It sounded as though I would stop at nothing to avoid knighthood. Even hallucinations.

"Never mind," I said quietly, tossing the items back onto the bed. "It was just a trick of the light in the corridor."

Again the wind was rising. It promised to be a hazardous night.

"There will be time for 'tricks of light' after you are knighted," Bayard maintained, stepping away from me and leaning against the mantel of the fireplace, his shadow long and dark against the window. "Time, no doubt, for other tricks, seeing as how you've spent the Night of Reflections. But now we are about other business, when the food has been prepared, the musicians hired, and the guests seated for nearly an hour."

"Somehow I do not think that you have things in their . . . order of importance, sir," I protested, picking up the dog whistle and turning it over in my hand.

"Brithelm's, this was," I breathed.

"I know, lad," Bayard said softly. He stood and put his hand on my shoulder. For a moment, we paused, our thoughts on my brother's little camp high in the storm-imperiled Vingaard Mountains.

Outside, the wind died down, and below us I could hear the musicians start up again, a kender trail song that showed they had been stretched to the end of all musical taste and knowledge.

"Remember, Galen," Bayard whispered, "that Brithelm is the Pathwarden with visions. You're as sane as anyone in this bedlam of a castle—as sane as Robert or Brandon or your father, and they're Solamnic Knights of the first order. Like it or not, you will be a Solamnic Knight of the Crown by tomorrow, Galen Pathwarden Brightblade."

"But—"

43

"And I do not care if you have some kind of problem with honor or decency or sanity or any other thing Solamnic. You will put on the armor, and then . . . well, we shall see what happens. I trust that the armor will do its job."

It did not sound all that foresighted to me. And yet Bayard's words were bolstering, as if he believed that something would come to pass when I put on the armor. Instantly I thought of legends: of Arden Greenhand, whose magical armor would change into a cloud at his bidding, or of Sir Lysander of Hylo, whose breastplate bore a map of the world that could transport him across the continent to any body of land he touched upon that map.

And yet, despite our tugging and tying, the armor I wore was secondhand, far too loose for me, and far too ordinary. Not only was it scarcely the stuff of legends, it was not a bit magical or fanciful or even all that attractive to begin with.

"The armor's job here seems to be to weigh me down and net me in its laces, sir," I argued. "But I am sure you have a deeper insight into this mystery."

"Luskinian ethics," Bayard said proudly.

"I beg your pardon, sir?"

"Surely you know the luskin, Galen? Surely Gileandos taught you that much."

"My education has been uneven, sir, guided by Gileandos's gin and whim, it seems. I obviously don't know what you want me to know about the luskin. A little gray bird, as I recall. A sometime singer who relies on the other birds to raise its young."

"Who in their youth behave as sparrows or starlings," Bayard added. "Or wrens or whatever, depending on whose nest their mother chooses to leave them in."

"All well and good, Bayard, and masterful natural history. But I don't see—"

"Luskinian ethics. 'If you look like one and are treated like one, the time will come when you act like one.' "

"This is not a great insight, sir."

"Nonetheless. Finish with the armor."

As I assembled myself quietly, giving last attention to the polish of the helmet, its crest, and its foolish feather, which looked as though a bird—a luskin, I hoped devoutly—had plunged to its death atop my head, Raphael returned bearing a sword the likes of which I dreaded he would bring back—a big, two-handed appliance as long as I was tall and heavy enough to set me unbalanced as I walked. I lifted it over my head with a grunt, then painfully slipped it into the scabbard at my waist, where it rested awkwardly, a good six inches of its blade still uncovered.

"I fear I have cracked through my eggshell into an eagle's nest," I complained to Bayard, who chuckled again and shook his head.

I shivered, and not with the wind that was rising higher and higher again, rattling the windows and coursing underneath the sill, where it staggered the flame of a candle and lifted a paper from my desk. Raphael moved quickly to shut the window more tightly as Bayard stepped to the door and, opening it, turned and beckoned to me.

It was an ominous image, as though again I was called into the heart of the stones.

Yet this ceremony was what I had trained and waited for, the moment I had achieved despite the predictions of almost everyone in Castle di Caela. Gathering whistle and gloves, I stuffed them into the pocket of my tunic and, my hands clammy but unshaking, pinned my cape about my shoulders with the opal brooch.

"Tonight you could almost pass for chivalrous, Galen," Bayard conceded as I followed him into the corridor and, in a swim of candles and music, descended the stairwell into the Great Hall.

* * * * *

I remember that night only fitfully. The torchlight from the sconces in the Great Hall of Castle di Caela shone brightly and deeply on the dark tables and the flushed faces of visitors—for after all, I had delayed matters, and wine had passed freely in the meantime.

It shone on the faces of my Pathwarden kin: my father, proud, rising to his feet in spite of himself with some of his old military firmness as Bayard handed me the sword. The others, noticing the old man's gesture and mistaking it for something we did at such times in Coastlund, stood also.

Nobody ever knew it was Father's private way of thanking the gods that one of his sons—even if it was the least promising of the three—had finally put on Solamnic armor. But Sir Robert stood, and Ramiro, and Brandon after them, and then even those self-important bluestockings Elazar and Fernando.

Dannelle di Caela stood also, though she did not seem to revel in it. She stared through me with those brilliant green eyes, and I hoped devoutly that she did not believe the rumors. In dismay, I realized I had forgotten her glove entirely and that the single foolish feather was my helmet's only adornment.

I remember the chant of an elven bard, the choiring women who heralded my approach to the place of honor on the raised platform. My brief but full enjoyment of the scarcely hidden contempt on the face of Gileandos, and the faint, surprising remorse I felt to see Alfric stand in my honor, his eyes dull, expressionless, and distracted, as though he labored under a strange and mortal disease.

I remember the ceremony itself. Remember kneeling as Bayard, Sir Robert, and my father stood before me, their large hands on the pommel of my sword, and the solemn words I must keep secret passed between us in whispers as the music swelled and deepened. Then the Vow of the Sword, the Crown, and the Rose—to defend, to adhere, and above all, to understand.

Then Bayard's hands pressed upon my shoulders and turned me to face those gathered in the hall, and my eyes passed over all of them.

Over Brandon, who stared toward the huge marble fireplace, unfocused and sad, as though he looked through the flames onto a distant, wronged country.

Over Ramiro, who stopped wrestling with a side of beef long enough to pay polite attention to what transpired on the platform in front of him.

Over Marigold, who mouthed something delightful and alluring and almost obscene when she caught my eye.

Over Dannelle, who turned away.

Then over Gileandos, distant and disdaining. Over Alfric, who looked up at me with a strange half-smile, then averted his eyes, staring disconsolately at the untouched food on his platter.

Bayard stepped down from the dais into the midst of my people, his big hands raised in solemn triumph. Flanking him, my father and Sir Robert marched to their seats, their years falling away with each measured step until, standing beside their chairs, softened and redeemed by the shifting firelight, you could squint and see them as they must have appeared a half century before in the pass at Chaktamir, the Nerakan army bearing down on their small but resolute band.

All eyes were on me now, all the guests facing me. I raised my borrowed sword, and like the older Knights had told me would happen, like none of the wise men—not even Gileandos—could ever explain, the blade of the sword shimmered with a thousand colors: through greens and yellows and reds into others I cannot name because I had never seen them until this night.

Through it all, the choir sang a ceremonial hymn as old as the Age of Light:

> "Beyond the wild, impartial skies
> Have you set your lodgings,
> In cantonments of stars, where the sword aspires
> In an arc of yearning, where we join in singing."

From the dark, color-spangled hall, a man's voice—Fernando's, I believe—joined in the chorus. Then Bayard took up the song, and Father, and the others.

> "Grant to him a warrior's rest
> Above our singing, above song itself.
> May the ages of peace converge in a day;
> May he dwell in the heart of Paladine.
>
> "And set the last spark of his eyes
> In a fixed and holy place,
> Above words and the borrowed land too loved
> As we recount the ages."

I tried to join in, but the words shifted in and out of my recollection. Instead of the images of the six ages of man, I remembered the scene at the heart of the stone: the Plainsmen, the pale hand, the knife at my brother's throat. The smell of old grasslands rose to meet me. That is the last thing I remember of the ceremonies.

It is only later I recall coming to, lying on the bed in my own quarters, my armor removed and arranged neatly on the table in front of me—no doubt the handiwork of young Raphael. There, surrounded by candles and silence, by my polished Solamnic trappings, I tried to sleep, and you would think it would be easy, having weathered a night and day of vigilance only to be assaulted hourly by spectral visitations.

You would think a lad would be too tired for thought.

And yet I lay wide-eyed until morning, and it was my brother and the Plainsmen who filled my dark imaginings.

Chapter IV

The servants had gathered at a distance outside my quarters. As I opened the window to let in the muffled light, I saw them down below in the courtyard, huddled together, murmuring, exchanging something.

It was later I found that Raphael had listened at my door for a good while, ear pressed against the wood, overhearing my claim of visions. Quite naturally, he had gone to his friends among the servants, bearing this new intelligence.

So the something exchanged was money. It seemed that a sizable wager had grown about the subject of my sanity. "Climbing the Cat Tower" was the servants' term for it, for those unsettling moments in family history when one di Caela or another would burst free of sanity and provoke castle gossip for the next generation or so.

The Cat Tower in question had to do with Sir Robert's Aunt Mariel, who had locked herself away in the tall southeast tower of Castle di Caela, holding everything at remove—responsibility, nourishment, hygiene, and as it turned out, the care of her pets.

She was stalked and eaten by her own cats after all of them had stayed a month together in the topmost room of the tower.

It was rumored in the servant quarters that the Lady Mariel's obvious madness was hereditary. That I was family by adoption made only little difference to the speculators, who, I understand, carried on a running wager as to which of us—Sir Robert, Bayard, Enid, Dannelle, or myself—would first stray from orbit.

To many of them that morning, it must have looked like a time to call in bets. I stood by the window as the milling and murmuring subsided, and looking down upon those assembled, I mustered all the solemnity of my newfound knighthood, crossed my eyes, stuck a finger in each side of my mouth, pulled my lips wide, and throttled my tongue at them.

I stepped back into my chambers, satisfied that behind and below me, more silver was no doubt flashing, more wagers being struck.

I stood on the battlements looking westward, the long shadows of the castle walls diminishing slowly as the sun rose behind me. Below, the farmlands of Solamnia shone green and gold.

There was noise and altercation somewhere in the courtyard. Apparently Sir Robert di Caela had chosen to discipline his niece Dannelle, who in return had chosen not to be disciplined. What had started as a mild disagreement, the nature of which I could not overhear, had risen in volume until it was ending in a series of elaborate southern curses involving poison and mothers and goblins and the entire Solamnic pantheon.

Where I had come from, family disputes generally ended in fisticuffs or breakage or glasses of Brithelm's lemonade. It had taken me a while to grow accustomed to the Solamnic bickering, though I had a talent for it myself.

For now, there was more serious business ahead of me. The image of Brithelm I had seen in the frieze, the knife-wielding hand at his throat, was a disturbing one. Indeed, the only good thing about such a vision was its plainness: The image of one's brother in mortal peril is hard to twist by interpreting into anything other than that one's brother is in mortal peril.

From as early as I could remember, Brithelm had a talent for tumbling into places where trouble had set up residence, yet he always managed to walk away without damages. Though the situation would collapse around him, he would be left standing, no more dazed and no more the worse for wear than when he had first found himself backed to the edge of disaster.

At first, some weeks back, when sentries reported that the foothills were glowing, it did not concern me at all. Even when refugee dwarves passed through Solamnia and, soon after, farmers around Castle di Caela began to complain of bears and panthers who had wandered out of the mountains and into their livestock . . . even then I did not worry all that much, resting assured that the wind would change or die down altogether, or that somehow before the fire touched a tangled hair of my brother's, rains or snow or something capable of extinguishing it would begin.

After all, when it came right down to it, refugee dwarves and complaining farmers were both common fare in this place and these times.

Still the fires persisted. My disquiet grew as the flames rose higher. Given the nature of my brother's encampment—the half-dozen wooden houses, the tents, and the lean-tos—fire was certainly a dire threat.

The omen that had invaded the ceremony of my knighthood resolved matters for me. As soon as possible, I was going to the Vingaard Mountains in search of my middle brother. Of course, it was something I had to discuss with Bayard.

Which was what had brought me to the battlements this morning. Bayard, dressed in the armor he had worn to last night's occasion, leaned against the crenellated wall as I approached him.

He looked westward, toward the foothills of the misty Vingaards. From a distance, he looked like the same Bayard who had hired me on as a squire three years ago—the mustache a little longer, perhaps, and the brown hair flecked with its first gray.

It took a closer look to see the difference. There are some Knights who are not fit for settled circumstances, and there had been something restless, something almost pent up about my old friend in recent months, as though he lay under house arrest in a castle of women and old men.

"Looking for omens?" I joked as I joined him at his post.

"Oh, awaiting visions," he teased gently in return. "Awaiting those Plainsmen, who, I am told, inhabit mountains as easily as they do stones in a brooch."

I leaned against the wall beside him.

"You don't believe me, do you, Bayard?"

He turned toward me, his gray eyes direct and penetrating.

"To be honest, Galen, I am not sure what I believe. I had my own night of reflections after the ceremony, in which I took serious stock of my conduct, wondering if I had made a mistake to strongarm you into knighthood."

"And what . . . what did you decide, sir?"

"I'm not sure," Bayard answered. "Except perhaps that your armor is beginning to work."

"I beg your pardon?"

Bayard smiled cryptically.

"I had a hand in putting that armor on you, lad. I have backed myself into a corner of goodwill. Now I must at least *act* as though I trust you with visions.

"So," he proclaimed simply, his gloved hand set upon the pommel of his sword, "together we must go to find your brother."

I started to speak, to thank him, but Bayard wasn't finished.

"Now, don't try to weasel out of this, Galen."

I shrank away from him, stung, my old name rising like a relentless pursuer. Bayard continued, his voice rising with eagerness.

"Vision or no vision, neither of us will rest until this

Brithelm matter is settled. I think we could use some adventuring—time away from Castle di Caela. I could see being rid of my father-in-law for a few days, and Sir Ramiro of the Maw has rendered himself impossible to endure once more.

"You, of course, might enjoy being free of your . . . softer entanglements. At least until you know which favor to wear on your helmet."

Bayard winked solemnly. I grimaced, knowing he spoke of the business with Marigold.

"That is the sum of it. What we are short of around here is adventure, which is why, two days from now, bright and early in that wonderfully quiet time before sunrise, our adventure will begin. We shall leave Castle di Caela—a handful of knights, accompanied only by horses and squires—on our way to the Vingaard Mountains, where we shall see to the safety of your brother Brithelm.

"It will be like old times, Galen," he exclaimed almost jubilantly as I thought of the winds and the distant fires and the road that was steep and rocky and untamed. Somewhere out there, at the end of a journey that was only now beginning to unfold, my brother and my courage awaited me.

"I shall have my squire by that morning hour, Bayard Brightblade," I promised, in a voice so ceremonial and dramatic that I could barely find myself in it.

I extended my hand, and Bayard nodded.

"And I, Sir Galen, will have chosen our companions, if there be any."

We parted company after a traditional Solamnic handclasp, each descending the battlements to his separate disaster.

* * * * *

"Never wed with a drunkard," my grandmother said, "if you wish to reform her. For instead of reform, there will be two drunkards."

She also told me that when I decided to get married, I should look to the ugliest one of my prospective in-laws, for that would be how my bride would look twenty years hence.

It was advice born of bitterness and the marshes of Coast-lund, of a world in which dire straits became more dire the longer you waited for them to improve.

Grandmama would have smiled to recognize the world of recruitments that Bayard and I faced once we descended the battlements.

No doubt Bayard believed that the mission at hand was an easy venture. Despite my bodings, we would find Brithelm and bring him back home. What he wanted, then, was good company along the way—good conversation, and no doubt someone up for a little hunting and hard riding.

Bayard politely asked Sir Brandon Rus to join us. That would have been good, for the most part. The young Knight, brilliantly promising, unmatched by any his age in skills or in resources or in downright physical courage, would have assured our safety against anything short of an army of ogres. Out in the hinterlands, there might be a chance to get him talking on something besides protocols and history, and maybe find out what it was that ate at the lad—why in the early morning hours at Castle di Caela the servants had heard him pacing the floor, as if despite all of the things in the world that did not frighten Sir Brandon Rus, something in his dreams or memory did.

Unfortunately, the young man begged off. He'd a quest of his own, he said, far to the east of here, past Neraka and Kernen. It was whispered that his journey would lead him to the Blood Sea of Istar, but Bayard, who had asked politely for Sir Brandon's company, was now polite enough not to ask his alternative destination.

It was disappointing to Bayard, but it came with the knightly territory. The world was filled with quests at that time—with quests and with the prospects of adventure. What Solamnic Knight, with the option of an eastward journey into dangerous country, would choose instead a sensible little search-and-rescue party in the foothills?

Ramiro of the Maw, evidently.

For the big Knight belched, wiped the crumbs from his

beard, and volunteered at once, setting his blunt sword at the feet of Bayard Brightblade, promising allegiance and insight and a strong right arm for the duration of the journey ahead. Bayard coughed and stammered and tried politely to deflect Ramiro's attentions elsewhere, but he was too late and too courteous. By the time Bayard came up with reasons, Ramiro was packed and ready for the road ahead of us.

* * * * *

Ramiro's hearty enjoyment of food and wine and women had made him good company in Sir Robert's time—the delight of holidays and festivals and tournaments. In recent years, though, the wine and the food had taken their toll, and heartiness had turned to clumsiness and stupor. Ramiro had almost drowned in a barrel of sweet port last spring, and had not Gileandos, sneaking to the cellars for a nip himself, uncovered the barrel and the thrashing feet of the big knight, we would have spent our spring in funeral.

It was not, however, the first of the food-related mishaps. A year earlier, Ramiro had nearly choked to death when he swallowed a whole chicken at a banquet honoring the anniversary of Bayard Brightblade and Enid di Caela. I remember *that* one myself: Sir Robert and Sir Fernando staring warily at one another, each trying to gather the courage to place a hand down Ramiro's monstrous throat to retrieve the wedged bird. Finally, with the big Knight purpling on the floor of the Great Hall, Bayard rushed from his chair and gave Ramiro a well-placed kick in the stomach, dislodging the bird and sending it skittering into the elvish orchestra.

Those were the highlights, of course, of Ramiro's seasonal visits. But each time he came, the farmers complained all the more as their livestock dwindled, and the di Caela women, forewarned of his hefty arrival, packed up and moved to guarded guest quarters on the upper floors of the Cat Tower.

This time had been no different. Two nights before my ceremonies, Bayard had found the big Knight tangled in an enormous harness, suspended from the top of that same Cat

Tower. Lowered by his laboring squire, Oliver, Ramiro had snagged himself in an ill-starred attempt to peek in on Dannelle di Caela at her bath. Bayard had been beside himself, but he fumed politely as Sir Robert explained away the conduct as "the energies of youth."

"There is a white-haired conspiracy about us," Bayard had whispered to me playfully, but one could tell that again he had begun to count the days until Ramiro's departure.

It was no wonder he was speechless when Ramiro decided to depart with us.

* * * * *

I, on the other hand, fared not much better.

Had efficient little Raphael been old enough, or even as big as he was efficient, my choice of squire would have been an easy one. Instead, he helped by introducing the candidates as I sat in my quarters granting audience to a dozen or so likely prospects culled from the Solamnic countryside.

You would be surprised how many unpromising younger sons of Knights will crawl from the woodwork when squirehood is in the offing. I tried to be attentive, to be polite, but my options were almost unbearable.

I remember some of them well—occasionally the names, and even more occasionally the face that went with them. And yet they all blend together ultimately into one big teenaged fool hell-bent on squirehood. . . .

"Fabian, son of Sir Elazar!" Raphael announced.

The boy's enormous feet filled the room—each the size of my forearm. It was as though one of those bandits from down near the Ice Wall—those men who sailed from the mountains on long wooden skis to plunder wayfarers and caravans—had found himself, surprisingly and uncomfortably, indoors with the skis still on him. Clumsily he skirted the furniture, backing into chairs, once nearly capsizing my table with a sudden turn. All the while he pled his case, concluding with the rousing statement that he'd "do well for the Knight in question when it came to a tight spot, sir."

I looked up at Raphael, who snorted and rushed from the room.

"I shall keep these things in mind," I replied neutrally.

"Gismond, second son of Bantos of Kaolin," Raphael announced. . . .

"No matter what the danger," the lad concluded, his good eye narrowed and twitching uncontrollably and his sword drawn, slashing menacingly near my hand upon the table, "I shall be quick with the sword and the dagger, gladly setting myself between you and the enemy warrior or the monster or the earthquake or fire or explosion."

"I find that reassuring, Gismond." I lied.

"Anatol of Lemish," Raphael announced.

"And you are the son of Sir Olvan?" I asked, fumbling through the papers in front of me.

"Yes, sir," the boy replied.

"Wait. It says here you're the son of Sir Katriel."

"Yes, sir."

"Well . . . which one, lad?"

"Yes, sir."

"Toland of Caergoth!" proclaimed Raphael.

"No matter what you have heard, sir," the boy began, striding into the room, "they were both dead when I found them."

Raphael and I stared at each other in alarm. I nodded, and he opened the door.

"Oliver of the Maw!"

"Why, Oliver! This is quite the surprise, seeing as—"

"Three years. I've been in Ramiro's service three years."

"And?"

"What with the lifting and lowering, the harnesses and pulleys, and draping him dead drunk over horseback and onto cots, I fear I've ruptured myself so many different times that . . ."

So it passed, until Raphael tired and the line of also-rans dwindled. I set down the papers, waved the page away, and lay on the cot. Pouring myself half a glass of wine, I took a short, relaxing sip and stared at the ceiling.

There was a knock at the door.

"Raphael, I haven't the time or the patience for another applicant. If you'd—"

"It's me, brother," a quite different voice replied.

"Alfric!" I said, sitting up on the bed. "Come in, please."

It was not the brother I remembered from my childhood in the moathouse or even from the early events of my squirehood—the blustering and bullying seemed to have gone right out of the fellow, and it was a quiet sort, bent and chastened, who seated himself in my chair and looked at me across the expanse of my chambers, disheveled and shy.

Once before, on battlements far from here in miles and in years, my brother and I had struck the terms of blackmail. At that time, it had been something silly: a simple boyish prank of mine, which Alfric's threats had magnified into the greatest disaster since the Cataclysm itself. I was only nine at the time, and gullible. I had believed my brother's dire bodings, and set myself at his beck and call for eight years—cleaning up after him, translating his Old Solamnic and Qualinesti, doing his mathematics, and taking blame for every enormity he managed at the moathouse or in the surrounding lands.

Eight years of such schooling had taught me caution.

My brother cleared his throat.

"Does this bring back memories, Galen?"

"I'm not sure what memories you have in mind, Brother dear," I dodged, alert to his most subtle movements through a long and sorry brotherhood. "Why is your hand on your dagger?"

Alfric uttered a surprised little laugh and raised his hands.

"I'm sorry, Weasel. I guess it's an old habit."

"Galen."

He frowned at me.

"From this day forth, I shall be known as Galen," I pronounced, then noticed how pompous and foolish and Solamnic the words sounded as they echoed sourly in the chamber.

Alfric nodded. "Whatever you like," he agreed. "I guess that's an old habit, too."

Alfric stared at his knees, then scowled at me.

"Father wants me to be a squire, no matter what it takes and who has to do it."

"And I appear to be what and who for the time being, since I'm expected to obey Father and gladly dangle a millstone around my neck for the next ten years or longer. I'm sorry, Alfric."

In a way, I *was* sorry, seeing as the Knight may not have been born yet who'd take my brother on as squire, and I might be a grandsire myself, gray and doddering, before he'd have another chance like this.

Slowly, his eyes fixed on his hands, my brother began to speak. Listening, I rose and walked toward the window.

"I expect I cannot blame you, Weas—Galen. No, I expect I cannot blame you at all, seeing as I have not been a good older brother and all."

It was hard to argue with him.

I opened the shutter. The thick air of the afternoon rolled into my quarters, bearing the smell of mud and of distant rain.

"So I cannot ask you as your brother, but for our father, Galen. On account of he sits up there in the moathouse and looks at my future, which he cannot figure out. He says it is a dark one, if there is any future at all.

"And I believe him."

My brother's head sank into his hands, and his shoulders heaved.

"But what's the *real* reason, Alfric?"

He looked up, expressionless and dry-eyed, a bit surprised that after a long absence I still knew his tricks.

"Why are you willing to be my squire and borrow trouble," I asked, "when you can inherit the old man's castle and spend the rest of your years squandering his patrimony?"

For the first time in years, my brother looked at me directly, with a gaze free of guile and meanness and malice and brutality. I almost failed to recognize him.

"Girls, Galen. I will become a squire to meet girls."

With a sinking feeling, I knew where the conversation was heading. Far better than his customary threats or blackmails, my brother had stumbled upon a ready way to squirehood—to appeal, simply and forthrightly, to my sense of the ridiculous.

"You see, the last of the serving girls left Coastlund a month before we came here. The peasants hid her . . . told me they'd rather die than tell me her whereabouts. The moathouse gets kind of lonely without women around. And I get to thinking . . . thinking, What would be more respectable than Knighthood, and all of them ladies like Enid and Dannelle and Marigold—"

With the last name, he shot me a sly look, then continued.

"With all of them flocking about you? So I think to myself, what is squirehood, anyway, but a time that you have to wait before the girls are a sure thing? And who would be easier on his own squire than my own brother?"

I looked out my window, over the wall into the bed of the huge moat Bayard had ordered dug around the castle to allay the pressure of the huge artesian well from which the castle drew its water. It was not yet completed, but the rain had half-filled it, and for a moment, I thought of jumping, of hitting the ground running and continuing to run to a country far away from ambitious fathers and philandering brothers and Marigolds of all sizes and stripes and appetites.

I suppose that land lies somewhere. Somewhere near the best of all worlds, no doubt.

The breeze picked up, warm from the west. There was the faintest hint of smoke upon it, like you might catch in the depth of winter from the chimneys in a town miles away, the whiff of dark evergreen and warmth taken up by the wind and passed your way by chance. But this was midsummer— terrible midsummer, with its morning heat and the dry days that promised to stay forever—and the smell of smoke at this time of year was the odor of unchecked fires.

To the west, the Vinguaards rose out of a bed of dark smoke, as though they floated on the backs of thunderheads.

"Very well," I said, my words suprising me more than they did my brother. "Your squirehood begins this moment."

Chapter V

So that was how I was visited with the squire some said I so richly deserved.

I will grant you that my decision to employ my brother did not arise from the purest of hearts. For it is hard going in the Order when one's relatives are scoundrels or fools—I had only to look at Father, to see how he had suffered for his sons' general wretchedness, to know that the knighthood was unforgiving and fierce. With history stacked against me to begin with, I could scarcely suffer a running tally of Alfric's misdemeanors.

Then again, neither could Father. I must admit that I felt for the old man, whose middle son was a mystic in the mountains, whose youngest son attained to the Knighthood only by Sir Bayard's finagling, and whose scion and heir was promising to be the sorriest of the lot. My taking on Alfric was in part for the good of Sir Andrew.

It would be even better, of course, on the off chance that my brother had a dash of the squire in him. So what if he aspired to knighthood for the simple and unproven reason that women are drawn to a man in armor? No doubt some heroes have begun under worse circumstances, with even more self-serving motives.

Cynical as I could be, especially with Alfric as the subject, I still held out hope that the boy could turn around, could make something of himself under the watchful eye of the Order.

That was until my brother went to work.

It was like a natural disaster. By noon, Alfric had torn one stirrup from my saddle and brought to pass the dismantling of three stalls in the stables when he curried my chosen horse too roughly.

It was only later that he lost my armor.

"Brother," I had begun in exasperation, as two grooms cleared the stalls of fractured boards. A third groom sat stuporously in the sunlight, stunned by his horse-propelled inspection of the barn's double doors. "Brother, I send you to prepare my horse, and you wreak havoc with the livery."

Alfric shuffled and tried to look repentant.

"And save that chopfallen look for someone who hasn't hated it since childhood. Father may forgive your monstrosities because you're first in line for the moathouse, but as my squire you'll answer to me, and I'll have no counterfeit anguish in the bargain."

"It was the damn horse you chose, Weasel—nothing I done. Why, if I didn't know better, I'd suppose you set this up in the hopes that the beast would kill me and solve your problem of taking me on as a squire."

"That is something you do *not* know better, Brother dear," I bluffed, hoping that somewhere in the deep recesses of my brother's thinking, something like healthy respect might emerge. "But the animal solved me no problems, despite his bucking and backlash. I suspect we are stuck with making you useful."

* * * * *

Being useful was how Alfric lost my armor.

I set him to the task of polishing the breastplate, although the page, Raphael, had done the same thing far better only the night before. Alfric's best efforts would do little to mar the workmanship, I figured, so I decided to risk letting him oil the leather straps of the greaves, so that they wouldn't dry and crack on the gods-knew-how-long journey ahead.

It was scarcely an hour later that I came upon my brother in the castle tannery, poised anxiously over a vat of oil kept to soften dry leather, silence squealing machinery, and hurl boiling over besieging enemies. Alfric stood by my helmet and breastplate, shield and sword, staring down into the darkness of the vat as though he had lost something.

"What was it I said about making yourself useful, Brother?" I began.

But Alfric kept on staring.

I called him once, twice. But he gazed at the glittering surface of the oil as though he were reading it for signs or omens. Finally he looked up, gasping and gaping like a large and ungainly trout pulled out of the Vingaard River at low water.

"Brother, I am afraid your greaves are sunk," he began meekly.

"Sunk? As in submerged? Underwater?"

He shook his head slowly, stupidly.

"Under oil."

I followed his eyes to the barrel.

"I figured it would save trouble if, instead of oiling all them leather parts, I just dipped the greaves into the barrel," Alfric explained, looking up at me dolefully.

"Dipped?"

"And I kind of lost hold on them."

His eyes returned to the vat. I reached for my sword.

"Alfric, you are going in after them."

"What?"

"The greaves. You let them slip to the bottom of that mire, and by the gods, you are diving into there and coming out with greaves or you are not coming out at all."

I raised my sword for emphasis.

For a moment, my brother turned toward me with the same old bullying airs that had served him well throughout my bludgeoned and blackmailed childhood. He rose to his full height and looked at me scornfully, eye to eye.

"Bluff and bluster as much as you like, Alfric," I whispered calmly, turning the sword until its nasty-looking point tilted up beneath my brother's stubbled chin. "I hold the weaponry."

Whether it was my newfound Knighthood, his complete and natural cowardice, or the simple good sense that urges you to cooperate when someone directs a sword at you, Alfric backed away. Reluctantly he looked down into the vat, then stopped short.

"Brother," he said frantically. "Kill me if you must, but by Sirrion, I'm not touching it! Look!"

He pointed down into the oil.

"The damned stuff is boiling!"

Indeed, the surface of the oil rolled and shuddered, then circles began to radiate within it, swirling outward as they do when you drop a rock into a pond.

It was then that we felt the first tremor. All about us the walls began to shake, the beams above us to shift and crumble. Dust and gravel dropped from the ancient ceiling, and for a moment, I entertained prospects of being buried alive under tons of rubble.

Alfric forgot his oath and was into the oil before the first gravel dropped, submerged in the vat like some grotesque muskrat or otter. The oil closed above him, and for a moment, I was left frighteningly alone, the walls tilting uneasily around me.

A torch fell from its sconce by the tannery door, shivered on the rocking ground, and sputtered out. The room fell into a curious gray shadow, streaked by light from the high windows, as the dust rose until it became difficult to see or even to breathe. All the while the building shook, and I grabbed for the side of the vat to keep my footing.

"Alfric! Alfric!" I shouted, plunging my arm into the oil and reaching down into its wet, heavy darkness for a handful of my brother. Twice I came up with nothing, but on the third try, I pulled him, sputtering, to the surface, my fingers entangled in a shock of red, oily hair.

"There's no safety there, Brother!" I urged, clutching his arm and pulling in a vain attempt to draw him out of the vat. Twice he slipped from my grasp, toppling over backward into the oil, lost from sight again and again as the dust rained and the floor rocked.

On the third time, I managed to tug him over the side of the vat, losing my balance with the effort and the slipperiness of the now well-lubricated floor. My brother landed on top of me, and both of us lay still for a moment as the light and air seemed to leave the room entirely.

Then Alfric was on his feet, pushing me back down in his scramble for the door, which he struck headlong and burst open as the tannery flooded with daylight. Gathering my breath, I followed him, diving with a yell into the open courtyard.

The whole castle rocked at the edge of disorder. It was like my memories of the Scorpion's Nest that nightmare afternoon in the pass near Chaktamir. All around us, the walls shook. Stone, mortar, and beam dislodged, and the bright afternoon air dusted over.

A shriek descended from the battlements, where a lone sentry dangled from the very ladder that I had climbed to speak to Bayard that morning. Suddenly, with the crisp, splintering sound that a quarterstaff makes when broken across stone, the ladder gave way, and the sentry fell and lay still, sprawled in an ungainly fashion in the courtyard.

All around us were the shouts of men and the screams of horses. You would think we had walked out into battle, or into the Cataclysm come again. I turned to see after Alfric.

Who was nowhere to be found.

Then I heard a familiar cry arise over all the others, and I rushed toward the source of the noise, fearing the worst. The cry was Bayard's.

I found him lying in the middle of the courtyard, surrounded by Sir Brandon, Ramiro, and the Blue Knight. Valorous, Bayard's black stallion, who it seems had provided the final touch to the disaster quite by accident, stood unsteadily only a few yards away.

As I rushed toward my fallen comrade, the rumblings stopped as quickly as they had begun, and Brandon turned toward me, his handsome face ashen, his eyes enormous.

"Quickly! Arrange for a litter!" he shouted. "I fear it's his leg." Nor did such a fear arise from special wisdom or insight. Bayard clutched his shattered leg tightly in his enormous hands.

*　*　*　*　*

It had all happened quickly, as disasters will. It seemed that as the aftershocks grew more frequent and violent that terrible morning, that Bayard, astride his most reliable mount, had set about to comb the castle grounds, trying to control damage as best he could.

It was a dramatic gesture and a brave one . . .

"But not altogether wise," Bayard chuckled, benumbed and bemused and stretched on his back across his bed, Lady Enid and two drawn-faced surgeons in attendance. "For ground that is unsteady underfoot is also unsteady underhoof, my hearties."

Ramiro, Brandon and I had become "hearties" after Bayard, who scarcely took even a glass of wine, had taken his third glass of dwarf spirits—Sir Ramiro's remedy for whatever ailed a Knight or even remotely promised to ail him.

As far as I could tell, the pint of Thorbardin Eagle had done as much damage as quake and horse combined.

Enid was of the same mind. She signaled to Raphael, who removed the bottle. Unaware of his pain—or of his surroundings, for that matter—Bayard continued to speak at bleary length.

One of the physicians brought forth a textral stone—the small, egg-shaped rocks from the Elian Wilds that are known to knit together broken things—that would mend his leg entirely in a month or so if applied constantly. The stone sputtered, as it was supposed to do, and while the surgeon passed it over the fractured leg and the smoke rose, smelling of burnt evergreen and clove and sleep, Bayard told us how the accident had happened.

"Valorous had not traveled a hundred feet from the stable

when he capsized," Bayard began. "Capsized most grievously."

He paused and stared at all of us dramatically.

"Most grievously indeed, falling heavily upon this . . . appendage."

He slapped his fractured right leg. Enid gasped in alarm. The surgeon jumped back, the textral only half burnt away.

"Are we going to have to restrain you physically, dearest?" Enid asked pleasantly, when she had recovered her composure, but Bayard was off on an elaborate story, in which he swore—by Huma and Paladine and everyone connected in any fashion with any of the gods that you swear by—that the accident had nothing to do with Valorous's footing, that there was nothing the poor creature could help or avoid.

That indeed the venerable stallion had been "ethereally startled."

"I beg your pardon, Bayard?" asked a puzzled Ramiro.

"Something spooked Valorous, Ramiro!" Bayard explained. "Spooked a horse that has stood firm before ogre and minotaur, hobgoblin and the walking dead, in earthquake and in fire. It was as though the poor beast had seen a ghost beyond its reckoning."

Red-eyed and drowsy, Bayard sank back onto the bed as my memory fixed on yellowed faces in the stones.

"And did *you* . . . see anything, sir?"

"Galen?" His mind floated back from some distant, abstracted place—the vats of Thorbardin, no doubt. "Had forgotten you were here, boy."

He smiled drunkenly at me.

"So now you're a Knight. Insanity and all."

I decided that now was not the time for interrogation, so I smiled and nodded.

* * * * *

Alone in my quarters, I thought long and hard upon Bayard's ghostly visitors.

Things about Castle di Caela had grown altogether too

supernatural for my tastes. I rummaged my memories of folk literature, taught to me at the wobbling knee of old Gileandos. Surely he had said *something* about ghost lore.

Or were his only familiar spirits distilled ones?

"Let's see . . ." I spoke aloud, seating myself by the faintly glowing fireplace and dabbing a rather hopeless rag at my oily greaves. "Spirits come back to . . . urge someone to complete a task he failed to complete while he was living.

"Well, if the spirits in question are those of Plainsmen, it's no doubt a dark and bloody quest that promises plenty of mileage and casualties. With my imperiled brother at the end of it.

"Sometimes, though, ghosts don't want a journey at all. Instead they come to urge the living . . . to avenge their untimely murder.

"I doubt that. If it's Plainsmen, they'd no doubt keep it in their own family like the Pathwardens do, or the di Caelas. Every family has enough intrigue and betrayal without calling in outsiders. And it's beyond me what Brithelm would have to do with a murky tale of vengeance."

I cast the greaves aside, rummaged through my other belongings, and picked up the brooch.

"Damn! Elazar and Fernando will drum me out of the Order if they don't have their self-righteous mitts on this at once."

But the brooch jogged my imagination, and leaning back in my chair, I held it to the light, speculating further.

"Then again, ghosts sometimes announce the prospect of treasure. . . ."

But those days were over. Though a faint greed stirred at the back of my attentions, I could not dwell upon it long. Avarice grew silent at the thought of poor Brithelm, spectral knife at his throat.

It was then that the centermost opal began to flicker. A faint light, fixed at the heart of the stone, expanded, deepened, until it seemed to split the gem like a column of fire in darkness. The room about me tumbled into blackness, as though the only source of light in the world came from the stone in my hand.

I gasped, breathed in moist, subterranean air, carrying

with it the chilly smell of mud and water and stagnant time. It felt as though I had fallen into the stone or lay submerged in sunless caverns.

The white light at the center of the opal took on shape, definition, resolving itself into a thin, pale arm, a pale hand clutching a long, menacing dagger.

I grabbed the arms of the chair and waited. No doubt it was the hand I had seen before—the hand at my brother's throat. I steeled myself and looked more closely into the stone, searching intently for movement, for other light, for any sign or clue or landmark that would locate the vision in the world I knew and understood.

Instead, I saw only the light and the hand and the dagger, and finally, beyond these a faintly glimmering visage—the pale face of a Plainsman, marred by a diamond-shaped patch over his right eye. Then a voice rose on all sides of me, whispering back and forth in the stunned darkness of the room.

Do not fear, it consoled, though the consolation was brittle, hiding beneath it a dark, icy current of menace. *Do not fear, young man, for your brother is free of harm. He is simply a way I have discovered to . . . gain your attention.*

"Forgive me if I find that hard to believe, having seen him last with a knife at his throat," I retorted. For all my attempts at bravery, my voice sounded thin, almost frail in the enormous, shifting vault of the room in which I felt I was sitting now—*felt* I was sitting, though for the life of me, I could not have told you how I had moved from my cramped little chambers into some monstrous, dark rotunda.

Your energy is most welcome, the voice explained. *For in energy is the beginning of commerce.*

I gripped the arms of the chair even tighter. "And what is *that* supposed to mean?"

Slowly the patch lifted, and the empty socket glowed with the dead light of phosfire—the pale green light that illumines nothing but the source of the light itself. It began to change shape, taking on a head, four arms, a tail, until a salamander glimmered and writhed on the black floor of the room. Turning quickly and more quickly in a rapidly tightening circle, the creature took its own tail between its jaws and, swirling yet more rapidly, became a spinning blur of light that suddenly became the face again, this time bright with sharp aquiline features.

His hair was dark, beaded, and disheveled. His unhooded eye was like a black opal, in the center of which lay a column of fire, wherein lay the same face. It seemed that the image in front of me repeated itself forever, each time smaller and smaller, like reflections in reflections, born of facing mirror to mirror.

It means it is time for commerce, Sir . . . The voice paused expectantly.

"No names. At least not yet," I whispered.

Except that of Brithelm, perhaps? taunted the echoing voice.

I leaned forward, cupping the brooch in both hands. The room reeled, then steadied.

"Just . . . just what is the nature of this *commerce?*" I asked.

Simple, the face responded, now moving its thin lips in accord with the words I heard around me. *My commerce is a simple purchase—your opals, if you wish to see your brother again.*

"I see. As ransom."

The face in front of me wavered, turned in the half-light. Behind it, if only for a second, I caught a glimpse of glistening rock in the darkness, of a pale cascade of stalactites or stalagmites—I never could remember which one was which.

"Ransom" is not our word for it. We prefer "reunion."

"I see." I fell silent and tried to avert my eyes from the stones. It was as though the face was everywhere I looked, reflected upon the dense and billowing darkness around me.

"Well, then, the opals are yours, obviously. I shall be glad to restore them. They are here, in my hands. Yours for the taking."

I am not fool enough to ascend among you, the voice scolded. *Instead, I would have you bring them to me.*

"But where in the world are you? Or where *under* the world, I might ask?"

For a moment, the face dimmed in the brooch. The room fell silent, and I could feel the closeness of the walls about me, as if I had been restored to my own chambers.

A clever one, you are. All brave and Solamnic and ever so bright.

"And altogether willing to hand over a mess of opals for my brother. Providing, that is, that I know where to hand them over."

You would like that, wouldn't you? To converge on a spot with dozens of your kind and to muscle your brother away from us.

Even the criminal, it seemed, mistrusted me.

"Yes, I *would* like that. But there are not dozens of 'my kind,' whatever that is. Nor would I wish that on the world. Look, this is something more basic than tactics, more basic than your deals and your transactions. Quite simply, I want my brother safe, and I have the opals that will assure his safety. You have my word for that."

The opals themselves will tell you what you need to know, the voice replied mysteriously and ominously. *In them lies the map of my darkness. In them lies the path to your brother. Follow the stone beneath the stone, and you will come to all of us soon enough.*

Suddenly the gems dulled, the fire in the center of the brooch extinguished, and the room was flooded in candlelight. I stood up, breathed deeply, and looked around me. The room was as I remembered it, but the window was ajar, and a faint hint of a chill had crept into my chambers.

Again I looked at the brooch, which a moment before had flickered and boded in my hand. Now it seemed harmless, quite lovely but useless for anything more than clasping a cape about the neck of a young and unsettled Knight.

"I am right on the edge of adventure," I told myself. "Or of disaster. Or maybe I am only talking to rocks."

Chapter VI

There is no telling when Bayard made his next deci-
sion, nor his state of mind when he made it.

I gathered that the surgeons broke the news to him
shortly after we left. Owing to his broken leg, travel was out
of the question, at least for the next several months. Horseback riding would be impossibly painful; the rocky foothills
of the Vingaards were naturally hostile to any travelers
aside from dwarves or mountain goats.

I figured that our adventure was postponed of necessity
and because my able benefactor would not fully trust me
out of his sight.

There had been times, back in my weaselly and misspent
youth, when this knowledge would have brought with it
waves of relief, a murmured prayer of thanks to the gods of

dry castles, warm beds, and especially to whatever deity fancied broken legs. Those times had passed, evidently.

Restlessly I stirred the fire in my quarters, thinking of Brithelm in the mountains, of the visions and threats I had seen in the opals, of what Bayard's injury meant to our plans.

Of how in the world I would get to the Vingaards alone.

It was almost a relief when Raphael came to my quarters that evening, bearing orders from Sir Bayard Brightblade that Sir Galen Pathwarden-Brightblade was to attend him at once. But that relief vanished when I entered Sir Bayard's chambers.

Given the shocks and tumbles of the past two days, I was not surprised to find Ramiro and Brandon seated by Bayard's bedside. It was, however, alarming to see both of them looking so glum and downtrodden and inconvenienced, like two old alchemists testing an ineffective laxative. My first guess was that they had just been appointed Brithelm's rescuers.

The conversation stopped when I entered the room. The three Knights stared at me intently, Bayard strangely curious and proud, the others blank and unreadable. Raphael, striding ahead of me, busied himself at once with some obscure and no doubt needless task.

"Sir Galen Pathwarden-Brightblade of Castle di Caela, gentlemen," Bayard announced, and I could tell he had rested, had slept perhaps, and was now quite sober.

His companions kept silent.

"Good evening, Weasel," Ramiro rumbled at last. I chose to ignore him out of both courtesy and caution, nodding politely to all present and taking a seat at the foot of my protector's bed.

Outside, evening was passing into night. I heard a pair of doves settle into the trees near the window, rustling and thrumming as they prepared for the rising storm.

"Galen, I'm afraid my news is hard," Bayard announced, raising himself in bed and grimacing. Ramiro took the flask of Thorbardin Eagle from the bedside table and offered it, but Bayard waved it away, his eyes remote and terribly melancholy.

"The surgeons have consulted, Galen," he continued, "and debated the fine points, on which they all disagree. But they have come to a general truth: that my travel by horse is impossible during the next six months, inadvisable at best for six months after that."

"But six months will be too late, sir!" I protested, standing up and knocking the chair out from under me. By instinct, Ramiro's hand went to his sword. Brandon, however, regarded me calmly from his seat by the fire.

"Too late?" Bayard asked. "Why 'too late'?"

The possibilities made me reel: Brithelm, ravaged by fire, injured in the earthquake, or lost in some underground darkness, at the cruel whim of a bunch of pallid Plainsmen. Whatever the situation, my brother was alone, at the knife's edge, and unschooled in survival.

"Who said anything about postponing the journey, Galen?" Bayard snapped, and my thoughts skittered and plunged.

What else could those words and this assemblage mean but that Bayard had decided to send out a party of Knights to the Vingaards, fully intending to leave me behind in Castle di Caela along with the disabled, the women, and the old men?

I would not have it.

" 'Too late,' " I announced coldly, "because I have had a vision that tells me 'too late,' damn it! And I *know* you've changed your mind, Bayard, and no doubt you will be sending Ramiro and whoever else has volunteered since your accident—anyone as long as it isn't the shifty, irresponsible Weasel! You've no idea how mistaken and foolish that is, for the opals have told me—"

"I beg your pardon?" Ramiro interrupted. "*The opals told you?*"

Now there was no turning back. My task was the simple and dreadful one of telling my brothers in the knighthood what had come to pass in the depth of the opals. I told it briefly, without ornament (I really *have* changed), told it all to an immense silence, to four pairs of widening eyes.

"So that is why I must go to the Vingaards, Bayard," I concluded. "Despite your good intentions of raising this party in my absence, it's an insult to me and to your belief in me and . . ."

Ramiro glanced at Bayard skeptically. Bayard winced as pain coursed up his damaged leg. For a moment, my heart went out to him—a man in the prime of his considerable powers, now bedfast and idle. Then I thought of what he was doing—shipping off virtual strangers to the Vingaards on a search for my brother, when I was the only one who knew of the danger. It was plain he did not trust me—had never trusted me—not as a squire and certainly not as a Knight.

At that moment, I devoutly wished the same condition for his other leg.

"I am sorry, Ramiro, that you, too, discount my visions," I said.

"No more, I am afraid, than I discount other things about you, Weasel. Still, you did show passable mettle in the mountains at Chaktamir, back when the Scorpion's Nest was crashing all about us . . ."

"I thank you for that memory, sir," I said, and stared ironically at Bayard. In the silence that followed, it struck me how shrill and peevish I sounded, like a schoolmaster badgering a whispering student to "share your secret with the other scholars."

It was what they wanted, evidently. Each one of them, looking at Sir Galen, no doubt saw only the Weasel in ill-fitting armor.

"Hold your tongue, Galen," Bayard said softly. "You would do your brother Brithelm a service to befriend these men assembled here, especially Ramiro, rather than doing your best to stir up discord and foolishness. Indeed, you would do yourself a service.

"Galen, your responsibility is a hard one to shoulder—greater than my own, than that of the men you see before you, greater even than the formidable duties of Sir Ramiro of the Maw, who will act as your second and confidante in the coming days."

"My *second?*"

Ramiro and I both gaped wildly, as though another earthquake had come, opening the floor beneath us and dropping us halfway into the center of the planet.

Bayard nodded, a strange half-smile on his face.

"Your second, Sir Galen. For in my absence, you are appointed to lead this expedition."

Even as Bayard spoke those words, the rain began, driving in thick sheets through the open window, which Raphael rushed to close, leaving the room in darkness.

It was as though the world wept at my leadership. For hours it poured, and where the Cataclysm had come before in fire and explosion, eruption and ruin, it threatened to come now as flood, as a deluge that would drown us all, given time and enough water in the heavens.

Behind the closed shutters of the infirmary, at a candlelit conference of Solamnic Knights, I learned what everyone thought of an expedition with Galen Pathwarden at the helm.

Ramiro belabored my failings at length. Brandon continued in tandem with him for about an hour, and soon I found myself nodding agreement to even the worst things they had to say about me, for after a while listening to such talk, you tend to believe the talkers and forget the specifics.

That the talk is about you, for instance.

There in the presence of bickering Solamnics, I unraveled a string from my tunic and settled down for another philosophers' duel, made only a little more interesting by the fact that I was the central subject in it all. The rain beat in waves against the shutters, and you could even hear it spatter the stone walls of the infirmary, it came down so hard.

Bayard was in full voice now, I discovered when I listened now and then, and the talk was of honor and obligation and staying the course. Of how much I could learn from this as regards responsibility and command, even though the chances were that Brithelm was untouched by the strange disturbances to our west. As the rain came down, so rose my sense of hope, for it became dimly possible that Bayard was winning them over, that by the time he was finished with them, Ramiro would follow me into the gaping maw of the Cataclysm or neck deep into the Blood Sea, for the pure and simple reason that he had promised Bayard some days back that he would follow someone somewhere.

In the midst of my musings, I saw Ramiro stand, saw that the big fellow was speaking.

Something about preparations.

" . . . tomorrow. We shall take the Plains Road due west, then ford the Vingaard and ride due north, keeping the mountains to our left. That way, if I recall, we can make steady progress without tiring . . . *anyone* unduly."

He glanced tellingly at me.

"Of course," he added, "this all depends on how . . . our leader figures it. I mean, if he has some little path of his own that he is all that bent on following . . ."

I could see I was completely accepted by my subordinates.

"Of course not, Sir Ramiro," I replied smoothly, also standing. "Indeed, I consider you an expert in terrain and travel, and it is a foolish leader who discounts the advice of his experts, now, isn't it?"

I was shameless, I know.

"And what is more, Sir Ramiro, if a lad must lead his first expedition as a Knight, must pass into unknown lands at the head of a party who become, tragically, his heavy responsibility, then I thank the gods that it is my lot to be thrown in with the most daring, resourceful, and formidable Knight Solamnia has to offer, in this time or any other."

Bayard blushed, and Raphael after him. The air in the room felt so laden with oil that I feared the candles would ignite us all. And yet I continued, crafting in the most indecent recesses of my imagination a way to compare my two companions favorably with Huma, while at the same time not comparing either favorably to the other.

But Ramiro raised his hands and cut short my groveling.

"Never mind, lad, never mind. It seems to me, Bayard, that the boy's intentions are good, and that perhaps his judgment . . . promises a likely future."

Bayard looked at me in disbelief.

"Thank you, Sir Ramiro," I replied. "Your kind words are an honor second only to my knighthood."

My protector winced as if I had broken his other leg, as Ramiro basked in my flattery like a walrus in warm water.

"Very well, lad," he huffed. "Very well. Now . . . ah, see to it that you're prepared for the road by tomorrow morning.

"That is," he corrected himself quickly, "if it suits you, being our commander and all."

It suited me, and I told him so.

* * * * *

It is a task to prepare for a journey, to see to the armor and horses and provisions not only for yourself but for those in your party.

It is a double task—a monumental one—when your squire is no help whatsoever.

Not long after the quake hit the castle, Alfric crawled out from under the rubble, none the worse for wear, but no longer quite as ardent for squirehood. In one moment, it seemed, he had discovered that peril was on all sides of him, full likely to rise from the earth itself. It could meet any of us unannounced and unexpected on the road from the stable to our bedroom or from our bedroom to the privy.

"There is just no need to go looking for things," Alfric maintained with high drama as he walked into the outhouse, hands filled with planks and hammer and nails, and proceeded to board himself inside.

It was a delaying tactic at best. Father, of course, was not buying it. Surely Alfric knew that, once he signed on as my squire, the old man would throttle him before he let him sign off.

While Alfric's hours were spent in the outhouse with the old man hovering angrily outside, I was left to my own resources, which seemed a loss only when I went down to the livery, intent on attending to last-minute details, and discovered that, thanks to the inattention of my squire, I had to start from the beginning—to arm and equip and supply myself, not to mention saddling all the horses. Cleaning the greaves alone took far too much time, and as the hours progressed into morning, I thought about the other duties that should occur to a Knight at the time of his departure—when he set out into unknown danger . . .

Perhaps never to return . . .

His second a man who mistrusted not only his leadership

but his good sense in general . . .

And his squire an incompetent elder brother who was spending the day and the night in cowardly dodges . . .

I sat roughly on the tannery floor, the greaves heavy in my lap. It had been a while since I was constrained to think about the odds against me, about the prospects of not returning from anywhere, and the prospect gave me ominous notions. I saw myself waylaid by bandits, turning on a spit over one of those mountain fires with a family of ogres gathered around me in expectation.

If that were the case, there would be others besides me. For not only was I responsible for my own skin in the days to come, but Bayard had put me in charge of the party—of Ramiro, his squire, and my own brother Alfric.

I stood up, oily and burdened, hoisting the armor over my shoulder and staggering across the wide courtyard toward the stable. Three horses were flawlessly saddled and appointed beneath a sheltered paddock, safely out of the rain—three big stallions belonging to Ramiro.

I knew I would be lucky not to be kicked to death by the children's pony.

All of a sudden, the largeness of what lay ahead of me grew larger still, until I was quite overwhelmed by it. I stood in the open bailey, in the pooling rainfall, my red hair plastered dark to my face and the water running in courses down my forehead into my nose and mouth. The stable ahead of me blurred for a moment, though I cannot say for sure whether it was rainfall or tears of pure terror that clouded my sight, for I was drenched by both of them.

"There is a saying about the sense to get out of the rain, Sir Galen," a sweet voice prodded from behind me, interrupting my reflection and self-pity. I jumped and turned swiftly, dropping the armor and nearly losing my footing in the water and mud.

Dannelle di Caela stood between horses in the canopied paddock, dressed in a light chain mail and holding a curry comb. It was neither attire nor pose that I generally found attractive, but the girl was flawless—brilliant green eyes and thick red hair, somehow untouched by these terrible southern downpours. Having caught my attention, she flashed the fetching smile that had kept her three years in my thoughts and had made her a factor in my most restless yearnings.

I felt myself grow warm about the ears.

"I am glad you are constantly about me quoting deathless philosophy, Lady Dannelle," I replied finally, stooping in the rain to pick up the greaves and carrying them beneath the canopy, into the warm, horse-smelling dark. "But I have adventures to saddle for."

Undaunted, the girl sidled next to me, glancing about her as though alert for spies or eavesdroppers. She smelled wonderful, as I discovered from this new distance. She bore a faint hint of lavender, which, when you've been in a tannery or the midst of a rain or simply around horses, can be a pleasant change from the general whiff in the air. The welcome fragrance disarmed me, and she saw that it did so and smiled, which disarmed me further.

"Saddle one more than you planned to," she whispered merrily, "because I'm coming with you."

"You are *what?*"

I tried to scramble to my feet, but I was surprised past scrambling.

"B-But, Danelle! Surely you know there would be conniptions through the upper ranks of the Order if they heard you'd even suggested such an arrangement, and worse still if they heard I had listened to your madness."

Her smile was steady and deadly serious.

"I can think of worse conniptions," she announced with bright menace.

At once, in a cascade of thoughts as rapid as floodwater, I rushed through my litany of wrongs, past the marked playing cards of my wealthy early days in the castle and on to the black-market selling of spices from the larder, even including the steady trade in rustled horses and hustled armor I had planned until fear, second thoughts, and Bayard's instructions had set in.

It was all accounted for. All, that is, except Marigold.

Who, when I had come to the castle a raw lad of seventeen, hungry for leisure and money and baked goods, had shared my interest in pastry with such zeal that croissants and pies had led to . . . other things. Many were the narrow hours of the morning when I scurried down the back corridors of the castle, seeking the darkest route from chamber to chamber, wrapped in a crumb-covered bedsheet.

It was a weak spot in my armor. For even when I signed on for a squirehood of chastity and service, I figured that it was too much to tackle both virtues right away. So the dalliance with Marigold continued until it became an embarrassment: The cakes she sent to my quarters with her maidservants took on naughtier and naughtier shapes until even the stable grooms would blush when they gossiped about it.

"Wait a half-mile from the castle, a little after dawn," I whispered. "On the Highland Road, out of sight of the battlements. Bring a good horse and a blanket and provisions for a week's ride."

Dannelle's eyes widened with each sentence. When I had finished she gaped at me, swallowed hard, and nodded.

"A half-mile from the castle," she whispered. "A little after dawn."

Then, like a vision, she slipped into the darkness of the paddock and, passing through the horses and the rain beyond them, found the entrance to the tower, closing the heavy door behind her.

Leaning against Lily, my old mare, who stood sleeping in her stall, I looked up through the downpour at Dannelle's high window.

Yes, it was best to take the girl along.

For if she broke the news about my evenings with Marigold, the mere aftershock of the telling might break a few more legs around the castle. Far better to cart her miles away, to avoid upheaval and her considerable talent with tales and rumors and revelations.

And she *was* pretty.

I chuckled to myself.

She would slow us down, of course, and no doubt cause further dissension in my ranks. I would have to watch Alfric around her, and Ramiro himself was not to be trusted.

And yet . . .

I remembered a time when this paddock had been a topiary, the window covered with vines. When I had looked up through shrubbery and night and watched the light in that window like a baying dog waiting for red Lunitari in the dark sky.

Could those moonstruck nights have really been years ago?

After a minute or so, a light flickered on in Dannelle's chamber. I smiled and propped my chin against Lily's cool, wet-smelling back. The old mare whickered, shifting her weight from flank to flank, dreaming no doubt of bitter-sweet memories.

"A long time ago, I thought she liked me." I whispered. "Is there still a chance, old girl?"

Chapter VII

Rain was general throughout Solamnia.

The waters had risen above the stone fences that portioned off the country south of the Vingaard River. Risen so high, in fact, that in some places the fences were submerged, and the servants said that from the heights of the Cat Tower one could look north and west to where the Vingaard had overflowed its banks and see only thatched roofs in the lowlands where houses had once dotted the landscape— thatched roofs afloat on a muddy, swirling tide of water.

We grew uneasy at home, of course, because of the well beneath us. For years, Castle di Caela had enjoyed running water, pipes, and plumbing, because one of Sir Robert's ancestors possessed the foresight to build the place above an enormous artesian well. Now good fortune rebounded on us with a vengeance, for those subterranean springs had dangerously little natural outlet to the surface, as the ground water slowed the customary seepage and flow. The more nervous of the engineers had nightmares in which all of Castle di Caela rode a monstrous geyser into the Solamnic skies and was dashed, inhabitants and all, when it hurtled to earth miles away.

Only the highlands, it seems, remained reasonably dry, a narrow ridge of waterlogged land that extended due west from Castle di Caela nearly twenty miles until it rose even farther into the foothills of the Vingaard Mountains. A traveler, it seems, could forget about fording the river and follow that ridge along its cobbled spine, known as the Highlands Road. From there, he might enter the known passes through the mountains by a way obscure and roundabout.

Legends emerge from this time: incredible stories of strange migrations and drownings. When the waters cleared finally, over a month after the ceremonial evening in which I was knighted, travelers and scavengers continued to find the bones of birds dotting the landscape—sparrows and nightingales and the heavier skeletons of owls and raptors. Tales arose that the trees in which the larger birds slept were overwhelmed by water, rapidly and violently, catching the sleepers unaware. And as for the smaller birds, why, they simply dropped from exhaustion, having flown in circles for days without finding a place to alight.

As for the folk who dwelt in the countryside of Southern Solamnia, it seems that for once the poor fared better than their more wealthy countrymen. For the poor built their houses of wood instead of stone, and many of them floated away north and east across the plains, where they settled on higher ground, some of them beyond the Vingaard Keep halfway to the Dargaard Mountains.

Whatever the circumstance, people vanished, people drowned. And people floated away, their far destinations a mystery.

There was little mystery, on the other hand, about our setting forth.

The next morning after the incidents in the stable, six

horses were assembled in the bailey and led to a plot of high ground where we did not have to mount them in ankle-deep standing water. Two of the horses were laden with supplies—food, dry clothing, and extra weaponry, all wrapped under canvas, from which most of the water ran in little rivulets onto the ground.

Our provisions were dry for now, but if the rain continued, I foresaw trouble in the making.

The other horses were for the four of us, of course: Ramiro and his squire Oliver, and the two Pathwarden boys, Alfric and me. Only recently pried from his rank-smelling hideaway, Alfric managed to do a fairly decent job of guiding Lily out of the unnaturally quiet stable, and into the brisk, damp air of the Solamnic predawn. He took his place with Oliver behind Ramiro and me, sullenly holding on to the reins of one of the pack animals.

I was drowsy that morning, having dozed fitfully in the stable as Oliver prepared four horses—Ramiro's, his own, and the two pack animals. I awoke now and then to the faint light of the lantern nodding against the flanks of horses, to the rush of rain on the roof, and Lily's blissful snoring. To the sounds of Oliver busy at some unattended detail with a voiceless efficiency that was almost frightening, making me wonder if this was how a real squire was supposed to behave.

One time I arose, walked out of the stable into the rain, ran across the bailey, and entered the keep, drenched and sputtering. It was my farewell trip to my quarters. Raphael had arranged all my belongings in full view, lest I forget something essential.

The brooch, the gloves, and the dog whistle lay on my bed in the darkness. I had no second thoughts about any of them.

Quickly I picked up the whistle and thrust it to the bottom of my tunic pocket. Brithelm would no doubt be pleased to see it when we reached him. The gloves followed quickly, almost an afterthought.

The brooch, on the other hand, I inspected carefully, making sure none of the stones was missing.

What was it the vision had said about the opals? *In them*

lies the path of my darkness. A murky sentiment, even as visions go. The opals caught the light of the torches and glittered as I counted them, and then the brooch joined the whistle in the depths of my pocket.

Elazar and Fernando would just have to wait for my earthly belongings, especially if anything I owned stood to be the key to finding Brithelm.

With my treasures gathered, I went back to the stable and to a short restless hour of sleep, where I dreamed of the voices of Plainsmen rising from the gargoyles in the cornices of the castle.

* * * * *

So we departed Castle di Caela, Ramiro and I riding abreast through the great gate of the castle onto the soggy western fields, our squires behind us and the gods knew what ahead of us.

Bayard greeted us at the gate, carried on a cot by two sweating surgeons, the third sullenly holding an umbrella above my reclining friend and master.

"Gentlemen," Bayard pronounced, in his best formal and ceremonial voice, "may the gods speed you on your journey. May you, Sir Ramiro, take gracious instruction from the Knight at the head of your embassage."

I wished devoutly I could tell Bayard to stop, having seen the sidelong glance that Ramiro gave me. But true to his Solamnic nature, the lord of Castle di Caela was in full flourish.

"And you, Sir Galen Pathwarden-Brightblade. May Huma buoy your spirit, and may you prove adept, resourceful, and worthy of the charge placed upon you. May you be gracious in the instruction of your subordinates, for the leader often learns from those who follow. But may your commands be iron. And let none question your wisdom or resolve."

So much for smoothing my path into command. Now even the horses would hate me. I smiled weakly at Bayard and told him to give my best wishes to Lady Enid and Sir Robert.

Then, with dire reluctance, I set out, men, boys, and horses falling in line behind me.

*   *   *   *   *

They always say in Coastlund that a long look back on the outset of a journey bodes ill fortune. If that is the case, everything disastrous, perilous, and strange that befell us in the following days was my doing, because I must have memorized my recent home—its towers and battlements—as we passed through the gates and rode westward, seeking the high ridge and drier ground.

What lay behind me were buildings full of monotony—a place that had driven me to distraction, not to mention Marigold. It was a place I had always told myself I would be delighted to leave.

But the prospects in front of me were frighteningly uncertain. The plains were so covered with water that following paths had become impossible, steering by landmarks difficult for anyone except those who could navigate by stars. Also, it was easy to imagine what would wash up when the waters subsided, and when it is easy to imagine things, my imagination is extreme and unkind. I fancied beached sea monsters in the process of learning to use fin and fluke as legs, monsters we would come across when their hunger was no doubt desperate. I imagined drowned men draped over the branches of trees. All of this, not to mention whatever was going on up in the mountains, and whatever catastrophe in which I would no doubt find my brother Brithelm, played out before me as we made our way though the murk of dawn and puddle.

All in all, it was a gloomy prospect, next to which Bayard's displeasure and Marigold's attentions and Dannelle di Caela's threats and approaching presence—and the strange phenomenon of the visionary brooch—all seemed worth the braving.

Several times I came close to turning Lily around and riding away from Ramiro and Alfric and Oliver, straight back through the western gates of Castle di Caela, to lose myself under quilts in my quarters for, oh, six to seven months,

Marigold no doubt tapping at my chamber door, hair sculpted and lacquered into the form of a yellow heart and arms laden with lurid pastries. So I would have done, were it not that desertion of one's fellow Knights is punishable by death under the old Solamnic codes. In his present mood, Ramiro, no doubt, would be more than delighted to interpret my refusal as such.

Therefore I looked a last time at Castle di Caela, then set my eyes ahead of me westward, toward the crest of a dark hill that marked the easternmost fingers of the highlands, faintly visible through the gray of the morning and the rain. There, in a misty little copse that stood at the beginning of the Highland Road, a small hooded form awaited us.

My troubles, I figured, were about to increase remarkably.

I had dreaded the moment when we would meet up with Dannelle, dreaded every question from my companions, every Solamnic sniff and headshake, every judgment passed in silence.

So I held my breath a moment as she led her horse out from among the trees. Her hair was tied up for the road, and she was blanketed and booted and armed, but already the rain had soaked through and the mud taken hold.

Nevertheless, she made all of us gasp—even Oliver, who was a young thirteen and no doubt considered a twenty-year-old woman to be ancient past recall. Pushing back her hood, she mounted her little gray palfrey, straddling it effortlessly like a cavalryman, her eyes already on the road ahead of us.

"Thanks be to Huma!" Alfric murmured. "The women are already following me."

Ramiro was the first of us to address Dannelle, bowing ponderously in the saddle. Roasted chestnuts dribbled from his pockets as he spoke.

"It is quite an honor, m'lady, that in such inclement weather you would venture so far to bid us farewell. But as m'lady no doubt is aware, the rain shows no sign of abating, and a downpour the likes of this is passing uncomfortable for the delicate and frail."

"I shall pass that along to the delicate and frail," Dannelle replied curtly, "when we return from this journey and see some of them."

Ramiro looked at me openmouthed. The overwhelming smell of very cheap cologne arose behind me as I heard a bottle break and Alfric swear.

We all looked back at Dannelle, who smiled winningly. And though I am sure that none of us thought she should join the party, each of us would be drawn, quartered, and boiled before he would suffer losing sight of her. Wordlessly she took her place beside me in the column.

Ramiro ogled her as though she were a pudding or a carafe of wine. Alfric, on the other hand, jostled his way ahead of poor little Oliver, sending the young squire bottom-first into the mud and positioning himself within earshot, intent that no word of intelligence nor endearment would pass his notice.

All in all, it was like a swarm of drone bees following their queen as we reached drier ground and set off westward toward the Vingaard Mountains.

* * * * *

Needless to say, Ramiro had no real intention of letting me command, especially not now, when there was a Dannelle di Caela to strut for and impress and bedazzle. True to form he was—to the Measure and to his promise to Bayard—but by the time we had traveled an hour up the Highland Road, it was clear how he had things planned.

"Shall we stop for a rest and perhaps a wee bit of midday sustenance?" Ramiro asked me, leaning back in the saddle as his large stallion grunted and bravely shifted its flanks to accommodate the change in burden. Beneath the broad brim of his "traveling hat"—a straw monstrosity that smelled of water and sweat and years of use—his broad nose peeked out of the shadows, and somewhere behind the water coursing over the brim I could make out the glitter of his little eyes as he sized me up.

Instantly I was on guard, for I remembered the castle wisdom, circulated among the cooks and the bakers: When Sir Ramiro of the Maw asks for lunch, be elsewhere and be occupied, or you'll be working on through supper.

From what I knew of Ramiro, one whiling would lead to another. The road would lengthen meal after meal, our travels slowing to a gorged crawl westward. We would be on the road a month, during a journey that should take all of three days.

"Why don't we go on a little more, sir?" I asked graciously, trying to slip a note of command into my voice. The rain seemed to subside as I spoke, and I caught myself almost shouting into Ramiro's ear, shouting into the quiet of softer rainfall and the wet hoof splatter of the horses behind us.

Ramiro reined in his big steed and looked at me slyly from under the drooped corner of that extinct hat.

"I mean . . . there's time aplenty this evening. For food. For fellowship. Even a warm fire then, sir, when we could all settle down to a good hearty supper among friends," I explained.

"That tree there is as good as any for stopping," he replied cheerily, as though my suggestion had been so much rainfall, brushed off readily into the mud beneath him.

"But, Sir Ra—" I began. The big stallion turned and cantered toward a gnarled old vallenwood. Oliver followed suit, as did Alfric behind him.

Dannelle, with scarcely a glance in my direction, followed the rest of them.

The rain picked up again, and with it a chilling wind for the summertime, borne out of the mountains and carrying with it the whiff of icy peaks and evergreen and thin air. But despite its freshness, it was cold, settling on me like a sudden shift in the seasons.

I was afraid for a moment then.

Things were tumbling rapidly out of my control.

I reined Lily toward the shelter and the others.

Whatever lay buried in Ramiro's provisions, one could trust it was not dried fruit or jerky. The big Knight drew an enormous ham from a sailcloth bag on the packhorse. Several loaves of bread followed, and two bottles of wine—a vintage no doubt pinched from Bayard's wine cellar with the sure knowledge that the host, who so seldom drank from it, would go years without missing it.

It was there that I heard Dannelle's story, told to us all between mouthfuls of ham and bread.

It was, as I had guessed it would be, a tale of gender imprisonment.

The three of us—Ramiro, Alfric, and I—rivaled each other to seem even more sympathetic to Dannelle's misfortunes, even more concerned and outraged when she complained of her mistreatment at the hands of a forbidding male world.

Respect and honesty were, as always, excellent disguises. So we wrinkled our brows with concern, brimmed with sensitivity, and, most importantly, interrupted Dannelle only rarely as she told about her rough week at the hands of her uncle, and how his restrictions had provoked an onslaught of tantrum-throwing and servant abuse never seen before in Castle di Caela.

"Things had reached a real impasse between me and Sir Robert," Dannelle began. "You see, I wanted permission to ride Carnifex, which he was not about to let a girl attempt."

Alfric and I looked at one another with alarm. My brother emitted a low whistle. Carnifex, you see, was a terrible half-wild stallion, a gift of some godforsaken nomad chief to Sir Robert five years back. The horse was nearly ten now, and no more docile or ridable than he had been as a colt. Sir Robert kept him as a huge, unmanageable trophy, a consumer of oats and, occasionally, grooms.

"The first time I asked," Dannelle continued, "I sidled up to him like we all sidle—said my 'yes, sirs' and set the matter aside for a month. Then I returned and used the old strategy Enid perfected while Uncle still ran things at the castle."

"Told him that he had approved it the last time you spoke?" Ramiro asked.

"Of course. It had always worked before," she explained. "But of course this was the time he picked to pay attention, and when he saw what I was doing . . . well, he threatened me, Galen.

"He told me that a few weeks of doing 'women's work' would remove all notions of riding Carnifex from what he called my 'pretty little head.' "

I smothered a smile. Of all the Solamnic Knights who were mired deep in backwardness when it came to the subject of what women could and couldn't do, Sir Robert was mired the deepest. For years, he had kept these sentiments in check, mainly because the women he dealt with directly were all di Caelas and all completely impossible to govern or even advise. But now, his duties as lord of the castle set aside, Sir Robert was saying what he damned well pleased, and I knew firsthand that he damned well pleased to offend just about everyone.

What Sir Robert considered "woman's work" would be just about anything the old coot found distasteful.

Dannelle looked long at me. I remained expressionless. She continued.

"He says to me, 'Niece'—he forgets my name when he's angry—'Niece, it seems to me that you're in some need of respecting a proper tour of duty about this castle, what with two dozen servants to fluff up your circumstances every time something ill suits you.'

"Then he says, 'Hear the thunder outside?' and of course I think he's off to the Age of Dreams again, and I smile and nod because I'm about to ask him once more about Carnifex, because I'm sure that if Robert's all abstracted, he's likely to think I'm someone else and let me ride the horse. But then I hear the thunder at a great distance and know that my uncle's hearing is perhaps the one faculty he hasn't lost. It's just then, like it's on cue or something, that the rain begins to fall and everybody hears it against the stones of the castle and the old man starts singing that 'rainy days are washdays, rainy days are washdays,' and the next thing I know, I'm down in the laundry with a handful of sheets, crouched over a washboard and tub."

It was all I could do to keep from laughing aloud, and I wished devoutly that I could have seen the dazzling Dannelle di Caela scrubbing the castle linens. But I governed myself, looked alarmed, even pained, and I encouraged her to continue.

"Well, it gets worse from here, Galen. Sir Robert fastened himself on the idea that I should do laundry as long as it rained, and as you know, it has been raining as though it will never stop. Two days into this, and I had lost almost all my interest in Carnifex. I was simply praying to any listening god that Sir Robert would not start taking in laundry from Palanthas or Kalaman just so he could keep me at the basin forever.

"I thought of all kinds of ways to deliver myself—things dark and violent, terrible things to wish upon an uncle. I must confess that my temper got the better of me when my servants escorted me to and from that soap-smelling prison at all hours of the day."

"Surely not!" I whispered, barely squelching my laughter, not trusting full voice.

Dannelle nodded gravely, taking me entirely seriously.

"I must confess that some of the linkboys did not fare well in my company."

I nodded in turn and cleared my throat several times.

"I thought dire things through long hours, Galen. But in the end, it seemed most fitting simply to run away. At any rate, you know the rest of the story, or at least it doesn't take a visionary to figure it out: how I went on the sly to the stable, intent on joining up with you and Ramiro, on leaving the castle grounds until Sir Robert—"

"Forgot about laundry," Ramiro finished, admiration in his voice. "Perhaps even forgot that you were missing."

I shook my head. Dannelle would have to be a fool to follow anyone into the prospects we faced. But it made no difference: With her gossip and veiled knowledge, and with my history of misdemeanor, the girl had me, and had me without options.

So I resolved to make the best of it. After all, the night would come soon enough. And after all, there was room beneath my trail blanket for two . . .

Possibilities, impossible and unthinkable under the watchful eyes of Robert and Bayard, now loomed inviting in the cloudy night.

*   *   *   *   *

We were there until late the next morning, despite my coaxings and urgings. Ramiro lolled over a dozen eggs and three loaves of bread until the sun was high, when he finally seemed to remember that we were not off on some May Day outing but fully intent to go somewhere and do something.

It was only then that our huddled little party took to the road. Dannelle, Ramiro, and I rode at the head of the column, with the squires forming a bedraggled line behind us. The ride was tedious and silent, for Ramiro and I were equally hostile and equally quiet. The only sounds were the movement and murmurings of the horses and an occasional grunt or uncomfortable sigh from Alfric.

Ahead of us spread the highlands like a wide, grass-covered bridge. Almost a mile across, they formed the only dry thoroughfare between the drenched Solamnic plains and the foothills of the Vingaard Mountains. Even so, the water was standing an inch deep on the ground beneath us.

The grass blades swam in a dark pool.

"People are assuming an awful lot on this expedition, Dannelle," I exclaimed when we stopped late in the afternoon. She, Ramiro, and I were still mounted, our horses nose to nose as the three of us waited for the squires to build a fire. As we spoke, a silent, efficient Oliver and a grumbling Alfric gathered whatever nearly dry wood they could find in this drenched terrain. Soon, on a damp spot under a thick-leafed vallenwood, with a horse blanket spread over the low-hanging branches as a sort of makeshift canopy, a smoky, halfhearted fire burned sullenly, while the rest of us smoldered on the rainy road.

"I mean, first of all it was you, stowing away in full sight of everyone," I nagged. "Then it was Ramiro, intent on perpetual dinner last night, and no doubt thinking of a ruse to keep us here until late tomorrow morning. I suppose the squires will tell me soon that they have appointed me to take care of our armor, and the horses will claim they assumed that I had volunteered to carry each of them. My authority is eroding rapidly around here, and—"

"Keeping the shimmer on your authority is not high on the list of my duties, Sir Galen," Ramiro interrupted, flashing a big, gap-toothed smile at Lady Dannelle. "Indeed, you might know from the Measure that 'it is the duty of subordinates to anticipate the wishes of their commanders,' and I assumed only that your authority would be . . . somewhat sensible about our travel and provision."

"Wait just one minute, Ramiro!" I snapped coldly as both of us bristled and preened before the female of the species. But at that moment, there was a noise from the woods, shrilling through the dusky air like the cry of something haunted and forlorn. Ramiro's head snapped up, and he reached for his sword.

The troll emerged from the forest.

Chapter VIII

I had never seen such a creature as this, and I hope devoutly never to see more of them.

From a distance, it looked like a moving stone, dappled gray and green and old-moss brown. It emerged from the landscape behind us as though the ground itself had swelled and erupted something fierce and unnatural. The troll was a good nine feet tall at the shoulders and had the strides you would expect from such a monstrosity. Rapidly it closed the distance between us, loping over the wet highland ground in a low crouch, at a speed most frightening because it was not at all human. Halfway to us, it dropped onto all fours to move even faster.

For an instant, things resembled those terrible moments in dreams when you cannot move as quickly as your attacker. Only alert little Oliver, the only one of us who was not preoccupied with Dannelle, saved us from being way-laid and disemboweled and eaten on the spot. Before Ramiro had his hand on the pommel, Oliver had mounted and reined his black horse toward the troll, his sword gleaming blue-white in his hand, a warning cry on his lips.

For a moment, the troll slowed down, almost paused. The sight of a boy on horseback, armed and challenging, was enough to be distracting, though the thing was probably too dim-witted to be frightened. The monster gaped, its large, fanged jaws dropping open stupidly like faulty draw-bridges. From where we sat on horse, only a dozen yards away, I could see its black, beady eyes widen.

That was all the time we needed. At once, Ramiro broke from the column, guiding his stallion in a wide circle around the creature. It took his rather heavily burdened horse a few moments to close on the troll, but once Ramiro had waded into combat, there was little prospect that anyone would ask him to wade out. A quick sword stroke downward, fol-lowed by half the big man's weight, crashed into the troll's right arm and sliced on through effortlessly, severing the limb at the shoulder.

The creature cried out—a breathless, dry crackling scream that sounded like the splitting of a monstrous vallen-wood. I would have thought dismemberment was suffi-cient. It usually is, in polite circles. Of course, that shows you how much I knew about trolls. With its good left arm, it clawed at Ramiro, who stopped the onslaught neatly with his shield. Still, the big Knight shivered and rocked in the saddle, and the shield came away dented and misshapen.

Nor was this some kind of last desperate surge of strength. Injured but by no means daunted, the troll turned slowly to face Ramiro, its little black eyes glittering with rage. The two of them locked into a careful, almost stately dance of violence, each one sizing up the other as Ramiro guided his horse in circles around the turning troll.

In the lull and balance before conflict resumed, Oliver dismounted and, creeping behind the troll, scurried within a stride or two of the monster. I started to cry out, to call the boy back, but he was moving so rapidly that had I shouted or spoken, my words could have done nothing but alert the troll to his whereabouts. Rushing across the muddy ground, the boy stooped, grunted, and lifted the severed arm to his shoulder. Staggering only a second under the considerable burden, Oliver sprang out of reach before the troll turned around.

Even as he carried it, the arm was sprouting a new shoulder, the shoulder widening and spreading toward the enormous torso it would regenerate in a matter of minutes.

The neck and head began to form and assemble, mottled gray ears and nose arising from the writhing flesh like a shape emerging from water or stone. With a last, heroic surge of strength, Oliver hurled the thing into the campfire, where the flames leapt hungrily over the knotted skin of the thing.

Alfric, Dannelle, and I let out a collective gasp. Safe on our horses, a gallop away from sword or fire, we stared at one another in consternation. Almost at once, my mind raced to more urgent questions.

Such as what earthly good I was serving Ramiro at this fainthearted distance.

There was no telling how long my indecision would have lasted had not Lily started and kicked out violently, almost throwing me into the mud; then, before I could do anything, she lurched forward into the mill of claw and tooth and metal that was rising again in front of me, as Ramiro wheeled his stallion and came at the troll again, sword raised.

A brief glance back over my shoulder before the action closed around me revealed Dannelle, still seated astride her palfrey, holding a riding crop in her hand.

With which she had no doubt basted my steed.

There was no time for prayer, or even profanity. I turned back around and looked into the mottled, enormous face of the thing, which had risen to full height, towering over Lily's head, its remaining hand poised above me, ready, no doubt, to descend and segment the newest Solamnic Knight.

I whooped, ducked, and felt a swift wind pass over my head.

Up against its dry, leathery chest, I set my hand and

pushed. Nothing moved. It was like swimming through metal. I wondered briefly how my body would appear when my head looked at it from somewhere over in the bushes.

The prospect was enough to send me tumbling over Lily's flank onto the soggy ground with a splash. I scrambled quickly to my feet and wiped myself off.

There were Ramiro and troll everywhere I looked, and as I spun around frantically, tugging at my scabbard for the sword that seemed riveted there, I discovered there was frenzy even in the places I wasn't looking.

I knew that what had been serious before had now fallen critical. For the troll had unhorsed Ramiro, and as the big Knight struggled for footing like a capsized turtle, the monster had suddenly turned its attention to me.

All nine feet of it towered above me, and it drew so close that I could smell the moss and ordure on its skin.

For the first time since I could remember, I was tunneled into a corner, without resource or lie.

As the big thing came at me, teeth bared, I fumbled with my sword.

It would not come.

I closed my eyes.

In that brown darkness, I heard the sound of scuffling and shrieks.

I opened my eyes, and Dannelle was astraddle the troll's back, dagger in hand. Down plunged the dagger into the fleshy neck of the monster, and up and down again, while the stupid, surprised look on the thing's face turned suddenly to something like understanding, and it twisted, tossing her into the mud.

I had no time for chivalry. One desperate tug at the sword broke the leather thong that had held my sword in the scabbard and brought the blade whining into the open air. I spun it above my head and lunged upward at the troll's midsection. Fully aware that the thing could easily handle a severed arm, I was looking to make contact with a more delicate appendage.

Instead, my blade glanced harmlessly against the creature's knee, shaving off perhaps an inch of its gnarled skin but doing little more damage. Still, it seemed I had been close enough to make the creature think I knew what I was doing. Quickly it backed away from me, gibbering. Off to my side, I heard Ramiro finally rising to his feet, and I drew my knife, standing my ground as the troll retreated.

As quickly as it had set upon us, the creature was gone. Growling, whining, scrambling over felled trees and slipping in the mud and the wet grass, it scrambled back into the woods.

In triumph, I turned toward the others. It seemed for a moment that the teachings of the Measure I had pondered and disputed were proven right at last—that an adversary, no matter its size and meanness, will back down when it is faced with spunk and stamina and, above all, righteousness.

So I was going to tell them all, until I saw Dannelle and Oliver, holding high the flaming torches that had scared away my monstrous opponent.

*   *   *   *   *

Most of them had accounted well for themselves in their first test. Ramiro, of course, had backed up his bluster with a good sword hand, and Dannelle had shown more courage than I was entitled to expect. Little Oliver, the best of us in this, whom I would have thought unprepared for either travel or troll, had shown himself resourceful, smart, and brave in knowing that the things regenerate and that fire was the weapon to use against them.

Others, however, were less impressive. Moments after we lost sight of the troll among rock and evergreen, Alfric came shambling up behind us, covered with mud and excuses. We all learned, to our great surprise, that another troll had been sneaking up on us back up the road, and that Alfric had met him single-handedly . . . and faced him down.

Alfric stared dramatically at Dannelle as he gave gruesome account of the combat that supposedly took place in our absence. She gave him rein, marveling at the wildness of the story, and cut him off only when he offered to show us all where his sword had entered the troll by touching corresponding parts of Dannelle's anatomy.

I recognized Alfric's strategy myself, having, at various times in my squirehood, stopped an army of satyrs, a giant, three goblins, and a dragon. Combat is easier against invented foes on a battlefield safe from the eyes of others.

Ramiro looked at me and smiled, remembering summers past, no doubt.

I, on the other hand, was not smiling as I hauled my brother by the arm away from his amorous diagrams, for the Pathwardens had scarcely conducted themselves with honor. While my brother tunneled from sight, I had fumbled with horse and sword and dignity until a child and a girl came to my rescue.

Disconsolate, I seated myself in the mud and rested my face in my hands. When I looked up, Ramiro was mounting his horse, hoisted into the saddle by Dannelle and two straining squires. He had donned his helmet, its gray ostrich plume drooped foolishly in the evening drizzle, and his sword was drawn, as though a struggle was in the offing.

"To horse, Galen!" the big man cried out triumphantly. "It hasn't had the chance to distance us yet!"

" 'It,' Ramiro? Just what is 'it,' if you'd be so kind?"

"The troll, of course!" Ramiro exclaimed. "There's an hour of light left us, as I figure it, and I've never known the animal who could outrun this stallion."

"I don't . . ." I began, unsure of what I would say next. But the big Knight had wheeled his horse about, and the two of them crashed through the water-black undergrowth that marked the edge of the woods. Off on a jaunt, they were, on a troll hunt, and those of us left behind were expected to gather ourselves and follow.

Sausages trailed from the saddlebags of the questing hero.

At once, Oliver was in the saddle, headed off after his protector. Alfric and Dannelle watched him blend into the trees, then looked at me warily.

"Do we *have* to go after the troll, Brother?" Alfric whined, and instantly I felt anger rising—anger at his cowardice, at my own lack of gumption that had allowed Ramiro to guide our exploits whenever he damn well pleased, and at Dannelle for standing there with a mysterious, disapproving look on her face.

"Your brother is right, Galen," she said. "This troll hunt is a foolhardy business."

But I was sure that what she meant was that she felt unsafe in the woods with her only guardians an incompetent Knight and his fainthearted squire.

I was tired of them all—of Father and Sir Robert, of Elazar and Fernando and Gileandos, of Ramiro, who was crashing through foliage in search of danger, and of Oliver and Alfric, who were no doubt thinking of disparaging things. Whatever I did and however I did it was subject to second guesses and blame and whispered calls of *Weasel, Weasel.*

Dannelle di Caela, it seemed, believed those whispers and the past they summoned. It would take high drama to show her otherwise.

"No, Dannelle!" I pronounced, the counterfeit strength and assurance in my voice almost making me think I believed what I was saying. "Foolhardy it may seem to the two of you, but it is Solamnic business, and by the gods, we shall pursue it!"

I turned to my horse, ignoring the girl's nervous snicker. Ducking under a hanging vallenwood branch, I guided Lily into the green and dripping dark, Alfric and Dannelle riding close behind me.

The woods that cover the foothills of the Vingaards are surprisingly thick and baffling and vine-entangled. Certainly they are more passable than swamps I have seen and traveled, but when you keep looking over your shoulder for pursuers, the way can be tricky and even downright confounding.

So it was that Oliver seemed to shout on two sides of us, Ramiro on another. We kept moving, however—moving away from the last sound we had heard, and keeping the campfire to our backs as best as we could manage, given the rising night and the shifting shadows of the foliage. It was an hour of rapid traveling and foraging, probably in circles. My eyes were half on the ground in front of me, half searching for the firelight to which I fully intended to return when Ramiro's energies—and with them, the hunt—subsided.

It was this rushing about, this hysterical wandering, that

brought us to a clearing I had not seen before. Suddenly the foliage around me dropped away, and I found myself standing on high ground. The grass beneath me was dry and wiry, bathed in red moonlight as was the whole clearing itself, and the wash of scarlet and deep green was broken only by the shadow that spread underneath the single small oak tree in its center.

It seemed like a good place to stop. My legs were tired from gripping the flanks of the horse, my face whipped and welted by vines and branches. But somewhere around us, Ramiro was plunging through marshy woodland in search of a dangerous quarry, following the fine tradition of Solamnic Knighthood: Serenely confident that you alone are in the right, you corner evil and do away with it, regardless of whatever or whomever else you injure.

It was a messy business, this breakneck pursuit. But Ramiro was my companion and, in a sense, my charge. I had no time for breath and speculation. I had to locate him before something vile happened to him at the hands of the troll.

Alone, bowed and cloaked against the soft rain, I waited for Dannelle and Alfric to reach the clearing. Together, the three of us waited as the faint halooing and the rustle and crack of branches told us Ramiro was headed our way.

The huge Knight splashed into the clearing shortly, dirty and bedraggled and cursing the cleverness of the troll. Oliver followed in the big man's wake, a dismal lump of mud on horseback.

Our party reassembled and stood together in the gloom, each one of us with his own sullen thoughts. The waters had risen over the hooves of the horses. If we tarried any longer, we would face not only the dangers of trolls by night but also slippery, unsteady blind footing.

"But there isn't a star to steer by," Ramiro complained.

Not that a galaxy would have availed a man with his lack of bearings. To Ramiro, all directions were the same, the trees identical, the ground of one level, and the paths wound in circles. Now, in the midst of nowhere, he gave over command gladly.

"Which way should we go, Galen?" he asked quietly and

urgently, drawing his sword as though a weapon in his hand could guide him through the green, entangling labyrinth in which we found ourselves.

"First of all, I intend to lead us out of this marsh," I declared and, dismounting into ankle-deep water, turned toward the single oak at the center of the clearing.

"He can do it, too!" Alfric insisted. "I have seen him navigate swamps before! Swamps worse than this, with satyrs in them!"

I looked back at my brother, who nodded at me encouragingly. As I sloshed through the high grass and water, it struck me that in my concern that others see my changes, I had overlooked those in my brother—how in that heart of meanness something had turned, perhaps indetectably to those who did not know him, but turned nonetheless, surfacing fitfully until now and again, if you looked at Alfric in a certain slant of light and with your eyes squinted in just the right way, you could see promise of squirehood emerging.

There would be time to explore that later. Hoisting myself onto the lowest branch of the tree—a sturdy one, as thick as my waist—I braced myself to climb as high as the thing would allow me. Perhaps from a lofty lookout the woods would open for me and our way back to the road emerge from this maze of greenery.

Clutching the next branch before I set weight on it, I noticed a crack—perhaps a quarter of an inch wide—snaking up the bole of the tree beside me. It often happens when the ground is wet, when the roots lose purchase in a clay-heavy soil.

Or so I have heard. Where I had heard it, I forgot entirely, for I stood rapt upon the branch, marveling that, despite the twilight and the shade, I could see small things so clearly. It was then I noticed that the opal brooch, pinning the cape beneath my throat, had begun to shine with a warm amber light, bathing the tree with a faint, steady glow.

I clambered down at once, lost footing amid roots, and fell to my knees in the water. Scrambling up, I splashed across the clearing to my comrades, holding the brooch aloft, my cape discarded behind me.

"I was right! I was always right, Ramiro! Look! The opals are on fire!"

"This does not inspire confidence in me, Lady Dannelle," Ramiro replied. I followed his pitying gaze to the brooch in my hand, dark and lifeless now, its magical light gone.

"M-Maybe the fall into the water . . . extinguished it or something. Maybe . . ."

"Maybe you're tired, Galen," Dannelle soothed. "You've scarcely recovered from the Night of Reflections, and now there's trolls and all."

"But . . . but they *were* afire, damn it!" I insisted, turning and walking away from them in my anger.

The stones began to glimmer again. Cupping the brooch in my palm, I looked into the opals. They showed nothing but a faint, opaque glow at their heart.

Another two steps toward the tree, and the light was detectably brighter.

What had the figure in the vision said to me? *In them is the map of my darkness.*

That was how, following the light of the stones like a half-mad diviner follows his dowsing rod, I passed through the clearing, beyond the oak, as the light in my hands grew brighter and brighter still. I heard a movement at my side and looked up.

Alfric was standing there, holding his horse's reins and Lily's.

"They *are!*" he shouted. "By the gods, the Wea—Galen is right! There's a light in the stones!"

Slowly the rest of them dismounted and followed. And as the light in my hands brightened further, so did our hopes.

For a moment, I felt like a genuine Knight, even if I had botched entirely the fight with the troll and let Ramiro lead us on a bootless errand somewhere in the soggy lowlands. For I was off on a journey of rescue, wielding magic at the head of my stalwart little band.

* * * * *

A map of my darkness, the vision had foretold.

Though far from their own terrain, in a country hostile to

concealment and surprise, they were Plainsmen after all, the handful of warriors who waited for us. We did not see them until they were upon us.

To this day, I am not sure that their intentions were lethal, but Solamnic Knights do not go easily, no matter the terms or the plans. When I felt strong fingers clutch my throat, I turned and, seeing Plainsmen rushing from the trees and undergrowth around us, fell to the soggy ground, breaking the hold of my assailant.

Without hesitation, the man leapt upon me, fingers prying at my clenched fist. Clumsily I reached for my sword and found that, in my haste to follow Ramiro, I had left it somewhere in the clearing where we had fought with the troll. I pummeled the man with my fist once, twice, but the blows were like raindrops against his leathery, heavily muscled ribs.

I struck him again, and this time the blow must have registered. Quickly and with the lean efficiency of a man taught to waste nothing, not even movement, he struck me with the back of his hand. My head rattled against the ground, and for a moment, I was in my boyhood room at the moathouse in Coastlund, it was winter, and a broom was in my hands.

Just as abruptly I regained my faculties to see Ramiro pull the man off me and hurl him through the air into an aeterna bush. I heard branches rending, heard the man cry out in a strange mixture of pain and triumph. Then he stood amidst the blue evergreen branches, his pale hand illumined by the opals in the brooch he was clutching.

I rose to my knees and yelled as Ramiro turned toward the thief in an ungainly, bearlike crouch. At that moment, another Plainsman leapt atop his back, and then another, so that the big man struggled for a moment beneath the weight of two of the enemy.

Whooping again, my attacker spun toward the darkness of the woods, and he might have escaped easily, taking the opals with him. But he gave a final turn and a final shout which gave my brother the chance to act. Hurtling through the air, Alfric wrapped his arms about the stunned Plainsman, and the two of them tumbled into branches and water as suddenly and as heavily as a felled oak.

By now I was standing and, after a brief glance to see that Dannelle was unharmed and attended to, rushed to my brother's aid. The Plainsmen atop Ramiro were getting the worst of it by now, but I could figure on no help from the big man for a least a moment or two.

Hurdling a downed Plainsman and a winded Oliver and skirting an old maple stump, I crashed through the aeterna bush and stumbled into the brawl in front of me . . .

. . . just as the Plainsman's knife slipped between my brother's ribs.

Chapter IX

It was midmorning the next I knew. I lay beneath the oak tree in the clearing, its branches drooping heavy with last night's rain. The woods around me were charged in a strange half-light, the unsettled gray of dawn.

I looked at the brooch, clutched tightly in my hand, as though all power of memory lay in the dark gems. It is a hard thing when you try to save one brother and lose the other one in the bargain.

I had reached Alfric's side as the Plainsman broke from his grasp and ran off through the trees. Carefully I groped through the shadows and the standing water, finding my brother wet and ruined amidst broken branches and torn cloth and leather.

"Galen, I was not running away. Not this time."

"I know that. Rest now, Alfric. Rest."

The sound of the conflict faded. Ramiro, I found out later, had gained balance and advantage against our attackers. The retreating Plainsmen were no doubt lucky that their pursuer was so large and ungainly, else they would have had too much to answer for there in the night-dappled woods.

"Rest now, Alfric! Ramiro and Dannelle will be over here directly, and so will Oliver with the horses, and then we'll see to patching you up and—"

"This is dreadful, Galen. Dreadful."

"I know," I whispered. The brooch glittered on the wet ground by Alfric's body, saved from the Plainsmen by his reckless heroism. As I spoke to my brother, the light went out of the gems.

"Rest now," I said. "Rest now."

Which is what they tell me I was saying over him when they joined us. Ramiro covered him up in those last moments, so he did not die cold, and Dannelle cradled me like an infant, she said, though she said it with no ridicule but with a deep and brokenhearted pity for me and for Alfric and for this whole botched trip into twilight. She knelt beside me, helping Ramiro, who poured something strong down me from a little flask, something I could not or would not taste, but only felt its warmth passing into me as the tears left me and I slept for a long while, clutching the stones won and made more valuable by my brother's blood.

* * * * *

The sky cleared just as we reached the foothills of the Vingaard Mountains.

The downpour had been so long and so terribly intense that it had virtually drowned the highlands. Shrubbery and small trees lay bent over, and the grass was matted and brown.

I hated to think how things looked down on the plains.

The air that was left behind when the rain lifted was not fresh and cleansed, like you find after a sudden, brief summer thunderstorm that washes away all dust and dirt. Instead, what was left was a cold and dead landscape smelling of rotten vegetation and small drowned things.

It was as though a week of rain had passed us from high summer to the borders of winter.

We climbed, and I looked down and behind me at the road we were leaving. Looked behind me in remorse, for my brother lay somewhere in that rain-washed country, in the makeshift grave we had made for him, under a cairn of stones and under the kind words of Sir Ramiro of the Maw and the singing of Dannelle and of Oliver, whose voice was young and yet to change. Unfathomably, my brother lay in the wet soil, untouched by light or air or the best of my intentions. He had followed my command, my leadership and visions, which had brought him to that last place below me.

Somehow the death of Alfric, which often I had thought would not affect me one way or the other, which sometimes I had thought I would even welcome, had left me nothing but this long ride, these shadows, and a trail that narrowed and narrowed ahead of us as we passed from the highlands into the sparse country of the foothills. It was indeed dreadful.

Dannelle and Ramiro tried, I think, but they were little consolation. My thoughts were not on them or on the journey ahead of us, but on how death had caught Alfric just short of changing. Had he been given one more month, even another week, who knew but that the strange turn of intentions I had seen—those moments of honesty and loyalty so fleeting and faint that I feared I imagined them—might well have amounted to something like knighthood or brotherhood.

As it was, not even my memories of Alfric could fashion him lovely: His blackmails at the moathouse and on the walls of Castle di Caela, the times he had manhandled me in the cellars of my father, strangled me in swamp and topiary garden, strung me up in the dark rooms of Castle di Caela, and nearly drowned me in the moat. How he had broken oaths and fine glassware, started brawls then run from them, lied to Father and Bayard and me and Robert di Caela, tried to seduce Dannelle and Enid and threatened them when his charms had failed.

All in all, it was a shadowy history of abusing horse and

servant and younger brothers, betraying the trust of comrades and superiors. Still, I found myself searching through memory for something remarkable, something that distinguished and redeemed this brother. I came up with Brithelm's turnips.

When we were growing up, my father had prized and savored turnips, and because *his* father had put every nonpoisonous root in Coastlund on a supper plate, then, by the gods, like fare was good enough for his sons.

Unfortunately, Brithelm had discovered at an early age that his innate love for nature did not extend to turnips. There were the long standoffs familiar to any family, when the child refuses to eat what the parent sets forth. However, Pathwardens are congenitally stubborn, and the struggles between Brithelm and Father took on proportions of terrible length and venom. Many mornings I found the two of them facedown in dinner plates, where they had waited out one another not from the *previous* night's supper, mind you, but from a confrontation two or even three nights old. The servants learned to work around them.

I do not know why Alfric decided to keep the peace on this matter. It was out of character in a brother who delighted in setting the whole family against one another. Perhaps it was only that Alfric coveted the same turnips his brother would leave on a plate until the Cataclysm came again. Perhaps it was a glimmer of kindness.

Indeed, as I thought about it there in the rising foothills, I could not recall clearly whether it *was* Alfric who scraped the turnips from Brithelm's plate and wolfed them down while Father was not looking. Other images came to my memory—perhaps a dog under the table, or a fold in the hem of Brithelm's robe that Father never checked for wandering tubers. I could not remember clearly for, after all, I had been scarcely three or four years old at the time, and not too concerned with those events that did not involve me.

It was now, when it had become important, that my memory sputtered and failed me. I sat back in the saddle, telling myself it was of little consequence, these turnips and childhood struggles. Telling myself to put it out of mind.

But out of mind it would not be put. And in the long,

haunted noontide, as we climbed past greenery into the rubble-strewn pathways of the Vingaards, I thought of all my doings, how perhaps one deft stroke of the sword or more experienced command, one different path chosen or even one less vision in the stones, and I would have had my brother beside me with all of his flaws and outrages and promise.

I used to say that you could see a miracle coming for miles if you just paid attention. But you can't when your mind is on other things. It is then that you get down and burrow in and follow your nose until something more reliable than attention or logic or common sense comes up to meet you.

I met Shardos in a pass leading toward the site of Brithelm's old encampment. My friends had lagged behind me, giving me generous space to wrestle with thoughts of Alfric, so Lily and I were quite alone as the pathway narrowed through rubble and sheer walls streaked with pink granite. I turned a corner and lost sight of the party. Indeed, Ramiro's usual racket of trumpeting and bluster, louder through the morning as he tried to cheer me up, faded into a whisper behind me as Lily put distance between me and their faint consolations.

It was a silence that bred suspicions.

After all, the talk behind me had touched upon bandits. And wasn't it a fact that bandits preferred a narrow pass for their villainy, raining arrows and rocks and the skulls of their previous victims down upon the unwary?

The first bowl fell, hurtling like a meteor from some concealed spot above me, splintering in the gravel and grit underhoof and sending shards flying in all directions. I yelped and drew sword, imagining an army of Nerakan cutthroats who had chosen this time and place to test their most ruthless and bloodthirsty plan of ambush.

The pass was too narrow to turn the mare around. Lily snorted and drew the reins from my hand with a strong twist of her head. A growl descended from the rocks above me. Amid my imaginings of wild beasts and their even wilder masters, of bloodlust and dismemberment, the unassuming form of the juggler appeared on the rocks above me. A big dog crouched at his side, its hackles raised.

"Be still, Birgis," he soothed. " 'Tis only a lad, and no enemy of yours."

The dog lay down at his feet, its growl receding. I breathed again and stood upright in the stirrups, trying my best to look knightly and offended.

The man had been dressed by a whirlwind. Pieced together by rags, a coat of yellow and purple and black draped over his shoulders. The coat had a yawning hole at its left side, not torn as far as I could tell, but seeming to be an oversight or the fancy of a mad tailor.

The tunic beneath this monstrosity was a lime green outrage that had once made a mockery of silk, no doubt, but its best years over, it had taken on a sort of magnificent ugliness. His shoes matched only in form. One was of black leather, the other of red.

I hid a smile, fearing he might be insulted and send the dog to do the work it was obviously more than happy to do, curled at his feet and baring its hundreds of sharp teeth. But the man paid little attention to me, staring blankly above me.

"I'm sorry, lad, that the bowl was so . . . proximate. Sometimes I lose them, even in a catch and carry I've done since before you were born. And my goodness, they do make a racket when they settle, don't they?"

"Begging your pardon, sir," I began politely, eyeing the dog, whose fur had risen in a wiry, aggressive mane about its frighteningly strong neck. I listened anxiously for the sound of approaching horses.

Ramiro, no doubt, had stopped out of earshot for a snack or a drink or a nap—for anything, in short, that would delay him.

The motley man above me made no movement, no sign of fighting or of running away. No sign, even, that he noticed the sword I was brandishing.

I waved my hand at him.

No response. Perhaps it was a trick of light or shadows in this rocky region.

I made the most hideous face I could imagine, flashed him the most obscene hand gesture I knew.

Growls from the dog only.

It was only then I noticed that the man held two other bowls.

"Are you in the habit of juggling crockery?" I asked uneasily, brushing the folds of my cloak to remove any stray shards that might discomfort me hours from now when I dismounted or crouched by a fire.

"Indeed I am, young sir," the man replied serenely. "The dog has learned to dodge bowls and to reconnoiter."

It was then I was sure the juggler was blind.

"So your companion, sir—"

"Birgis."

"So Birgis is . . . the eyes in your alliance?"

A long pause filled the cool mountain air while the man awaited the obvious next question, while I debated whether I should give him the satisfaction of asking it. But I had to know.

"Doesn't your . . . lack of sight pose a problem in juggling?"

"Indeed it does, young sir," he replied, stroking the bristled back of the dog beside him, who growled once more and lay still, waiting no doubt for a sudden movement or loud noise on my part—anything that might justify his dragging me from my horse and disemboweling me.

I heard the clopping of hooves on the trail behind me. Ramiro and Dannelle came into view, then Oliver close behind them, leading the riderless horses. My big, blustering companion tipped his traveling hat politely at the sight of the juggler.

"Indeed, it is a long story. Times have been," the blind man went on heedlessly, "that I would have given my earthly goods for a set of eyes. But I shan't trouble you with a drawn-out and tedious tale."

"Why, nonsense!" Ramiro boomed merrily, already halfway dismounted. "What better time for stories and lore than when you have stopped for the day, ready for a meal and rest and a whiling of hours?"

"Ramiro . . ." I began, but there was no stopping it. The big man sat and motioned to Oliver, who sighed, retraced his steps to a notch among the rocks, and set about to build a fire.

"You could stand with a bit of distraction yourself, Galen," Ramiro added, "and what good is a story if not to while away all heaviness and woe?"

"What good indeed?" asked the juggler, stepping cautiously down the rock face, the dog scrambling nimbly onto his shoulders. Together they hopped lightly onto the surface of the trail, the story beginning before the blind man had crouched by the fire to warm his hands.

*   *   *   *   *

"Mine were the sharpest of eyes," the juggler began, "in my early years, when I juggled torches and knives in a floating palace on the edge of the Blood Sea . . ."

And on it went, through an hour of silliness and farfetched stories of some notorious performing career that spanned Ansalon from one end to the other. As he told his story, the juggler stood and produced three bottles from somewhere in those patchwork robes. It was like sleight of hand to begin with, and I caught myself watching for secrets, for distractions and misdirections as though he were intent on pocketing our coins rather than bedazzling us.

Bedazzle us he did, for as his life unfolded, the bottles flashed brightly in the mountain air, first green, then red, then blue. Then as he tossed them more quickly, the colors combined, green and violet and yellow from somewhere unexpected, until I think I saw the entire spectrum, and the colors moved quickly into transparency as the blind man seemed to juggle ice and light over our marveling heads.

The youngest son of a circus family, Shardos—for that was his name—had been born in far-off Kothas beyond the Blood Sea, by the strait that easterners call the Pirate's Run. He said he had come west over its waters with his family "not long after the Cataclysm."

I looked skeptically at Ramiro. If my history and reckoning were correct, the old man was claiming to be over two centuries old.

Ramiro sat by the fire, as wide and complacent as a huge toad, rapt with interest as Shardos continued his story.

Through the Death's Teeth Shardos's family had come,

and once ashore, down to Ogrebond, where the audience had eaten his oldest brother and set afire the family tents.

West through Neraka they had traveled over the span of several years, their tented wagons heavy with bottles of cure-alls, with potions and trained animals and fireworks. It sounded like the most wonderful boyhood life to me, for you could name the city—from North Keep all the way to Zeriak by the Ice Wall—and Shardos had been there. He had stories that went with the places, too: from the Cracklin Coast, where he was burned and blinded by a cruel duke who distracted him while he juggled torches, all the way west to the Gnome Kingdoms under Mount Nevermind, where his middle brother was dismantled by an explosion in a wagon full of rockets.

More than that, he had collected the stories of the places themselves: He knew by heart seven versions of the Tale of Huma, and creation itself was different, it seemed, depending on your town or country or race. He knew the stories of Istar and the Cataclysm and more recent stories, too, such as that of the Battle at Chaktamir in which my father had fought.

Shardos claimed to know the entirety of di Caela family history, and within it, the Scorpion's tale. He knew Bayard, and somehow was familiar with the bleak and desolate childhood of my protector.

Solemnly the blind man told us that he knew the true story of Brandon Rus and the arrows, and that at some time, given greater leisure and our kindly attention, he would tell us why the young easterner let his brilliant gifts lie waste in memory and brooding.

Shardos claimed to know two thousand stories, stories that had served him well as his hands slowed in later years.

"For I have found," he claimed, "that jugglery and story-telling are cousins. It is the illusion you're after—the moment when the juggler and the teller fade from the sight of those who are looking on, when all you can see is the objects rising and falling and the story completing itself on its own."

In puzzlement, I looked at Ramiro, who shrugged back at me in turn. As men of action, we were used to being left in the dark by comparisons.

At any rate, Shardos had become a bit of a poor man's bard, fabling and gossiping supper from hovel to castle through a century of roads. Up until a time, that is, when seeking rest, he had chanced upon a small encampment in the Vingaard Mountains.

"There I had fancied on staying," he claimed. "To be done with the travel and to think on my stories for a while. For they all must fit together somehow, wouldn't you think? At least, that is what my host in the mountains told me before he disappeared."

In an instant, we were all alert, eyes so intent on the blind man in front of us that Birgis the dog became uneasy and growled menacingly at Ramiro.

"And the name of your host?" I asked, my voice almost a whisper.

"Why, Brother Brithelm, I heard them call him," the juggler replied.

Briefly and urgently I told him that Brithelm was *my* brother.

"I see," Shardos said, his tone a little more somber. "I can imagine what has brought you to the mountains, then."

"Yes, I suppose you might guess why we are here," I conceded. "Brithelm's camp is but a day's ride away, as I remember it, and we were on our way to see if he has weathered the earthquake well."

"*Were* on your way, you say?"

"Yes, Master Shardos," I replied guardedly. "For though I surely intend to visit my brother in the days to come, this talk of disappearance has . . . given me pause as to where I should venture next. That and the Plainsmen. Pale fellows. Wearing beads and skins. Most of them armed. Perhaps you've seen—I mean, noticed them."

"So that's what they look like. Their clothing rustled like buckskin and leather, but the skin color—I had no idea. They've made quite a commotion in the surrounding woods this evening."

"Who are they? What are they?" Ramiro asked.

"No idea there, either. But whatever they are, it's your brother Brithelm you're after, is it not? And well you should be, for he's been kidnapped."

"Kidnapped?"

"Whisked from the world as we know it, I'd wager. That camp of an abbey is as empty as the City of Lost Names northward. Scarcely a sign that Brithelm or any of his fellows have ever been there."

"I . . . I can't believe that," I protested. "Who would want to kidnap Brithelm? So, Shardos. You are saying that my brother's abbey—"

"Is deserted. Yes, Galen. When the quakes arose and the seasons shifted and the elements burst their bounds, the kidnappers came out of the earth . . ."

"Lead us there, Shardos," I stated before I thought, teased out of caution by bewilderment. I stared down the apprehensive look flashed at me by Ramiro and continued. "I have lost one brother too many in these mountains, and by the gods, the hills will open before I lose another."

" 'Tis simple enough," Shardos observed cheerily. "Birgis and I can find him for you. He is unharmed, I am sure, though no doubt distressed by his new surroundings."

Chapter X

"AND this bROThER," the NAMER said, waving his hand dramatically in the direction of a fire, low beneath the Sign of the Antelope—a whitened, antlered skull propped on a tall spear. "To what have they carried him, and what awaits him there? It is dark where he is going, but there is torchlight."

He crouched before the fire, passed the strand of metal over it, and resumed the story.

* * * * *

Soon, thought the man on the mottled throne. Soon the stones will be brought into my presence, brought from above like a sweet black rain cascading from the hand of a god.

And why not? he mused, resting his head upon the cool moistness of a sheet of stalactites. Did not the hand of a god guide me here to begin with?

Below him, in the great cavernous hall called the Porch of Memory, white-haired Plainsmen milled about their tasks under the torchlight. Some—stout men, as a rule, their shoulders knotted—pushed wheelbarrows sagging with rubble and sediment, to a place well lit beneath the torches, where folk more dextrous and nimble—young women and smaller men—sifted through the fragments for the opals that had eluded all of them, century by century.

But soon, Firebrand thought, closing his one good eye and smiling blissfully, the rattling, chipping sounds of mining and sorting fading below him into faint sounds he imagined that he only remembered. Soon all this pushing and sifting and hoping will be . . . outdated. Yes, outdated when the Knight brings the stones to me from his tall castle.

Then I can tell my people that I . . . found the opals. That a vision told me they would be . . . where they would be.

For visions have spoken to me before, spoken unerringly out of the silence and the light in these very stones.

He held a silver crown in his right hand. Slowly, with a sort of mad elegance, he placed the circlet upon his head. Between the twining strands of silver, seven opals nested in an irregular, broken pattern.

The crown was still hot from his burning touch.

His eye opened wide as the chanting began beneath him, echoing off the walls of the Porch of Memory until the great room resounded with the voices of children. His eye was as deep and as black and as flickering as the opals above it, and brimming with tears as it focused on a far point and a far time. From beneath the diamond-shaped leather eye patch, tears trickled grotesquely, mixed with soot and the recollection of blood.

The voices poured like dark rain down the walls.

"You pass through these, unharmed, unchanging
but now you see them
strung on our words on your own conceiving
as you pass from night to awareness of night

> *to know that remorse is the calm of philosophers*
> *that its price is forever*
> *that it draws you through meteors*
> *through winter's transfixion*
> *through the blasted rose*
> *through the shark's water*
> *through the black compression of oceans*
> *through rock through magma*
> *to yourself to an abscess of nothing*
> *that you will recognize as nothing*
> *that you will know is coming again and again*
> *under the same rules."*

Whether he joined in or only listened, Firebrand often wept at this chanting. He shed soft tears on the tenebral necklace he wore, upon each little hooked claw, each little silvered tooth that stood for a vanished, long-dead year the Que-Tana had spent underground. For the Chant of Years was a map of sorrow, a chronicle of time forever wasted in a mission of darkness.

Oh, the Chant of the Men was sorrowful enough, Firebrand could tell you, with its heavy alternation of names and of teeth and the claws of cave bears. And the Chant of the Women was a testament to the terrible ruin of innocence, as the people knelt and prayed, touching leopard tooth, leopard claw, as their hands raced along the necklace and the litany raced along the roll of names.

All were names of those who had died underground, in search of the dark wisdom of the godseyes, of the black glain opals that held five thousand years of memory intact, like a fly preserved for eons in the heart of amber. And the names were mourned indeed, for many of them Firebrand recalled—the faces of the old and of the children, the soft movement of the young women who died beautiful and much too soon, all buried in the search for the stones. The children below him intoned the Chant of Years, the most sorrowful of all, wherein the People recorded the time they had irretrievably lost, while the others—the Que-Shu, the Que-Kiri, the self-important cousin Que-Nara—lived carefree in the light and the wind and the rain.

Quickly he collected himself and reached up to touch the tight collar about his neck, from which the teeth and claws hung.

How like the tenebral we are, he thought, casting his mind away from the chant as again the hot tears threatened. How like the small, yellowed squirrels that swoop through the subterranean abbey, their leathery wings aglow with the strange lumen, the secretion that burns when touched by the sunlight.

For Firebrand knew what happened to the tenebrals when, by accident, their path of flight took them out of the caverns into a sunlight they had mistaken for the light of torches or for the lumen that glowed in their strange hanging nests. Indeed, one of his men had carried one back to show him—its body shriveled into half its size, the wings also shriveled, ravaged by the phosphorous riding in the clear streams of lumen.

The animal was consumed by its own fluttering heart.

Such things happened quickly, the People maintained. Sometimes it was a matter of only a second.

How like the tenebral we are, Firebrand thought once more. Or at least how like them are my people. For they would burn and dry and wither away in the Bright Lands, in the Nations of Light. Why, even the moonlight blisters the very young.

He shook his head, and the beads and leather thongs braided in his dark locks rattled like the tail of an ancient crotalin snake—the creature who warns before he strikes, but strikes nonetheless. For a moment, the miners below him paused, wan faces lifted to the sound, for judgment and punishment rained down from that throne as suddenly and as unexpectedly as rockslides or cave-ins.

This time they received neither judgment nor punishment. Instead, they saw the dark-haired man, who was always smaller than they remembered him, seated atop the natural chair formed in the Age of Dreams by the continual rush of water over rock. Firebrand's dark eyes were closed now, his face flushed with some strong emotion. His hands each clutched a free stalactite vaguely, as though he lay entranced in the fanged mouth of an enormous beast.

His lips moved along with the chant, but his memory, swayed to the chant of his own years . . .

* * * * *

There was no Porch of Memory when he came here, flying from the anger of his own unforgiving people. The Que-Tana had built no great halls yet, choosing to tunnel like leaderless termites in their endless, winding search for the godseye. They had built no throne from the rock and the moist darkness. Then there were only small chambers aglow with candles, smelling of tallow and smoke.

He had turned his back on the surface and scurried like a rat into that stinking smoke as he followed the passage that only he knew, down into the darkness, guided by candle and one eye. So had he come out of the sun, alone down narrow dark corridors into the embracing silence, where he was lost for good in the heart of the mountain, prey to accident, or to starvation, or to the long fur claws of the vespertile, the huge flightless bats that scour the bottommost recesses of the caverns.

He drank of the stagnant pools, gobbled the small crawling things he stepped upon in the loud blackness, and nothing he ate and nothing he drank could taint or harm him.

For the dark god had a hand in his traveling. That much Firebrand knew from the start, from the moment he put on the Namer's Crown, admiring the dozen flawless black godseyes set in its intertwining silver knots. "Visions," the old Namer had said to him. "The crown will bring visions, then knowledge, then wisdom."

He had held the silver circlet in his two strong hands as the old man spoke. Over the years, he could still remember the last words of his old predecessor.

"Visions, then knowledge, then wisdom," the Namer repeated. "And perhaps long years between each. But do not despair, my boy, and above all, grow not impatient. For it is said that 'sometimes the waiting is the doing.' "

Idle thoughts of a mind in its dotage. He learned later to laugh at the old man, to be glad of his passing.

The god in the stones taught him that, taught him also

that prophecy was easy. For after all, was he not the youngest of the Namers? And a Namer among the Que-Nara, where even the infants touched the hem of Mishakal?

For beyond knowledge and wisdom lies prophecy. Of that Firebrand was sure. So he looked into the opals deeply, into the godseyes, and as the name of the stones should have foretold for him, the eye of a god looked back.

"Sargonnas," it called itself. And "Consort of the Dark." Quickly it taught him to prophesy, to leap over knowledge and wisdom straight into the fire and the glamor of things foretellable.

He sat at the edge of the fire, peering into the crown as the others—the simple ones, unskilled in philosophy and lore— busied themselves with the menial things, with setting and striking the camp, and with the gathering of food. There, alone where the firelight stopped at the edge of the darkness, he pondered the mystery of stones, saw the seas roll and the moons wink out.

He saw a dark woman rise from a deeper darkness, her hair spangled with ice and winter stars.

All of these were yet to come, the god in the crown told him. He was not sure what they meant, these visions, but they were his, and they foretold something grand and terrible. Of that he was sure, and the god agreed.

And when he had seen them all, the countless visions and portents from that moment three centuries ago to the time in which all things will end, the voice in the stones whispered hauntingly, sweetly:

"Now they will follow you . . ."

Of course he had thought it was the Que-Nara that Sargonnas meant. But they were a dirty, hide-smelling people for whom a young man's prophecy was raving and ambition. "The future is deadly," the elders warned, "because we expect so much of it."

He scorned them. Their words were the howling of toothless jackals.

So it became the young to whom he prophesied. They came to him with troubles that he thought to be of little consequence, with questions about a flickering romance or the outcome of a first hunt. He told them what they wanted to hear, said, "Yes, the girl loves you" or "Yes, the antelope waits for your spear," and the children liked what they heard and followed him.

Until the gaunt little boy—the youngest son of the Second Chieftain, a lad who had not seen his tenth summer—got it into his head to hunt the wild dogs and came to receive the blessing of the Namer.

He prophesied the best of fortunes and blessed the lad without ever looking up from the opals in the crown. He told himself later that he would not have changed his mind even had he looked up and seen the boy, nine years old and the size of a child of five. When the boy had asked his blessing, he would still have granted it, for the god in the stones was saying, "He is ready, he is ready, let him go . . ."

They returned the next morning carrying the boy, stretched out on a leather shield, his neck opened by the feeding dogs, his eyes staring blankly into the red moon, and the white, and then into the black moon that only philosophers know. They brought home the boy, and the chieftain, beside himself, had summoned the Namer.

Banishment is simple enough among the Plainsmen. In the center of a circle they placed him. The elders surrounded him and recited his wrongdoings, then the tribe left him. It was the most unceremonious of ceremonies.

Except for the taking of the eye.

Even now, as he sat three miles below and three centuries after, Firebrand remembered the blade, held over the fire till it reached a blue hotness, and how it felt as it passed into his eye, blinding him and searing the wound closed in one motion as the women looked on and chanted the Song of Lost Sight:

"Let the eye surrender, if it offends the People,
Let its last song ride on the blade of the chieftains,
Let it fall like a dark stone into memory,
And in memory let it reside and dwell,
Phantom of light on the wall of the heart
Stored like a dead thing in amber.
Let its last song ride on the blade of the chieftains . . ."

He remembered the song, and the last sight of the blade, then a dazzlement of stars that preceded the pain and the darkness.

Then the darkness lifted, and he was walking.

It was a rocky country, its farmlands tilled and settled. Just where it lay, he did not know.

Nor did he know how the crown, stripped of all opals but one, had fallen back into his hand.

One gem was all he needed, though. For through it, the dark voice explained everything: how taking the crown was not theft, and the death of the boy not negligence, but both were the tests he had passed to enter the prophecy.

"Enter the prophecy?" he had asked bitterly as he wandered the pastured land like a monster, scrambling painfully over fences, hearing by the distant farmhouses the outcry of wary dogs. "I left a dead boy and a home and a people and even my eye behind me . . . to enter a prophecy?"

But the stone was silent. There was dark, and daylight, and again dark before it spoke again.

These mountains toward which you are traveling . . . it whispered as the Namer looked up through the foothills north into the rough, violet rays and above into mist and cloud. *The Vingaards. Do you remember the Vingaards?*

He remembered the knife. Nothing more. And yet . . . something the old Namer had taught him . . .

"The Que-Nara," he said. "Those who dwell under the mountains . . ."

The stone was quiet. A taut silence played across its surface.

"But the Que-Nara remain the Que-Nara," he protested, kneeling to drink from a creek that tumbled out of the foothills. "They will see that my eye has been taken, and they will turn me away."

They call themselves Que-Tana now, the stone replied. *But whether Que-Tana or Que-Nara, they will take you. Of that be sure.*

"But how do I find my way to them?" he asked.

Remember, the stone replied. *Remember the old Namer's teachings.*

And under his damaged sight, a light rose from the center

of the opal. Within it, he saw a clearing: four vallenwoods, their branches intertwined above an ancient dolmen and a path running between the stones down a hill into a network of vines, which covered . . .

A hole in the cliff face. Darkness lay at the bottom of it.

"But even if they take me in, those who wounded me will know, will see it in the stones they took from me."

But you have the crown, the voice soothed. *Those who wounded you will see no more than you will let them see.*

A raptor wheeled overhead, its feathers black on brown on white. It shrieked and swooped, and in a moment rose out of the tall grass, something small and gray in its talons.

The shriek sounded like a call to the Namer, and for a moment, he mistrusted his senses. But the bird circled above him, drifting lazily westward and westward. He followed it dreamily, losing it once as it passed over a strand of poplar but finding it again weaving among bush and evergreen over higher ground, its prey now motionless in its clutches.

Once he looked down into the opal, and within it saw the fiery image of the same bird passing over the same trees in the same country. There would have been a time years ago when he would have dismissed it as coincidence or illusion or even temptation, but now he had followed the call of the stone too long to question. He took the godseye at its word and followed the design of the dark one within it, as both birds—the real one in the air and the cloudy one in the stone—settled at the same time in the branches of a vallenwood . . .

One of four vallenwoods, their branches intertwined above an ancient dolmen and a path running between the stones down a hill into a network of vines, which covered . . .

A hole in the cliff face. Darkness lay at the bottom of it.

*   *   *   *   *

It was a dry season in which he found the way to the land of the Que-Tana. The twigs he tied together with dried grass and reed popped and sputtered as he passed his hand over them.

For as if to give him solace at the loss of his eye, the dark god had given him fire in his hands—a slow, flameless burning that had guided him by night when touched to a torch, had warmed him at his solitary campsite when he had touched kindling. But now, as he held the dried grass, the fire passed through it, burning it far too quickly to provide a lingering light.

He was not twenty paces down the passage when the light gave out.

Disheartened, he crouched in the canceling darkness, breathing rapidly and angrily. From somewhere ahead of him, he could hear the distant sound of voices and metal on rock. But he knew sound carried deceptively in the dark, that distance and direction tied themselves into knots. Following his ear alone could lead him over precipices or into the lair of the vespertile.

Fearing to go forward and resolving not to go back, he crouched there for what must have been an hour. Only then did the stone begin to glow.

Soon the godseye gave off enough light to see by. Placing the crown on his head, the Namer descended the narrow corridor. Twice the passage forked, and both times the light fluttered and went out when he followed the path he had chosen, only to rekindle when he retraced his steps and followed the other path.

The walls of the corridor were painted with old designs, scratched with old graffiti. Plainsman was the language, and the drawings were of creatures the Namer knew well—the antelope, the leopard, the wild boar, and the hawk. It was only when he passed the first fork in the passage that the drawings began to change—at first gradually, then rapidly, birds on the wing transformed into strange geometrical swirls, the familiar form of the leopard now no more than the bright play of color on color. The writing changed, too—the phrases and language and finally even the letters.

From the changes, the Namer knew that generation by generation, the Que-Tana in this underground kingdom were breeding away from the memories of their time in the light. Like heartfish, he told himself. Like heartfish in a cavern.

He had heard of the tiny red fish, once river dwellers in

the sunlight of the Age of Dreams, who entered the underground and evolved without eyes there in the dark recesses. For the first time, he had seen them in his travels as the passage he had followed crossed by the edge of a slow-moving subterranean brook. A kind of changing, of breeding away, had taken place among the Que-Tana, too, as their history filled with darkness and moisture and endless search for the stones until that story was the only story they had, their brothers in the Bright Lands mythical, almost forgotten, reached only through the magic of the stones for which they searched incessantly.

And now the stones had vanished, torn from them by a dark and mysterious hand. There was no explaining it, no consolation but the simple fact that they had seen it coming in the stones for years—that years ago, a voice in the stones had told them the story of Firebrand, of how he would come when the stones were gone and the darkness at its closest about them.

It was the legend they chanted to soothe themselves, and it was that chant that echoed up the hidden corridor, finding its way by coincidence or evil design into the ears of the approaching Namer.

"In the country of the blind," it began, and as he heard it, he marveled at his dark and uncommon luck.

> "In the country of the blind,
> Where the one-eyed man is king
> And the stones are eyes of gods,
> Are pathways to remembering,
>
> "There three centuries of gloom
> Pass under rending, drought, and wars,
> Until the Firebrand comes to us
> Upon his brow a dozen stars.
>
> "Out of his wound the stones will speak,
> Will lead us from the groves of night
> And with the power of life and death
> Restore us to forgotten light."

Circumstance this might have been, he told himself now, eye half-closed, reclining like a basking reptile in the damp and the darkness of the Porch of Memory, his subjects smiling about him on their tireless business. Coincidence, perhaps, that, like the Firebrand of their legends, I had been grievously, unfairly wounded. And that when their stones and their hopes were lost, I descended to them, carrying a stone and the first glimmer of hope reborn.

But if it were only circumstance, only coincidence, why then did the stone flare in the palm of my hand and strike their faces with a fierce and godly light?

And why did I refuse it at first when they bowed to me, saying, "No, good brothers, oh, no," but then consenting to wear the crown—my crown—for the Que-Tana?

And how, in the midst of my visions, could I discover the opals that over these three hundred years have come to replace the ones the Que-Tana had lost? How indeed, unless I am the prophet that the stones have told me I am?

How indeed, unless I am the Firebrand of whom they sing?

Tell me that, if you challenge my place on this throne.

* * * * *

Madly he looked about, his eye wide and its pupil a flashing, stellar black in the torchlight.

"Well, then," he breathed hoarsely, his people continuing at their tasks below him, as accustomed to Firebrand talking to himself as they were to the flights of tenebrals through the caverns, to the musical dripping of water and the vast silences of the black recesses beyond and below them.

"Well, then. I see no challengers."

He laughed a nervous little high-pitched laugh and squinted into the darkness, where torchlight approached and there was the sound of warriors and of triumphant return.

They carried a robed figure, bound and blindfolded. Framed by the torchlight, his wild shock of red hair tumbled in all directions, as though he had been caught somehow in a monstrous wind.

There had been no trouble finding the red-haired man, the messengers had said. Camped not a mile from the entrance, he was in a rickety house on stilts decorated with holly and paper lanterns and an odd, foul-smelling old stuffed parrot that frightened the youngest Que-Tana out of a year's growth.

Other than the simple fright of the boy, there were no wounds, no casualties. It had all been terribly easy.

If this was the man he wanted. The brother of the one with the opals.

He looked like the one in the stones—the flashing image of the cleric in the makeshift camp, high in the mountains amidst the snow. But it seemed too easy.

"Brithelm?" Firebrand asked quietly, repeating a name he had heard while wearing the crown.

The blindfold was lifted from the eyes of the red-haired man, who blinked in amazement as he looked about him.

"Oh, my!" he exclaimed. Then he looked up the cataract of stone to where Firebrand was seated, silver crown blazing on his brow.

"Oh, this is not how I pictured the afterlife!" the man announced, to the bewilderment of his captors. "I always thought it would be less gloomy, a little greener! But at least Gileandos was wrong about the whole thing, and that's gratifying beyond belief!"

He smiled foolishly at the Que-Tana assembled around him. Several of the older men stepped away from him, making the warding sign against madness. He stepped toward the closest of the warriors, extending his hand in that old, Solamnic gesture of acquaintance that Firebrand had learned to despise over the centuries.

"Brithelm Pathwarden, I am!" he announced. "And I suppose we should be friends, seeing as we'll no doubt be here for eons and all!"

Chapter XI

The Namer stirred the fire, and its sparks rose to illumine the crags and furrows and green eyes of a nearby face. Slowly he took yet another cord of metal from the weathered hand.

"In the Bright Lands," the Namer murmured, "the young Knight had not foreseen other meetings."

* * * * *

We traveled much of the afternoon, snaking north over broken trails and around rubble-clogged passes, over terrain I would have imagined impassable.

Our destination was still Brithelm's camp, a little beyond the site I remembered from my former visit. For according to Shardos, my ethereal brother had settled less than a mile from the underground entrance through which these nocturnal Plainsmen were wont to come to the surface on rare occasions. Leave it to Brithelm to wade into dire circumstance. Unfortunately, it appeared that on this occasion, no fool's luck had arisen to spirit him away from danger.

It was to this entrance we traveled, guided by a blind man. I did not have time to stop and laugh at these ironies, for my brother Brithelm lay endangered somewhere below us, and who knew what the coming days would hold for him if I was not quick and resolute?

We rode in a column, sharp-eyed little Oliver at the head, leading by the reins the stocky little pied packhorse on which we had seated the old juggler. Though the young squire guided the horse, he was more on the lookout for adversaries than for directions since we steered ourselves by Shardos's dark sense, by the smell of the evergreens, and the soundless pressure the old man felt in his ears as the landscape altered, rising and dipping around us.

Birgis weaved merrily through the legs of the uneasy horses, his thoughts no doubt on squirrels and his freedom. Indeed, there were several occasions when the dog wandered completely out of sight, and then, for the first time in my recollection, the dog whistle Brithelm had given me came in handy, bringing the beast back over the rocky terrain at full waddle, lugging along a stick or a bone or whatever else had struck his foraging fancy.

I watched him approach merrily and marveled at how even the most obscure and apparently useless things—whistles, it seemed, and certainly opals—came into their power if you endured their keeping long enough. Perhaps I would feel that way about Shardos and his dog soon.

Behind this unlikely trio—Shardos and Oliver and Birgis—came the rest of us. The trip had reached that juncture when adventure wears off, when the first blush of excitement fades into fears and the drudgery of making daily mileage. Dannelle complained as though she carried all our belongings, horses included, on her own back. Dannelle di Caela was no trooper, as we were learning to our discomfort and chagrin.

As the path ahead of us wandered through country long favored by troll and bandit, my traveling companions were also rapidly growing tired of my hand at the helm of things.

As if all of that weren't ominous enough, there were the visitors that Oliver saw in the distance, pacing northward parallel to us far down in the waterlogged lowlands.

We did not think they were following us at first.

At least such thoughts did not occur to Shardos or Ramiro, and since it is a bad Solamnic habit that Knights seldom consult with squires or women, nobody knew or even cared what Dannelle and Oliver thought.

So when we first sighted the Plainsmen a mile or so east of us, wading through ankle-deep water at the edge of the foothills, most of us were alarmed. After all, our history with Plainsmen had not been good of late.

They outnumbered us at least three to one. And they moved like specters or wraiths, gliding smoothly across the rough and forbidding landscape east and below us.

"How do they keep going at that speed, Ramiro?" I asked.

"I beg—oh, the Plainsmen. Where are they now?" The big man looked behind us and far to the right of us, squinting.

"Not there. Look parallel to us, Ramiro."

He shifted in the saddle. The horse grunted and staggered a bit before recovering its pace.

"By the gods, you're right! I don't like the looks of this at all, Galen!"

Of course, Ramiro was ready to move upon them full tilt, regardless of odds. He had his sword drawn, his shield raised defiantly, and would have been galloping out of the foothills heedlessly had Shardos not laid a deft old hand on the stallion's reins.

"Look to the south of them, son," the juggler whispered. "Then consider the . . . arithmetic of this whole adventure."

We were sighted and had not known it, but the old man was right. Another dozen or so Plainsmen were rushing to join the others.

The numbers involved cooled even the most Solamnic ardor. Ramiro sheathed his sword and drew instead a cheese. He gnawed on it uneasily as we took to the road again.

As we all had expected, the Plainsmen pitched camp

when we did. From our vantage point, we could see them, shadowy and tall, milling about in the business of building a fire. It was Shardos who suggested that we establish contact to see who they were and what they wanted.

Ramiro had tired of the monotony of riding and waiting, and had started pulling at the wine flask. Given a man of his size, wine took a terribly long time to splice the main, as they say in Kalaman. Nonetheless, he was remembering songs by the time the juggler suggested negotiations, and by the time our fires were blazing, he felt somewhat belligerent and otherwise invulnerable. In full bluster, his sidelong glance on Dannelle, he volunteered himself as our ambassador of peace.

"Or worse," he said ominously, "if it comes to that."

"I'm not so sure that's altogether wise, Sir Ramiro," I cautioned. "You're much too . . . valuable a member of this party to lose if the lot of them—and remember, there *are* a lot of them—decide on mayhem."

"Then you will go with me, sir," Ramiro commanded merrily. Then, remembering Bayard's sickbed orders, he changed his tone and bowed comically in the saddle, his horse grunting and rolling its eyes.

"That is, if such embassage is to your liking, Sir Galen."

Well, it was not. I had seen enough of Plainsmen in the last week to take me through several years of knighthood and whatever journeys came with those years. Nonetheless, I had cornered myself in leadership. Now I could not back out of the little jaunt he had in mind without saying to him, to Shardos, to the world attendant, and especially to Dannelle that the threat of Plainsmen was a bit too much for my liking.

I sat back, scooting to the edge of the saddle, almost on Lily's haunches, as though backing up on the horse would get me out of what I had to do anyway.

"These are day travelers," Shardos said quietly. "Not the bunch that carried off your brother Brithelm or . . . or killed your brother Alfric."

"And what tells *you* such things, grandfather?" Ramiro asked with an icy smile.

"The whiff of 'em, boy," Shardos replied calmly. "Aloft on

an easterly wind, can't you smell it, boy? Why, the horses can, I'll wager you."

I looked closely at the old man, who cocked his head like an enormous owl, listening down in the lowlands for movement. Could he know what he claimed to know? I had always heard, of course, that a blind man's other senses intensify.

If Shardos was right, and these were a different lot of Plainsmen entirely, I might learn something. As Ramiro said, most Plainsmen generally meant no harm to the likes of us, and I was eager to find out what had brought these so far north and why they kept to the plains alongside us. If they were friendly, at worst I would return to an easier night's sleep.

If they were unfriendly . . . well, the odds were that they would find a way to close with us after nightfall anyway. Then it would be on their terms and in their choice of terrain, and with companions like Ramiro, the outcome could be disastrous.

"Do you speak their language, Shardos?" I asked.

"I beg your pardon?"

"Do you speak Plainsman?"

"Well, young fellow, that's a tall order, for many's the kind of Plainsman to speak—Que-Shu, Que-Teh, what have you. What you call your dialects."

"But with all of those, there's a sort of common Plainsmen, isn't there? Else one tribe couldn't talk to the other, and—"

"Yes, yes," Shardos interrupted, waving his hand. "And I speak it passing well."

"I see. Well, Ramiro, if there is no other recourse, things should take place the way the *leader* of our party suggests, and he suggests as follows: You stay in the foothills with Dannelle and Oliver, while Shardos and I descend to dialogues."

"If you say so, Sir Galen," Ramiro said ambivalently, no doubt relieved to be off the hook but sorry for the missed chance of braving it before the lovely Dannelle di Caela.

As we left the trail for points downward and east, seeing the look of concern on her face was a prize worth having.

Worth having, but not worth dying for. I shuddered as I handled the reins of Shardos's pony and made for the low fires east of us.

*   *   *   *   *

One of the Plainsmen ahead of us—a young man not quite my age—watched us from the time we broke from our companions. I saw him crouched in a cluster of rocks above his fellows but still a great distance below us. He was dressed in a loincloth, armed only with a sling. As we approached, he moved off into the open, amid low brambles and downed ferns, as if he did not care at all whether we saw him.

Shardos nodded and pointed toward the boy and the rocks.

"How do you know?" I asked.

"I can feel his breath on the east wind," the juggler avowed, blank eyes on the ground ahead of us. It made me uneasy, as if in that sightless world of sense and guesswork Shardos could reach into you and draw out your dreams.

The Plainsman watched calmly from his outpost amid the rocks as we rode by on our uncertain way to talk with his comrades.

I thought of Alfric, wondering if I could find peace with the boy and his people.

"You have the command here, Galen," Shardos whispered behind me. "The command you secured from Ramiro, when he challenged your ways and your going, is yours alone. From this point in our journey, you are the strategist, the tactician. I shall step in only if you bring us to the brink of massacre—which, of course, you will not do."

He grinned spaciously.

"From this point on, Sir Galen Pathwarden-Brightblade, yours is the leader's voice."

*   *   *   *   *

The tallest of the Plainsmen was my counterpart, evidently—the tribal spokesman. The rest of them gathered casually behind him, each holding his weapon, but with the spears pointed earthward, the bows unnocked, the slings unloaded.

Nonetheless, I did not fancy a long engagement.

As we reined in our horses in front of him, the tall Plainsman set down his weapons and gestured to a dry spot amid the surrounding rocks.

"Dismount, commander," Shardos muttered to me. "It's an insult to them if we talk centaur."

"Centaur?"

"What they call talking downward to them while you're on horseback."

"How, Shardos?" I asked in exasperation, turning to stare at him across Lily's rump. "How do you see silent gestures, having no eyes?"

The juggler chuckled.

"Lore, my lad," he replied. "Simple Plainsman lore. For the story makes up for the eyes and the senses. It is their way. It is how they have greeted visitors since the Age of Might."

"If you know so almighty much about Plainsman protocol," I snapped, "why don't you conduct this meeting?"

Shardos smiled merrily. "You might want to dismount, Sir Galen. That is, unless you have another strategy."

What could I answer? I dismounted and followed the big Plainsman toward the dry spot, where his followers had spread skins for our comfort.

Longwalker—for that was the Plainsman's name—cut an impressive figure. Que-Nara he was, which you could tell, supposedly, by the robe's design, by the feathers of raptors and eagles woven into the tough horsehide.

Not that I knew him from Que-Shu, or Que-Teh, or Que-anything, not until I had asked his tribe and received the answer—in surprisingly fluent Solamnic. I knew only that he w : s a Plainsman and far north of his customary country. Even with the sudden change in the weather wrought by the rainstorm, Longwalker was dressed too warmly for our balmy country. The smell of horsehide garments unsettled our horses, and as a result, they were leery of the Plainsmen, so Shardos had to tether them to a half-rotten oak that had sprouted, grown, and died unexplainably, all in this hard and merciless terrain.

Then the two of us joined Longwalker on the dry campsite, where his followers moved about quietly and gracefully, building a fire in our midst. The lookout boy came down from the high ground and began to help in the gathering of kindling. A lone woman produced dry grass from nowhere and, striking flint, ignited wood I thought too wet to burn.

For a long time, I watched her. It seemed . . . unusual, a woman in the midst of all this hardship and endurance. I had heard that the Plainsmen were like bandits in this, making no difference between men and women in the tasks and duties and adversity. I thought of Dannelle at Plainswomen's business and for some reason found it hard not to smile.

Then I felt Longwalker's eyes on me, and I looked into the green, unreadable stare of the Plainsmen leader.

He was older than he had seemed from a distance—on the edge of sixty years—but as dark-haired and straight-backed as a man half his age. Angular and lean, he was, as though years of travel and fasting had burned all softness and leisure from him, leaving only what was necessary.

I could imagine him looking through rock and darkness.

Around his neck, he wore animal teeth and claws, the feathers of hawk and falcon and raptor, not to mention some I had trouble naming. About him was the smell of woodsmoke and endless grasslands, and something beyond that—of memory and dream and deep imagining.

What was more, a blue light, almost like corposant fire on the masts of ships at sea, lingered about his shoulders and face, upon the leather pentagons and circles tied to the braids in his hair. It was like an aura, that light, and he looked like a damaged god in an old painting.

All of which made our meeting even more eccentric, more unsettling. I had heard that some of these Plainsmen had one foot in the spirit world to begin with, especially the Que-Nara, and chances were that anyone appointed to lead such a visionary band would be downright at home in the ether.

A faint smile flickered across the face of the Plainsman, then lost itself again in the strange, impassive gaze, which grew suddenly focused and intent, as if Longwalker had been searching for something on the horizon and at last had found it, faint and maybe undefined, but present nonetheless.

I shifted cautiously as his stare settled upon me and softened.

"We met in a night of stones," he declared quietly, and at once I knew that he was speaking of the opals and the visions. Longwalker's eyes appraised me as though he were sighting me down the long shaft of a nocked arrow.

I glanced at Shardos, who was suddenly poised and alert.

If Longwalker meant what I was sure he meant, if somehow he was friends with those who, pale and unsubstantial, walked through the walls of Castle di Caela and those who had killed Alfric, then the danger was most certainly mine. If I was right, we knew the same ghosts. But he evidently was on first-name basis with the lot of them.

"The stones," he urged, leaning toward me, his largeness menacing in the deceptive firelight. Instinctively my hand went to my throat, covering the brooch. I had not come this far and lost my eldest brother only to hand these stones to the first Plainsman that reached for them. I saw no Brithelm in this camp, and my price for the stones was my remaining brother's safe return.

Quickly I moved away from Longwalker and stood up, my hand moving rapidly toward my sword. In an instant, the rocks were alive with a dozen Plainsmen, who stood silently about me, bows and slings at the ready, like hunters when the quarry is brought to ground.

"Let him see the stones, Sir Galen," Shardos advised from his seat by the fire. For a moment, I thought that the worst had happened, that the amiable blind man who had followed me into the camp had turned traitor or coward, siding with the same fiery brigand who had kidnapped my brother in a cruel attempt to gain these very jewels.

"Nonsense, boy!" the juggler snapped, as if he had heard my thoughts. "Look about you! Do you think that if the man wants your jewelry that a single sword will stop him?

Let him see the stones, I urge you. They will return to you made more powerful by your trust."

"I've no fondness for mystery at the moment, Shardos," I replied. "Especially if I'm about to be stripped of my where-withal. No, if Longwalker intends to take these stones, he'll have me to reckon with, because the death of one brother and the life of the other are wrapped up in that reckoning."

"These words are power to me," Longwalker said, still crouched and staring into the heart of the fire. "These words are a sign that the stones are in trustworthy hands."

Flattered, I let my hand uncover the brooch. Longwalker lifted his eyes and regarded the stones from a distance. They seemed to glow under his gaze, as they had in the rainy dark of the woodlands.

"Yes," the big Plainsman pronounced. "There are six of them. It may be all Firebrand needs."

I returned to the fireside, glancing once over my shoulder in a vain attempt to catch a glimpse of Ramiro, Dannelle, and Oliver, who waited somewhere in the high foothills. Instead, there was the sun descending, blazing red and obscuring everything westward but the mists of night rising on the nearby lowlands and the play of sun and long shadow. Throughout the bare countryside, the cries of birds rose into the darkening air— birds stunned by the downpour of rain, who took to the wing now, seeking high wind and drier lodging.

I had not realized how late it was. Suddenly I felt cold, vulnerable. I leaned toward the fire, extended my hands to warm them.

"I'm sorry, Longwalker. I'm perilously at sea when it comes to the spiritual. I have no idea who this 'Firebrand' is, or how many stones he needs or what he needs them for. I'm not quite sure what worth these opals are to begin with, but I've seen things in the bottom of them, and I know there's more to them than the adorning of a cape."

The Plainsman nodded. He smiled faintly, picked up a branch, and stirred the fire. The blackened kindling at the heart of the flame broke at his touch, hurling red sparks and ashes harmlessly into the air.

"You have never seen the bottom of them, Solamnic. For

the bottom of them lies with the gods, since the Age of Dreams. So has been the story since that time," Longwalker said as the boy—the lookout—approached us quietly, handing each of us a cup containing a clear, fiery liquid that made Thorbardin spirits taste like weak tea. I sipped once and thought I had made a cultural error—had swallowed a lamp oil or a tanning agent or some exotic explosive. But across the fire from me, Longwalker tilted his cup back and drained it.

I thanked the gods that Ramiro was not here in my place.

"Since the Age of Dreams, Solamnic," Longwalker continued. "As everything did in that distant time, the story begins with a god. For the gods had brought us these stones in the time before the Telling—before the tribes assembled in Abanasinia to renew our stories. The stones go by many names—glain opals, godseyes, wishing stones. Whatever men call them, they are magical and rare, and showing us our visions and dreams and words, and the visions and dreams and words of others. Used in wisdom, they helped our scattered brotherhood, the Que-Shu, Que-Teh, Que-Nara, Que-Kiri, and the others, to know each other over miles and years."

"I'm not sure I follow you," I confessed. Longwalker paused and explained patiently.

"In our tribes, there were always the Namers—what you might call clerics, but more than clerics. For the Namers remembered the histories of things—the wanderings of our peoples for a hundred generations back, unto a time when the gods walked among us and there were as yet no stories to remember."

"A weighty calling, that of the Namer," Shardos said.

"The burden was lighter because of the opals," Longwalker continued. "For placed in the Tribal Crowns—the great circlets forged by Reorx in the Age of Dreams, one for each tribe and one alone—the stones would hold memory. The Namer could look into the godseye and see what had passed and what was passing. Que-Kiri could speak to Que-Shu through the opals, though mountains and waters lay between them. And through them, we spoke to the past."

"There in the crowns lay the memories of our peoples, the memories we sang of and shared at the Telling."

"The Telling?" I asked.

"A Plainsman conclave," Shardos explained. "A great get-together of the tribes that takes place every seven hundred years or so. They tell their tribal histories there, set aright any mistakes in them, so that the lore of the Plainsmen gets passed down correctly and the deeds of the ancestors are re-membered."

Longwalker nodded. "A crown to each of the twelve tribes," he continued. "Each crown with twelve opals. A sign of our unity, but also magic itself, they tell us. Whatever the power of the stones, it is only when they are set in a god-forged crown that they bind and spark a greater power. In the godforged crown only."

"But what about . . . those in my brooch?" I asked. "I can see things through *them* without this crown."

"The visions that two opals provide are fleeting. They go wherever they wish, like the shape of a face in a cloud, so that they mean one thing to one eye and something else to another. The more stones that are set together, the clearer the vision. The best of all numbers is twelve, and twelve was the number in each of the crowns. It is said that the wisdom of twelve stones abides with the Namer for years—that once he has worn the crown, he is never the same again.

"I cannot say for sure that is true. Nor can I tell you of the danger, for it is also said that if *thirteen* opals were set into one of the crowns, then the wearer would have power over life and death."

I looked at Shardos, who shook his head and frowned.

"Power over life and death?" I asked. "What does that mean, Longwalker?"

"I cannot say for sure," the tall Plainsman answered. "Nor could I tell you why anyone would want such a power. For I have heard that the dead come back at the bidding of the thirteenth godseye, and I am told that in each of the Naming Crowns is a thirteenth setting, always left empty, to remind us of that legend—to tell us that it was our choice not to seize what is forbidden. Not until now."

Longwalker raised the sleeve of his deerskin tunic. Beneath the sleeve lay a rawhide armband, glittering with black eyes in the firelit night. "For someone is about to take that power, Solamnic. Indeed, someone has waited for you to bring him that power."

Chapter XII

"*Not so fast!*" I warned, the worst of my suspicions returning. For what could someone waiting for the power of the opals possibly mean but that he had been waiting for me all along, had followed us this far and set up camp, knowing that I would fly to his fires and to my destruction like a dim-sighted, dim-witted moth?

I leapt away from the fire toward the darkness, where I knew my horse was tethered. But Longwalker stayed close to the flame and called out to me, his level voice reaching me suddenly and softly, as though I was thinking his words to myself.

"Not so quickly, Solamnic. I have been waiting for you, but I am no thief."

I paused, my back to the fire and the Plainsman.

"Now," he said, after a silence. "Linger awhile longer and listen to the rest of my story. Your brother, lost amid stones and darkness, would thank you for hearing me out."

I turned to face him, breathing more slowly, my hand relaxing its grip on the hilt of my sword.

I could not have left anyway—not without Shardos, who had not stirred from his place, intent on Longwalker's tale. I muttered an oath at the circumstances: Everywhere I looked, I was responsible for someone, it seemed, and though I had known the man scarcely more than a day, I could no more abandon him than I could Dannelle or Ramiro. Or Brithelm, for that matter.

The sudden flight toward the horses, away from all of this history and magic, was simply the ridiculous first of my options. I sighed and returned cautiously to the fire. When the Measure orders you to defend the rights of the poor and oppressed and the helpless, it never says how large and powerful and downright frightening the oppressing forces can be.

"I was speaking of the crowns," Longwalker said. "Of the crowns and their powers, and a time in which the people held them and used them wisely."

I nodded and sat beside Shardos, who still had not moved.

"The Ogre Wars," Longwalker continued, "back in the Age of Might, made that happier time but a memory. All of the crowns were either destroyed or damaged or vanished, suffering the loss of most or all of their stones. The last Telling, four hundred years before the Rending—what you call the Cataclysm—was a time of great sorrow. Terrible gaps lay in the years, for even the wisest of Namers could not remember the stories without the crowns and stones to guide them. So the People were cut off from their fathers, from the memories."

"It could not end that way," Shardos whispered quietly and urgently. The firelight played over his dark, grizzled face, his vacant eyes. "Your people could not let the wars steal their memory."

"And, of course, the duty fell to the Que-Nara," Longwalker said.

"I have heard little of the Que-Nara," I said, "except that

yours are the most priestly and visionary of the Plainsmen."

"Or the luckiest, perhaps," Longwalker added, his face breaking into an enormous, jagged grin. "Ours was the only crown that survived undamaged, so ours was the task of rescuing memory.

"Half of us went below the earth, into the dark of many voices, there among the swimming lights and the great snake that bears all Solamnia upon its back . . ."

I hid a smile at the creaking poetry of the old legends, but Longwalker was watching nothing but the flames.

"They wandered under the earth through a passage known only to the Namer and passed down from one to the next, as the young Namer adorned his hair and put on the crown, and the old one passed into silence. Once the Que-Nara were there in the darkness, they hunted the stones in the veins of the ground."

"To replace the ones that were missing?" I asked. But Longwalker kept at the telling.

"The rest of us stayed above, as guardians, and to assure that the Que-Nara would survive rockfall and tremor and flood and the changes of the earth. And for the lives of six chieftains, the Que-Nara below spoke to the Que-Nara above, for six of the stones were in the keeping of the Que-Nara below, and six of them we kept with us."

Longwalker paused. He looked up at me and extended his hand, his fingers as long and knotted as branches. I knew without words that he wanted to hold the opals. Silently, with only the slightest doubt and reluctance, I handed him the brooch.

He stared into it deeply, as though he looked beyond it into something murky and imponderable. As though he had found the bottom of the stones.

"Now is the time to tell of the one who awaits you," he said, handing the brooch back to me. "Tell me what you see in the godseyes, Solamnic."

Instantly my suspicions returned.

"You're not . . . up to some Plainsman hypnosis, are you? I mean, is there some kind of trick your tribe has to lull enemies to sleep?"

"Most certainly there is," Longwalker admitted, "but this

is not that trick. Look into the opals, Solamnic."

I did so reluctantly. Like black pools they were, reflecting the light of the fire, of the rising red moon, and yet underneath the reflection, something was moving. I leaned forward, squinting against the firelight. The stones began to glow as they had last night in the clearing, and I shuddered, remembering where the glow had led me and where I had led Alfric in turn.

Suddenly I saw figures shimmering and moving in the depths of the stones. It was as though I watched them through a crystal, as though in a core of fire there was a window or door through which they walked, faint shapes in the rippling blackness. The world inside the stones was a world long vanished, and I watched the vision and knew I was looking back through the years, into the depths of the past.

* * * * *

There were twenty of them easily, perhaps two dozen. The cloud in the stones obscured the shapes, made counting difficult. But the feathers and the symbols they wore were Que-Nara.

The country around them was forest—an unbearably bright forest that shimmered sea-blue. Perhaps it was the woods or southern Hylo, doomed by the Cataclysm that would follow in the years to come. For I knew without being told that this was an older time, before the Kingpriest's decrees and the Rending, though for the life of me, I cannot tell you how I knew such a thing.

As I watched, the Que-Nara established camp in a woodland clearing. Quickly and with great skill, the old ones and the children gathered the wood, kindled a slow, smokeless fire that shone gold on green, and the stones in which I watched this scene glimmered at the edges with a borrowed light.

One of them, a young man, leather diamonds and bone stars woven into the thick web of his hair, crouched some distance from the fire, his attentions on something cupped in his hands. For a moment, I disregarded him, my thoughts on the campfires and the families huddled about them, but the stones would not show me those fires and families, fixing my sight instead on the young man at the edge of the light.

I did not know his name. Why I should expect to know it, I could not tell you, but the stones were firm in this, and the first thought that rose to my mind as I watched him about his obscure business was that I did not know his name.

The second thought was that the young man was the one who spoke to me in the vision—the one who claimed to have kidnapped my brother Brithelm.

I had spoken to this one not four nights ago, and yet this scene was two centuries, three centuries old. It was like the light from distant Chemosh, which the astronomers say reaches the eye decades after it rises from the surface of the star.

I felt Longwalker watching me as I thought this. His presence was of little concern: My thoughts were fixed on the young man I saw in the stone, on the past unfolding, as though a mural in the halls of Castle de Caela sprang suddenly to life, and history moved in my marveling sight.

The nameless youth held a crown in his hands—a crown of woven silver, into which four, five, six opals were set. It was difficult to tell how many.

I shook my head, and the stones I was watching directed my eyes to the stones in the crown. Stones within stones within stones, like mirrors facing each other at the ends of a long hall, in which the eye is swallowed forever into something like eternity.

My eye plunged downward into the dark of the opals, and the scene before me was swallowed up in darkness, and darkness was all around me. . . .

"Wait," Longwalker said, and I felt a strong hand on my shoulder. "Follow no further. That is how Firebrand lost himself, in sounding the bottom of the stones."

Sounding the bottom of the stones? It was all mystery, all Plainsman hocus-pocus. And yet there was something in those depths that called me further, so that it took everything I had to resist it, and yet I was not sure I had resisted it, not sure. . . .

The pressure at my shoulder increased.

"Good," Longwalker said. "Now you will see what happened."

Again the young man was in view, the crown on his head and a faint, fanatical smile on his lips. The children of the Plainsmen shied from him, adults turned from him in the councils, until his only companion, his only confidant, was the crown he talked to by the fire's edge.

His people looked on in suspicion, drawing signs of warding on the ground before they lay down to sleep.

Soon he traveled a mile behind them. They would not permit him to venture any closer. A voice traveled with him, cold and obscure and insinuating. I could hear it talking to him, could hear it saying . . .

So it always is with the gifted, with the god-ordained. For your eyes see into the time to come, and if you look long enough, my friend, you will see a time in which all the Que-Nara understand your gifts and hearken to the words of your prophecies.

Then, the voice said, and the ground over which the young man walked was suddenly covered with glittering blades of ice, *then I shall tell you what to say to them; they shall hear the words of your mouth as prophecy, and in the time that follows, we shall be among you.*

"According to your will, Sargonnas," the young man said.

"Sargonnas!" I exclaimed, tearing my gaze from the stones.

"Sargonnas the Consort," Shardos said quietly. "Prince in the Dark Pantheon."

"I know where you are in the story, Solamnic," Longwalker said, "because I have seen it so many times. What they transacted in that ill hour, Namer and god, only the gods themselves know."

We looked at one another uneasily. At last the big Plainsman smiled faintly.

"Tarry but a while longer, Sir Galen, for the story has a middle and an end."

And in the stones were the rocky foothills, a circle of boulders in a bleak country.

The Plainsmen surrounded the Namer, and a chieftain

pronounced the charges and the crimes.

"False prophecy," they said, and "corrupting the young." "Conjury," and "rending the earth."

" 'Rending the earth'?" I asked.

"Who is to say that the tremors in the mountains are not his doing still?" Longwalker asked. "His, and that of the evil prince he serves."

I started to return my eyes to the stones, but the Plainsman waved his big hand.

"You have seen enough," he said. "Do not look into what follows, for the ceremony is private when a man is cast from the tribe.

"The stones in the Namer's Crown were divided among the elders, his eye was taken according to the Old Ways, and the wound seared by the white-hot blade of the spear."

I gasped and swallowed hard. It was all a bit fierce and nomadic for my tastes.

"Wh-Why the *eye*, Longwalker? Why not just . . . muster the poor lad out? It seems a little harsh, this ceremony of exile and the cutting that goes with it."

"It's actually kind, Galen," the juggler added, stirring from his place by the fire and stretching his spindly old legs. Not for the first time, I wondered how Shardos had learned all of these tales.

"Kind in a rather stark, Plainsman way, that is," the old man continued. "For though it maims the outcast, it also protects him, in an odd fashion. It is an outward sign to the other Plainsmen among whom he wanders that, though he is an exile and cannot be taken in, he is not to be harmed, for perpetually he suffers for his wrongdoings."

"It still sounds harsh to me," I insisted, and Longwalker frowned.

"What," he asked, "would Solamnics do to one who betrayed their Order?"

I was not sure, but I admitted that the Measure would call for something drastic, something with a taste of high drama, no doubt.

"As I thought," Longwalker replied with satisfaction, and he told me the rest of the story: how the outcast left the Que-Nara, but not without stealing the crown and one of the opals. How he wandered for months, guided alone over the desolate landscape by hints and suggestions from the voice that had taken up residence in the cold silver of the crown on his head, which spoke to him somehow through the single, unnaturally glimmering opal.

How after weeks of wandering, the young Namer was not sure whether the voice in his ear was that of a god or a stone or a crown, or perhaps the softer voice of his own prophetic gifts, and how he praised himself for his "insight and foreknowledge." How the wanderings would take him by the way he knew as the Que-Nara Namer—the secret way unto the rest of the tribe, buried deep under the ground.

"Almost at the moment he reached them," Longwalker said, his dark eyes bleak and ominous, "the Rending raced along the spine of the world and the earth burst open, and nothing has ever been the same. . . ."

"You don't believe," I insisted, "that this Namer, this—"

"Firebrand, he calls himself."

"Did this . . . Firebrand . . . have anything to do with the Rending?"

Longwalker shook his head. "I cannot say. It also puzzles me how he has lived through the lives of six chieftains."

It puzzled me, too, but there was a whiff of mystery and murk about anything to do with the Plainsmen.

"How . . . how do you know he is with them? I mean, with the Que-Nara beneath the ground?"

"In the last few weeks, I have seen him, spoken to him," Longwalker said, with a quick motion drawing a warding sign in the dust by the fire. "He laughs at us and says that his wounded eye has stared down our weapons."

"What does that mean?" I asked.

"That the people below took him in despite his wounded eye. That his eye must have deceived them, then his words, for now they follow him without question, and that the time will come when his crown is complete—complete beyond the twelve, he says, for it is his plan to set the thirteenth stone and bring forth the power of life and death."

"And I am walking right into his hands, bringing him the very thing he seeks?" I asked apprehensively.

"The very thing he seeks may be his undoing,"

Longwalker mused. "You see, Firebrand is right, for I am powerless against him. His taken eye is *my* undoing, in a way. For even if I knew the way beneath the mountains into his dark kingdom—which was a way lost to us when Firebrand took the knowledge with him—I could not harm him, for the blade that marked him has stayed my hand."

I crouched in a puzzled silence. Beside me, Shardos cleared his throat uncomfortably and stirred the fire with a stick.

"Do you mean you cannot lay hands on Firebrand? Not even to save your people?"

"Not even if he harms my people. For he *will* harm them by stealing their memory, and if I lay hands on him, I am saying that memory is not worth the stealing.

"But," he continued, green mischief deep in his eyes like fire in the opals, "that is not to say I cannot sit back and let someone else—someone not of the People—lay hands on him. Nor that I would not be pleased to do so. For the hands that destroy Firebrand will carry history. They will bind wounds and unite a sundered nation. Perhaps it is my task only to watch them at their business. Sometimes the doing is the waiting."

Moths sailed through the baffled attic between my ears.

"I'm sorry, Longwalker," I said finally, "but I don't really have the stuff of history and all. I'm afraid that all I'm after is my brother Brithelm, and once I have him, my quarrel with this Firebrand is more than likely over. I am no hero."

As if to prove my point, I told the Plainsman the whole unsavory story of *my* opals: how the stones came to me long ago from the coffers of an evil illusionist, as a bribe to betray Bayard Brightblade, not to mention my family. I dragged the gems through the whole adventure with the Scorpion—from the dusty rooms of my castle to the illusory rooms of his, and despite their time in my possession, I knew little more about them than I did when I first grasped them in my money-hungry clutches.

"I survived, of course, Longwalker," I concluded, squinting into the darkness of the tall shape now standing just outside the firelight's edge. "But it took all my ingenuity and soft words and courage, finally, to pry me out of the Scorpion's clutches. I fear I am just about spent of all those virtues."

"But you survived, of course. And that in itself is something. The night is long," he added abruptly, "and ahead of you a longer journey. By now you must know we have no intent to harm you. Trusting that, you should sleep calmly in your camp tonight."

He smiled his ragged, broken smile and said, "We heard about these stones, that Firebrand awaited their coming. It is our nature to be concerned when such things take place. So we wanted to find them, to see that the hands into which they have fallen are . . . gentle hands that may guard that stillness well."

"I know of these things, too, Longwalker," I said. "I have seen the fires from a distance, in the mountains and in the gems. A brother of mine is somewhere beneath those mountains, and another . . ." I choked.

It was still too soon to talk of Alfric. Longwalker rose from the fire and moved slowly and graciously toward the edge of the light, leaving me with my thoughts for a moment.

"Longwalker?" I said at last, having gathered myself together again. "What have you heard from my brother—the one Firebrand has taken?"

"Only what you have told me now, Solamnic," he replied, moving back into the light.

He looked down on me almost gently, and I stood, helping Shardos to his feet. The three of us walked toward the edge of the camp. Between two tall rocks far to our west, a faint fire was glowing, and from that region I heard the sound of Ramiro's laughter, carrying over miles and no doubt fueled by a flask of Thorbardin Eagle.

"I believe you now, Solamnic," Longwalker said quietly. "You will care for the stones and for my people wisely."

"But why? Why should you believe in me? I wish your people and their history well, but it is my brother and only my brother I am after. And I shall do *anything* to win his freedom."

"That in itself is something," the Plainsman said bluntly. "I believe that the gods always send my people something. You seem to be the one tree on the plain."

"That is not encouraging, Longwalker."

"Then you have more of encouragement to learn," Longwalker said mysteriously, leading me to the horses.

* * * * *

It was a lonely trip back to our campsite. Lily plodded, worn down, no doubt, by her fear of the Plainsmen's clothing. I led Shardos's horse, puffing and snorting, through the rising rocks, the old man snoring in the saddle.

I labored under my own burden. The stones weighed heavily in my speculation, for at heart I have always hated responsibilities that offer me no chance to order about those around me. And the whole murky business of this Firebrand and his crown and visions made me doubly uneasy.

Waiting may be doing, but to me, that night, it seemed too much like doing nothing.

There in the darkness, as the path we were on began to ascend more steeply toward the faint light of our campfire, I thought about planting the stones on Shardos.

But the old man's moon of a face smiled in serene sleep behind me, and I knew that my thoughts were idle—that I was not going to take the coward's way out. But damned if I knew what way I would take instead.

Chapter XIII

"What about the others?" a small child asked, crouched over several little piles of stones and sticks he moved along with the Namer's story. "What of those who stayed at the castle and those in the Namer's caves?"

The Namer nodded and smiled. Slowly he twined the two strands of metal together over the fire, bending them gracefully in his gloved hands.

* * * * *

Here is the story as the Lady Enid told it to me, as I gathered from what others said, what servants said, from what Sir Bayard let fall in moments unguarded. It is the tale of what took place in our absence.

At first, Bayard was his old self, handling in his customary and courteous manner the wave of hysteria that passed through Castle di Caela when Dannelle was discovered missing.

All of this ruling in justice and wisdom is well and good, but Bayard was quickly restless, having dispatched all the daily duties he could notice, foresee, or even imagine by the end of the first day after our departure. That is not to say there wasn't much left to do around Castle di Caela. It is just that Bayard, by temperament an adventuring Knight, had neither the patience nor the skills to attend the details of castle maintenance and government.

It is then that the real story begins.

Only three nights passed, it seems, until Bayard was climbing the Cat Tower. The whisper went from servant to servant as the Knight lay in the infirmary, attended by Enid, who was beyond herself with managing a restless husband and an even more restless estate. The three surgeons stood constantly and irritatingly over the injured Knight, rubbing his leg with their textral stones. The stones steamed and emitted sweet odors, but they lost their early fascination for Bayard and were now part of the boring daily landscape.

On the other hand, Bayard found young Brandon Rus the only bright spot in the bleak hours. It was Brandon who talked to him about hawking and horses, who knew more about those cherished subjects than half a dozen Knights twice his age. However, Brandon knew such things because he was at them constantly, and so he spent most of his day in the castle forest beyond the east wall, restlessly riding and hunting.

Sometimes in the morning, when the wind lifted, Bayard could hear his horn echoing over the grounds of the estate. It was then that he turned uncomfortably, filled with a most un-Solamnic jealousy, and shouted at the surgeons.

Still, Sir Brandon was always welcome. Bayard looked forward to his conversation as a cherished relief from the mournful Sirs Elazar and Fernando, the gloomy Solamnics whose talk was only about violation of rules and missing opals. Nonetheless, when the surgeons left at night, when the hard-pressed Enid napped in her brief rest from enter-

taining and attending to her husband, Bayard was left alone
with his discomfort, with his loneliness and his boredom,
with the distant metallic sounds of the one cuckoo clock
Enid had not dismantled in her campaign to redecorate the
palace old Sir Robert had defaced years ago by absentmind-
edness and bad taste. Bayard longed for even Elazar's company then, in those bird-haunted and lonely hours, though
he knew he would regret it in a matter of minutes.

So the hours passed until the third day, when Sir Bayard
Brightblade decided to do something picturesque with his
surroundings. He began with an archery range set up
through the infirmary window.

After Enid had opened the shutters and moved away from
the half-light of noon, drenched by the continuing downpour, and after the three surgeons left dripping with sweat
and rain, having carried Bayard, bed and all, to a towering
view of the courtyard, an equally soaked servant gloomily
set up two targets in the center of the bailey. Then Brandon
Rus, perhaps the only dry person in that wing of the castle,
pulled up a chair at Bayard's bedside and brought forth a
crossbow.

"You have to allow for the height and the distance and the
rain, Sir Bayard," he explained politely as he and Raphael
nocked the arrow and drew the string, tilting the bow ever
so slightly. Calmly he loosed the shaft, and it flew out into
the downpour.

Raphael's shout rose above the steady rushing sound of
the rain. Sir Brandon's arrow struck the bull's-eye.

Brandon smiled faintly and handed the bow to Bayard.

Sullenly he handed the crossbow back to Brandon.

" 'Tis an impossible device to load from a sickbed, sir," the
young man explained as they reloaded for the embarrassed
Knight.

" 'Tis also my damned leg that's ailing, lad, not my arms!"
Bayard snapped. After which there was an uncomfortable
silence, a stillness in both men. Then Brandon handed the
bow back to the recumbent Bayard.

Who missed and missed and missed, the first arrow sailing long, passing over the targets and into an awning of the
paddock. The canvas, already sagging with rainwater, burst

open and spewed water onto an unfortunate groom currying a mare beneath it. The mare galloped off, leaving the boy behind her, soaked and still clutching a comb.

The second arrow fell closer to its mark, but not close enough, the arrow shivering in the very spot where only a second before a sentry was standing sullenly.

The third arrow hit the top of the windowsill and darted back into the sickroom, ricocheting between Raphael's legs and pinning Bayard's blanket to the wall.

Bayard looked at Sir Brandon, who scooted his chair away from the bedside. Archery, it seemed, was over for the day.

* * * * *

It was time, instead, to bring on the dwarves and the dogs.

For on the third day of Sir Bayard's living in, a party of five dwarves, making the long trek from Thorbardin north into Palanthas with five barrels of Thorbardin Eagle to barter, trade, or sell at impossible prices, was waylaid by the heavy rains and forced to seek shelter at the first roof, which happened to be that of Castle di Caela. According to Solamnic custom, Enid saw to the quarters of the five from Thorbardin. According to custom, she was also supposed to be responsible for their entertainment.

A duty that Bayard took eagerly out of her hands.

The rooms in the infirmary underwent a bizarre transformation. Doors were opened, in some cases removed. Tables were stacked and ordered, as were the linen cabinets. The result of all these arrangements was a wide, circular path that passed through four of the sickrooms, having its beginning and ending directly in front of Bayard's bed, which was moved, again by the gasping and perspiring surgeons, back to its original site.

A wide, circular path. Makeshift, but good enough for a dog track when money and dwarf spirits circulate.

And circulate they did, the second night of the dwarves' stay, as the races began. Bayard bought one of the barrels of Thorbardin Eagle at a price Sir Robert denounced as "banditry"—at least until his third drink, when the "bandit" became a sober-faced bloodhound who sat down at the final turn of the dog track, allowing a beagle and a pug to pass him, and forfeiting the large amount of money Sir Robert had placed on his promised speed and endurance.

Sir Robert asked Brandon for his bow, preparing to shoot the animal in a fit of gambler's rage. Brandon and Bayard exchanged glances; by now they were the only two sober folk in the room, and their sobriety told them that it would be a real game of chance to determine where Robert di Caela's arrow would lodge, and that the stakes in such a game would be terribly high.

Robert was escorted to bed by Sir Brandon, who gave up escorting after a few steps and hoisted the old man to his shoulders when the two of them reached the stairwell leading to the fourth floor and Sir Robert's quarters.

This left Bayard downstairs, alone in his sobriety, but not without company. Sir Andrew was there, as was Gileandos. Elazar was snoring under the three-legged table that completed the first turn of the dog track, while Fernando, dressed in the ornamental armor worn by old Simon di Caela before he decided he was an iguana, tried in vain to order around anyone—dwarf, guard, page, or dog.

Enid entered the room as the second race began and was faced with this sorry sight. Fernando turned to her. In a booming voice, he proclaimed that she should return to where she belonged.

The whole room dropped into silence and every eye, drunk or sober, snapped around to Fernando. Enid turned icily, haughtily toward the litigious old fool, who had just crossed a boundary that nobody—Knight, dwarf, servant, or dog—could cross without dire peril. For Enid Pathwarden was Pathwarden only through marriage and love for her husband. By blood and by a thousand years of heritage, she was all di Caela.

She was, indeed, *the* di Caela.

And the dog races were declared over. Memories are blurred as to how Fernando managed to ride twenty-five miles south toward his holdings near the Garnet Mountains that very night. What is more, he was wrapped in yards of

linen and was terribly bruised about his head and shoulders.
The bruises somehow matched exactly the carving on the
missing leg of the table at the first turn of the dog track.

Sir Elazar, though still at the castle, was also badly
bruised, having been found by Raphael the next morning, a
victim of collapsing furniture.

The dwarves were gone by noon on the next day, Elazar
was packing, and the dogs were kenneled once again, their
night of celebrity passed into di Caela history. And so, deprived of sport and diversion, the master of the castle again
lay splinted and confined to the infirmary.

*   *   *   *   *

It was enough to drive Bayard Brightblade to the di Caela
family papers.

For two years, he had promised his wife that, "given the
time and the leisure," he would gather together the volumes
from the library—the ledgers and histories, the journals and
logs and lists and registers in which the di Caelas of old kept
all kinds of records. Enid hoped that the whereabouts of the
missing well cap would come up after desperate page-
turning, and the danger of flood could be averted. But she
also delighted in her husband's newfound interest in the
daily business of the estate and the balance of credit and
debit.

Within an hour, the poor man was overwhelmed. Numbers hurtled by him like hostile arrows, and he soon decided
that the single most happy advantage of wandering knighthood is its freedom from budgetry and arithmetic.

"Mathematics is for gnomes, anyway," he muttered, setting aside the account books and moving to the wills. Wills,
of course, make for better reading, having been principal
weapons in di Caela family combat for centuries.

It was here that Bayard Brightblade read of family feuds
and disputes that had passed down through the generations,
as each di Caela, on his or her deathbed, seems to have re-
served a posthumous slap for one or more descendants.
Most clerical older sons inherited the father's favorite pros-
titute, while fastidious nieces inherited their uncle's privy.

Some bequests were not as jolly: Evana di Caela received only a side of beef from her mother, which, the old woman said, "should serve as a reminder of what happens to heavy, bovine creatures"; Laurantio di Caela received from his uncle a single dagger with the murky instructions to "do what needs to be done."

The Lady Mariel passed down to Enid herself, who was an infant at the time, fifty cats. Bayard thought of how the mad old woman met her fate and laughed wickedly.

"Wonder how she proposed to feed them all?" he asked in all mischief. Then his eye stopped on an older scrap of parchment—centuries old, perhaps, and no larger than the palm of Bayard's hand. And yet it was written in a polished script that was strikingly, unsettlingly familiar.

Now where . . . ? he thought, then recognized the writing of Benedict di Caela.

You again, old enemy, Bayard thought, for it was the Scorpion's writing, reaching out to him beyond four centuries and the villain's several deaths.

Having nothing to inherit, I have little to pass to my descendants. My father and that brace of vultures who call themselves my brothers have seen to that.

"We saw to it also, you brigand!" Bayard hissed, surprised at the anger he still felt toward the dead illusionist. Bayard snorted and lifted the parchment to the light.

So I resolve to bequeath chaos and disaster and a curse on generations. Castle di Caela will be mine eventually, for I shall return to it until it falls into my hands.

"Or the curse is lifted," Bayard pronounced triumphantly, then frowned at the document's conclusion.

And if you who read this have lifted my curse, congratulate yourself no further. If you have been triumphant, prepare to have Castle di Caela snatched from your hands by the rending of the earth. Eventually it will come, as foretold and unstoppable as the rains of autumn or the awakenings of spring. For I have seen to that. Beneath your feet and your thoughts, your histories and even your imaginings, I have set a device in motion. From the wakening of time, from the Vingaard Mountains to the Plains of Solamnia, even unto the foundations of this murderous house, there were forces that awaited my guidance, and you will know of them soon enough. Though you may uncover my devices, you will never strike the mark nor hit the target. And though I may be dead when you read this, be assured that in some dark and comfortless corner of the skies, my laughter mocks you and those who follow you with the fond and foolish hopes that my powers are spent.

Bayard's night was sleepless. The shooting pains in his leg mingled with unsettling thoughts, more baffling than any numbers, as he tried to decipher the will, to plumb the mysterious "device," to stop the dark laughter. He worried, too, about the young man in the mountains and his ragtag group of followers.

* * * * *

It was almost a week before Bradley, one of the castle engineers, inspecting the foundations and cellars of the castle for flaws and damage the earthquake had wrought, stumbled across the gap in the dungeon.

It was not a large opening, he insisted to an alarmed Bayard and a half-dozing Sir Robert, but dangerous enough. For the great well that lay under the castle, subject to strain and pressure through the extraordinary rainy season, was no doubt brimming and bubbling in the deep recesses of rock, where only a sudden twist of the earth could unleash a flood through the floors of the towers and leave them awash in their own cistern.

To Bayard, it was still a question of plumbing. He soothed himself, thinking, I shall attend to this later. Until the young engineer added that beyond the opening lay a network of tunnels.

Now he was far more concerned as to the state of the castle, for there was no telling what vermin or darker thing might emerge from the deep silences of the earth. And, of course, the Scorpion's will returned to his thoughts, and he wondered if this indeed was the beginning of the last unworldly threat.

It seemed far-fetched, too much of a coincidence. Finally it was something from the deep silences of boredom that called Bayard Brightblade into action.

"I shall have to see this fissure," he demanded, rising painfully in his bed. The surgeons, who had moved to the far corners of the room in respect for the master's privacy, scurried toward him now, textral stones in hand.

"Enough of this quackery," Bayard ordered, waving them away. "If I cannot have entertainments, by the gods, I must at least have order!"

Having donned a mask of sternness, Sir Bayard Brightblade smiled inwardly at the prospects of adventure. He tried to stand. The leg was incredibly heavy, weak, laced with a pain that was endurable but sharp.

Now he sat at the edge of his bed. One of the surgeons approached again, his hands fluttering. Again Bayard waved him away.

The engineers stepped forward, offering to help the master rise.

The surgeons backed away. One of them sidled toward the infirmary door, out of which he intended to run when Bayard was not looking—to run in search of the Lady Enid, who was the single soul in the castle who could calm the master.

"Not another step, surgeon," Bayard snapped, "or I shall watch you drink every purgative in those bags of yours."

All three of the surgeons stood where they were, their white robes wavering, settling to a stillness. They looked like gaunt, bearded flagpoles.

"Bring me Brandon Rus," Bayard snapped to the bewildered engineers. "It's high time we cleaned the cobwebs from this castle, and I shall need stalwart companions to help me do it."

I shall need the others, too, he thought ironically. Andrew and little Raphael, perhaps, and—the gods forbid!—maybe even Sir Robert here. Though if that is the case, I'd be hard-

pressed keeping them from getting lost or scattered or
crushed or dismembered. Even those I might want beside
me, if for no other reason than I cannot abide the disruption
and whining and threats of swordplay if I pass up one for
another.

*   *   *   *   *

Descent into the dungeon of Castle di Caela was hard
enough for a healthy man. The steps were narrow and
steep, almost sheer—designed at a time when either the men
took longer strides or fancied themselves larger than they
actually were. They were wet, these steps, and moss-
covered, as slippery as the ground outside after twelve days
of rain.

Even the engineers, who were young and nimble, had
troubles of their own descending the stairs. It went without
saying that those who followed them were hard-pressed indeed.

Brandon Rus, bracing himself against the walls, was
younger than most of the Knights and more nimble than any
of them, and had insisted on going first, in order to "break
the fall" of anyone unfortunate enough to lose footing behind him.

Brandon, though, was not doing so well himself. Twice he
stumbled, and as he did, the engineers, who had long since
passed him, jumped and shuddered, fearing the cascade of
metal and leather and Knight that would strike them square
in the back if Sir Brandon lost his purchase completely.

Behind young Brandon Rus was the most haphazard crew
of Solamnics it was ever Bayard's misfortune to muster. Or
so he thought as, his arm draped over the shoulders of Andrew Pathwarden, they descended uncomfortably, pushed
together by Bayard's disability and by the narrow walls of
the stairwell.

Sir Andrew descended, coughing and cursing the darkness and dampness of the air. As did Sir Robert di Caela,
who had invited himself along over Bayard's better judgment. Bayard mentioned to Sir Andrew in private that he
would appreciate some help in making sure that Sir Robert

neither wedged himself in some remote underground cranny nor caused a cave-in or rockslide due to his high spirits. Sir Andrew promised that Robert was "in good hands."

Bayard Brightblade was not assured.

Comprising the rest of the group were servants— linkboys and bearers. There were two men trained as sappers, whose talents Bayard thought he could put to less military use. There was also Gileandos the tutor, who hovered about Sir Robert and Sir Andrew, prattling about the differences between stalactite and stalagmite and how one remembered the difference, until Sir Robert suggested that the scholar carry a lantern and make himself "useful for once."

All in all, there were nearly twenty of them—"a small army," Bayard muttered, a little resentfully, because his visions had been of adventure—of a solitary Knight, or at most a band of two or three or four, off into the bowels of the earth, where unknown peril awaited them.

With his group, the numbers were stacked against the lurking dangers. And Bayard admitted he was disappointed by the odds. His followers pressed together around him until he felt like a schoolmaster or a governess off on a jaunt with unruly children in tow.

* * * * *

"What . . . what does it look like inside there, Bayard?" Sir Andrew asked, squinting over a lantern held much too high by Gileandos.

Together the Knights peered into the fissure. Andrew shifted uncomfortably under Bayard's weight.

"I cannot see a thing while I rock like a boat, Andrew," Bayard replied curtly, and the old man settled himself.

Brandon Rus leaned forward and, taking a lantern from one of the linkboys, cast light into the fissure.

A tangle of roots, no doubt from the huge hackberry and vallenwood parks just outside the castle wall, spread across the door as though the very veins and arteries of the world lay exposed. Beyond the network of tendrils, there was a greater darkness—some tunnel, no doubt, or a passageway formed where the roots churned and shifted the ground about them.

The explorers, all twenty or more of them, stood gaping at the edge of the darkness. Bayard tried to move forward for a closer look, but the reluctance of his bearers held him back.

"There is nothing of . . . passageways . . . in the histories," Brandon whispered.

"Oh, I have seen them in a chapter or two," Bayard murmured ominously as startled eyes turned toward him.

Gileandos moved forward and faced the party, his back to the cavity in front of them.

"Gentlemen, you are looking into the mouth of an accident. A quirk of geology. All that's left for any of us is repairs, if you ask me. Nothing a good stonemason cannot mend and refashion into dungeonry."

Bayard regarded the old tutor curiously but said nothing. All around him, the servants voiced their agreement with the scholar. No doubt they were anxious to be upstairs in warmth and dryness and light.

Among all assembled, Bayard was sure of only one stout heart.

"What do you think, Brandon Rus?" Bayard asked, leaning heavily on the wall at the mouth of the tunnel, one foot already stepping into the tangled darkness beyond the light of the lanterns.

The young man paused, poised between Solamnic courtesy and the truth he was coming to suspect—that indeed, Sir Bayard knew more of this underground mystery than he was letting on, for whatever reason.

"No doubt," Brandon Rus said slowly, tactfully, "the schoolmaster is correct when he claims this to be an accident of nature. All the more reason we should go forward and explore it—for the sake of science, if for nothing else."

"And," Sir Andrew added, "a body can never tell when something like this spreads beneath his foundations and undermines his whole damned architecture."

Bayard breathed raggedly and rested against the strong arms of the younger man. As Sir Andrew stepped behind him, the faint unsavory odor, the smells of unwashed trail dirt and the heavy odors of soured wine, was lost in the smoke of the torch.

Bayard sighed. Hygiene may not have been among Sir Andrew's virtues, but courage and loyalty took its place most gracefully.

The Knights stood together at the lip of the fissure, waiting for something they could not quite fathom.

"As . . . as . . . the only accredited scientist in this group," Gileandos began, "I assure you that whatever discoveries you might expect in the bowels of the castle grounds would be minimal at best. Why, this area has been excavated, plowed under, apportioned, and surveyed for a thousand years. There is nothing new beneath Castle di Caela—"

"Enough, Gileandos," Sir Robert insisted.

"Why, indeed, if there are tunnels, most certainly—"

"That will be *enough*, Gileandos!" Sir Robert thundered, and the whole party stood silent. There was a scuffling sound and the clatter of metal behind them as one of the linkboys dropped his lantern and scurried back up the stairs toward daylight and safety.

"Well . . ." Sir Robert began, this time more quietly, a note of resignation and almost of sadness passing over his voice as he joined the three others who were preparing to pass from the cellars into the thicket of roots and sliding dirt.

"Give me your lantern," he said to the nearest linkboy. "The rest of you tend to business upstairs. Tell my daughter where we've gone."

"Then we're off for it," he said, grinning exultantly. "It's a glory how so many things come down to a crawl in a dungeon."

His companions looked at one another curiously, then back at Sir Robert. Trained Solamnics all, they waited politely as the rest of the party filed up the stairs toward the Great Hall and fresh air and light. Bayard glanced coldly at Gileandos, who stopped for a moment on the stairwell and leaned into the shadow, no doubt hoping to overhear whatever transpired when the entourage left. The old scholar snorted and cast his eyes downward.

Finally Sir Andrew had enough.

"Damn it, man, if you're going to blubber or pout, I'd rather risk all our lives and take you with us."

The tutor scurried back down the steps. Now the darkness in the room grew deeper as the cellar door closed above the six of them. Sir Robert lifted the lantern, and each face was bathed in orange light.

"So here we are," Bayard said with a smile. "One fresh young Knight little tested, one seasoned but somewhat banged up, and three others—"

"Old. The word is 'old.' Like cheese or wine." Sir Andrew chuckled, and Sir Robert laughed gamely.

There was something in the zest and movement of these old Knights that Brandon could not yet understand. Nor Bayard, for that matter, though something in his leg would whisper it in the rainy seasons of the years to come.

Now it was two old men, facing one another at the brink of yet another adventure. Both of them were weary, longing for repose and rest and featherbeds and wine and blankets and the aimless chatter of grandchildren.

Yet both of them knew that whatever lay beyond the walls of the cellar was yet to be encountered.

Bayard raised his hand suddenly. "Hark! Something back in the . . ."

Great silence filled the cellar. Footsteps rustled across the floor overhead, and a rat skittered into a darker corner, its eyes glowing red for a moment as they reflected the torchlight.

For a long time, there was no sound.

Then there was a faint light at the head of the stairwell. Someone was descending, hand on the railing until the railing ceased. Then the steps became more cautious, more unsteady, as whoever it was continued the slow descent toward the Knights.

"You have been ordered back!" Sir Robert shouted. Something small and accustomed to the dark shrieked in the corner of the cellar, and Gileandos leaped again, the light in his hand bobbing badly.

"Hold that thing steady, Gileandos, or you'll ignite yourself!" Andrew snapped.

The tutor whimpered but held as steady as possible.

"I am afraid I cannot answer to you, Sir Robert," a voice piped down the stairwell.

It was Raphael.

"Raphael, go back up with the others," Bayard ordered impatiently, his eyes already back on the fissure in the cellar wall.

"I am afraid he cannot answer to you, either, Sir Bayard," echoed another voice, even more familiar.

"Enid!" Robert and Bayard exclaimed in one voice. "Get back up—"

They stared at one another stupidly.

Chapter XIV

"No," the lady of the castle declared musically as she stepped into their presence, draped in a gray wool cloak, her high cheekbones and deep brown eyes bathed suddenly in candlelight as Raphael stepped apologetically out from behind her.

With her also was the Lady Marigold, large arms crossed over her ample bosom. Her glowering look made even Brandon step back. Marigold saw the young Knight shy away from her, and her glower softened.

The big woman was ready for adventure, it seemed. She carried two enormous bags, one of which bristled with brushes and combs and netting, along with machines and devices foreign to all of the men. The other was tied tightly, heavily laden, and smelled of sausage and cheese. Marigold's hair was tiered and woven with flowers. Long-stemmed irises perched on the back of her neck, and the flora changed from nape to forehead, where dainty pansies and namesake marigolds adorned her brow.

"She looks like a wandering hothouse!" Brandon Rus exclaimed beneath his breath. Coyly Marigold winked and kissed the air. He flushed and sank into his armor.

Enid was, as usual, breathtaking. The old men thought of elf-women, of goddesses.

Bayard, on the other hand, knew she was from anywhere but the heavens. Enid glared at him angrily and took Raphael's candle into her hand.

"No, dear Father, dear Husband. No to any of you, for that matter. I am not 'getting back' anywhere."

"But this is no place—" Brandon began, then stopped himself in midfoolishness as Enid's eye caught his.

Sir Robert snorted, turned, and walked to the far side of the room, his ceremonial armor clattering. Bayard closed his eyes in dismay.

It was like being in the eye of a hurricane. Skittering sounds echoed through the darkness. Even the rats were leaving the vicinity.

" 'No place for a woman,' you were going to say, dear boy?" Enid di Caela began sweetly.

The other Knights coughed, cleared their throats, looked at their feet. Only Bayard stood firm and attentive, half smiling as he stared levelly at his wife.

"Well, let us just take stock of this 'no place' verdict, Sir Brandon. I see five males in this cellar—not counting, of course, any of the standard underground fauna. Of these five males, I believe I can say that you alone are capable of serious exploration. Look at your companions. Raphael is a boy. My husband has been waylaid by natural disaster and has a leg that rough terrain will ruinate.

"Of the three remaining, you are all marvelous gentlemen, with over two hundred years of experience among you. Those years, though, will become heavier as the climbs grow steep and the tunnels long. But I am not here to discourage anyone from a little jaunt, in which you can eat things that are bad for you and get your armor dirty."

Bayard looked at Brandon in amused consternation. It seemed they had forgotten all provisions.

"Indeed," Enid continued, "something *should* be done to determine what damages we have suffered in quake and deluge. However my two beloved men may preen and brandish and plan their adventures, I am *the* Di Caela. The title passes down to me, and the name and the castle and the holdings are *my* inheritance. Indeed, I found myself rather set upon not long ago for being an heiress, and since that time, I have felt entitled to know just what everyone wanted to marry or kidnap me for."

Enid seated herself firmly at the foot of the steps, smiled glamorously at the assembled Knights and retainers, and announced: "So, my dear. And so, my father. And so to all of you. I shall go."

Marigold and Raphael smiled in unison.

". . . and all of us will abide with you through the duration."

The older men gasped at the effrontery. The younger men remained silent, and soon the cellar was altogether quiet, the faint sound of water dripping somewhere along the far wall, and the shuffling sound of Sir Robert's feet as slowly he moved back into the light to join the rest of the party.

Bayard began to laugh.

"Begging your pardon, sir?" Brandon inquired nervously, jostling the big Knight draped over his shoulder.

"Did you know, Sir Robert, that I married your daughter for her temperament?" Bayard asked finally.

"What a surprise," Sir Robert replied brusquely, folding his arms.

"Eight is a lucky number, my dear," Bayard said, "and the three of you will expand our number, and, it is hoped, our luck. And you are entitled, by inheritance and, more importantly, by simple fairness, to know what has befallen your estate. I shall expect you, however, to follow my orders implicitly."

Beside her husband now, Enid crouched, staring intently down the long tunnel behind the collapsed wall.

Gileandos alone was interested in going inside. He took the lantern from Sir Andrew's hand and stepped slowly through the fissure. Suddenly he stopped short, for deep in the tangled darkness ahead of them, something rumbled deeply.

"What might that be?" Bayard asked, his voice sinking to a natural hush, as a trained soldier's will at a distant sight of the enemy's lines.

Gileandos scrambled from the passageway and crouched behind the Knights, trembling.

The others shook from their revery and listened down the musty, root-clotted corridor.

"Can't hear a damn thing," Andrew declared, which surprised nobody. The old man's growing deafness became more famous the longer he stayed at Castle di Caela.

"A door opening above us?" Brandon asked, but all of them knew that was wishful thinking.

Sir Robert shook his head.

"It's coming from beneath the far tower. No cellar or dungeon in those parts."

"Hand me that lantern, Gileandos," Sir Andrew insisted, stepping boldly into the fissure. "All you can light from there is the hem of our cloaks. And take courage, man! For at its worst, it is no doubt the product of nothing more than the altogether natural workings of the elements."

Gileandos rose slowly, timidly. He was obviously not consoled by science.

Without another word, Andrew, Robert, and Bayard drew their swords. Gileandos raised the lantern, and the procession into the black roots of Castle di Caela began.

* * * * *

The world beneath Castle di Caela was wet and hollow.

At least, so it seemed to the Lady Enid as she walked behind her husband, who was propped on the stout right shoulder of Sir Brandon Rus, who plodded dutifully ahead, clutching a lantern in his left hand.

Hollow, and also confusing. It was a world in which one could become quickly and forever lost. The network of tunnels branched and doubled back on themselves, as elaborate as an anthill or a hive. For that was what came to mind—

some kind of lair or warren. It was not the kind of tunnelry born of the seepage of water, the shifting of earth. There was something more intentional in all of this, more designed, as if it had been burrowed by something menacing.

Except that there was no dreadful smell, no hot stink of terror or panic or lust or simple sleep or stirring or hunger. The smell of the tunnels was the smell of something remote and unearthly.

If nothing had a smell, Enid thought, it would smell like this.

Bayard wished he had not given in, Enid knew. He wished he had put down some masculine boot and sent his wife back up the cellar stairs to light and safety. His father-in-law would have supported him. Indeed, none of the Knights would have stood against his decision.

But he chose to be fair, chose faith in Lady Enid's resources, in the simple rules of justice and reason, in the Measure and Oath the way he had always read them.

Now she was in for the duration, for any danger. Because of this, the poor man was worried to distraction.

The lantern dipped in Brandon's hand, and quickly the Knights recovered their fragile, shared balance. Enid and Raphael and Marigold followed, their cloaks wrapped tightly against the cool still air and intrusive damp.

Behind them, the other three straggled and splashed through roots and rubble and tilting shadow. Already the shallow breathing and the grunting and the occasional brilliant oath leapt like sparks out of the shadows.

All at once, the party came to a juncture where the tunnel branched. Without hesitation, they took the left branch, which sloped downward past two small eddies of water circling beneath where they had stood but a moment before. Behind them, the old men followed laboriously. Now the tunnel circled back on itself and back yet again, descending in a tight spiral, its earthen walls giving way, surprisingly, to walls of hewn stone as Bayard and Brandon led the party deeper below the castle.

Sir Robert swore he knew nothing of this lower masonry.

"It's before my time," he declared. "Before the castle itself, unless I am mistaken."

Bayard reached across Brandon, took up the lantern, and raised it high, until its light tumbled onto the crumbled bricks.

Strange letters were scrawled across their surface.

"The spidery hand of magic," Gileandos whispered reverently, and Sir Andrew rolled his eyes.

"Gileandos, you say that every time you find something you can't read."

Bayard looked more closely at the writing.

"Plainsman, I'd wager by the shape of the letters. Other than that, I'm lost."

For a moment, the party collected itself before the wall in question. Each of the Knights squinted, mumbled, and conceded he could not read it either. Gileandos crouched behind his companions, his mind far from magic, listening no doubt for animals and geysers and rockslides. The other lantern, his responsibility, flickered and dimmed because his constant, nervous fumblings with its mechanism had retracted the wick.

"Look!" Gileandos exclaimed, holding the sputtering lantern aloft. "We are faced with a shortage of air down here!" The Knights looked at one another curiously.

"The time has come for hard decisions," Gileandos babbled on, pointing frantically to the faint glow in the lantern globe as some kind of mad evidence. "One of us will have to . . . give his life so the others can breathe." He glanced into each puzzled face around him, looking, no doubt, for a volunteer.

"Gileandos, are you having trouble breathing?" Sir Andrew asked coldly.

"Quick, sir. There's little time remaining, if my calculations—"

"Damn your calculations! I asked you a simple question, man. Are you having trouble breathing?"

Gileandos coughed, stammered, then shook his head.

"Then I would suggest we hold off on slaughtering our ranks. Meanwhile, you might see to extending the wick in that contraption we've been foolish enough to put you in charge of."

Shamefaced, Gileandos slinked into a corner, leaving his

companions in an orange half-light, framed by gloom and shadows.

"Well, now, Bayard," Sir Andrew said, "before Gileandos sacrifices us all to the great god of panic, we should have an idea of where you are taking us."

"To be honest, Sir Andrew," Bayard said, leaning against the weeping wall of the tunnel and smiling winningly, "I have never really considered it."

All of his companions—even Brandon Rus—looked at one another in astonishment.

It was Enid's turn to smile. One would think she approved of such a shot in the dark.

"You mean," Sir Andrew finally ventured, "that we've been shanghaied into the bowels of the planet on some sort of whim?"

"On some sort of adventure, Andrew. It's not by accident when the world beneath you opens."

"It's a curse," Sir Robert pronounced.

"It is clearly tectonics," said Gileandos.

"How strange," Sir Andrew observed. "It seems like accident to me. Or the will of the gods, which sometimes looks like accident. Sir Brandon, what is your philosophy?"

"My philosophy is that the dark is for philosophers," Brandon said curtly, his eyes on the descending spiral in front of him. "I agree with Bayard because we are already down here."

It seemed that Brandon Rus had hit the mark once more. His companions nodded, puffed, grunted, and shouldered their weapons and burdens for the descent. Here where the tunnel corkscrewed down into the blackness, there was time for reflection and for long thought. The stone of the corridor curved leftward, beetling over the Knights as they descended, blocking their view of each other.

We are below the Southeast Tower by now, Sir Robert thought. He never called it the Cat Tower.

He thought of Mariel, his mad aunt. Thought of the smothered laughter her story brought to his visitors—the laughter that even the family shared now, the years having spiraled old Mariel into a faint, small form at the edges of memory, someone remembered because of this story only.

But Robert remembered the door opening onto the room in the top of the tower. Mariel's red door, the silver fleur-de-lis fast in its center. He remembered how they waited outside the door for a moment, how his brother Roderick set booted foot to the door.

It had been like flies swarming.

The cats boiled across his aunt's body, covered with dust, cobwebbing, and wet, hot-smelling things that he could not name if he dared. They were feeding hysterically, their tails whipping through the air as if a hostile wind was moving them.

Years later, when he saw the scorpions settle on Benedict di Caela, there in the Pass at Chaktamir, Robert had remembered his aunt, had felt nausea rise and had told no one.

Again the image arose, banishing the dark and the torchlight ahead of him, banishing the curve of the rock, the downward incline of the muddy tunnel floor. For a moment, Robert di Caela thought he was climbing steps. He shook his head, saw rock, darkness, and torchlight. Saw the descending tunnel ahead of him, Bayard and Brandon huddled together, moving from shadow to light to shadow. His daughter following them, at her side the young page, Raphael.

"I am getting old," Sir Robert said to himself and resumed the descent.

The tunnel curved once again, and Robert lost the Knights ahead of him behind another wall of rock. Moving forward resolutely, with that alert, discouraging feeling that one gets when walking alone at night in an unfamiliar house, Robert turned the corner cautiously.

The corridor, empty of his companions, ended not five feet in front of him in a red door, a silver fleur-di-lis planted firmly in its center.

*　*　*　*　*

Brandon had seen no door. Indeed, he had passed farther down the corridor, he and Bayard. He heard Sir Robert stop behind him but thought little of it because the old men had stopped repeatedly since they had entered the darkness. Instead, Sir Brandon Rus thought of the sea.

How the tunnel was like the whirls in a seashell. For a moment, Brandon stopped. He listened for the sound of breakers in the corridor below him.

Once he had seen the sea as a boy; his mother set her bright blue tents by the waters. It was a story that Brandon did not tell.

The Solamnics and landholders from here to the Virkhus Hills had heard the stories about his gift for archery. It was said that he missed but once, and in missing, hit the target at which he should have been aiming all along. But they had not heard this story.

The sea was devouring, terribly strange. The Blood Sea of Istar, they called it, though his tutors had told him that its waters are red only at midocean. Still, there was an unfamiliar cast to the waves—a blue that bordered on a deep violet, a disturbing warmth to the tide.

Nonetheless, his sister Almia chose to swim. Far on the horizon, he could see her, her light hair rising and falling on the violet waves.

Brandon shook his head. Was there something in this tunnel—some gas, some closeness in the air—that was stealing his wakefulness? Bayard coughed again at his shoulder. Why these thoughts of the sea?

Yet . . .

Yet there, as the sun dropped low on the water, its light settled on his sister's hair, spangling it gold and silver and red and violet. She was out a perilous distance, near the Road of the Dolphins, where the ships catch the strong northern current and sweep up the eastern coast like iceboats.

Brandon sat on the shore, lulled by sun and the regular sounds of the tide, the ugly and wonderful smell of kelp. Nearby, he watched a pelican hunt, watched the huge bird sail awkwardly over the purple crest of the waves and then, its quarry spotted, wheel over to stall and plunge headfirst into the water, suddenly, limply, as though the bird had been dropped by Brandon's crossbow.

He looked up then and saw his sister gliding across the face of the water. At first it seemed she was caught in the

Road of the Dolphins, drawn northward by the powerful surge of the current, her long hair golden in the wake of her passage.

Already there was an outcry on the beach. Mother's retainers were stripping off their armor. One, a large man named Venator, was already knee-deep in the water, striding out to sea as though something would lift him onto the surface and he could stride out over the waves to rescue Almia.

Brandon fumbled with his bow. For some reason, whether youth or fear or the whim of the gods, the arrow was too large for the bow, then too small for his clumsy fingers.

It was then that Almia went under. Where she had been, the huge red back of the creature twisted angrily above the water for a moment. Finally Brandon fired the weapon, watching in horror as the arrow skipped harmlessly over the purple waters.

And into the breast of his sister.

Then the thing dove, its man-sized flukes turning once, high in the air above the Road of the Dolphins, and the sea was smooth once more.

He had run away then, in rage and sorrow and hatred for himself, marveling at his stupidity and its result. When they found him later, they had tried to console him—the viziers, his mother, the old Knight, Venator.

It had been too late, they said. There was nothing he could have done to save the girl. The creature had destroyed his sister and then taken her form in the water.

He had done what any archer, any brother would do, they claimed. The creature would not kill again. To this day Brandon Rus did not believe them.

*   *   *   *   *

By now the pain in Bayard's leg was consuming his thoughts and his strength. Weaving on Sir Brandon's shoulder, he stood hollow-eyed at the front of the party, his stare fixed on nothing in particular as Brandon guided him through the toothed and silent landscape of the cavern.

Something drove Bayard Brightblade that he could not put words around. It was a journey by night, he thought, with the road marked uncertainly, the signposts old and weathered and wordless.

It was like the streets of Old Palanthas, where as a boy he wandered, orphaned and cast away.

The buildings became stone in Palanthas at the point where the great South Road narrowed northward into the city's heart. Oh, there were some brick, some wattle, and some simple wooden lean-tos back in the most forsaken alleys. But mostly it was stone there, and fourteen-year-old Bayard Brightblade, fresh from an overthrown castle and the sight of slaughtered parents and retainers, found a moment of peace in its craggy stillness.

Though to a lad from the countryside, the city streets were as strange as the face of a moon. As strange as the black moon nobody has ever seen, that legends and odes and metaphysics claim must be there for things to make sense.

So he had followed the road north, and the buildings crept closer to the curbside. North and ever north he had traveled, the smells of garbage and spice and sweat all fading into the distant breath of salt water as, ahead of him, the moonlight raced across the marble of public buildings and the flickering Bay of Branchala.

There had been a tower off to the west—whether he passed it or was passing or only approaching when it came into notice he did not remember now. Only that it was a tower, suddenly on fire, white flames coursing up its sides as if it had been doused with oil and ignited. Fresh from the devastation of grounds and manor, the boy stopped, marveled, awaited alarms, the smell of smoke.

The tower burned yet was not consumed. It burned briefly, then faded until he could barely see it, a black silhouette against a gray darkness.

Corposant, they had called it. Branchala's fire. But he did not know these things when he saw the light, the strange and wonderful incandescence in the western sky.

He thought instead that the sun had set in the tower.

He had taken this as a sign. Though he still did not know

what was expected of him, he thought that something had been given to him. That Palanthas was the place where the tower burned made it extraordinary, different from the faceless plains and foothills and mountains he had passed through to get there. It was at least something. And though in the months to come he would question that "something," whether it meant anything at all, it must have had meaning in some mysterious way. For living in Palanthas, under carts and bridges and occasional lean-tos by night, by day in the network of tunnels that made up the Great Library of Palanthas, soon he discovered the book that revealed to him the curse of Castle di Caela and the part he would play in lifting it.

All this from a pure accident of weather.

* * * * *

There is no telling what the others were thinking. What went through the mind of Sir Andrew, of Marigold, of the boy Raphael, was as mysterious as old writing. Within the hour, despite Enid's better judgment and the urgings of the older Knights, Bayard had led the party even farther below the foundations of Castle di Caela. Masonry had given way to earth and igneous rock. Even the taproots of vallenwoods did not go down this far, though the water was here, hissing about them and dripping from crevice and outcropping as though the whole earth was a sodden sponge.

Gileandos leaned against the cellar wall, which felt cool, mossy, uncomfortably moist. "Indeed," he asserted, eager to support the judgments of his employer. "In my humble opinion as physicist and alchemist, I should have to insist that nothing I have seen or heard or otherwise observed here is necessarily the product of anything more than the altogether natural workings of the elements."

Bayard, Robert, and Brandon stared at the tutor with contempt. Suddenly Gileandos's eyes wided. His thin, pale-fingered hand slid over the wall behind him and pulled away in disgust.

"What is it, pedant?" Sir Robert snapped. But the tutor was speechless, staggering to the center of the corridor.

Brandon steadied Bayard, moved quickly past the old man, and set his hand to the wall.

He felt a give, a wet leathery surface that pulsed under his fingers. His voice thin and wavering, he turned to the party, struggling for composure.

"It—it cannot be, Bayard," he said, his words rising scarcely above a shaken whisper. "The wall . . . the wall is alive!"

"And I am the Kingpriest of Istar!" Sir Robert snorted, stepping forward to rid the world of nonsense. But Bayard's hand stayed the old man, and slowly Bayard hobbled toward Brandon, removing his gloves as he approached.

The wall was pliable and moist. From a distance, it was indistinguishable from stone, and indeed at some time others had made the same mistake, for whatever the thing was that lay in front of the huddled Knights, it was covered with drawings and scratches and fabulous designs. Only at close quarters could one see the pores and the leathery contours of what appeared to be skin.

"Gileandos!" Bayard hissed. "Quickly! What are the legends, the lore about great creatures under the earth?"

"Arrrh . . ." the tutor replied. Then "Arrrh . . ." again as his wits and resources failed against the prospect of danger. Sir Andrew slapped him with a glove, but the old tutor continued to gargle and stammer.

"If I might be so bold, sir," Sir Brandon Rus offered, peering intently at the rippling surface in front of him. Bayard turned to the young man and heard the others close ranks behind him.

"In several collections of lore," Brandon began, "I have seen mention of the daergryn, as the elves call it. The giant worm that bears the surface of Ansalon on its back. 'Tellus,' the creature was called in the times of Huma, and the dale worm is its name in the common speech."

"You have heard of this, too, Gileandos?" Bayard asked.

The old man swallowed and nodded. "Mythopoetic way that the less scientific times explained the rumblings and tremors of the earth. 'The dale worm stirring,' they were wont to say. Hence the expression 'the worm has turned' to denote great change and reversals."

Emboldened by his knowledge, the scholar folded his arms triumphantly, then remembered that the worm in question was neither myth nor poetry and began to stammer again.

"Gileandos," Bayard said, his great hand calming the scholar with a simple touch on the shoulder. "I suppose we can all say that the worm has turned now. And I fear we're in for a turn or two more. It is time you all learned what I read in the papers of Castle di Caela. Perhaps, with luck and the favor of the gods, we can avert the promises and threats we have inherited."

There, crouched by the side of the dale worm, Sir Bayard Brightblade revealed what he knew. That "the rending of earth" was part of a dead man's plan, seized upon in vengeance four centuries ago. That somehow a device—some gnomish machinery, no doubt, or an ancient unfathomable mechanism—was set in motion by the anger and hatred of the very Scorpion destroyed by Bayard in the recent past. Now it was set to arouse this creature, to disrupt everything "from the Vingaard Mountains to the Plains of Solamnia, even unto the foundations of this murderous house."

What that meant, and how the arousing would take place, not even Bayard Brightblade knew.

Chapter XV

SEVEN STONES WERE SET IN HIS CROWN. SEVEN GODS-
eyes: one brought from above, six mined in the dark recesses of the Vingaards.

For Firebrand, it was not enough.

Are there not places for thirteen stones?

Oh, the timid had warned against it, shaking their fingers
and saying, "The power over life and death belongs to no
man, nor should any man try to take it. For what right has
man to govern the plains and the caverns, the places that
give birth to him and nurture him and receive his body
when he is no more?"

A weakling's argument, in which a false mysticism hid
one's fear. One might as well ask what right a man has to
govern himself.

But it was more—indeed, much more. For recently Firebrand had felt it, as the visions grew sharper, more consuming, as the stories of those around him came to painful and vivid life in his thoughts. There were times when Firebrand thought he was becoming transparent, when torchlight shone through his extended hands, when he could look through his palms and see the carvings on the stone walls of the corridor. It was only a matter of time, he thought, until he rose beyond himself.

All the more reason for the thirteenth stone, for the power over life and death. For when the prophecy was fulfilled and Firebrand led the Que-Tana back to the surface, he would rule over all the Plainsmen as history renewed itself.

Slowly Firebrand rose from his throne. The Que-Tana below him continued in their tasks, tirelessly combing the stones for the godseyes. He turned from them, his bearskin robe stirring the lifeless air in the Porch of Memory, rocking the flames of the candles, and he climbed up the stairs that were carved in the sheeted stalactites above the throne. He entered the corridor that took him past the Hall of Chanting, where the women recited the Song of Firebrand continuously.

Two miners met him in the corridor, carrying the stone-crushed body of a child between them. They stopped and knelt before the Namer. Firebrand touched his eye patch absently and stepped over the boy's broken body.

One of the miners thought of a curse as the Namer passed, but he cowered, and the words died in his throat.

Past the library Firebrand proceeded, where at his orders, the children had removed the last of the books and destroyed them, because soon all history, all thought and science and poetry—all of anything worth knowing—would reside in the stones on the silver crown.

He stopped and touched the carved writing on a torchlit wall. A poem in Old Que-Nara—a love poem to a dark-haired woman.

Blue light flickered in the Namer's hand. His fingers coursed over the words of the poem, and the stone smoked beneath them. The words vanished, and in their stead, the wall was glassy and black like obsidian.

Firebrand admired himself in the reflection.

Deeper into the caverns he went, his duties calling him to his own cubicle, where the warriors had taken the kidnapped cleric. He came to the Gates of Flame, the yellow row of stalactites and stalagmites that marked the boundaries of his private quarters. They were long, sharp, and irregular, like teeth of fire.

Stepping through the gate, Firebrand entered the long, narrow part of the underground cavern wherein he resided. He was no longer surprised at the uncanny warmth of this part of the caverns, the wind as regular as a heartbeat, soft against the face of those who approached, carrying upon its back the cloying smell of decay, the floors and the walls of the corridor wet with centuries of sediment.

The voice in the stone has told me how it will come to pass, Firebrand thought as the opals began to glow more brightly, guiding him gently toward the cubicle. I shall rise at the Telling, the Que-Tana at my command, and I shall have not only the Crown Fulfilled—the twelve stones that store the memory of the People—but the forbidden thirteenth stone, forbidden, the voice has told me, because it steals the memory of others.

And there on the Telling Ground, I shall take the years from the People who took years from me. With all of our history in my thoughts, I will start it again. I shall remember what needs remembering, forget what needs forgetting, and history will begin and end in Firebrand.

I shall become a god, no doubt. I expect that now in the Bright Lands there is a starless gap in the skies, awaiting my constellation. And once those stars are placed there, shining like opals in the black heart of the heavens, not even Sargonnas himself will govern me.

*　*　*　*　*

Two of the younger warriors helped the captive travel the shifting passageway from the Porch of Memory to the library, where they seated him among empty shelves and desolate tables littered with old manuscripts. They had combed the straw and dust from his hair, mended his tattered red robe, then brought him to the Namer's quarters for an audience with Firebrand. Finally convinced that it was no longer the afterlife in which he found himself, Brithelm had returned to his favorite pursuits: eating, sleeping, and odd studies. Even now he was poring over a zoological volume brought with him out of the wreck of the library.

Within days, Brithelm had become firm in his conviction to study the tenebrals he had observed dangling from the ceilings of the caverns and corridors. He was convinced that the creatures were a lost species of raptor.

Firebrand stooped at the door to the cubicle and entered. Brithelm did not stir, his face above the book, an odd pair of triangular spectacles perched on the bridge of his nose.

Firebrand cleared his throat. "So it was an abbey you were building up there? Up in the Br—the Vingaard Mountains?" he asked, leery of this eccentric young man in front of him.

The fellow continued to ponder the text, which he had spread on his lap, the red thicket of his hair bent over the pages, his ruddy hands coursing rapidly over the text. Scrawled Plainsman letters reflected nervously up into the glittering triangles at his eyes.

"The book says, Father Firebrand, that these . . . *tenebrals*, as you call them, cannot abide sunshine. Is that so?" he asked, looking up from the book at last.

"Indeed it is far worse than that, Brother Brithelm," Firebrand explained, seating himself with a rustle of robes and furs in the single, hardbacked chair in the sparsely furnished quarters. "The sunlight kills them, shrivels them at once, burns their wings. I would imagine it is a horrible death. But I asked about your abbey. Tell me of your abbey."

"What do they live on?"

"I beg your pardon?"

"The tenebrals." Brother Brithelm's face was aglow, fastened on a peculiar interest that he did not want to abandon just now.

Firebrand's memory stirred, returning to the image of a frail young boy, intent on the first hunt. The Namer frowned and wrestled his thoughts back to the time at hand, to the disheveled lad seated on the floor in front of him.

"What do tenebrals eat?" Brithelm asked.

Firebrand shifted uncomfortably on the chair. Apparently the captive would not be satisfied until he knew all about tenebrals. Nor would Firebrand be satisfied in turn, not until he knew all about this mysterious sanctuary in the mountains, about the Knight who was coming with the opals in question.

He longed for the ceremonial stool, the soft, crackling give and take of its woven reed.

Already, it seemed, they had reached an impasse.

"I don't know what they eat, Brother Brithelm. Now as to your—"

"Do you suppose tenebrals could live on the surface after nightfall?" Brithelm interrupted. "That's why I asked about their feeding habits, for if whatever they eat can be found above ground, why, then . . ."

* * * * *

Firebrand did not hear him.

Instead, he was remembering something else: the ill-fated assault of the night before. He had tried to wrest the stones from the one who brought them, and to do so by surprise. It would have been safer that way, before the young Knight and his entourage drew near enough to the entrance to find their way down among the Que-Tana.

Firebrand had ordered the Que-Tana warriors not to fear killing the Knight nor any who rode with him. No time could have been better than the time they attacked, when a twist of the knife in the foothills of the Vingaards could have done the business quickly and easily. He would have had the opals by now.

And the young man seated before him would be disposable.

But even the moon was a treacherous light for the subterranean Que-Tana. Lurking in the dark woods, they had ambushed Sir Galen and his followers, but the light was confusing, threatening, and they had failed at their mission.

Those who had failed paid the price. They now dangled by their braided hair in the Chamber of Night, the deep and enormous cavern that underlay the Porch of Memory. There they awaited the vespertiles, the huge flightless bats that roamed the darker margins of Firebrand's kingdom.

The vespertiles were always hungry.

I am a vespertile myself, Firebrand thought with a smile. No. Better yet, I am a spider. Dark and subterranean, weaving elaborate webs in my chambers, my only companion a daft captive cleric who is bait and brother to the approaching quarry.

To Sir Galen Brightblade, the bearer of the opals.

"Tell me," Firebrand repeated, his mood much better now, "of your sanctuary, Brother Brithelm."

"My sanctuary?" Brithelm asked, his shimmering eyes returning to the book. "Oh. I suppose I've never thought of it as *mine*, actually." And as the young man spoke, his eyes still fixed on the book in front of him, Firebrand gazed into the maze of stalactites in the vaulted ceiling above him and became lost in the web of Brithelm's words.

Brithelm told of an array of wooden houses on wooden stilts, a cluster of tents and lean-tos that looked more like a way station for vagrants than a holy place. It had about it the melancholy frailty of a child's play fortress, vulnerable to invasion and fire. To faulty architecture and falling crossbeams, for that matter.

All around it birds rose into the air with the strange, skidding sound doves make when they take wing. They reeled overhead and flew southward and away, the cold mountain air whistling behind them.

One by one they came to Brithelm, out of the foothills and the plains of Solamnia and Coastlund. Braving inclement weather and rocky trails and the ever-present dangers of goblin and troll and bandit, they came to his ramshackle mountain sanctuary. Brithelm spoke warmly, lovingly of each of them.

From Palanthas came two elderly women, who brought nothing with them except a set of fine china and a stuffed parrot they swore could predict the weather. On their third day in camp, they were thoroughly drenched by a surprising downpour, and the resulting head colds had kept them confined for a week.

There was a pirate captain from Kalaman, whose dreams of shipwreck had plagued him so much that his sleeplessness forced him to retire. In the quiet of the mountains and in Brithelm's calming presence, finally the man slumbered, though his bad dreams were really none the better. He slept in a wooden lifeboat suspended from the stilts beneath one of Brithelm's makeshift huts, his cabin boy above in the hut proper. At every hour of the night, the boy had orders to ring a bell through a trapdoor in the floor of the hut, directly over the captain's head, awakening him so that he would not drown in his dreams.

There was a beautiful blonde woman of about Brithelm's age—Evalinde, she was called. She seemed to have designs on the metaphysical brother and took no discouragement from the fact that he did not notice her, occupied as he was with the summoning of birds and some other strange form of meditation that involved dangling a lizard over an elaborate parchment design and searching for enlightenment.

It might be hard to believe that a bright woman like Evalinde put up with such foolishness, much less kept an interest in Brithelm. Nonetheless, she visited him at night, slipping from her tent into his lean-to when the two moons, red and silver, shone together.

The old Palanthan women consulted their parrot for details of the tryst. It told them, evidently, that Evalinde brought visions to Brother Brithelm. The pirate captain, of course, had other theories.

There were a few more displaced souls in the encampment, perhaps a dozen in all, including an odd-looking dwarf who cames from the gods knew where to sell Brithelm parchment and lizards.

Strangest of all was the blind juggler. Of him, Brithelm was peculiarly silent, though Firebrand plied the lad with questions—idly at first and then more intensely when a mystery rose and surrounded this man called Shardos. But he learned nothing, really, of the juggler.

"How many," he asked the young cleric, "were at your sanctuary at its height?"

" 'Its height'?" Brithelm asked, reclining on the cool floor of the cubicle, steepling his fingers behind his head.

"Its most populous," Firebrand urged, leaning forward in the hard chair.

"Oh . . . one or seven, depending on how you count. Eight, if you count dogs. Do you count dogs, Father Firebrand?"

Firebrand did not count them. Brithelm nodded and explained.

"You see, there was only one, if you count me, who was after all the only one who had really decided to stay there and all. All of the others were visiting for a while. There was Evalinde and the dwarf, the captain and the cabin boy, the juggler and his dog—but you aren't counting dogs—and the two old women from Palanthas. Do you count stuffed parrots? There was one with the women, and if you count it there were nine of us . . ."

Firebrand did not count parrots either.

"Who . . . provided for you while you lived there, Brother Brithelm?"

" 'Provided,' sir?"

"Food. Protection."

"Bayard Brightblade came once, sir. With my brother Galen. I think they brought loaves and eggs. Perhaps some potatoes and some cheese, too."

Galen Pathwarden, then. Sir Galen Pathwarden, who roams the surfaces above us, who has dispatched scout and skirmisher.

Like so many mercenaries.

When he invades us, dares to come below, he will find the dark not to his liking.

"Are there any . . . stories about these tenebrals of yours?"

"I beg your pardon?"

"Any lore," Brithelm explained, staring at the ceiling. "I take to lore well, you know."

Firebrand sighed.

"If there is, it will be in the volume before you. Fauna is not a strength of our library."

He cleared his throat. Brithelm looked up at him innocently.

"On the other hand, minerals are. Rocks, both igneous

and sedimentary. Gypsum and limestone. Gems such as . . .
these."

Carefully he took the crown and showed it to Brithelm. It
was an impulse, really. Something told him it was only right
that the man should see the stones that would cost him his
life.

Perhaps.

Firebrand had not decided how useful the Lightdwellers
would be, once the opals were placed in the crown.

It was more than fairness, though, that guided the hand
of the Namer. Something in him yearned for a kindred
spirit, for another bearer of visions, who would see these
stones and know that the Namer of the Que-Tana stood at
the borders of prophecy, at the edge of the greatest power
imaginable: the power over life and death.

Brithelm rose onto his elbow and examined the stones.
Handing the crown back to Firebrand, he reclined once
more, his left cheek pressed against the coolness of the stone
floor of the chamber.

"Have you anything to eat, sir?" he asked finally. "Being
kidnapped surely gives rise to an appetite. Just anything will
do—nothing fanciful or strange or rich, and nothing with
turnips in it, if you don't mind, Father Firebrand. You see,
the turnip is the one thing that jars my internals. If by mistake I eat a turnip, I have to lie on my right side for an hour
with my left arm raised over my head. That way the organs
return to their proper and natural arrangement."

"I see," snapped Firebrand, his hopes and confidence tumbling. Surely the boy was more cluttered than clairvoyant—
all this addled talk of tenebrals and turnips. And yet
Firebrand had not given up hope entirely.

"I show you the stones, Brother Brithelm," he announced,
cradling the crown in his left hand, "because through them a
god speaks to me."

Brithelm lifted his face from the floor and raised an eye-
brow. And in loneliness Firebrand told him of the commands of the god Sargonnas—of the prophecy he had been
granted and of the powers to come that the god had promised him.

He would need followers, he explained. Men of forthrightness and courage, and above all, of vision.

After Firebrand finished, there was silence in the room for a long while. They were both surprised by the direction the talk had led them.

"This is quite an undertaking you're about, isn't it, Father Firebrand?" Brithelm asked finally.

Firebrand sat in silence. There was no answer to that question.

"What I'd like to know is this, though," the young cleric continued, his face pressed again to the floor of the chamber, his voice muffled by stone. "What if this Sargonnas is lying?"

*   *   *   *   *

Firebrand rose, bid a cold farewell to Brithelm, and left the cubicle. Back down the hall he strode, the long crosier of his office clicking woodenly on the stone floor of the cavern. Cursing the Lightdweller and his blasphemy and thickheadedness, Firebrand paused beneath a torch guttering in its sconce, and in the light, yellow on green on yellow, examined the crosier idly.

It was carved with the shapes of plains animals, the names of which Firebrand no longer remembered. Surprised at his own lapse, he leaned against the wall and began to weep.

He was forgetting the Bright Lands.

He had been right all along. The times were urgent, and the worthy few. Indeed, as he feared, he was the only worthy one, and he was alone and not yet come into his power.

But the godseyes were scarcely a mile away, and approaching with the speed of an oncoming storm.

A tenebral flashed by the torch and into the engulfing darkness.

Chapter XVI

"Meanwhile," the Namer intoned, his voice lowering to almost a whisper yet still carrying, through skill or magic or trick of the wind, to even the farthermost of the assembled fires. "Meanwhile the young man descends into darkness, where there are eyes among the stones."

Quietly he reached into the folds of his mottled robe, producing a handful of dark gems.

* * * * *

As the trail at last began to widen and the rocks to become familiar, I hoped what I had seen in the opals and heard from old Shardos had been utterly wrong, that somehow everyone's senses had been jostled by fire and flood and earthquake. That when we arrived in the clearing where I last saw Brithelm, things would be as I left them: the camp surprisingly unchanged, my visionary brother standing precariously at the top of one of his stilted cabins, trying to draw birds to the site with handfuls of seed and suet so he could read the omens in their patterns of flight.

But the camp had vanished. It had been here, I could tell by the boards and the stilts, the thatch and the canvas. In the clearing, a boat hung desolately from a single frayed rope, the shambles of a cabin forming a circle about it.

Nothing else had been left standing. A huge black spot lay at the center of the clearing, as fresh and unforgiving as a wound. The smoke still rose from it, and I wondered what anyone could find at my brother's encampment that was worth burning. On either side of the fire-scarred ground lay rubble, pitiful relics of the odd but wonderful community.

We all sat quietly on horseback, struck into silence. Finally Shardos stood in the stirrups and breathed deeply.

"The whole place smells of dust and collapse," he pronounced much too loudly. "Bear with me, friends. Our destination is but a mile from here. As the story says, 'It is where four vallenwoods grow, their branches intertwined above an ancient dolmen. A path runs between the stones down a hill into a network of vines, which covers—a hole in the cliff face. A hole with darkness at its bottom.' "

Brithelm would have looked on a place like this, bare and colorless and altogether dismantled, as a country of hope and promise.

"Look around you, brother," I could imagine him saying—imagine as sharply and vividly as if he, not Dannelle, were seated on horseback beside me. "Look at the . . . the absence of distraction!" I thought of the hundreds of times he had listened for my prospects in bleak circumstances, how over the childhood years, I had confided it all—Alfric's bullying, Gileandos's stupidity and injustice, Father's thickheadedness.

My own ungovernable weaseling.

How through all of this he had seemed not to listen, had drawn my attention instead to birds in the courtyard, to some fortunate turn in the moathouse architecture or a particularly lovely autumn moonrise. And how after all his distractions, I had returned to Alfric or Gileandos or Father more anchored and sane for the distracting.

He was the best one in the many sides of my families. There was no way that I was going back without him.

"There's another story this reminds me of," Shardos said with a smile. I must have sighed, for he cocked his head curiously in my direction. His hearing kept astounding me.

Not that I cared altogether. For since we had left Longwalker's camp, Shardos had been a compendium of tales, spread before us in an elaborate weave where the thread of one plot entangled with that of another, where the hero of a minotaur bandit saga locked horns, so to speak, with the brother of an hourglass-eyed mage in a gladiatorial conflict that did or did not happen, depending on which version of the tale you listened to. There were stories of ice-reavers, of Huma at the height of his powers, of even a kender romance mixed in with a Plainsman's search for a crystal staff and a Solamnic siege in the dead of winter. Somehow all of these stories were connected, though none of us could follow them through all their complications to see how legend fit with fable and fable with tale. Shardos saw to the bottom of them all, evidently, juggling them all as deftly as he juggled crockery or torches or knives.

"Brithelm," I said. "Brithelm is hostage somewhere under all of this, and . . ."

For a moment, the strong tears surged again, and I drew my hood over my face.

"There, boy, there," Shardos soothed, his milky eyes turned in my direction with a hollow stare that was unsettling. "If your brother's whereabouts has you all that bothered, then I'll take you to find him straightaway."

"Enough, juggler," Ramiro cautioned, then turned to me. "It's no country for hope nor for jest. I'd rather not lose the rest of us if you're bent on guiding us down among these underdwellers. If you're risking five lives to recover one, then you'd best allow that this Firebrand has done the worst he can do and leave it alone at that."

"You need not send us packing right away, Sir Ramiro," I said sharply. "I shall stay the course. I have decided that if

Shardos claims he can find my brother, why, the least I can do is a little of what he says."

Ramiro turned ponderously toward me, looking at me candidly and a little unkindly.

"I await your orders," he said through clenched teeth.

"Shardos?" I called, and the blind man stepped forward.

"It is near sunset," the juggler offered cheerily. "The bird-songs are changing, and the wind dying down. 'Tis the best time to embark."

Ramiro began the demanding process of dismounting. Oliver rushed to his side, grunted, and wrangled him down. Owls called in the high rocks that surrounded us, and with a nod from Ramiro, Oliver moved away from the fire and walked quickly toward the horses, stripping a long over-hanging branch from an aeterna tree as he made his way back down the trail to guard the skittish animals from the ominous sounds of the approaching night. One of the horses whickered behind us, and you could hear Oliver faintly clicking and cooing and consoling the creature.

Only Dannelle remained near me. I could feel her eyes on me.

I took a deep breath. In went the thin mountain air, fresh with its icy edge and a faint whiff of aeterna. Out came the orders.

"So we follow Shardos," I said. "And we shall see what happens. Leave the horses here, neither tied nor tethered. They're no good to us under the ground, and perhaps they'll find their way back to the plains if we don't make it too hard for them by harnessing them to this and that."

"There was little generalship in that decision," Dannelle whispered teasingly as Shardos crossed the campsite and took a narrow path through the undergrowth beyond it. Ramiro and Oliver followed reluctantly.

"It is all the generalship I've got," I confessed.

* * * * *

So we fared, each of us burdened with rope and lantern and hand axe and piton—whatever necessary things we could gather from the horses we were leaving behind us. It was not fully dark before we reached the vallenwoods. Sharp-eyed little Oliver, walking with Shardos at the head of our column, returned to us with the news.

"A place there is, like the juggler spoke of, Sir Galen," the boy announced breathily, apparently winded from the longest sentence he had spoken since we departed from Castle di Caela. "The trees with the dolmen and the opening beyond 'em, and something flying out of the dark there."

"Flying?"

"Yes, sir. Some of 'em fell once they came out. It was like they were diving or something. They leapt into the sky and . . . and folded up. It was like something in the air crushed them. They fell straight to the ground. From up close, they look like burned squirrels or something."

"Tenebrals," Shardos announced, slipping silently back into our midst.

"I beg your pardon?" I asked.

"Harmless, really," the juggler said. "They tell me the things glow underground. Their blood is luminous, but their wits are dim. I have heard that dozens issue from caverns before the sun goes down, and the action of sunlight on their skin is fatal. I'm not sure of the science involved. But that's another story, and neither here nor there."

Shardos paused, tilting his head as though he listened to Oliver's movement and breath. "Be most vigilant now, friends, for soon we pass through the gates of the Que-Tana, and on those faculties of yours will hinge the fate of Sir Galen's brother."

He led us into the clearing, past the vallenwoods and the dolmen, down a narrow trail, amid bramble and undergrowth, to a fissure in the side of the mountain.

The old blind man stood at the opening and looked up at us merrily.

"For a while in this coming darkness, I shall see as well as any of you. Perhaps even better."

With Birgis in tow, and clutching the dark rocks upon the walls of the fissure, he edged down the hewn stone path.

In the next few moments, we all must have looked at one another a dozen times, each of us sizing the situation, wrestling fear and misgiving and pure common sense, exchang-

ing glances, a few muffled words, and no doubt a supersti-
tious prayer or two—Get me out of this alive, and I'll rush
to the door of the nearest monastery.

I waited a long, troubled moment above the fissure, saying good-bye to the wind and the twilight. Then, catching
my breath, I followed, listening hard for pale Plainsmen or
for trolls or for something inexpressibly worse.

What I heard was the uneven breathing of Dannelle following me. Behind her walked Oliver, and towering over
the both of them, I could see Ramiro. And then, as complete
darkness closed around us, I said a brief prayer to whatever
god favored the luck of fools and the nerve of shaken
Knights, and I followed the sound of Shardos's careful steps,
the snorts and whuffles of Birgis.

"Let me tell you a story . . ." Shardos whispered back to
me, and the mountainous night engulfed us.

*　*　*　*　*

Had there been light to see us by, I am sure we would have
looked awkward and strange.

Shardos ranged below me on the downward climb,
scrambling nimbly from rock to rock, clutching Birgis under his left arm. The dog, it seemed, hated enclosed spaces,
and on occasion a loud rumble or whimper or yelp rose up
to me through the windless, damp air.

I was ready to rumble or yelp myself. Twice Ramiro had
slipped, shaking dust and rock down upon the rest of us
from above. We all would stop, shiver, send prayers or
oaths flying though the darkness around us, and then continue. I figured that at any moment he would fall, and
hoped that when he did, he would make the supreme sacrifice and not grab out for purchase and drag someone down
with him, but plummet to his death quietly and solitarily.

Dannelle and Oliver, on the other hand, descended gracefully, soundlessly, sandwiched between me and the puffing
Ramiro, who, amid stumbles, was cursing his own lack of
foresight for following me anywhere, especially to the center of the world.

The silence around us grew even more still at our passing.

Occasionally something would burst into flight by my face, erupting with squeals and light and burring and the sound of frantic wingbeat as it rushed by on its way to the surface.

"Tenebrals," Shardos whispered, and I thought of the strange, collapsing creatures that had rushed on wing from the mouth of the fissure. I hoped, for their dim-witted sake, that it was dark on the surface above us.

* * * * *

Almost an hour later, the guidance I had hoped for from Shardos came remarkably to pass. For in the candlelit, lanternlit recesses of earth, we stumbled about like blind things while the truly blind found resource in his other senses.

For a thousand feet down (or so it seemed), Shardos guided us by touch. His skilled hands and feet scrambled over jutting rocks, and he would pause, pointing dramatically at unstable shelves, at notches in the fissure wall too shallow for purchase.

Twice I shifted my lantern from one hand to the other, moving the light for a better grip on the rock walls around me. Everything that lay more than twenty feet from me was lost in the darkness beyond the pathetic glow of the lamp I carried. Twice we reached tunnels, branching away from the fissure into even a deeper dark. At the lip of those tunnels, Shardos would stop and tilt his head, as though listening or smelling or feeling the moisture in the air. Twice he shook his head, again dramatically.

That way lay danger, evidently. Or at least a dead end, a passage leading nowhere—especially not to Brithelm.

On occasion, a noise from below us made Shardos pause. Nimbly he hugged the wall of the fissure, motioning for silence or stillness or just plain attentiveness. His signal was relayed back up the line of followers, and whatever it meant in particular, I am sure we gave it to him.

After those pauses, he would move again, downward and downward, sometimes far more quickly than the full-sighted oafs behind him could manage. When his hearing told him he was losing us, he would stop and allow us to catch up.

At the third passageway, he whispered, "This is the one, Sir Galen." I joined him on the wide shelf of rock that jutted out into the chasm. Dannelle climbed down to stand beside me, followed by a nimble Oliver. Ramiro hung on the rocks a step or two above us, conscious of his weight as always, how it might be the last thing an overhang would need.

I stepped into the passage, lifted my lantern, and the tunnel in which we stood emerged out of darkness into a low, orange light. Three or four tenebrals who had been dangling from the roof of the tunnel shot out into the chasm, chittering wildly, their pale wings glowing more dimly as they flew away from us.

For a moment, I thought of phosfire, the dim light of decay that ranges over swamplands in warmer country north of here. But my attention soon returned to the situation at hand.

Ramiro grumbled. I looked up to see his enormous backside, hanging out into the chasm like some kind of clownish awning.

"Would you rather keep scrambling down the walls like a bunch of salamanders until we reach the core of the planet and our flesh is burned away?" I chastised.

Slowly, doubtfully, Ramiro took the step or two to the lip of the cavern, then let his weight down carefully.

Of course, the floor of the tunnel held.

What the lantern displayed was no less unsettling when we had joined each other on the landing. We found ourselves at the entrance to a large, low room of rock, stretching for hundreds of feet in all directions, but never any higher, it seemed, than ten feet or so above our heads. Stalactites drooped from the low ceiling, here like fangs or a row of teeth, there like a smooth stone curtain, making the room difficult to negotiate—well nigh impossible without the light my lantern provided..

"Birgis?" Dannelle whispered. "Galen, where's the dog?"

Thinking only that I'd be damned before I lost yet another member of the party, never considering the danger it could bring, I reached in my pocket, pushed aside the gloves, and wrapped my fingers around the dog whistle. Placing it to my lips, I blew three short, brief bursts into the stagnant air of the cavern. At the opposite end of the enormous room, the sound of rustling wings and of wild, pained chittering arose as the tenebrals stirred uneasily, alarmed at the noise we could not hear.

Something belched at my feet. Birgis appeared out of nowhere, snuffling at my shoes. I stroked him behind the ears and seated myself on a low, rounded stalagmite.

"Well, where do we go from here, juggler?" Ramiro asked aggressively, leaning back against a huge stone drapery. A silence followed, in which we heard the flapping wings of a bat or tenebral—or *something*—dodging through the stalactites at the far edge of the light. "Here we are, half lost down a crack in the earth, not even close enough to our destination to draw enemies."

Dannelle stirred angrily.

"It is grand of you to be so concerned about enemies at this juncture, Ramiro," she observed ironically. "Nonetheless, I think what we do is up to the leader. Who, if my understanding is correct, is not you."

As if to second her words, Shardos gestured in my direction.

"I believe the choice is Sir Galen's," he murmured.

All eyes—even the blank ones of Shardos—turned toward me. I looked around me, then behind me, where Birgis sat on a flat rock, scratching his ear and staring simply and expectantly.

I looked up, pretending to be mulling a great decision, though in fact I was searching frantically, desperately, for anything that would make sense of this underground labyrinth.

A trio of tenebrals fluttered overhead. They circled rapidly, began to descend and, seeming to sense the presence of the lantern, dodged its light and warmth in a blind rush back into the darkness toward the far end of the cavern. Off in the dark, the large room filled with the rustle of innumerable wings.

Through the frayed cloth of the pouch in which I had placed it, I saw a faint light as the brooch began to glow.

Chapter XVII

By following the waxing light of the brooch, we found our way over stalagmites across the dark, vaulted chamber. This cavernous world was chaotic, grotesque, as if patched together by formations of rock.

Shardos walked beside me, Dannelle and Oliver directly behind us, and Ramiro tailing them, straddling the stalagmites perilously and squeezing and finagling past corner and rock formation. The dog Birgis brought up the rear, snorting and whuffling merrily.

Ahead of us, the tenebrals fluttered and dove, glowing with an unearthly light like huge, darting fireflies. Soon their presence became a part of the environs, beneath our notice or beyond it, so that when Shardos cried out and pointed above us, I had almost forgotten them.

Above us, a host of the small creatures—ten, perhaps, or even as many as fifteen—circled away from us and poured into a wide tunnel twenty feet up the wall of the cavern, losing themselves once more in the dark.

"That's it," Dannelle said calmly, confidently. "A way out of here foretold by the stones in your hand."

She moved against me for warmth in the cold, cavernous room, and for a moment, I was greatly afraid for all of us.

It was not heartening, following the godseyes, when following them before had led us on a trail into ambush—an ambush that had cost me my brother Alfric. It was all I had to go by, though, the strange and ominous directions of the light in the gems, for I had burrowed us to a crucial point in our journey.

The prospects were not cheerful when it became obvious that there was still some rugged climbing to do before we put this underground chamber behind us. The large room we had crossed ended in a sheet of yellowing limestone, wet and glistening in the torchlight, as though a waterfall had frozen in midplunge before us. Atop the cascade, some twenty feet or so above our heads, lay the black, gaping mouth of yet another tunnel. Through it the tenebrals swarmed like a river of unhealthy light. The stone in front of us had a certain beauty, but it was a beauty that only a mountain goat could have stopped to appreciate.

Resignedly, I held out my hand for whatever passed for climbing gear in this group.

Suddenly, inexplicably, Birgis growled low and menacingly, the rumble beginning deep in his chest and passing swiftly through his bared teeth.

The juggler was moving before the dog's hackles rose. Deftly he slipped a rock in his sling and pivoted, sending the stone hurtling to the margins of light, where it struck the first of the seven creatures emerging from the darkness. The thing whined, staggered, and kept coming. The others came after it. Uncanny, unnaturally white, as swift as illusion, they darted into the light, chittering and snapping the air.

Ramiro, Oliver, and I drew swords.

"Vespertiles!" Shardos breathed.

And they were on us.

The first of them surged by the juggler with a brief, high-pitched cry and barreled into Ramiro. There was a dull, leathery sound as the two collided and tumbled into the stone cascade. I turned back to face the vespertiles and saw nothing but teeth and hot red glittering eyes as several rose from below me, one climbing up under my tunic, thrashing its way to my throat.

I cried out and tried to push it down, but it scrabbled up my chest, its claws scraping and tearing through my shirt, and then we were fighting under the same ragged skin.

I looked up, and Oliver was rushing toward me, knife glinting in his hand.

"Don't move, Galen!" he cried as the dagger plunged into the front of my tunic, and the vespertile spasmed, stiffened, and softly fell out of my clothing. A blue spot widened around the place Oliver's blade had torn my shirt.

I had time to raise my sword. In a stride, I was next to Shardos, who was grappling with another of the creatures. I slipped my arm between them, shielding Shardos's face, and sunk my sword into the thorax of the vespertile. The blade wrenched in my hand, and I brought it up through bone and gristle and entrail as the monster on the end of my weapon writhed and shrieked, its scream ascending into shrill, barely audible sounds and finally into silence.

I set my foot to its neck and pulled my sword from its body in a swift, grating movement, bringing a course of thin blue fluid up the blood gutter.

I turned to see one of them envelop Dannelle's head, the outline of her face faintly visible through the veins and translucency of its enfolded wings. Swiftly she brought up her dagger, splitting the wing's leather. The creature shrieked and fluttered from her grasp, and Birgis leapt onto its back, grabbing its neck in those long, badger-breaking jaws and worrying it back and forth until it was limp and still.

Oliver and Ramiro drew their swords out of the third vespertile as blood streamed from the ragged cut on the big Knight's forehead. Their companions put to dagger and sword, the remaining monsters turned and scurried back into the darkness, some of them dragging ruined wings.

By the time I had caught my breath, Dannelle was already walking confidently to the foot of the formation as though someone had appointed her mountaineer. She tested its surface for holes, for shelves, for purchase.

"Just what do you have in mind, Dannelle?" I asked in my most commanding voice. She did not heed me. Up the rock face she scrambled, and though she was no monkey, no goat, but still a dazzling girl brought up in luxury, in social grace, she had managed somehow to become a more than adequate climber.

What was more, the view from below was certainly fetching. I marveled as I watched her ascend, the view as round and perfect as distant fruit, and as desperately out of reach.

For a moment, there was peace amid all this tumult and darkness.

I felt a hand on my shoulder. Ramiro raised the lantern to provide a better view for the both of us. It was as if he had intruded, had parted a veil with his thick, meaty hands.

"You bring up the rear, Ramiro," I said coldly as I grasped the line Dannelle cast over the edge of the stone cascade. Staggering up the slippery rock, I left the intruder fuming behind me.

The corridor at the top extended endlessly into the darkness and rock, or so it seemed from a quick sweep of the lantern I carried up the rock face.

At first, there was no time to investigate nook and cranny as the two of us helped first a puffing Shardos to the mouth of the tunnel, and next Oliver, who was wrestling with a nervous and wriggling Birgis, wrapped quite securely and safely in a makeshift litter of cloth and rope.

Ramiro himself came last. We lowered the rope for him and steadied him as he swung frantically over the chamber below us. Finally his feet touched solid ground. He knelt, recovering breath and balance.

"I refuse to do *that* again," he announced, leaning against the tunnel wall.

Three or four tenebrals rushed by us on their way to the chamber we had just left behind.

As we stood between dangers, figuring the odds and the options, all of a sudden the passage ahead of us filled with light and noise. A dozen Plainsmen approached, Que-Tana from their markings, bearing torches and bows and spears. In the midst of them walked their leader, a tall dark-haired man, a diamond-shaped patch over his right eye.

He was older than any of the other Que-Tana I had seen, probably about Shardos's age, and he looked different from the others. His one good eye was smaller, lighter, and though he was pale by Plainsman standards, he was downright ruddy among this underground people. What was more, he had plentiful dark hair, beaded and locked like Longwalker's. Indeed, he looked like a very pale Plainsman—like a Que-Nara priest just recovering from a ghastly illness.

The crown he wore was silver and glowed with the deep violet light of the opals.

The grub-pale tenebrals flashed across the path of the Que-Tana, squeaking desolately as they burrowed into the darkness.

"Of all times to meet them," Ramiro muttered. "Our backs to a freak of nature and our faces to superior numbers. Our best hope lies in the blades of our swords when they close with us."

He smiled fiercely at me, drawing forth that long, double-edged monstrosity he handled like a carving knife.

"There's never been a time," he claimed, "when a Plainsman could hold his own against a Solamnic Knight in close quarters."

It was then that the rain of arrows began.

Clattering onto the stones around us, they came like a menacing avalanche. Under the direction of their leader, the Plainsmen aimed some five yards short of us, and volley after volley drew nearer and nearer, until Ramiro and I were forced to raise our shields above the party, forming a canopy of leather and metal over them.

It was all designed for terror's sake, this relentless barrage of arrows. Pinned down we clearly were, and in open terrain, and as far as I could figure it, at any moment they could have lowered their sights and riddled us with straighter and more deadly shots.

We extinguished our lantern at once, then huddled together, the five of us, shivering as though we were caught in a mountain blizzard.

"That does it!" I finally exclaimed, as yet another wave of arrows swept over us, jarring my hand on the shield. "Whatever befalls the rest of us, I'm finding a way out of this for Dannelle!"

"Indeed not!" the girl exclaimed bravely, but her voice quivered, and I could feel her tremble next to me. "By the gods, I can stand here with the best male among you!"

"Standing here is no real feat of courage, my dear," Shardos explained, his voice a trifle too high-pitched to be taken for calm. "I could guide you readily back the way we came, then send you for help. The only thing is that our visitors may still prove great fanged flies in the ointment."

I thought of the waiting, hungry vespertiles and shuddered.

"Well, then," Oliver announced with a sigh, reluctantly but fearlessly, as though it was his part only to rise from bed in the wee hours of a winter's morning. "Well, then, there should be a sword hand to secure the lass the length of the chamber below."

Ramiro and I looked foolishly at one another. As fortune would have it, at that moment, there came a lull in the shooting, and Oliver slipped from beneath the shields and raced toward the ledge and the lower cavern.

"No, Oliver!" shouted Dannelle. Shardos, turning, groped for the squire but came away clutching nothing as Oliver slid down a stalactite and into the chamber below us.

It was too dark to see what was unfolding down there. I heard Oliver shout once from directly below the ledge, then again at a distance and once more at a still greater distance as he drew the giant bats away from the stalactites.

Dannelle grasped my arm, and I took her hand.

"You have no choice now," I said to her bluntly. "The boy is moving the monsters away to save you. You have no choice but to use the time he is buying to get to the surface, then hasten toward whatever help you can find us."

It was a fiction, and we both knew it. The help Dannelle went for would almost certainly arrive too late. And yet it was good to think about, that help, and with all of our thoughts upon it, at least we could act, could be busy at something when the enemy overwhelmed us in the dim caverns and the dim times. Meanwhile, my directions would surely take her back to Castle di Caela, to the safest place I knew in these troubled parts.

I placed her hand into Shardos's.

The rain of arrows began again as the juggler burst toward the ledge, shielding Dannelle's body with his own. In the half-light from the Plainsmen's torches, I saw the blind man lift an arm above the both of them and, when one or another arrow came too close, swat it from the air in an old juggler's movement that was remarkable and totally unexplainable. It was as though they passed through a downpour without getting wet.

Birgis trotted along merrily after his master, hugging to the safety of ledges and Shardos's cloak.

Dumbstruck, Ramiro and I watched all three of them slide over the ledge. Then we lifted our shields and followed to the lip of the tunnel.

Below me, I saw them blend into the darkness at the far end of the cavern, safely out of the reach of bowshot or vespertiles. Loudly to my right, Oliver shouted again and rushed back in our direction, one of the monsters not far behind him. The boy's intention, no doubt, was to climb the wall and join us. But there was something deceptive about the beast that pursued him, something as subtle as quicksilver and as shifting in form, for its speed propelled it faster by far than the movement of legs or hand, and we learned that at its most fleet, it surpassed the eye itself. The boy was halfway back to us when the vespertile turned and rushed him in a white blur.

Oliver screamed and raised his sword in desperation, but the big, sail-like wings were already covering him.

"No!" Ramiro and I cried out in unison, our eyes fixed to the terrible scene below us, to the vespertile lowering its face like some horrible lover to the boy's unprotected neck. The Que-Tana, shrewdly commanded, chose that moment to rush us, and as I watched the unspeakable fate of Oliver, a solid blow from a Plainsman quarterstaff struck me from behind, sending me skidding toward the ledge after the lantern, which dropped ahead of me, struck the stone ground, and shattered as I hurtled after it, clutching desperately for the ledge, for stalagmites, for anything, somehow righting myself so I managed to hit ground feetfirst but losing my sword and my sense of direction in the process.

Half-dazed, I sat against smooth stone, looking up toward the dodging torches at the high mouth of the tunnel. Above me, I heard the sounds of struggles—thrashing and wrestling and Ramiro bellowing—and here around me in the gibbering darkness, the high-pitched cries of the vespertiles.

Oliver moaned somewhere off to my left, and I heard the scraping sound of something monstrous moving across stone and rubble.

There was nothing I could do.

Whatever had happened to Oliver would happen next to me. There was no telling about Ramiro, whose curses grew more elaborate and powerful as he wrestled a dozen Que-Tana above me, nor about Shardos and Dannelle, whom I could only hope had escaped.

For a moment, I felt worse for my friends than for myself, even though I had brought them here.

Above me suddenly a shout burst out of the darkness. It was Ramiro, I was sure, and something in the shout spurred me to action, for there was no pain or panic in that cry. Instead, there was something like triumph.

There in the caves, where we all lay blinded, something above me was passing for hope.

My fingers moved into my pockets, past the nuisance of those old leather gloves, and closed thankfully over metal and reed.

I drew out the whistle—the old dog whistle that was a gift from Brithelm all those many years ago. What impelled me to blow it, I cannot say for sure: something in my childhood schooling, perhaps, or the way it had disturbed the tenebrals when I had used it to call Birgis before.

Whatever my reasons, Huma's dog whistle, as Brithelm and I had called it laughingly, shrilled its silent note through the caverns, and I heard strange, humanlike shrieks above and about me, and the sounds of scurrying, of rustling, of of something running away, leaving us alone.

Soon Ramiro called my name down the cascade of wet stone, and I answered, and above was the glimmer of torchlight.

But here about me, the silence was deep, complete. It was like some blackness before the world began, like there was simply nothing here but nothing.

Ramiro stood at the lip of the ledge above me, flanked by a handful of Que-Tana. From behind this little tableau rose a voice I had heard only once before yet remembered clearly. It had come to my ears on that day that seemed years ago, when the quake rocked Castle di Caela and I looked into the opals of my brooch and spoke to an apparition.

"You may rest now, Sir Galen," the voice said, and within it, I heard the desolate rush of wind over a lifeless plain. "You may rest now. Your long journey is over. Welcome to the Kingdom of Firebrand, the country of the Que-Tana."

One of the Plainsmen dropped a torch into the gloom beside me, and the cavern took on shape and dimension in an elusive light. I was uncovered, and four of the Que-Tana above me leveled their bows and gazed at me coldly down the shafts of their nocked, barbed arrows.

They lowered a rope then, and I climbed up to join my captive companion, all the while under the sharp sights of the bowmen.

Halfway up the cascade, I looked behind me, over Oliver's pathetically broken body, to the opening at far end of the cavern, through which Shardos and Dannelle had passed in their rush to escape.

The brooch glowed in my hand. Soon it would pass into the hand of our dreadful host. I looked deep into the stones.

There I saw Longwalker, camped in the hills miles above us, staring calmly and resolutely into the stones he carried. Then Bayard, lost somewhere in rock-hewn walls, propped on the shoulders of Brandon and my father, moving in ominous torchlight.

I saw a darker vision yet, in which some large, snakelike creature coiled within shadow and slate, its length extending across the continent and his ageless sleep shallow now, and restless.

"Tellus the dale worm," I breathed. "What was it Longwalker said? 'It bears all Solamnia upon its back'?"

But that vision faded, too, and finally I saw my brother Brithelm, somewhere in a room of towering shelves, reading alone and undisturbed by candlelight, those absurd triangular spectacles on his nose.

The stones winked out like stars behind a cloud, and I was afraid then—afraid for the chieftain that my incompetence had betrayed, and for a brother whom I had failed to rescue. I feared for my friends and father, drawn underground and in obvious peril, and most of all for the innocent Dannelle di Caela, whom unknowingly I had sent to find them.

For all of these, I was dreadfully sorry, and whatever Firebrand could devise seemed slight punishment at the moment.

"May the gods speed them," I whispered as I continued to climb. Strong, pale hands clutched my forearms and dragged me up into Firebrand's presence. "May the gods speed all of them, all of us."

Chapter XVIII

With deft little twists of his hand, with a strange, beaked tool of iron, the Namer scored the entwined circlets four, six, ten, twelve times. Then a thirteenth time, the only noise in the far-flung encampment the crackle of the fire that illuminated his delicate work.

"There is a place for each of these stories in a larger story," he told the rapt Plainsmen.

* * * * *

Through the darkness she raced, holding the hand of the blind man.

The faint light from the Plainsmen's torches, from the few feeble lanterns Galen had thought to bring with them, faded suddenly behind her, and she waded through black silence, through the desolate night-struck caverns.

Dannelle di Caela wished that she could avoid all the duties that no doubt would follow. In the darkness, she imagined the path ahead of her, steep through the caverns, then down from the mountains on foot, across the rain-soaked, troll-infested plains, and back to Castle di Caela.

A journey of days, if not weeks.

By which time the hope that glimmered under the mountain would fade, she feared, as finally and completely as the lights had faded behind her.

"Come now, girl! No dawdling!" the juggler whispered ahead of her. She realized she had stopped moving.

"Oh, Shardos!" she exclaimed, much too loudly, her voice echoing through the corridor, raising, she thought in a panic-stricken moment, all kinds of creatures out of the rocks, next to which, no doubt, the vespertile would seem like a sparrow. "Shardos, whatever I can do is going to be too late!"

"Nonsense!" the old man said with a chuckle, drawing her on up the corridor. "As long as you're breathing and fit to be doing it, it is never too late. Let me tell you a story you should know—a story of a great tournament at a castle not far from here."

Shardos could feel the electric pulse of the girl calm in her wrist as, despite herself, she became lost in the tale of the reason behind Bayard's late arrival years ago at the tournament for Enid's hand, a story she enjoyed all the more, the old man thought, because she knew the actors, knew it was true and that it ended happily, despite the power of the villain and the mistakes and stumbling of the hero.

From there, Shardos moved to another story, and then another. Released from paying attention to anything else by the absolute dark and the absolute quiet, Dannelle abided in the world of his telling as the old man fabled the girl toward the surface and the air and the light.

"We have passed through the Veins of Sargonnas," he told her finally, the darkest part of their journey behind them. "The Veins of the Red Fist."

"The Veins of the Red Fist?" she asked, knowing she

would be drawn into yet another story as readily and completely as she had been drawn down the tunnel ahead of her.

"It is a dark name," the juggler began, "and one of mystery, for the bards and the Namers and even the priests themselves have come near forgetting the god. Vengeance he governs, and fire, but beyond that, little is known of him. It is like those gaps in manuscripts where pages are illegible, or blotted out, or torn and destroyed. . . ."

"Lacunae," Dannelle said, taking the old man's hand again as the passage narrowed and darkened. "They call those gaps 'lacunae.' "

"Gaps or lacunae or mysteries, the ways of Sargonnas are more unknown than known. The Plainsmen pair him with the great snake Tellus, who is said to lie in timeless slumber beneath the continent of Ansalon, only to stir at the end of all things. Others see him as a scavenging red bird—a vulture, perhaps, or an enormous condor who dines on the entrails of those who offend his consort, Takhisis."

"This is not pleasant fare for a dark road, Shardos," Dannelle protested. And yet she marveled at Shardos's steadiness, the occasional "Step over, miss," and "Lower the head here, miss."

Around them, small creatures cried out in the darkness, surprised by the strange noises and speed of the two rushing by them, the big dog at their heels. Once Dannelle heard a flutter of wings, once a terrified whirring sound directly under her feet.

So by a dark sense the juggler steered, a sense born of sad years wandering blind over the face of Krynn, Dannelle figured. It was one of those times, rare though they may be, when loss becomes advantage, and weakness strength.

She was surprised to think of Galen in the same thought, surprised to find herself smiling in the darkness.

Years ago, Dannelle di Caela had taken on the betterment of Galen Pathwarden as a kind of quest, for he had come to Castle di Caela in need of every imaginable improvement.

When he seated himself on the mahogany chairs in the Great Hall, he would fling his leg over an armrest, and formal dining was a complete embarrassment, for it seemed that up in Coastlund, they had never heard of the fork, thinking it was placed on the table as aesthetic balance to the very real and useful knife and spoon on the other side of the plate.

Like a gully dwarf he ate, or how she had imagined a gully dwarf would eat. In the first months of Galen's stay at the castle, before he looked around him and began to catch on to the etiquette, Dannelle di Caela would shudder when the lad shoveled gristles of pork beneath the table for the benefit of his most recently befriended dog.

Indeed, befriending was one of Galen Pathwarden's greatest skills. Marigold, Dannelle di Caela's most distant cousin, had befriended the lad when she had grown tired of befriending two of the younger and more handsome palace guards. Galen had been next in line, for some unknown reason, but Dannelle suspected it had something to do with his knightly prospects. Marigold did love a man in armor.

For months, Dannelle had stewed while the two of them simmered in the chambers of the other tower. Galen, it seems, had found the whole arrangement entirely new and altogether fascinating, and Dannelle would watch with rising irritation as lights went on and off in various windows across the courtyard.

And yet that dalliance, too, had gradually stopped, like the sport with the dogs and gristles. Nonetheless, Dannelle had thought to herself not a month ago that the young man's Night of Reflections was coming right on time, that the knighthood within him was growing and blossoming. A knighthood of the new generation, which would not recoil at a girl's desire to hawk and hunt and ride and be something beyond a bauble in the castle like old Sir Robert's tuneless mechanical birds.

She had continued to dream of that knighthood, through the stumbling in battle and the uncertain command, through the misguided visions in the opals and the disasters that seemed to follow when the boy was guided by stone and brooch and omen.

It had been a world of the possible, even when faced with monsters and the dark Que-Tana. That was why it could not end the way it was preparing to end.

In Shardos's stories, the promise of a boy was always realized, the magical sword was eventually unsheathed and its power displayed, and the talking bird had something magnificent and important to say. The lost book was found, the wandering ship came home, and the third son prospered despite his unlikely inheritance.

Dannelle di Caela would see Galen again. It was the way that stories ended.

The trail turned sharply upward, and the three of them, dog and juggler and lady of the court, embarked on the last half-mile or so that would bring them to the surface and to as much safety as they could expect here at the borders of imperiled Solamnia.

Dannelle could discern the outline of stone and corridor in a deep, settled grayness. Now she could follow the juggler without being led like a child or a donkey.

"We are nearing the surface, my dear," Shardos said. "Can you smell it?"

Dannelle breathed more easily, taking in the sweet, metallic smell of rain, and beyond it the green of juniper and aeterna.

It was midnight there in the upper mountains, but even the light of the moon seemed unbearably brilliant. Dannelle shielded her face for a moment, covered her head with her cloak. Beside her, Birgis sneezed, no doubt bewildered by the brightness himself.

Shardos took the girl's hand once more and whispered to her kindly.

"Rest, my dear. But only awhile. Though the odds seem longer than the distances, I'll wager you have a part to play before the story has ended. But you'll not do it alone, that's for certain. Rest awhile, and aid will come to you."

Her head still covered, her eyes still closed against the moonlight, Dannelle heard the old man turn and descend. He was going back down into the darkness.

"Shardos!" she cried turning around to follow him. He was already at the mouth of the cavern, once again half-hidden by shadow.

"Did you think I would walk you home, m'lady?" he asked, pausing at the edge of the entrance. "Though the prospect is charming, more charming by far than returning to Firebrand and his pasty underlings, it is nonetheless a walk I cannot make. I am afraid I am needed more below than above."

She took one step toward him, but with a broad wave of his hand, he motioned her back.

"Be of good heart!" he urged. "The time is fast approaching when all of us are called upon to do the hard things. You have a breathing space, Dannelle di Caela, before your hardest travels are at hand. As I said to you but a moment ago, rest awhile and aid will come to you."

Dannelle sat with her face in her hands for a long while. Birgis looked up at her with a strange, wise look of concern, cocking his big head and resting his long, badger-killing snout on her lap. Finally she rubbed the animal's ear in an idle, circular motion, as heedlessly as if this journey, this adventure, were all a daydream over the laundry tubs in Castle di Caela.

Longwalker found Dannelle rubbing the ears of the dog, her eyes staring off into high country. He smiled and led her into the clearing to the little mare—the one who had stayed behind when the other Solamnic horses scattered.

Dreaming girls, he realized, are not the most durable of riders. And the road to Castle di Caela was a long, rough one for a cavalryman, not to mention a sheltered girl used to the attentions of servants and finaglings of courtiers.

But then, he told himself, he must trust on all counts to the most unlikely of heroes: a blind juggler, a bedazzled cleric, and a long-nosed dog. An unlikely trio, who trust their safety to even more unlikely Solamnic Knights: a four-hundred-pound epicure more bent on sirloin and sherry than sword and shield, and the leader, who seemed anything but skilled and experienced and resourceful.

Trust in the likes of these, Longwalker thought, is the beginnings of the strongest faith.

The girl started as he laid his hand softly on her shoulder.

*   *   *   *   *

Sargonnas saw them all as he looked up from the bottom of the Abyss, in his eyes the fire of black opals. Saw them all and laughed, his laughter the croaking of scavenging birds.

Below tenebral and Que-Tana and vespertile he waited.

Below Firebrand, and below the depths of the opals.

Below darkness itself, below vision and imagining and somewhere even below belief.

And the tunnels under the Vingaards were known as his Veins.

Let Firebrand gather his stones, the dark god thought. Let there be ten, eleven, twelve, but let there be thirteen finally.

Firebrand is fodder, is kindling. But his one eye is my light upon history.

He is like all mortals, all of them caught in their cravings for power or vengeance, or love or recognition or simple respect or something—anything—to lull the pain of their serious wounds.

It does not matter what they want, for it all amounts to the same thing.

Sargonnas reclined on a swirl of dark air in the center of the Abyss. He laughed again, the smell of ordure and smoke and blood rising from deep within the laughter and mingling smell with sight and sound, until even the things that fluttered about him in the Abyss recoiled mindlessly from the stench and the noise.

Their desires change from day to day, Sargonnas thought, and often grow larger and darker.

Why, now Firebrand imagines that godhood lies in the heart of a simple stone. He even believes there is space in the heavens for his stars.

Sargonnas's laughter faded to a glittering red smile. Firebrand, he concluded, is no more than a spyglass. For years, I have watched the world through his eye, known the history he knows. And indeed, it is valuable.

But it is not yet enough.

Out of a whirlpool of blackness, Sargonnas sighed. Three thousand years was a long time, even for a god. Three thousand years, in which the only mortal voices he had heard were those like that of Firebrand— those with the foolhardiness or the greed or the anger to call upon him.

There had been a dozen or so, perhaps.

A mad mage from Neraka, who fancied himself to be the

god Chemosh, wearing the skull mask and the hood that hid his terribly mortal anger that he would have to die.

A traitorous Solamnic Knight, who had slain both his children and still found no harbor for his anger.

A cleric or two, or perhaps even more than that.

Between them, the times were fitful, fragmented.

Sargonnas had forgotten most of the visitants, for they were inconsequential—little men who trusted in nothing until it became unbearable, then trusted in Sargonnas.

Who betrayed them as quickly, as readily as he could, according to their weaknesses. Who reopened the wounds that had brought them to call on him in the first place, and let them watch as the old wound festered and spread and devoured them like fire or acid or vengeance.

Firebrand was the most recent, though not the most distinguished. Nonetheless, if things came to pass as Sargonnas had foreseen and planned, the Namer of the Que-Tana would be the last of the visitants. Any day now the dark gods would return to Krynn.

For along with the self-styled king of the Que-Tana . . .

There was the worm.

Under the surface of Ansalon the dale worm Tellus slept, dreaming of light and movement and terrible arousal.

Back in the Age of Dreams, when the dark gods fell into the deepest of banishments, the door to the bright world was sealed after them. All of them—Morgion and Hiddukel and Sargonnas and the Dark Queen Takhisis—spun and tumbled in confusion down into the depths of the Abyss, where falling ceased to be falling, because like everything else around them, it, too, had become nothing. They rested on nothing, there in the center of nothing, and they thought long thoughts of exile.

At their banishment, Tellus, who had hovered at the edge of awakening, had trembled once beneath the surface of the world and settled back into a sleep of nearly three millennia.

A sleep that was about to end. And when the dark gods flooded the world, only one of them would know its peoples. Only one would have . . . a history with him. And to him all worshipers would flock. For the dale worm was power, but the eyes in the crown were knowledge.

Consort of Darkness no longer, he would be Darkness itself.

Sargonnas closed his predator's eye, a rumble of contentment rising from his throat as the ground above him trembled. Slowly he remembered once again his triumph, for exile in the Abyss led even a god to repeat his thoughts.

The device, he thought, was set millennia ago . . . by Huma himself. How sweet and ingenious! But its intricacy hides a simple magic.

When its time comes, it will rouse the worm. Nothing more than that.

And the worm, awakened, will rush toward the surface beneath which it has slept since the Age of Dreams, tearing open the continent from Palanthas to Port Balifor.

The Cataclysm come again, it will be, and it will be our portal into the world.

Quickly Sargonnas rose in the Abyss like a vulture on a thermal wind, wheeling slowly over a battlefield as a wounded bird for water.

He wheeled over history, circling and remembering.

I thank my fortune for that fool the Scorpion, he thought. Just one more visitant who thought—as every visitant thinks—that he could make the gods do his bidding.

When his thoughts first reached in my direction, I returned with them as a small voice in the recesses of his imaginings, as I do, sooner or later, to all of them.

It took me years to convince him that my voice was a part of his thinking.

And when I did, the rest was easy.

Again Sargonnas laughed, and the earth trembled in grim accordance.

* * * * *

"What was that?" Gileandos asked nervously, leaping away from the wall as though it were molten metal.

"Perhaps," Bayard replied apprehensively, "it is the promised Rending."

"Well," Gileandos announced, turning quickly and striding back into the shadows, toward the way up and the castle and the light. His footsteps echoed down the corridor and stopped.

Nobody was following.

Instead, the rest of them—Andrew and Robert, Bayard and Enid, Marigold, Raphael, and Brandon—stood in a circle, pondering the creature beside them, the quake above and below and around them.

Whatever the creature was, it was as black and impenetrable as onyx.

"It's like . . . the thing is as big as the castle," Enid whispered, slipping her arm around Bayard. "Or even the Vingaard River."

At Bayard's other side, Sir Brandon nodded.

"Right you are, m'lady," he said, "and I for one would rather not chance a tangle with it."

"How about . . . a stroll *around* it, Brandon?" Bayard asked, his face unreadable, turned away from the torchlight.

Behind them, Gileandos whimpered in the darkness.

Brandon stood there silently for some time. His face, too, was obscured, but from the tilt of his shoulders, you could tell he was reluctant, that Solamnic honor wrestled with good sense in his faculties. Finally he nodded.

"Around it, it is, if you say so, Sir Bayard. Though I find it hard to think of it as a stroll."

He took a tentative step forward into the corridor beyond them.

"Not so quickly, Brandon," Sir Robert protested, chivalrously hoisting Marigold's bag of food to his shoulders, where he tied the cords securely in a knapsack of sorts. "Whatever the creature is beside us, the way in front of us bears closer inspection before you wade blithely into it."

"Sir Robert is right, Brandon," Bayard admitted. "What is more, we shall need your stout back to carry me along. After all, it will just be the two of us from this point on."

After Bayard's words sank in, it was Enid di Caela's turn to protest.

"I know there's something all knightly and manly in this, Bayard Brightblade," she said. "I also know that I'm not supposed to understand. You'll *say* I don't understand, and you'll leave it at that. But I cannot stand here and let you get yourself killed for a posture."

"You don't understand, Enid," Bayard replied with a crooked, brief smile. He gestured to Raphael, and the boy drew from his pack a strong, light cord—a Plainsman twist, good in a traveler's hands. Bayard tied the cord once, twice about his waist.

"You have heard the stories about the mazes of the minotaurs?" he asked his dumbstruck companions. "How a light cord taken in to the labyrinth can be followed out to safety?"

"I am not about to be widowed by my husband's damned recklessness," Enid insisted.

"Nor does he intend to widow you thus," Bayard replied formally, absently, tightening the third knot. "Now, Brandon, if you'd be so kind as to help me along, we'll find where the worm ends, or where the device lies of which the chronicles speak. And I'll wager from the shaking of the earth about us that we aren't far—that indeed, we will not need all of the rope we carry.

Brandon took the rope in hand. He stared at it long and intently, as though it were a thousand years old, a relic the use of which had been forgotten. Bayard gave the cord a short, playful tug, and it slid from the young man's hands.

"I hope you plan to maintain that thing a little more ardently, Brandon," Sir Robert muttered, and the young man muttered something back—inaudible and fierce. He picked up the rope, tied it tightly around his own waist, and nodded brusquely to Bayard.

Suddenly, Sir Andrew stepped forward, grabbed onto the far end of the rope, and bound it tightly around his own hand. The stocky old fellow tested the strength of the cord, then nodded to his young companions.

"Well, boys, I can't say enough about how foolish this idea of Bayard's strikes me," he said. "But he's going through that corridor come Cataclysm again. Such places are known for the worst of footing—the ground can fall away from under you with a single false step in the shadows. I cannot speak for any of you, but I'll be damned if I'll see Solamnic knights let one of their own take a tumble."

Andrew braced himself and gave the rope a brisk yank.

"I suppose," he concluded, "it's as the deer hunters say up in Coastlund, where I come from. 'Them not skinning can at least hold a leg.'"

Reluctantly, straining beneath armor and cheese and sausage, Robert di Caela clutched the rope as well.

Gileandos whimpered again, then put hands to the cord.

Bayard limped toward the edge of the darkness, left arm over Brandon's shoulder, right hand clutching an unsheathed broadsword. He felt foolish with weapon drawn, for the creatures he had met in the subterranean corridors were either too small to bother with or too large to disturb. And yet somehow to step into the darkness armed and ready seemed just and right and proper . . . seemed Solamnic and Measured.

"Your leg, Bayard!" Enid protested, but by now she knew that those protests, the urging or argument or even the begging, were useless, except in the small comfort of having set forth a warning.

"I shall be careful, my dear," Bayard tried to reassure her. The words sounded superior and smug.

Those words were drowned out by a small voice in Enid's dark imagining, a voice growing louder and louder, seeming to rush from the walls around her and the rock beneath her and most of all from the oily dark of the fissure.

He is going to die, the voice repeated. He is going to die, and you will be a widow at twenty, alone in this terrible, unsteady castle with memory and misgiving. You are right: You should not have said those words about widowhood. Your words and his foolishness will leave you bereft.

"A little slack there, Robert," Bayard called back out of the shadows. "A man can't venture that far into certain doom when you're holding the rope like there's a tug-of-war in the wings."

The earth rumbled once more about them, this time more loudly. And suddenly, as though the world was collapsing, exploding in upon them, the roof of the corridor caved in behind them.

Sir Andrew released the rope and lunged toward Enid, gathering her into his arms and shielding her with his body against the tumbling rocks and surge of water. Marigold screamed, pulling Sir Robert down on top of her. Raphael tumbled pathetically into a ball on the floor, while Bayard and Brandon rushed back up the corridor, back into sight of the others. All were shouting and embracing and colliding as everyone huddled together, expecting the worst from the ceilings and walls.

But the awaited collapse never came. The corridor tilted about them, clouding with gravel and debris. Bayard reached his wife and embraced her as Robert and Marigold disentangled and the ill-matched band of adventurers gaped and gasped and choked in the dust-filled air.

"Nothing but rubble in that direction," Robert observed, gesturing at the corridor behind them. He ducked under Marigold's knee and wrestled laboriously to his feet. "Rubble and Gileandos."

There was a yawning moment of silence, in which the horror of what had happened to the tutor descended on the lot of them like a rockslide.

Chapter XIX

While Bayard and his followers huddled in rubble and fear deep beneath the foundations of Castle di Caela, Dannelle was riding south into the highlands, barely atop the game little palfrey that Longwalker had brought her.

She rode homeward, traveling through the night, uncertain of what she would find when she got there and even more uncertain as to what she would do about it.

She was a comical sight. A young woman scarcely out of her teens, scarcely five feet tall, her hood blown back by the brisk wind and the wild ride, her red hair billowing behind her like a banner.

It was like something from a painting, from a legend or romantic myth, if it were not for the dog behind her on the horse. For Birgis rode with Dannelle, tethered to her back like a Plainsman baby, though the creature weighed nearly as much as the girl herself.

His long snout rested on her shoulder. His tongue dangled blissfully as he tasted the air and reveled in the wind passing over his face.

"It's all beyond my understanding," Dannelle said over the sound of wind and hoofbeats, her only listener the dog draped over her shoulder, his short front legs braced on either side of her neck. He closed his dark eyes and grumbled in her ear. "Beyond my understanding why a strapping old veteran like Longwalker can't gather up his charges and descend on the whole bunch of them down in that warren. I'll bet you *he* could come back with Galen and Brithelm and Ramiro and leave a lot of smoke in his wake."

She paused a moment, blushing because she was talking to a dog. Birgis sniffed her neck serenely, his long, badger-breaking snout poked seriously under her chin.

"All this talk of ban and bane and cannot lift a hand! Why, the Plainsmen out-Solamnic Solamnics with their promises and posturing."

Birgis snorted and whuffed. It seemed to Dannelle di Caela that he was answering her, saying, "You are right, Dannelle. You are right, and there is salt on your ears."

The girl snorted, too, as Birgis licked her. She nodded her head and flicked the reins, and the palfrey quickened to a gallop on a smooth downhill slope extending for miles into the Vingaard foothills, leaving behind the bare and rocky terrain.

Down into greenery the girl rode, past the spot where, days or years ago—things happened so fast and so far underground she was unsure of time—she and Galen and the others had met the troll on the road.

"It's like forever ago, Birgis, no matter how long it has been by calendar or clock," she mused, and they rode quickly past, the dainty hooves of the pony flinging turf and mud behind them now. "And now the clock has begun to move again—now that I have to ride for help and all. And you know, it's like that clock is making up for lost time, because Galen's in danger and so the hours are shorter and shorter still."

She looked into Birgis's muzzle, and he licked her nose solemnly.

"Oh, and the others, too, Birgis!" she corrected, "though I expect that of all of them, your master Shardos can take care of himself. It's just that Galen . . . he . . . means too much to me."

They rode together in silence, and the road seemed to be turning east, though it was hard to tell under the moonlight.

"The one thing that troubles me about all of this," Dannelle confessed as they left the highlands and descended onto the still soggy plains of Solamnia, "is that I haven't the first idea what we shall do when we get to the castle."

Birgis yawned colossally at Dannelle's shoulder. Resolutely she clicked her tongue at the pony beneath her. It was galloping gamely now, stretched far beyond its usual duties as a lady's or child's mount.

Nor was Dannelle aware when the gait of the little horse changed, began to waver and tire. The resting and watering and airing of animals had always been the groom's job, or on long trips the job of the man escorting her. It had been Dannelle di Caela's job to order those men about.

The first she noticed of the palfrey's distress was when the animal slowed to a trot, then a walk, then stopped and refused to move.

The three of them were like a tableau, standing there below the blue fragrant branches of a huge aeterna tree: the stubborn, winded palfrey, the angry young woman, and the dog who sniffed the branches above him for squirrels, unconcerned by the conflict between horse and rider.

"Damn!" she shouted, rifling her saddlebags for a whip or crop or spurs, none of which were to be found since, after all, a Plainsman saddled the horse. Finally, disconsolate and immobile, the girl scrambled out of the saddle, staggered under the heavy dog on her back, slipped in the mud, and fell facefirst in a heap, clutching frantically at the reins that dangled above her head.

Birgis licked the mud from her ear, snorted, and nodded off to sleep atop her. No doubt he dreamed of rabbits, of scraps under a table in a great and generous hall.

Propping herself up on her elbows, Dannelle muttered an

oath famous among infantrymen regarding cavalry horses and their imagined ancestry. It was not a pretty phrase. Galen would be astonished to know that she even knew such words, much less that she found occasion to use them. Even Birgis stirred at the sound of it, his hackles rising at its venom and anger.

"This is a sorry excuse for a rescue," she confessed and started to rise, but the weight of the relaxed dog held her down.

*   *   *   *   *

When the tremors around Castle di Caela had caved in part of the underground labyrinth and trapped Sir Bayard and his followers, there were others who fared better for the disruption.

The engineers, for example, exhausted with inspections and miffed at being sent back to the surface by the liege lord, had agreed to take the afternoon off and, having hauled a barrel of Thorbardin Eagle into their quarters on the ground floor of the Cat Tower, rode out the quake in singing and the swapping of lies, and none worried about anything for several days afterward.

Then, of course, there was Carnifex, Sir Robert di Caela's celebrated stallion.

In the close confinement of the castle stables, the big animal had been restrained by his own size. Where a smaller beast could turn in its stall and find purchase for bucking or kicking, Carnifex was forced to settle for standing there, shifting his weight, and contemplating the biting of passing grooms.

That is, until the quake rocked the grounds, shaking the door of the stall off its hinges.

It was as though he had planned what followed for years, rehearsed it in his imaginings and refined it to a brutal economy of three swift movements. Smoothly the big horse stepped from the stall, backed toward the door of the stable, and with one resounding kick, the whole damned means of access—lock and bolt and thick board—erupted in splinters across the rain-soaked courtyard.

The grooms outside the stable froze, as though they had been caught in some capital theft. Carnifex turned again and cantered out of the hay-smelling darkness, snorting and nodding, his black eyes glittering.

The four young men assigned to the livery did not look back until they were safely up stairs or ladders and shivering atop the battlements, braving tremor and misstep and rusty or frayed ladder in the process of climbing.

One of the young fools scaled the west wall by the chain of the drawbridge. The boy was clinging to the latticework above the great gate when Carnifex backed up to it and, like some powerful walking siege engine, subjected the thick oaken portal to the same deadly motion with which he had dismantled the entrance to the stables.

"Whoa, 'Fexy boy! Gee! Haw! Settle down . . ." the groom began weakly. Then he gritted his teeth as the great door splintered below him, and Carnifex was through and into the moat, whinnying and breasting the thick water with an almost lunatic calm, stepping out on the far side dripping stagnant water and moss, then striding into the Solamnic distances at a full gallop, erasing the world under his long, effortless strides.

"It's just as well," the boy mused as the big stallion galloped away, a red shape dwindling into a speck on the western horizon. "You was always too fierce for the keeping."

* * * * *

Of course they had to meet. It is the way of adventures and of stories.

Only a few hours passed before the jubilantly free Carnifex, capering across the wet lowlands, came to a stand of blue aeterna where rested a strange, swearing, ten-legged entanglement of girl and pony and dog. He stopped, whether in confusion or curiosity, or simply to catch his breath.

And the muddied girl wobbled out of the puddle and walked toward him, a large, ungainly, and oddly dry dog strapped to her back.

"You are what brought me here," Dannelle said to the stallion. "No. Not you, as much as it was knowing you were there that caused all the problems."

She fumbled with the elaborate network of ties and straps and knots by which Longwalker had bound her and Birgis together.

"For all the times I have said to my Uncle Robert that I was bound and determined to ride you, I suppose I never thought that the chance would come and the options would narrow to the point that I could do nothing else *but* ride you."

Birgis growled over her shoulder, a lazy, short-lived growl with little or no conviction. Slowly the girl approached Carnifex, lifting her hand.

"You were much less . . . daunting in the wish world."

She stretched across uncertainties of space, her fingers flexing, extending. Finally she stroked the long, threatening, velvety muzzle.

"They say you run faster in flesh than you run in the legends," she mused. "That words cannot surround the speed of your coming and going."

Her hand was at his withers now.

"You must prove to be faster than words, my Carnifex. You must prove to be faster than time and catastrophe."

With graceful indirection, as though she were approaching a viper, Dannelle sidled to the great horse's flank, and in one strenuous vault, straddled the back of the steed never mounted, never bridled or saddled.

It astonished the both of them. For a moment, Carnifex planted himself solidly in the middle of the muddy road, his ears pricked and his eyes wide in his stiffened, high-borne head.

Then, beyond his own expectation, and certainly beyond that of Dannelle, the big horse turned and galloped toward the castle, the strides lengthening until Dannelle felt as though the two of them hovered above the drowned land itself and a hundred miles had collapsed into one.

"Ride him," muttered a voice at her ear. Or "Ride him" she thought she heard in the hoofbeats and rush of the wind.

But there at her shoulder was Birgis only, his eyes closed and his nose tucked into her hair.

*   *   *   *   *

There was neither rest nor movement beneath the cellars of Castle di Caela. Bayard and the Knights picked through rubble in a futile search for the buried Gileandos, coming up instead with a boot and a pair of spectacles and shards of a ceramic flask that carried upon it the faint but unmistakable odor of gin.

They gave up soon, with leaden and downcast faces. The tutor was never a favorite of any of them, especially Andrew, who knew the old man best of all. Nonetheless, there was a real reluctance to their leavetaking—especially to Bayard, who felt that Gileandos was in some way his responsibility.

" 'Tis all we can do, Sir Bayard," Sir Robert consoled, laying a bracing hand on the commander's shoulder. "The next order of business is finding us another way out, if there's one to be found."

"Oh, but that's not it at all, Robert," Bayard protested, turning his reddened eyes toward the older man, both of them dappled in shadows by the wavering light from the lantern young Raphael held. "The next order of business is to keep the worm from turning. It is as simple as that. And now that I cannot send the rest of you back, it's all of us down to the heart of these tunnels, if that is where we find the Scorpion's device."

They were all silent at the thought of the dread mechanism. It had lurked in their worst imaginations for a day now—perhaps two days, for the hours bent and broke in the unchanging subterranean darkness. Each of them, no doubt, had an elaborate, monstrous machine in mind, whistling and rumbling and flinging sparks and oil like a gnomish nightmare.

On the other hand, Bayard remembered the Scorpion well and knew that no device he had fashioned would be a loud dramatic thing. Or if it was loud, it was only to call the wrong attentions to the wrong places. The one cog or gear or mechanism that seemed to run all the others could in fact be nonessential—even irrelevant—and to the last the trouble would be where you least expected it.

"Wherever it is to be found," Bayard offered, "the one way we can go is farther down the tunnel. Brandon?"

He extended his arm, and the young Knight slipped beneath it, offering himself once more as a crutch for the older man. Slowly the party began to collect itself.

Enid glided to the other side of her husband, the lamp-carrying Raphael in tow.

Muttering something about mulish nieces, Sir Robert pushed the hefty, reluctant Marigold into the marching order behind the bunched Brightblades and their escort. Only Sir Andrew tarried, sinking into the darkness as the others turned into the corridor and became a fading light in the distance.

"Damn you, Gileandos!" he whispered. "If you hadn't been fool enough to get yourself buried . . ."

He spun on his heels and strode off to join the party.

"I'd give you the moathouse if you'd only had the sense to come out alive!" he muttered.

* * * * *

Somewhere a million years beneath them, where distances tie themselves together and height and depth are swallowed in darkness, the big god stirred.

He is only a hundred yards from the Scorpion's device, this Brightblade, Sargonnas thought, and a gust of stagnant air smelling of stone and carnage buoyed him to a higher level of the darkness. Only a hundred yards.

There was something in the huge raptor's eye of the god that wavered for a moment. If you were to see it in a human eye, you would recognize it as misgiving, but a god is not accustomed to misgive, and the wavering soon subsided, dispersing like smoke into the Abyss around him.

A hundred yards or a hundred miles, Sargonnas mused. It is all the same when one proceeds in the wrong direction.

He hummed contentedly, and a glaze of ice formed at the rim of the Abyss.

* * * * *

Within the hour, despite Enid's better judgment and the urgings of the older Knights, Bayard had led the party even farther below the foundations of Castle di Caela. The tunnel now widened into a huge, vaulted hall littered with stalagmites and stalactites, both upright and broken, glistening yellow in the light of the lanterns.

Brandon gasped under Bayard's arm and stopped suddenly. Sir Robert, plodding along absently behind them, walked straight into their backs before Enid could stop him. All three men jostled, started . . .

Then stood still, looking down into the crevasse not a yard in front of them. A narrow bridge of rock, scarcely a foot wide, spanned the yawning gap in front of them and led away into the thick and climbing gloom.

They could not see the bottom of the pit in front of them. Sir Robert picked up a small fragment of limestone and tossed it into the darkness.

The sound returned with surprising speed, for the fragment dropped quickly into the bottom chasm. It was not thirty feet deep.

"Then why," Bayard asked aloud what they all were asking to themselves. "Why does it seem so bottomless?"

All of them looked into the crevasse, seeing only a short way into its abiding darkness.

The room felt palpably colder. Somewhere in the distance, near the other side of the stone catwalk, there was a faint whirring sound, like a distant chorus of cicadas. Bayard squinted toward the source of the noise but saw nothing.

"It is the device, sir," Brandon stated matter-of-factly, shielding his eyes against the lantern light and peering across the breadth of the chamber. "By the gods, it could be nothing other."

"I . . . I am afraid that the light in Raphael's hand has blinded me momentarily, Brandon," Bayard said, flushing. "Would you be so kind as to describe the device in question? I mean, for the benefit of those behind us."

"It's . . . it's . . . glittering, shining, crafted of metal, I believe," the young man ventured, "though it is impossible to tell at this distance. No doubt of dwarven make, to have survived this long in the dampness of these caverns."

"Of dwarven make, you say?" Sir Andrew huffed, joining the other Knights at the lip of the mysterious chasm. "How can you tell from fifty yards?"

"A hundred yards," Brandon corrected. "And I cannot tell. My eyes aren't as good as they were when I was a boy."

Andrew and Bayard glanced at one another, hiding embarrassed smiles.

Brandon smiled himself, shook his head.

"Then again, I'm quite the one for 'dwarven make' and 'cunningly wrought,' aren't I, gentlemen? As if the blasted thing is not fabulous enough just being down here."

"Go on, Brandon," Sir Robert urged. "Describe the apparatus. This is no time to come down with a case of self-knowledge."

Brandon Rus snorted in amusement.

"Well . . ." he began again, his eyes intent on the veiled shadows as the older men hung on his arm and words. "There are concentric circles on the thing. Not unlike an archer's butt."

For the first time, Marigold showed an interest in the conversation. Facedown in a bag of silks and cosmetics, her hair newly fashioned into the shape of a sailing ship, she looked up in passionate curiosity. "Whose butt?" she asked innocently.

" 'Tis only an archer's term for a target, Cousin Marigold," Enid explained curtly, never lifting her eyes from the murk beyond the huddled party.

"Oh." Somewhat disappointed, the big woman sank back into contemplating her sundries.

"Or like an eye," Brandon continued. "Indeed, quite like an eye. About the target is an old stone painting, that of the scorpion who swallows his tail, the circle and cycle of life, as the old legends have it." His voice rose in excitement at the mythology. "It is the center of the thing that draws your attention, though. Within those concentric circles there is a dark, immoveable center, a darkness next to which the surrounding blackness is gray, almost light."

"As if it led into absolute nothing," Bayard murmured.

Brandon nodded. "As it well may, sir, what little I can make out."

He turned, regarding Bayard directly.

"Whatever it is," Bayard observed, "it becomes more dangerous by the hour. It is set here to waken the worm, on that I'd wager. But as to how it will do so I can only guess."

Enid took her husband's hand, as though she was about to guide him through unfathomable dark.

"Well, why in the name of the twenty-seven gods are we prissing here at the edge of this inch-deep chasm like a flock of embroiderers," thundered Sir Robert, "when we could see to our liking if one of us had the simple fortitude to take a closer look?"

And holding high a brightly glowing lantern, he stepped forward onto the footbridge, marching securely toward the sound ahead of him.

"Wait!" Bayard cried, reaching for the rash old man. But his leg gave beneath him and he started to fall, pulling Brandon with him. Sir Robert took ten steps, and fell suddenly from view as the rock gave way beneath him. Clutching the lantern, he tumbled in the dark like a small subterranean shooting star.

"Father!" Enid shouted and stepped to the rippling edge of the chasm.

"Be still, all of you!" Bayard cried out and, steadying himself against Brandon, grabbed for his wife and held her.

Behind them, Marigold trumpeted in dismay.

"Uncle Robert has vanished with my sausages!" she exclaimed. "If we are trapped, I'll starve!"

Icily Enid stared at her most distant cousin as all about them, the men flinched involuntarily.

"Then I can only suggest you lower yourself into whatever lies in front of us, Marigold," Enid said through teeth impossibly clenched, "and retrieve them, casings and gristle and all. And do try to rescue my father if you can find the time."

But Marigold had anticipated her. Already she was waist-deep in the chasm, lowering herself into the whirling darkness with the ungainly grace of a manatee. Soon the big girl had nearly vanished, complete with bag of cosmetics, as the lacquered ship of her hair sank into the murky country below them.

* * * * *

Sir Robert di Caela lay spread-eagled on a stone table, wondering how by all the gods it had managed to cushion his fall.

Even the light in the lantern was intact.

It was welcome to Robert, this sense of his life being spared. Instantly he felt younger—thirty or forty years younger, at least as young as he felt when, as a lean and dangerous swordsman, he traveled east from Solamnia, joining a band of Knights in the Khalkist Mountains, at a little pass called Chaktamir.

It was a feeling he had almost forgotten in the habits of his old age.

Robert breathed the gray mist eagerly. It was cool, harboring the clear blue smell of ozone and imminent water, as though, beyond all possibility, this chasm lay somewhere under the sea.

Was it a shipwreck around him? Robert squinted, struggled to his feet for a better view.

Above him there were shouts, as though all of his companions were speaking to him through blankets. Someone was descending. No doubt they were concerned for his well-being.

Which is better than it has been in decades, he thought with a smile.

About him, the landscape was littered with glass and barrel staves. A sour smell rose on the charged air, reminding him of centaurs, of singing.

What were the words of the song?

> As hungry as a dwarf for gold,
> As centaurs for cheap wine.

It was a wine cellar, or the remnants of one. Robert waded slowly through the rubble. At first, he leaned against a broken-down wine rack. Slowly he examined himself for bruises or breakage. Shadows swirled above him, and a form descended through the tumbling dark until he could make out its girth and its shape and its absurd hair.

"Marigold!" he breathed in exasperation.

Robert felt his own ancient limbs. He was surprisingly intact. For a moment, he thought there might be some restoring magic to this cellar.

What seemed to have happened was that the cellar had dropped. From its previous site at the base of the Cat Tower, where a single flight of stairs had led from the light of the surface down no more than twenty feet to the finest wines in southern Solamnia, the cellar had tumbled, wine racks and barrels and all, into these depths.

Fragments of glass, covered with old wine, stuck to the soles of his boots. Nothing was intact here.

It must have fallen hundreds of feet, he thought. Almost by reflex, he looked above him, as if from this depth and this darkness, not to mention through the mist, he could see the walls of the cellar, left hanging when the floor dropped into the earth.

A clay pipe jutted from the floor beside him, rising out of sight into the darkness. But there, where pipe met floor and seemed to disappear into the rock, lay an enormous clay shield, gnomish letters inscribed on its circumference.

"The well cap!" Robert exclaimed in delight. "The cellar must have fallen through onto the damned thing!"

The well cap was cracked and moldy. Water seeped from the crack, and beneath its strained surface, Robert could hear the rumble of the mighty well.

This is a chamber of miracles, he thought triumphantly. Now losing the castle papers rests more easily on these poor old shoulders.

He looked up toward Marigold—still descending— toward his other companions, prepared to trumpet his discovery.

Someone—Brandon? Bayard?—signaled frantically. There was something dreadfully wrong up there.

Then Robert heard the yowling issue from the fissure walls. He looked about him and saw over a dozen slick white things as they crawled, orange-eyed and hissing, from the rubble and the dust and from notches and holes in the stone.

"Mariel's cats!" he marveled. "By the gods, I was right!"

But this was no time for congratulating himself. Quickly he drew his sword and crouched, lantern held high in his left hand, his seasoned blade low in his other, but far too light to an experienced hand.

He looked down. His sword was broken.

Enid watched from above as the white forms crept closer to her father, wavering and wailing.

"What in the name of Hiddukel—" Andrew began.

"Enough speculation," Brandon announced flatly. "I'm going to kill them."

The first bolt from the bow sailed through the rippling mist and pinned one of the things to an overturned barrel. It screamed like a child, that shrill, rending sound of something skidding across glass. Two of the others lunged toward it, reducing it to bone with quick, ravenous tearing and chewing.

Brandon started. He moved away from the edge of the fissure, as though the ground he stood upon had become suddenly too hot.

"Get back here, damn you!" Enid said through clenched teeth, clutching the young Knight's arm. "Killing one doesn't stop the rest of them!"

Robert straddled the well cap, crouched in an old Solamnic battle stance. The cats flitted about him, between barrel and table and crate. He could not keep track of them, but the two that were feeding he could see quite clearly.

They were pale, hairless, with the skin of a grub or a rat's tail. Their ears were large, cupped, batlike, their orange eyes bulbous, too large.

Also too large were the fangs, as though lost in the subterranean darkness, the creatures had reverted to old generations, to the saber-toothed cats whose skulls miners and gravediggers found on occasion.

One of the creatures burst from a hole in the crevasse wall and hit the floor in stride, rushing at Robert, who raised the lantern in front of it.

The cat thing slowed, bent its path around the old Knight, and ran full tilt into the stone wall with a wet, crackling sound.

Robert looked once, looked away, then looked back. It

had killed itself through its own momentum.

At once one of the cats was on the old man's left arm, biting, rending, burning in the white light of the lantern. With a quick, painful move, Robert broke the grip of the thing, hurling it across the room. It tumbled into a wine rack, then, dazed, scooted off into the dark.

Unfortunately, the lantern, too, went flying from Robert's hand as he fell. It clattered onto a shelf, rocked there for a moment, its wick sputtering, and then—miraculously—remained lit.

"Thanks be to Huma," Robert breathed, then looked to his damaged hand as the cats circled slowly.

And unaware of the danger below her, Marigold set foot on the floor of the chamber.

* * * * *

They looked like ghosts from her vantage of height. Like phosfire or moonlight rippling on gray water.

And yet they are substantial, Enid thought. Brandon's bow had shown us that.

Substantial and fierce, for the one who latched itself to her father's arm had emerged from the shadows and weaved about him with the rest of its kind.

There were more of the things every time Enid looked. Though Brandon had fired again and again, dropping creature after creature with his flawless aim, it seemed that at least one more came to take the place of each one that fell.

She shook her head as Brandon fired again, the bolt passing through two of the screeching things below him. As for Robert . . .

Robert di Caela had stretched his injured hand toward the boiling rock beneath him, felt warmth, uncomfortable warmth and wetness, and drew his hand back.

Now up with the sword hand he reached, touching the hilt of the broken sword to the swimming surface of the rock. Across the floor, Marigold approached him, her skirts lifted, the square-sailed vessel nodding atop her head. One of the cats broke out of the darkness, rushed at her madly, then balked at her heft and her withering stare. It seemed that even starvation and generations of inbreeding had not deprived the animal of its most basic instincts of survival.

Robert snorted in amusement, scooted himself against the cap, which was warm but not uncomfortable against his back. The way up the rock face lay ironically at a distance over Marigold's shoulder, the cat-things milling behind her.

Soon they would have the numbers.

Wearily Robert drew up his gauntlets from where they dangled by a rawhide cord at his belt. He put on the iron-studded gloves, wincing painfully as the leather pressed against cut and blister.

I am beyond rescue, he thought. Even if Brandon and Bayard rise to their highest heroics, they cannot possibly get to me in time. And so these gauntlets, which will be better than bare hands when Mariel's cats close in.

He smiled and braced himself, and as the lantern dimmed, he silently prepared himself for Huma's breast.

*   *   *   *   *

Above Sir Robert di Caela, things unraveled steadily. His friends looked on as the floor of the chasm milled with white, larval creatures.

"What is going on down there?" Bayard muttered with a rising fury. He had been picking up stones, heavier and heavier, and dropping them upon the flitting pale things below him. Now, winded and clutching at his leg, he leaned against Sir Andrew, his eyesight spangling with pain.

Turning from Bayard and Andrew, Enid looked desperately to her father. He leaned against the well cap, smiling grimly, resolutely, as Marigold approached him and stood beside him bravely, giving but one sidelong glance to the possibly fatal sausages she had come to retrieve. Meanwhile, the white hissing things crawled nearer.

As Enid watched, the air seemed to go white about her, and for a moment, she reeled unsteadily at the edge of the chasm.

It was Raphael who reached her first, but he lacked the weight to pull her back from the ledge. Together, locked by the arms, the two of them hovered over the gray and pooling darkness. An eager chittering rose from the swarming things below them.

And Brandon Rus's strong arm closed about the boy, dragging the two of them to safety.

For a moment, the three of them, Brandon and Raphael, with Enid atop them both, lay in a shivering heap on the solid stone of the ledge. Bayard and Andrew rushed to them, lifting the woman to her feet as Brandon scrambled up.

"Where . . . Father!" Enid shouted at once, broke from Sir Andrew's grip, and rushed back to the edge of the fissure. For a moment, Raphael, lying on his stomach, looked up and became furious as he saw her totter again, saw all his courage and risk about to amount to nothing.

Then she gained balance, squinted, and looked to the far edge of the cellar.

A light was spreading across Robert's face.

Four days ago, when he had sat half-dozing in the castle infirmary, watching as the servants danced attendance about his son-in-law and the engineers fretted in their oily sobriety, there was something . . . something . . .

"For the great well," they had said, "that lies under the castle, subject to strain and pressure through the extraordinary rainy season, is no doubt brimming and bubbling in deep recesses of rock, where only a sudden twist of the earth could unleash a flood through the floors of the towers and leave us awash in our own cistern."

And what, indeed, might this humming crack in the well cap beside him be but deliverance?

Robert laughed as Marigold swatted away one of the cats who hurtled at her and at Sir Robert's knapsack.

Well, then, Sir Robert thought. This might be a chamber of miracles, after all! And mustering his strength, he drove the hilt of his sword solidly against the crack in the casement.

Not even old Sir Andrew had seen its like. Water surged forth into the fissure like a deluge, and before he could even begin to strip off his armor, Sir Robert found himself knee-deep in a warm sulfurous tide from the artesian well.

He caught himself, rose suddenly from idleness, and

slipped off Marigold's knapsack and his breastplate.

Around him, white spectral forms scurried into the cracks of the rocks, screeching and yowling. Whatever they had become through the years and the permanent darkness, Mariel's cats were still cat enough to harbor a healthy fear of water.

Now, stripped to a linen tunic, Sir Robert rose with the water, looking once beneath him to see if Marigold was following. The lantern went out as the water reached its shelf, but in his last glimpse of the girl, he saw her neck-deep, straining to remove her knapsack of cosmetics, wedged between two solid rocks.

Robert caught his breath and tried to swim for her, but the light was gone and he could no longer locate her. Instead, his lungs burning and his muscles cramping, he treaded water, floating toward the faint light above him until, as bereft of worldly goods as a man can be without being completely naked, Sir Robert di Caela rose to the surface of the fissure, where Brandon's strong arms reached out and dragged him onto the stone.

"Marigold?" he gasped as the waters continued to rise, reaching the edge of the crevasse and brimming over. Painfully Robert gained his footing and stood beside his friends and family. Enid embraced her bedraggled father, and Bayard lifted high the lantern he was holding, its light fracturing on the surface of the rising water.

Five minutes they waited. Then ten.

Then, in the middle of the newly formed underground lake, a yellow lacquered schooner broke the surface of the water, floating absurdly at a middle distance atop the drowned, mountainous girl, who clutched her bag of cosmetics in a terrible grip that would no doubt last forever.

"The device, sir!" Brandon muttered, his voice uneasy and puzzled.

"What of it?" Bayard asked impatiently, staring across the rocking surface of the pool. The darkness swirled and congealed, permitting no vision.

"The device, sir. It remains unchecked for all this water and commotion."

Slowly, Bayard slid from the young Knight's grip and

knelt on the pooling floor of the cavern.

They had lost Marigold and gained in return less time in which to figure out the workings of whatever machinery lay across the fissure in the blackness. Disconsolately, Bayard lifted his eyes and stared into the darkness, hoping to catch a glimpse of the thing he needed to see.

"If it can't be seen, it can't be managed," he murmured.

And below him and above him—indeed on all sides of him and somehow, unexplainably, even within him—a low rumbling rose, as though the whole subterranean world was laughing.

Chapter XX

Now calmly, almost reverently, the Namer set a dark stone in a notch of the circlet. He set another, and again one more. Soon six stones lay in a glimmering field, and the Namer continued, setting and naming.

"There are all kinds of traps," he said, and his listeners shifted uneasily and looked about.

* * * * *

The vaulted room wherein Ramiro and I found ourselves was lined with nearly empty shelves, littered only with an occasional ledger, scroll, or manuscript. Leather volumes sat precariously high out of reach, their spines scrawled with lines and patterns that were either some incredibly random form of decoration or an indecipherable alphabet. Some were moldy from the ever-present damp.

It made Gileandos's library look small and shabby. What was more, since the leather was regularly oiled on most bindings, I gathered that these volumes had been read at one time or another, unlike those we had back home in the moathouse, which our tutor had collected for their thickness and mustiness and ponderous-sounding titles.

Under Gileandos's tutelage, I had never been all that much of a book lover, so for me, these volumes, too, were just interior decoration. Far more to my interest were the Que-Tana themselves, the dreadfully pale creatures who glided in and out of the room on obscure duties.

They were not much more attractive in daily activity than they were as hillside assailants. They were sort of blue-skinned, with bulbous eyes and sparse waxen hair—at first glance, more like exotic tubers than humans. Their speech was indecipherable when they addressed each other, though it sounded, as you might expect, faintly like the language Longwalker had spoken to his followers, full of hard consonants and little breathing. Yet it was no longer Que-Nara Plainsman that was spoken, but a darker tongue, filled with enormous silences and echoes and deep watery vowels that rose from the depths of the throat.

I heard the same music in their common speech when they spoke to us, their fluency drawn into the dark undertow of their subterranean accents. I thought of hot springs and geysers.

Quite abruptly, the business and noise around me died down. Adorned more formally, with beads and necklaces and carrying a tall hooked staff, Firebrand himself approached me from the far end of the porch.

"I trust you have been made comfortable?" he asked, pulling a reed chair to my bedside and seating himself.

Ramiro sidled casually within earshot. The Que-Tana, on the other hand, moved quickly away before the man was seated, attending shyly to some task on the other side of the room.

"Oh, as comfortable as can be expected," I answered in common speech.

"I see," Firebrand replied. "I fear there's little I can do regarding either your departed brother or the vespertiles, but perhaps we can see to it that your . . . remaining brother is restored to you."

"It would be about time," I said. "A whole day and a half we've been confined here, by my reckoning. And after all, my brother's release *was* the deal we struck through the opals."

Firebrand gestured dramatically, and through the door strode Brithelm, as disheveled as ever, but looking all right considering kidnap and submergence. Brithelm smiled amiably, bumped into a lectern, and sent rolls of parchment flying about him.

"Excuse me," he murmured, as Plainsmen rushed to retrieve the skittering rolls. Brithelm bent over, picked up one leaf of a manuscript, and scanned it as he walked to a sconce on the wall to get some light firmly at his back.

"Brithelm!" I shouted. "Thank the gods you're alive!"

He lifted his eyes from the page in front of him, and stared reverently toward the rock ceiling of the room.

"I thank the twenty-one gods that I am alive," he pronounced solemnly and returned to his reading.

"History!" he exclaimed delightedly. "My favorite!"

A young woman, her patience stretched beyond restraint, snatched the paper from his hand.

"Does it just go on and on about architecture?" Brithelm asked her disappointedly. "When I read history, I do love a good sword fight!"

"Well, then," Firebrand broke in, his fingers twitching with impatience. "About the deal we struck. As I recall, you have something to hand over to me, Sir Galen." He leaned forward, his dark hair spreading over his face, covering dark brow and leather eye patch and burning solitary eye.

I stood my ground. We had come to a place where neither fear nor courage made any difference. Firebrand had us—my brother, Ramiro, and me—and he would do whatever he wanted, regardless of my cowardice or bravado.

"As I understand," I replied, "you have waited centuries for what I bring you. Wait but a while longer, while I greet my brother."

I had no time for further words: Brithelm was on me, glad-handing me, thumping my back, and saying over and over again how happy he was that I had "dropped in for a visit."

His happiness, of course, made it clear that he had not heard about Alfric. But this was hardly the time for telling him. The way I had it figured, he stood to lose another brother in the coming hours.

"Actually, Galen," Brithelm said into the fresh silence as the Que-Tana drew near us and listened, "there's little else to do down here besides read and answer Firebrand's many questions."

"Many . . . questions?" I asked, looking over my brother's shoulder into the menacing eye of our captor.

"I trust, Sir Galen, that the . . . amenities have ended," he said coldly, an edge of anger in his voice. He extended his hand, palm up, and the air about us was charged, incandescent.

Slowly, reluctantly, I handed him the brooch. He trembled briefly and sighed when it lay in his hand. His Que-Tana bodyguards closed in a tight circle around him, their black eyes fierce and expectant. Ramiro, reclining all this time on a cot, rose to his feet and stood by me, looming.

"Now," I said as Firebrand lifted the brooch to the light, examining it ecstatically, "there is the matter of our leaving. . . ."

"You have seen one another again, have you not?" he asked gruffly, his eye never leaving the glittering opals. "That is all I promised, if I remember correctly."

"Why, you mountebank of a . . ." Ramiro began, but the presence of a dozen glaring bodyguards rendered him discrete and silent.

Lowering the brooch and pinning it delicately to the shoulder of his robe, as smoothly and effortlessly as a woman prepares her jewelry for a banquet, Firebrand fixed his eye on me, regarding me directly. An ironic smile flickered across his face.

"You would make none too good a lawyer . . . *Weasel*, isn't it?" he asked playfully. "Oh, yes, I know all of that business, for the stones in my crown allowed me to watch you finagle your way about that little backwater castle as you came into knighthood. You were better as a weasel, lad, with your sly-ness and gutter smarts. If you had left Brithelm where he was, had backed off from your foolhardy venture while you had the chance, you'd still have another brother in the Bright Lands. Indeed, you'd still have years ahead of you."

He paused, rolling the staff in his dark hand.

"As it is, the years compress into minutes, and the Pathwardens themselves dwindle rapidly. I expect that your father back in Solamnia will think little of that honor of yours when he measures it against the lives of three sons and the death of his name."

I started to answer him, but the words fled down a dark corridor, leaving me alone and speechless and downright miserable, knowing that beneath all Solamnic show and glitter, my father's heart would agree with this villain, that through the years remaining for the old man, a part of him would hate me for my high-minded stupidity, for the chiv-alry that cost him all his heirs. Firebrand stared at me and nodded, assured that his words had drawn the deepest blood.

"I'll take him for you, lad, entourage or not!" Ramiro whispered at my shoulder.

I shook my head disconsolately as the captor's words con-tinued to sink and settle.

"Hardly the talk of a philosopher-king, Master Namer!" another familiar voice called out heartily behind me. I turned to see Shardos, his hands tied, escorted by two Plainsmen into the swimming light of the library.

"What would you know of philosophy, sirrah?" Fire-brand growled, gripping the staff tightly.

"Oh . . . not that much," Shardos replied, stepping away from his guards and walking cautiously across the chamber. He came to the very lectern against which Brithelm had stumbled and stepped around it deftly. "Not that much. Only that it keeps a man from twitching after visions."

"Is that so?" Firebrand asked, the anger rising in his voice. Then suddenly the anger rushed from him. His shoulders slumped and his eye softened, and he stared at the old jug-gler with a look of surprise and fascination.

"Attend to the gentleman!" he snapped at the guards. "Can't you see that he is blind?"

Gruffly brushing aside the pale helping hands, Shardos seated himself atop a library table, his large hands gripping the yellowed wood. His blank eyes scanned the room.

I coughed loudly, intentionally. His gaze uncannily fastened on me.

"Sir Galen," he said quietly, a strange half-smile on his face. "It appears that we are all together again."

"Except . . ." Ramiro began absently and caught himself. His meaty faced flushed with embarrassment at the prospect of almost having betrayed Dannelle's escape to the Que-Tana.

But Shardos caught the words and juggled them gracefully. "Of course," he said quickly. "Except for my dog, whom I shall miss sorely."

"Who is this man, Galen?" Firebrand asked, walking slowly toward the old man.

"Shardos is my name," the juggler replied. "Traveler, jongleur, purveyor of history and lore, and juggler to the courts of seven kings."

"I see," Firebrand said, a note of suspicion creeping into his voice. "A juggler, you say?"

The Que-Tana Namer stood his ground now, a good knife's throw from the table and from Shardos. It was as though a wall of light lay between them, transparent but impenetrable. Firebrand circled Shardos, staring at him from every side, and it occured to me that our captor was afraid.

Afraid, no doubt, because he had not seen this man in his vaunted visions.

"A juggler? But—"

"It is every man's question," Shardos interrupted. "And there is no answer but in the juggling itself."

The Plainsmen guards moved toward the blind man, but Firebrand raised his hand, waved them away.

"Juggler and . . . purveyor of lore?"

"Balance and sleight of hand are more common than they used to be, sir," Shardos replied merrily. "Nowadays a man has to branch out—to sing and tell stories while the bottles tumble butt over neck in the air. Mere jugglery is a poor man's trade, but you can eat when you throw in song and tale amidst the fruit and crockery."

"Shall we escort him somewhere, Namer?" one of the guards asked.

"Song and tale?" Firebrand asked, ignoring his underling. Absently he walked to the obstructing lectern, his back to the juggler.

Almost as absently, Shardos began to sing:

> "In the country of the blind,
> Where the one-eyed man is king
> And the stones are eyes of gods
> And pathways to remembering . . ."

"Enough!" Firebrand shouted, clutching the sides of the lectern. The silver circlet he wore on his head flickered with a dark light, and smoke blossomed from beneath his grasping fingers, singeing the wood.

Ramiro and I glanced sidelong at each other, and my big companion emitted a low whistle.

"Not fully mounted, this one," he whispered to me as Firebrand spun toward Shardos with a rattle of bead and bone and a creaking of leather.

"So a snatch of old song comes back to you, juggler?" Firebrand asked, and what little civility was left in his voice he had banished entirely. "But your primary talent . . . is *legerdemain*, is it not?"

Shardos said nothing, his gaze fixed somewhere far beyond his adversary. With a quick, powerful lunge, Firebrand stepped directly in front of the old man, gathering objects from the lectern as he moved—an ink bottle, a book, a piece of parchment, and finally a small, sharp, glittering penknife. Extending his hands to the juggler, the Que-Tana Namer smiled wickedly.

"Juggle these," he hissed. "Juggle these, or you shall find things most . . . excruciating for your comrades."

Though I knew nothing of the juggler's art, I knew that the task before Shardos was a formidable one. Four items, each of different shape and weight, made for a clumsy performance, and the introduction of the piece of parchment, which would flutter and catch on the slightest breath in the chamber, was surpassing cruel to any man in Shardos's line of work, much less a blind man.

But Shardos took the objects with a smile and, standing atop the library table, held them aloft while he surveyed the room with that penetrating, vacant stare. Almost instinctually, the Que-Tana began to crowd around him, Firebrand included, until only four of our captors remained beside us.

Almost instinctually in turn, Ramiro and I glanced at one another, reckoning the odds.

Three of our Plainsmen escorts were formidable enough, in their paint and leather, their sharp spears at the ready. But the fourth one, a man at least a head taller than Ramiro, looked as sturdy as a vallenwood, though I doubted he was much brighter. Nonetheless, his line of work did not partake of higher mathematics. Even the usually dauntless Ramiro looked once at the menacing hulk beside him and shook his head.

We would have to wait for other options to arise. But what was it Longwalker had said, miles above me and days away from me, by a fire at the foot of the mountains?

"Sometimes the waiting is the doing."

"It will be a feat justly celebrated!" Shardos began, holding the strange, disparate objects in plain sight above the nodding heads of the Plainsmen. "These objects, as unlike as poet and soldier, no more kin to each other than godseye miner and forest-dwelling elf, will find their way and their proper place in the great turning of things, where the wheeling path of the book in the air crosses that of the ink bottle."

Quietly, as Shardos held the attention of his audience, Firebrand slipped from the edge of the crowd and moved to a far point in the dimly lit chamber, where he was lost among shadows and leaning shelves.

Frantically I tried to see where he had gone. With the opals in tow, he was no doubt looking for a private spot, away from the eyes of his people and his prisoners, where he could be about the ensorcellments that Longwalker dreaded so. And surely with the opals in tow, he would no longer find any of us useful.

My thoughts were darkening quickly, and I might well

have sunk into the stupors and sorrows, had Shardos's act not become suddenly interesting.

"In my travels," the juggler said, "I have found it often a delight to sing for my hosts while I juggle." He cleared his throat dramatically.

"A delight indeed," Ramiro whispered ironically.

"Oh, yes, Ramiro!" chorused my brother, on whom all irony was lost. "I love a singer as much as a sword fight!"

"Hush! Both of you!" I muttered, and Shardos continued.

"Unfortunately, I have fallen on hard times in my travels, and fallen in with a rather . . . rough-hewn company in my later years. I am afraid that the only juggling songs I remember are a bit on the racy side for the women and children among you. . . ."

"That's absurd!" Ramiro commented. "The old bastard remembers *everything*!"

"Hush!" I repeated.

"Therefore," Shardos announced, "I shall sing the salty chorus in its original language, so as not to offend the more delicate ears in our midst."

Ramiro looked at me and frowned. I winked at him solemnly. For the "slyness and gutter smarts" that Firebrand accused me of were spinning and focusing like elaborate gnomish machinery. Something was afoot, and we would not be long in the finding out.

I looked back to Shardos just in time to see the ungainly juggling begin.

How Shardos was able to send that paper tumbling through the windless air, wrapping bottle and book and knife around it, is beyond me to this day. Perhaps it was more sleight of hand than jugglery. Whatever the case, my attentions were fixed not on the objects, but on the words of the old man's song, beginning, as you might expect, in the common speech.

> *"Your one true love's a sailing ship*
> *That anchors at our pier.*
> *We lift her sails, we man her decks,*
> *We scrub the portholes clear."*

Then, atop the same old marching tune, the song slid into
Old Solamnic, a language familiar to only three of Shardos's
listeners: Ramiro, Brithelm, and me.

> *"They do not understand this part,*
> *They stand around and gape,*
> *They think I'm after dirty things*
> *Instead of your escape."*

A dozen sets of eyes turned to us. I confess I was gaping
myself, stunned at the old man's brass.

Then my brother, the innocent fool of my imaginings, began to laugh. He looked at me, repeated "your escape" in a
loud Old Solamnic, punctuating it with an ancient, obscene
hand sign that would have made even Marigold blush.

The Plainsmen had not been underground forever. They
began to laugh at my brother, and I found myself laughing,
too—not at the gesture as much as the sheer bizarreness of
seeing my brother make it.

Meanwhile, Shardos continued in common speech, the
bawdy trail song filling the room.

> *"And, yes, our lighthouse shines for her,*
> *And, yes, our shores are warm;*
> *We steer her into harbor—*
> *Any port in a storm.*
>
> *"The sailors stand upon the docks,*
> *The sailors stand in line,*
> *As thirsty as a dwarf for gold*
> *Or centaurs for cheap wine."*

Then, in an ancient and surprisingly graceful dancer's
turn, the old juggler spun himself about on the stage. Uncannily the piece of parchment flattened itself in the air, lying steady as though it still rested upon the lectern from
which Firebrand had taken it. About it, the book and the
bottle and the knife wheeled on their own, as though set in
motion by some primordial design, and Shardos sang more
verses, again in Old Solamnic.

> *"Follow where you saw him go*
> *Out through the corridor,*
> *The legends say his allies*
> *Are those you've fought before,*

> *"I can't make hide nor hair of that;*
> *You should expect the worst,*
> *There is a legend tied to this*
> *I'll save for the final verse."*

He smirked, painfully aware that his rhymes were straining. But we were after directions, not aesthetics. All three of us laughed, and the dark-eyed Que-Tana nodded and smiled among themselves, sure that some naughtiness lay in the Old Solamnic.

With a flourish, Shardos pocketed the paper, then the ink bottle, as he sang yet one more verse in common.

> *"For all the sailors love her*
> *And flock to where she's moored,*
> *Each man hoping that he might*
> *Go down, all hands on board."*

The adult Plainsmen chuckled at the suggestions of the verse, as did three of our guards. The fourth one, the dense enormity at Ramiro's side, stared in wonder at the book and knife, which continued to circle one another in the air.

Shardos smiled, stamped his foot, and pocketed the book as he began a final verse in Solamnic.

> *"No matter what you see or hear*
> *Avoid the thirteenth stone,*
> *And no matter what you think*
> *Leave the crown alone."*

As the last Solamnic "alone" crossed his lips, the juggler plucked the knife from the air. But instead of hiding it away, as he had all the other objects, Shardos wheeled toward us suddenly and hurled the blade end over end through the cavern.

It glittered in torchlight as it tumbled through the air and lodged in the chest of the big bodyguard.

For a moment, everyone was stunned. The enormous Plainsman looked stupidly down at his chest, then, as though his wound was only then dawning on him, tumbled to his knees and, with a wordless outcry, onto his face.

There was a brief, familiar pause, as there often is when first blood is drawn in a skirmish between inexperienced fighters, when both sides stop, see what has been wrought, and take in the knowledge that this is real, that the fighting is for keeps and is only beginning.

Then, like some enormous fluked monster rising from the depths of the Blood Sea, Ramiro lurched free of the guards, grabbed the nearest Plainsman by his long, braided hair, and sent the man hurtling into the nearest wall, rattling a torch from its sconce in the process.

Throughout the large stone room, lights were extinguished and things hurled, and the dry curses and calls of the Que-Tana bounced off the tricky walls. I threw my first stone—at the nearest of my foes, of course, for I figured there was no point to any jugglery of my own.

The rock clattered harmlessly past the dried grass stool on which Firebrand had sat, and my target crouched and loaded a sling.

With a deft move of his hand, now glowing with a simple but surprisingly powerful clerical magic, Brithelm seized the wrist of a large Plainsman who was choking Shardos. In my brother's grip, the Que-Tana passed at once into deep, snoring sleep on the cavern floor as Brithelm turned to face further onslaught and Shardos caught his breath again.

Something blurred in the air in front of me, a dark thing flying out of the dappled torchlight, and I had no time to move or fear or even reflect . . .

And a dark, deft hand plucked the stone from the air, as neatly as it had once caught crockery in the wealthy halls of Palanthas and in floating palaces on the Blood Sea.

Quickly Shardos hurled the rock back into the milling Plainsmen, end over end into the rising shadow. In the vanguard of that mass of robes and pale skin, one shadow fell, clutching at its side.

Then Ramiro rushed in the wake of the stone, scattering Plainsmen as he waded in among our adversaries. His meaty fist found the face of a Plainsman warrior. Blood spouted from the pale man's septum, and his eyes rolled back in his head as he fell to the stone floor, scattering beads and teeth.

Bellowing with delight, Ramiro dodged the downward arc of a Que-Tana club, and as the wielder staggered, the big Knight planted his wide, hobnailed boot squarely on the backside of the Plainsman and propelled him headfirst into three of his approaching comrades, who toppled like drunks at a country fair. Caught up in the rampage, the big man hurdled a downed stalagmite, felling two stalactites when he leapt too high in his enthusiasm. Staggering, he caught one of the stone icicles before it hit the ground and brought the heavy thing whistling up into the groin of yet another approaching enemy. Another he struck, and then another, until his dangerous path brought him to a dropped sword. Puffing, he crouched over, picked it up, and came up in the stance that the ogres call "the Feminator."

Twenty Plainsmen crouched involuntarily and took a step back, which gave Brithelm a chance to reach Ramiro's side. Together the two of them, a most unlikely tandem, backed toward the shelves at the far end of the chamber, forming as they did a narrow passage through the windmilling confusion of robe and armor and weapon.

"Go on, lad!" Shardos shouted in my ear above the cries of the Plainsmen. I resisted his push, for since the Solamnic Order was closing with the Que-Tana at last, it seemed that the only fitting action was to answer their blows.

Shardos restrained me.

"We can hold them back only a little while," he said merrily, a curious smile spreading over his face. "And after all, who better to send burrowing after vermin than a weasel?"

He pushed me again, and this time I was on my way, straight toward the ponderous shelves at the end of the chamber.

I slipped behind Brithelm and Ramiro, the bluish arms of the Plainsmen reaching for me, clutching, grabbing. Brithelm had spread a green, unnatural spellfire through the chamber, and for a minute, our adversaries recoiled, overwhelmed by light.

Blinded a little myself by the brilliant glow, I staggered until my eyes adjusted, until the shadowy outline of the shelves emerged from the dazzlement. Recovering my bearings, I raced toward the far entrance.

But I had lost valuable time.

Ahead of me, racing to cut off my escape, a lean, fierce-looking Plainsman half again my size positioned himself and raised a glistening onyx war hammer. I took a long, gathering step and leapt into him, and the two of us crashed to the floor, the hammer skittering harmlessly into the wall in front of me.

Then, for the first time in a long time, I had my eldest brother Alfric to thank. For in the forgotten arenas of the moathouse, he had sharpened my wrestling well, in a childhood when to be a little brother was to dodge, to scramble, to grapple with things larger than yourself.

Larger the man was, but also surprisingly fragile. In a moment, I was atop him, his head in my hands. I twisted my arms abruptly, and the snapping sound that followed seemed to echo in a deep and silent chasm far from the shouting and clash of metal around me.

As I knelt there, the imagined silence gave way to the outcry behind me. Then two strong hands lifted me, and I recognized my brother Brithelm's voice as he coaxed and assured me with words that I could not recognize then nor remember now, and together we rose and raced from a land of chaos and knives into the far shadows and the cold corridor beyond.

Chapter XXI

"Steep" and "formidable" were indeed the words for it.

With Brithelm leading, we took every downward path imaginable, all of which seemed to circle as though we descended through the whorls of a shell. My brother guided us through the torchlit passages that crisscrossed and doubled back on themselves, and when a sudden gust of wind from a side corridor extinguished the flames ahead of us, he guided us by an unexpected glow from the tips of his fingers.

The walls of the corridor were scratched with graffiti in the swirling alphabet of the Plainsmen. Names, Brithelm said they were mostly, as we hastened by them—names and religious slogans in which he said he could find no clear theology.

As we descended even farther, the letters gave way to pictographs and drawings of bats and tenebrals. There was one disconcertingly deft drawing of an enormous vespertile closing its monstrous, leathery wings around a band of Que-Tana. The drawing was abstract, almost childlike, and it summoned a deep and rousing fear within me, and evidently also in Brithelm, for he clutched the front of my tunic when I stopped to stare at the scene, then pulled me onward.

I thought of Oliver, shuddered, and doubled my pace.

Those drawings gave way to yet others of surface animals such as horses and leopards and, occasionally, birds. The two moons, red and silver, careened over a herd of pegasi. Finally a city lay toppled to its foundations, surrounded by designs and patterns only, abstract and geometrical, squares and spheres and rhomboids and a strange, geometrical man astride it, his head among the clouds and a swath of soot from a nearby sconce obscuring his face and eyes.

It was the final drawing; the walls were bare as we descended even farther. We had gone too deep for tenebrals, into the very core of the mountain.

Deeper still we went, past where vespertile guano caked the walls and floors of the corridor, to a depth where bone and shards of strange pottery were all that kept the tunnels from a sort of smooth sameness of milky brown rock. Then even bone and broken earthenware gave way to clean tunnels that were unnaturally dark and quiet, as if at some point we had crossed a border into a region where living things could not long abide.

"So this leads us to Firebrand, you say?" I asked my brother, who weaved in and out of the light.

"Surely it does, Galen," he replied. "I've been in those very quarters, but they blindfolded me on the way there and back. So instead of firsthand experience, I shall rely on a sort of . . . scholarly pursuit."

He smiled and looked at me directly.

"I saw the maps in that library back there, and I have pieced together the directions from the library to Firebrand's quarters with only a little research and common sense. This is the way, I am reasonably certain. It leads not only to Firebrand, but to his quarters and no doubt to the Namer's Tunnel and the secret passage back up to the surface."

He stopped in the tunnel, pausing in movement and thought until I nearly lost balance trying to keep from running into him. He looked at me wryly and frowned.

"At least I suppose so," he concluded.

"At a thousand feet beneath the surface," I snapped, "one does not rest well with supposings, Brother."

To that he was silent, dodging ahead of me like something frayed and insubstantial.

Now, Brithelm was never all that reliable in a library.

To him, a wealth of books was like a mountain range tunneled through by an army of mad dwarves—much like the terrain we found ourselves in at the time. For just when he would get going in his research, would follow a fact or a thought or a phrase from one book to the next, something new and more interesting in that next book would catch him off guard and lure him away as though he had followed an interesting side tunnel, until he would lose himself in the maze of his own interests, having forgotten entirely what had brought him to the library in the first place.

As a result, my brother believed that the Cataclysm was the result of the "double cellars" popular in Istar almost three centuries ago, and that although legend blamed the Kingpriest of that city for the disaster, true blame resided in the architect who, in a reckless attempt to create space in cramped properties near the center of town, chose to build one basement under another and undermine the foundations of block after block of ancient buildings.

Brithelm also believed there were walking trees in Estwilde and that the men of Ergoth had eyes in the back of their heads, through which they could see the past. He believed in a third black moon.

Nor was my brother's research any better on things closer to home: As a boy, growing up in a house where religious observance was rare, he decided that he would celebrate major religious holidays, but he never could figure out or understand the idea of movable feasts. Yes, the feasts moved, but not according to anyone else's calendar. Sometimes we would celebrate Yule in summer, sometimes in spring.

It turned out that Brithelm began to confuse regular holidays with those movable feasts, until he would wake each of us on odd days with the announcement that "Today is your birthday." And though each of us recognized the mistake full well, none of us ever corrected him, eager as we were for the presents. Brithelm, after all, was the only generous Pathwarden.

Though I am not quite twenty, by his tally and because of my greed, at last count I have celebrated fifty-seven birthdays.

All of this is a long way of saying that I was afraid that the research had misfired again. Here we were, a quarter of a mile below light and fresh air, trusting in a common sense that had not displayed itself as all that prominent a Pathwarden quality, and a sense of direction that might well lead us back into the jaws of vespertiles or worse.

My legs were tired, and the air was fetid. I was feeling my fifty-seven years.

After a while, our wandering became an issue. There in the bare corridors, I completely abandoned my hope in my brother's judgment.

"Suppose with me for a second, Brithelm," I suggested as we came puffing to a junction of tunnel and tunnel. "Just suppose. What if . . . those rooms are no longer a Namer hideaway of sorts? What if they're used for something entirely different? Or used not at all—those rooms you read about?"

"It will not matter," Brithelm stated flatly, coming to a sudden stop in the corridor so that I nearly ran into him. "It will not matter, because this is not the way to the rooms I read about."

He turned to me sheepishly.

I imagined us there in the corridor—lost entirely and completely and no doubt forever, white bones moldering into the history of the caverns and tunnels as our small intrusion into the lives of the Que-Tana faded to a footnote in one of the massive histories we had seen in the Porch of Memory.

I hadn't the heart to rail at Brithelm, who could not be blamed that his readings had gone awry. Our mission, I am

afraid, was further imperiled by the fact that we had no
weapons. In our ignited exit from the Porch of Memory, we
had left anything fit for menace lying among papers and
crumpled Que-Tana.

"There is, however, another way to find the path to Firebrand," Brithelm said, squinting into the corridor ahead of
us.

I looked at him expectantly.

"Let us stand here until we can figure out what it is," he
suggested. He sat calmly on the floor of the corridor, drew
forth his spectacles, and put them on.

"Brithelm, I really think that—"

"Hush, Brother. Hush. Sit here and join me."

I seated myself at his side. I fidgeted as I thought of the
Namer somewhere, fixing the stones into his crown, preparing to receive the power of life and death while I joined my
brother in wool-gathering.

"Have you a scarf, Galen?" Brithelm whispered.

"I beg your pardon?"

"A scarf," Brithelm repeated, graciously but firmly. "Or a
bandanna. Or even a sleeve that you do not need."

"No, I'm afraid I— Stop it!"

I clutched him by the shoulders and spun him around to
face me.

"Listen to me, Brithelm! We are not in the best of straits
here. There are a thousand Que-Tana who would gladly
skin us alive, and their leader is somewhere on these prem-
ises thinking he's about to translate himself into a deity and
is ready to destroy the lot of us in the whole harebrained
venture, and we are the only ones who can stop him, and we
are seated in the middle of an empty corridor discussing fabric and accessories like a damned pair of ladies-in-waiting!"

"I want you to blindfold me, Brother," Brithelm replied serenely. "If scholarship alone does not work, I shall have to
recreate the circumstances under which I visited the Namer's
quarters. It is the best of our hopes."

In resignation, in fatigue, perhaps in a bit of despair, I lay
back on the floor of the corridor, resting my head against
cool stone for a moment.

Then voices arose—a strange echoing in the rock, rising

from the stone itself, as voices in a closed room will reach you when you set the mouth of a ceramic cup to the door and listen.

Voices I could not untangle from each other.

"Nor will we tarry that long before the light returns and the mountains settle . . .

"Here the text speaks of fire, of fire and stone and memory . . ."

"They are not edible, those tenebrals, and the sooner you . . ."

". . . and of course it will be the best of hunts, for you are sturdy and strong and of age and a chieftain's son . . ."

"It is pretty bad, Weasel . . ."

Then, above all of these, a last voice rising shrill and mournful and filled with the music of a cold, impassable desert.

" . . . does not lie. But this might be the first. Oh, find them, find them. Together we will learn their language. Together the darkness will take away shame and fire and the hurt, hurt, hurt in your eye and spreading through your veins now, so that you cannot eat. And when you have found the stones, when you have found them, none may return to tell them where you are. At least for the girl and the old blind man, make it painless as the god has taught you . . ."

I started to my feet, and the voices stopped.

There was no waiting this out.

"Just close your eyes, idiot!" I snapped. "Close your eyes and follow your homing instincts, and if we survive this and you ever breathe a word of it to anyone in the Order or out of it, for that matter, I shall . . . I shall . . . fashion something that makes igniting Gileandos look like a purification ritual!"

"Now," Brithelm whispered, and closed his eyes as he stood up. The faintest green glow arose from his hands, which were clasped behind him as casually as if he were out for a morning stroll.

Where we were going, and what it had to do with Firebrand, for that matter, I had yet to figure out. But I followed my brother's lead, the luminous green hands stretched out ahead of me, weaving and floating like a tenebral.

It was no more than a brief span before the outline of my brother—shoulders, shadowy robe, jungle of unkempt hair—rose out of the darkness in complete silhouette. Which meant, of course, that somewhere ahead of us was another source of light.

It shone from beneath a warped oaken door, marred by stain and rot, by what time and water do to the things we build. The door was barely ajar and probably could never be closed completely anymore.

Frantically I watched as closely as I could—for details, for signs, for clues as to what we might be up against—and awaited my brother's direction.

"I do not know what we have been led to," Brithelm cautioned from the murk ahead of me, "but it's as likely the Namer's quarters as anything."

By the dim light, I saw him drop to his knees and crawl forward until he reached the door. There he stayed for the longest while, his face turned from me.

From his posture, I assumed he was praying, meditating, or otherwise observing, so I waited the proper and reverent time, though I must confess that I grew impatient.

"Remember us also in your prayers, Brother," I urged. "Then remember us *here*, if you would, for I await your instruction."

"Firebrand is behind the door," Brithelm whispered without turning to face me. "He is alone and reveling, having affixed most of the stones to his crown."

"Why, that's . . . *astounding*, Brithelm!" I breathed. "How . . . how can you be so sure? Visions? Augury? Some kind of telepathic trance?"

He turned to me, smiling, a short beam of light cast across his face as if it rose from the door itself.

"Keyholes, Galen. The future unfolds through keyholes. I would have thought you remembered *that* much."

Outside the door, we readied ourselves. Brithelm crouched again in the keyhole light, while I searched the walls and floors for substantial stones—stones for throwing, in case the circumstances called for such.

"It has been my experience," Brithelm whispered, "that surprise will succeed on almost any front, in almost any circumstance. And usually weapons are not needed."

"I do not recall asking you to draw on your considerable battle experience, Brithelm," I hissed.

We both stood silent outside the door of Firebrand's chambers. From within, the light dipped and altered as someone passed between it and the door—someone moving in directions and paths we could not see, intoning something dreadfully important, no doubt.

I could swear there were two voices in the room.

"It's like Father says, Galen," Brithelm offered, moving toward me in a rustle of red robe, placing his hand on my shoulder.

"I know, I know," I muttered, eyes on the stone floor, which I feared would soon pool with my blood.

"I know you know, but say it with me," Brithelm urged.

"I am no doubt going to die with you, Brother. Grant me the dignity of not repeating Father's rural slogans."

"Now, Galen," Brithelm cautioned merrily, ruffling my tangle of red hair. For a moment, it was as if there was no danger approaching. It was as though we were somewhere back at the moathouse—oh, sixteen or seventeen years ago—and he, the only Pathwarden with a talent for caretaking, was coaxing little Weasel to take his medicine.

Brithelm and I looked directly at one another and spoke in unison one of Father's most time-honored sayings.

" 'Them not skinning can at least hold a leg.' "

I opened the door and we burst suddenly into the room, armed with gathered stones and courage and not a small portion of folly. Dazed for a moment by the bewildering array of torches in the chambers, we looked about aimlessly, stumbling over rock and declivity, searching for Firebrand, for anything or anyone.

Then the light receded, and Firebrand was revealed sitting on a wicker throne in the far corner of the chamber, an unfathomable smile upon his face. Above his head he held the silver Namer's crown of the Que-Nara. And in the midst of that circlet were set thirteen black, gleaming stones.

"We're too late!" I hissed to Brithelm, who nodded in alarm.

"Now from these stones will arise my greater power," Firebrand intoned, his voice rising hysterically as he raised his arms. "I am disappointed in you, Brithelm. Disappointed that, when you might have been my first priest in the Bright Lands, you chose to bury your nose in books of physics and history and . . . and fauna, idling away your hour of greatness."

"I have been known to dawdle," Brithelm agreed.

Firebrand's eyes rested keenly on the two of us.

"But now your high tide recedes, as they say," he announced. "Your little rescue story comes to a close, Solamnic. For my translation awaits me."

With that, he set the circlet on his head.

He smiled. "All quiet," he said. "Even the Voice is silent before the power of life and death."

Something echoed through the caverns around us—something deep and sorrowful and altogether bereft. Above me and below me and somewhere else in the distance, I heard a great wail and outcry, and before me Firebrand's good eye rolled upward in the socket, its iris and dark pupil vanishing into a milky whiteness as though the Namer was in the midst of trance or seizure.

They tell me that above ground, in the Bright Lands that the Que-Tana had almost forgotten, the namers and chieftains and those with a bent toward wisdom heard wailing, too, but their wisdom was not great enough to understand what had just taken place. As far south as the Eastwall Mountains and the Thar-Thalas River they heard it, mistaking it for the distant cry of birds, and yet at the edge of the Plains of Dust, a group of herb-gathering Que-Teh stopped, bewildered, and stared at the greenery in their hands. The cry faded away somewhere far to the north of them, and they could no longer remember how or why to concoct with the herbs.

Hunters from the Que-Shu tribe, it is said, lost the ancestral trail into antelope country even as they traveled upon it. The people wandered for weeks. Several of the old ones starved. I have heard also that Longwalker's opals flickered and went dull and dim.

Almost as quickly as he had lapsed into abstraction, Firebrand recovered, his good eye dark and alert and piercing.

"Oh, I see it all now," he murmured, as quietly as you would speak if you approached a rare and timid bird in a clearing, where even the slightest disruption and noise would set the discovery to wing. "I see it all. . . ."

No matter how quietly he spoke, though, the words carried in the echoing chamber, buoyed by the emotion in his voice and the cavernous, reflecting walls.

"And now from these walls will arise my great people," Firebrand intoned. "Will arise those whom the Rending took, and the years, and the wars and the fires and the floods and the search for the stones themselves."

"Climbing the Cat Tower," I whispered to Brithelm.

But Firebrand continued, his voice lower now, and calmer.

"Those taken and perhaps not taken, but those that your memory summons in a night of bad dreams. And the choices you make, as always, will be wrong."

He waved his hand, and through the walls of the cavern it came, passing through smoothly and readily, as though the rock was mist or smoke.

In front of us was the troll from the rain-soaked highlands. In its eyes was a terrible, surpassing weariness, as if it had been called from something more than sleep or labor. From something we could not know yet.

Firebrand folded his hands ceremoniously. As he began, I started for him, stone in hand, but Brithelm grabbed me by the shoulders.

"Whatever it is, it is over, Galen," Brithelm explained. "He called this troll to life hours ago."

"You are right, Brother Brithelm," Firebrand whispered. "Go to your death knowing you could have shared in this glory."

Firebrand chanted yet again, something in an old and corrupt version of the Plainsman tongue, and a hot wind passed through the room, carrying on its waves the sound of an ancient wailing.

The troll came toward us, its yellowed teeth bared.

"He's conjured this up, Brithelm," I whispered urgently. "All you have to do in circumstances such as this is not put faith in the vision."

"The eyes can be deceptive, Brother," Brithelm agreed uneasily. "And yet I do not believe—"

"You taught me this long ago in 'Warden Swamp," I declared confidently. "You taught me that the way to deal with illusions is simply to disbelieve them, simply to go about your business and let them break like waters around you."

Brithelm cleared his throat, but I was halfway to the throne and Firebrand before he could speak. Swiftly the troll stepped between me and the Namer, but I looked beyond the formidable image and kept walking straight into the glaring, leering product of my enemy's imagination. And bumped into tough leathery skin, into muscle and gristle and claw.

"Galen!" Brithelm called out as I tumbled through the air into the rocks some twenty feet from my enormous and tangible foe. Dazed, I recovered my faculties just in time to see Firebrand climb a rope ladder into a tunnel halfway up the far wall, then pull the ladder up after him.

Just in time to see the troll turn and lurch toward me, finger-long claws switching and lashing in the dead air of the chamber.

Chapter XXII

*I came to as Brithelm crouched over me in the Nam-*er's chambers, as Firebrand vanished in the dark of the tunnel above us. It was still possible to get to the villain—my years of pastry and idleness at Castle di Caela had not yet slowed me to the point that I could not catch a one-eyed man in the dark.

There was, however, the matter of the troll in front of us.

"I thought you said that thing was an illusion," I whined, rising painfully to my feet.

Brithelm smiled and shrugged. "You have it mixed up with all those satyrs back in 'Warden Swamp," he said and backed away as the troll approached, smacking his lips, breaking a long stalagmite from the chamber floor, then waving it above his head like a baton.

I looked about me. Suddenly the rocks I could gather and throw seemed much too small, my brother much too weak an ally, and all that vaunted Solamnic training was like Dannelle's riding instruction—well and good in the thinking about it, but dangerous in the face of the real thing.

The troll rushed between us, striking the stone floor a shivering blow. The chamber shook, and for a moment, I thought the troll had shaken it. But it shook again, and the monster lost its footing, stringing slobber through the air as it staggered and turned.

Serenely Brithelm picked up a rock and bounced it harmlessly off the troll's leathery nose. The monster's eyes crossed in consternation, and it looked up in search of its assailant.

"Over here!" Brithelm warbled. And then "Over here!" echoed in the cavernous chamber from somewhere behind the troll. Stupidly the monster turned toward the sound of the echo.

Brithelm winked and called out again.

"Oh, yoo-hoo!"

The troll pivoted left in a complete circle and staggered a little.

I crouched and picked up a couple of stones. Then I saw that my brother was spinning the creature again and again, in slow circles, toward the rockface and the tunnel.

Brithelm sat down, crowed, and flashed green flame from his waving hands, and the troll, who had crouched for a better whack at its target, paused for a moment, dizzy and uncertain at the prospect of this fire.

In a split second, I understood Brithelm's tactic.

The troll crouched, and its gray, knotty back formed an incline of sorts, its shoulders no more than a good athletic leap from the mouth of the corridor above us. Before I could consider further, I was running, building up speed across the floor of the cavern, and the monster had only started to turn when I vaulted onto its backside like a kender acrobat, my legs still churning and arms windmilling, the sheer momentum carrying me up the steep incline of the back onto its shoulders and, in a leap sparked more by fear than by strength or dexterity, headfirst into the mouth of the tunnel.

* * * * *

Firebrand's putting on the crown had done more than muster trolls from the masonry. I have heard that down the hall from us, where Shardos and Ramiro were failing against impossible numbers of Que-Tana, the skirmish stopped as suddenly as it had begun. Blearily, the Plainsmen gaped at one another, thoroughly lost and distracted by a wave of darkness that passed through their hearts. All around the echoing library, staff and sling and spear toppled to the floor as the Que-Tana fighters struggled to recover their bearings.

Ramiro, of course, was battle-hardened enough to know an advantage when he saw one. Despite fatigue and bruises, at once he grabbed Shardos's wrist and lurched in the direction Brithelm and I had gone, intending to cut a path through the Plainsmen around him on his way to rejoining us.

Shardos, however, was having none of it. To everyone's surprise, but especially Ramiro's, the old juggler braced himself on the stony floor of the chamber. Ramiro stopped, puffed angrily, turned to berate the blind man . . . and discovered a chamberful of wide dark eyes, staring at the two of them expectantly.

The caverns began to tilt then, to shake and rumble ominously.

"The one-eye," one of the Plainsman said tentatively, looking about him uneasily as dust and gravel tumbled from the dome of the chamber. "The one-eye. The Namer. He is not . . ."

The lean, pale Que-Tana paused, his brow wrinkled.

"I do not remember a Namer. What is he supposed to be?"

"Look around you," Shardos said confidently. "Where is the one-eye when the world shakes?"

"But he is the Namer!" a young woman protested. "He keeps . . . keeps . . ." A look of profound uncertainty passed over her face.

"Keeps *what?*" Shardos pressed eagerly, freeing his gnarled arm from Ramiro's grasp.

"I . . . I do not remember, except the Namer knows," the

woman replied. "He also knows the way to the Bright Lands."

Several of the Que-Tana looked nervously toward the roof of the chamber again.

"If one . . ." Shardos began cautiously, ignoring the impatient tugging of Ramiro at his sleeve and the shudder of the earth at his feet, "If one were to show your people the way to the Bright Lands . . . and know the things that the Namer keeps . . ."

All eyes turned to the juggler eagerly.

"He would be the Namer," a small child piped.

It was exactly what Shardos wanted to hear.

"I am not sure such a conclusion follows, my dear," Shardos said with a deep breath. "What I *am* sure of is that there is more than one version of every story and more than one way out of every cavern. Sometimes even more than two ways, two versions. These caverns are old, worn smooth by water. I know many ways out of them."

"Shardos!" Ramiro hissed. "What—"

"Would you like me to show you one of those ways?" Shardos asked, his blank stare still leveled on the Que-Tana.

"Follow the juggler," the woman said quietly. The lean Plainsman who had spoken first now chimed in, followed by the little girl, an ugly, squat axeman near the lectern burned by Firebrand's angry grip, then two of our guards.

Shardos turned to Ramiro, smiling.

"Get ready, my portly companion. We are about to lead an emergence and bridge the abyss between darkness and light."

Ramiro snorted. "If that involves getting out of this godforsaken place, would that I could be right behind you, Shardos! But there's the Oath to reckon with, and one of the Order is no doubt neck-deep in Firebrand at this very moment."

"There are some things larger than that blasted Oath of yours, Ramiro!" Shardos replied sternly. "Do what you like, but look around you first and see if the Oath goes deeper than you imagined."

Ramiro scanned the faces of the Plainsmen in front of him, resting his gaze on the vulnerable pale skin and its terrible fragility. The floor shook again, and a huge cleft opened between him and the passage down which he had seen us go.

"As for Firebrand," Shardos urged softly, "well . . . 'tis high time you trusted in the gods and in Galen."

"Neither of which has been that reliable, as I recollect," the big man grumbled and, taking the hand of a Que-Tana girl in his own meaty paw, followed the juggler from the chamber as the library filled with dust and rubble behind them. -

So together they passed through, juggler and epicure and a hundred befuddled Plainsmen. And that hundred became yet another hundred, and those two hundred a thousand, as the corridors shook and crumbled and threatened to collapse.

*   *   *   *   *

Meanwhile, I lay against the far wall of the passage, my feet still absorbing the shock of landing. Below me, Brithelm whooped merrily. The troll snorted, and the sound moved away as the two of them skirted the Namer's room in their dangerous game of taunt and pursuit.

The wall behind me trembled once, then stood still. Gravel tumbled into the corridor in front of me, and the sound echoed on down the passage. I braced myself against the side of the tunnel, started to rise, and felt the leathery wall pulsing beneath my touch, as though deep within it, a great heart was beating.

The wall was alive! And it was growing restless.

"Tellus!" I whispered, and thought of the old legend—of Longwalker's tale of the worm beneath the continent of Ansalon, whose great turning wrought the mountains.

And who would turn again, in the last of times, to undo what he had wrought.

There is no telling how long I would have stood there, speculating and gawking, were it not for the troll's arm shooting into the mouth of the corridor, its claws clicking and grabbing for me.

It seems that Brithelm had been able to hold the monster's attention only so long. Something glimmered on the edge of the big thing's memory, and it recalled, though faintly, that another small creature had shot past it only a few minutes ago.

I was drawn from contemplation when its groping fingers brushed against my ankle.

Yelping, leaping into the air as though an enormous spider had just crawled over my foot, I was fifty feet down the corridor before the hand had closed on empty air.

It was dark here, and the footing was treacherous. I swallowed hard and listened ahead of me.

From somewhere down the passage, borne to me as if it rode on the back of a drafty echo, came the sound of someone falling and an accompanying curse.

Firebrand. Stumbling in the darkness himself, and not yet out of my reach.

Blind, I scurried toward the source of the sound.

If Tellus indeed was here, dormant amid the caverns and mountains of the Vingaards, was this rumbling and shaking, this turning of the earth, a sign that he was preparing to waken?

I resolved not to think about it. At least not yet.

Now a faint light glimmered in front of me, and the smell of sulfur reached me. I knew the Namer had touched hand to something dry and flammable.

Swiftly, silently, my energies renewed, I rushed toward the light, running like a weasel, confident and deep in its own burrow.

The floor of the tunnel shifted beneath me, and I came down hard on one knee. I resolved not to think about it yet.

He had not made good time. When the darkness engulfed him and he became unsure of his footing, he had reached toward the walls and found the remnants of torches, dried by the years in ancient, rusty sconces.

The torches went up like thatch in a village fire. He must have watched them in fascination, no doubt sure that the creature he had unleashed on his pursuers was back in the Namer's chamber, finishing a grisly business.

No doubt Firebrand thought he had all the time in the world.

I followed the guttering lights, the smell of smoke, and

turned a corner in the passage just in time to see him sixty feet or so ahead of me, his hands encircling a torch just beginning to flare strangely.

He looked over at me, his eye flaming like an opal, like a torch of anger and rage.

"Persistent, are you?" he asked in a level voice. "Most vermin are."

I took an angry step toward him, then remembered I was unarmed. I crouched and fumbled around me in the corridor for something hard and edged that might pass for weaponry, but my hands raced over smooth, weeping stone.

"Weasels and stoats and little toothed things are practiced grovelers, too." Firebrand spat, and I started.

"How did you—"

"Know to call you 'weasel'?" he asked. Though the torch made shadows thick and mottled, I thought I could sense a smile in his voice.

"Oh, I know many things, Weasel. The stones tell me, and the eye in the stones tells me more." He folded his hands in a graceful, almost saintly manner—even more frightening a gesture because it appeared so tender.

"The past is inescapable, Weasel," he intoned, and the godseyes at his brow began to glow, as they had in the Namer's room. "You cannot salvage or cleanse it or even forget it, much less make it right. It is always there, and when you add up your little heroics and measure them against the worst you were, you will be hung on your words, on your own conceiving, as you move from night . . ."

He paused. In the shadowy distance, I saw his hands rise.

". . . *to awareness of night*," he intoned.

And Marigold walked out of the corridor wall, her hair angular and drenched like a wrecked ship, her white gown muddy and dripping. From behind her—indeed, *through* her, for she was glowing and strangely translucent—I saw Firebrand turn and rush down the passage until he was lost in the darkness.

"Robert!" she cried. "Where is Sir Robert?"

She looked around her stupidly, water flowing down her in rivulets onto the floor of the tunnel, which remained completely and remarkably dry.

"My combs?" she asked uncertainly, painfully, turning toward me slowly. "My face paint?"

Our eyes met.

"Lacquer?" she murmured, and we stared a long while at each other.

Despite myself, I started to laugh.

Somewhere within me, I had added up the evidence—the translucency, the walking through walls, the simple fact that Marigold of Kayolin was supposed to be miles above me and miles away—but it had not sunk in yet. The only thing sunken, indeed, was the horrid little schooner atop the woman's head, run aground on what rocks or reef I could only imagine.

"*Paaastriiiieeees!*" she shrieked, and her eyes began to glow, to pinwheel in red fire.

"*I'm dead! I'm dead!*" she shouted, her hands rushing ineffectually to straighten her shipwrecked hair. "*And it's all your fault!*"

I raised my hands, shook my head, and looked frantically for side tunnels.

"But this is better," Marigold said, suddenly calm. "This is better, Weasel. *Mm-hum. Yes, oh, yes.*" She stepped toward me, her white robes gliding inches above the floor of the passage. Menacingly she extended her arms.

"This way," she said, her voice almost musical, "we can be together *forever!*"

Her mouth opened, and yellow troll-like fangs protruded, dripping water and lacquer and blood. I backed down the corridor, with Marigold floating after me, as close as fog, a hint of cheap cologne borne somehow on the stagnant air. Then the Weasel of my beginnings resurged in my here and now, and I panicked and turned to run . . .

And collided with Alfric.

It is lucky I have a sound heart. Not good or compassionate, I fear, though in my last several years, I have tried to render it so. Nonetheless, it is sound and able to bear a shock or two. Shock one: Marigold. Shock two: my dear, dead brother.

There, sandwiched between the departed brother and the evidently departed other, I was speechless, unarmed, and tracked down, as Firebrand had prophesied, by the ghost of my ruinous past.

"Well," I said, my fears giving way to despair, to a bleak bravado of sorts, "I expect there is nothing in the world that you can ever live down. Once you do it, it more or less runs at you till it has you at bay, then guts you and skins you and hangs you on a wall. . . ."

But neither of them was interested in my gibbering philosophy. Impassively Alfric stared over me and met Marigold's gaze.

"Why bother with him," he asked her unexpectedly, "when you could have me?"

Marigold's face softened. The burning whirl of her eyes slowed and faded, the fangs receded—all but one, anyway, which she pulled her lips over daintily. For a moment, she looked as she always looked in life: burly and selfish and a bit overdone, but strangely compelling in a tarty sort of way.

She snorted and vanished into nothingness, and I turned to my spectral brother with something approaching gratitude. For Alfric had called her off, it seemed—had saved me from an eternity of badgering and ethereal pastry.

"Thank you, Brother," I began in all sincerity.

"We will see if you're inclined to thank me, Galen," he said, "after you have reckoned with me. For you and me have got scores to settle."

I stepped back one stride, then another. My heel touched stone behind me.

"We have odds to even, Galen." My ghostly brother came closer. "And the reckoning begins now."

With the flat of his broadsword blade, Alfric struck my head. Then again and harder he struck, as my vision burst into a hundred glittering flames and I reeled up the corridor.

"You done this to me, too, Weasel!" he shouted, the shrill rise of his voice blending with the rumbling around me and above me.

The dale worm was stirring. Old Tellus, foster son of Chaos and Night, was lifting his lidless eye.

Alfric raised the sword again and stepped forward.

All my weaseling could not avail in this cramped, narrow

passage. I was cornered, brought to bay as I had been so many times in the nooks of the moathouse and beneath the beds of unswept guest chambers. But here there was no place to hide or dodge.

There was not enough room to grovel.

So I stood to my full height, and my older brother seemed to shrink a little before me. Perhaps death had diminished his stature—I cannot be sure. For instead of the Weasel who cowered before a formidable larger brother, I was every bit as big as the oaf in front of me.

The punch surprised me, even though I threw it. My right fist hurtled through the dark air of the corridor and caught my brother squarely on the left side of his prominent nose. He reeled, shook his head, almost regained his footing . . .

And then my left fist came calling, surging out of the shadows below him as it hooked up into the underside of Alfric's chin.

"Whaaa—" he began, but he was falling backward, his arms spread out like the useless wings of a vespertile. Into the wall he tumbled, growing suddenly transparent, almost liquid, as he passed into mud and rock, his sword clattering to the corridor floor behind him.

He looked back at me as he faded, once and for all, into the stone of the tunnel. He smiled—not the wicked grin that had harried me over the past two decades of brotherly abuse, but a smile considerably warmer, perhaps even apologetic, carrying with it the faintest hint of respect.

The most generous moment of his life, it seemed, had come when that life was over.

"I'm sorry, Alfric," I breathed. "But I will avenge you."

I hadn't the time for good-byes. Around me, the corridor was collapsing, filling with palpable dust and fist-sized boulders, while before me somewhere was daylight and air and Firebrand with the opals.

The options were clear. I picked up the sword and began to run with new strength toward the last wavering lights in the burrowing distance.

Chapter XXIII

A SEVENTH, AN EIGHTH, AND A NINTH STONE FOLLOWED
into the twining silver, until the twelfth was in place. With
confident fingers, the Namer tested each setting, shifting the
stone once, twice, until it held fast.

"Now they are all together," he announced. "Each fixed in a
holy permanence, bound to each other always in memory."

* * * * *

As she slept in the saddle, Dannelle di Caela dreamed she
was riding with Sir Galen.

The two of them, astride the enormous Carnifex, galloped into a clearing of towering pine and aeterna; the light
was blue and white about them.

She was proud to ride with him, behind him on the back of this formidable horse they had broken together. Carnifex snorted and steamed, but he was bested and knew it, his wild strength bridled in obedience to the combined will of man and woman.

In the dream, the horse reared up, its forelegs pawing the misted air. Galen twisted in the saddle and reached for Dannelle . . .

But she was falling . . . falling . . .

As she jerked awake, riding with Birgis atop the racing Carnifex, it seemed to Dannelle that the trees she passed were blurring, transforming themselves into huge swaths of blue and green. It seemed that the landscape around her was dissolving, that only she and the dog—who sniffed and rumbled amiably at her shoulder—remained from the world she remembered.

She was relieved to see the Cat Tower pierce the horizon. As the walls of the castle and the fluttering pennants atop it became clear in front of her, she lowered her head and pressed the strong flanks of the horse with her knees. Birgis stirred a bit in the harness on her back.

"Sit back, damn it!" she started to exclaim, but the wind rushed into her face, choking her and drowning the words. Her thoughts moved quickly over the ground ahead of her, outrunning Carnifex and the wind and even the reddening sunlight breaking across the pennantry.

Now the walls loomed before her, the crenellation and windows sharply defined. Now she made out the arms of di Caela, of Brightblade and Pathwarden and Rus on the fluttering pennants.

Good, she thought. They all are here. And fifty miles of riding has come down to the next half hour.

For Dannelle di Caela intended an arrival that was showy and brilliant, nothing short of completely spectacular.

Riding Carnifex over the drawbridge she came, full speed across the courtyards, amid a flurry of hoofbeat and color and the shouting of heralds, straight to Sir Robert di Caela, who in her dreams of this moment stood agape before the double oaken doors of the Great Tower, scarcely believing his eyes.

For this red-haired slip of a girl he so often disparaged had not only arrived in time to save her companions beneath the Vingaards, but also arrived on the back of Carnifex, the horse Sir Robert had claimed she could not ride.

There were two problems with this just and wonderful vision: First of all, the Lady Dannelle di Caela was uncertain as to how she would dismount from her horse.

And secondly, the drawbridge in question was boarded up by makeshift carpentry. Behind it stood engineers with little better to do than weathering hangovers and speculating as to how to repair the mechanism kicked asunder by a big stallion not two days before.

For several years, everyone in Castle di Caela had marveled at the lack of foresight or intelligence shown by the fabled nomad chief who had given Carnifex to Sir Robert.

"Such a fine piece of horseflesh," they marveled. "As a gift outright."

And they shook their heads at nomadic stupidity.

All but the grooms in the stable, who had known for several years that Sir Robert had the worst of the deal—that the real stupidity lay in part with the old lord of the castle, but chiefly with the big horse itself.

Carnifex did not shorten his stride. Ignoring the cries of the woman atop him, her frantic tugging at his long silver mane, the animal lowered its head and whickered, its speed increasing until a panic-stricken Dannelle scarcely noticed they were airborne.

The horse and his two passengers leapt from the far bank of the brimming moat and splashed into the mud on the other side. Birgis, by far the most practical of the three, untangled himself and plunged into the water, as with a short, powerful surge, Carnifex strode up the incline and charged toward the half-repaired entrance, Dannelle hanging on desperately atop him.

It is hard to imagine the surprise of those engineers who, still aching from their bout with Thorbardin Eagle and settled in for a safe, undemanding afternoon of examining gears and pulleys, were confronted suddenly by a wild horse surging through the woodwork, a long-vanished noblewoman astride it.

In a moment, everyone scattered. Engineers and carpenters dove from their path, and whether by reflex or foresight or simply damned good luck, Dannelle di Caela grabbed the dangling chain of the drawbridge mechanism and swung acrobatically from the back of the horse, landing ankle-deep in the sucking mud and precariously, dramatically gaining her balance.

She looked cautiously around for an audience. She seemed disappointed, but decided that the engineers would do.

Dannelle was telling her story before Carnifex was out of sight, before Birgis had shaken the water from his coat and trotted merrily through the shattered drawbridge. She told them the lengthy story as, filled with alarm, the engineers carried her between them toward the infirmary, terrified that they would be blamed for any of her bruises or breaks or discomfiture.

Birgis tipped along behind them, yawning and wagging his tail.

"Which brings us to this juncture," Dannelle concluded, "where I guided the stallion over the moat outside and in through the drawbridge . . ."

"A daring exploit that must have been, m'lady," the head engineer commented absently, shifting the girl's weight in his bony arms.

"Not so daring, that," she objected, well schooled in false modesty. "The moat was full, after all, and would have cushioned my fall from the saddle, and then there was the mud . . ."

"I beg your pardon?" the man said, his beard trembling, his eyes suddenly intent.

"There was the mud in the courtyard that—"

"The moat was full, you say?"

Dannelle nodded. "I suppose the lot of you have been busy in my absence. Where are the others?"

Without waiting for her answer—indeed, dropping the young woman perfunctorily at the steps of the infirmary—the engineer turned and raced toward the cellars of Castle di Caela, where the brimming moat had told him that the underground was filling with water.

Birgis trotted up to the indignant young woman and

again most reverently licked her nose. He murmured in her ear, something that sounded like words again to the jostled Dannelle.

"You are muddy," he seemed to say, "and you smell like salt."

Birgis charged off jubilantly around the corner of a guardhouse, and something squawked and fluttered from the direction he had taken.

*   *   *   *   *

Down in the tunnels below the castle, something stirred in the rubble. Gileandos, tutor to the Pathwardens, scrambled out from a rockpile, trailing gravel and dust.

He did not know he had been unconscious for a day.

"Oh, dear!" he exclaimed. "Oh, dear! I fear that my companions have been . . . submerged past all recovery."

His hands fluttered like bats in the darkness. He could not see them.

After scrambling and worrying and exclaiming and fluttering, the tutor groped in the darkness, found a large rock—one, in fact, which missed his head by inches in the cave-in—and seated himself upon it.

"Now, think clearly, Gileandos," he told himself. "There is . . . there is a lantern in these whereabouts, and if the gods are kind, it is still in working order."

Like a mole, he turned and dug in his subterranean blindness, his soft, thin fingers scrabbling through rock and dust.

*   *   *   *   *

Above Gileandos, the engineers stopped at a fork in the passage and caught their breath. The dozen or so castle servants they had brought along—grooms, sappers, a cook or two—ran into one another in the gloomy, lamplit corridor. Following behind the stumbling wall of men, Dannelle stepped through the crowd and laid a muddy hand on the shoulder of the younger and more promising engineer.

"You've been this way before, Bradley," she said. "Where from here?"

The young man blushed. Dannelle's touch, it seemed, was volatile in many quarters.

"He has no idea, m'lady," the head engineer replied testily. " 'Twas long before this that Bayard Brightblade made the lot of us turn back."

Dannelle nodded in the shadows, being accustomed to unwelcome protection.

"And yet," the young man said, his eyes on the two passages, "after a brief inspection of incline and breadth and the mathematics thereof, I would venture that the leftward passage leads toward Sir Bayard and his party."

"Nonsense, Bradley!" the head engineer sputtered. "Surely you are aware that the workings of the well lie south of here. If Sir Bayard knew aught of engineering and matters hydraulical, he would surely have pursued the passage to the right."

"Then I would venture that Bradley is right," Dannelle interrupted, and the old man gazed at her with something approaching contempt.

* * * * *

"I shall be food for bats!" Gileandos murmured, fumbling hysterically at loose things. "Or giant rats, or lizards, or huge flightless birds that have evolved into something menacing, or . . . or . . . that *worm I touched!*"

Hysteria turned to blind panic as the tutor flung rocks in all directions. As he raised dust in the blackness, he coughed and sneezed and continued to burrow deeper into the rockpile until he reached the floor of the corridor, until his right hand struck solid rock . . .

And his left hand metal.

Panting, squealing, fumbling with the lantern, he juggled it from one hand to another, heard the splash of lamp oil on the dark rocks around him. Fumbling in his robes, he came up with a tinderbox, wrenched it open, and drew out flint and tinder. . . .

There were times years ago, in Coastlund, when Gileandos was said to be careless with fire. It was a reputation he did not deserve. Frequently ignited by the youngest and oldest Pathwarden boys—who worked sometimes separately, sometimes in tandem—the tutor spent much of his time in the infirmary, nursing burns and the ill regard of Sir Andrew Pathwarden. In those long, reflective hours on his back (or on his belly, depending on where the fire had struck him) Gileandos had come to believe that he had set the fires himself, or walked into them as part of some huge and fatal design established in the cloudy past of the Age of Dreams.

That was why he was not surprised when his sleeves burst into flame in the corridor and, shouting and spinning like an enormous fireworks display, he pinwheeled up the corridor, straight into a geyser rising from the artesian well, which whirled him about and extinguished him.

And yet, in that blaze of glory, an obscure tutor had saved a shimmering array of Solamnic knighthood and nobility, for the sharp eye of Bradley the engineer caught a glimpse of light wavering down the corridor—the *left* one, it was, to the young man's great delight—and, pointing out the glimmer to the head engineer and the Lady Dannelle, he proceeded to guide the expedition to its source in the smoldering, smarting tutor.

From there, it was a matter of pickax and shovel against rock, a task taking less than an hour.

* * * * *

Far below the clamor of metal and stone, below the rescue party and below those they had set out to rescue, below the great dale worm Tellus, who stirred uneasily in his hundred thousand years of sleep, the caverns dropped away into nothing, and nothing dropped away into the Abyss. Where Sargonnas waited, watching events unfold.

The dark god frowned. There was a whining at his ear, thin and incessant, like the choiring of mosquitoes.

Something was wrong.

He had plotted so carefully all that had come to pass: hundreds of years ago, setting a dark passage in front of the Scorpion and even darker thoughts in his heart, and at almost the same time finding the Namer through the depths of the opals . . .

It was all so elaborate and beautiful.

And yet, Sargonnas thought now, turning uncomfortably in the black vacuum of the Abyss, and yet there are too many of them. Wherever I look are unforeseen people: the sharp-eyed, mournful Knight and the merry blind juggler the girl and the priest and the dog. . . .

And since he put on the crown, I have not heard from the Namer anymore. Too variable these mortals were, and something was about to happen that was beyond contingencies.

He stirred, anxiously scanning the Vingaards and the plains and the subterranean cavern beneath both.

He could not figure it. Too many and variable they were

*　*　*　*　*

"Something the Scorpion said in the parchment . . ." Bayard began thoughtfully, scrambling urgently for answers as the fissure brimmed over and the chamber around his party began to fill with water. "Some clue to that damnable distant machinery . . ."

His companions paused expectantly, their gazes moving from the dark mechanism faintly seen by some, only imagined by others, until every eye was on Bayard, who frowned, shifted himself on Enid's shoulder, and turned to Brandon Rus.

"*Though you may uncover my devices*, the note said, *you will never strike the mark nor hit the target*. It's easy and direct, and wouldn't that be the Scorpion's greatest joke, that for all his machineries, the key is not subtle at all but is in fact the simple head of an arrow? That spot in the center of the device, Brandon," he urged as the fissure before them spilled water over their feet and the ceilings rained. "The dark spot, like the pupil of the eye. Can you shoot it with a bow?"

"I don't . . . Well, it's a terrible long shot from here through cascading water."

"And yet it seems what we must do," Bayard pressed, his gray-eyed stare intent on the younger Knight.

Still Brandon Rus hesitated, looked to the shadowy distance.

"Then step out to knee-deep and hold your breath, damn it!" Sir Robert roared. "You heard Sir Bayard, boy!"

Brandon leapt at the old man's order. In a moment, he was at the edge of the fissure, drawing the powerful bow.

"I'll have to figure weight, and distance, and differences in height, and who knows how thick that mist is across there."

"Brandon!" Enid urged. "I saw you hit a target through a second-story window in the middle of a rainstorm! Is this talent of yours good for anything besides tricks?"

Brandon stepped back, wounded. "There was the one time, though . . ."

"*Damn the one time!*" Enid screamed, reaching out and grabbing the young Knight by the sleeve. "Either make the shot or give me the bow and I'll do it."

Brandon Rus paused for a moment, then sprang toward action, his feet in the water before he thought too much about it. One step out, then two steps.

Then his submerged foot felt nothing beneath it.

How can I shoot through this obscurity? he thought, his strong hand trembling as he raised the bow.

The light behind him shifted over the gray mist like the light over a desolate sea. It flickered on the far wall before him, and the wall seemed to recede, to brighten and dim.

Brandon raised the bow, aimed at the turbulence, and was seized again by doubt. What if he missed?

Enid called out something unintelligible from behind him. She leaned over his shoulder and sighted along the shaft of the arrow as the young man aimed at the dark center of the thing at the far end of the chamber.

The lad took a deep breath and closed his eyes. Silently, with the archer's accuracy and skill that made him legendary, he shifted his aim, and the arrow rocketed into the head of the carved circling scorpion that adorned its border.

For a moment, Enid and Raphael cried out in dismay as the others squinted for a sight of the target across the dark distance. Brandon turned away, bowed his head.

"No, Brandon!" Enid shouted. "By the gods, try again!"

"What—" Sir Andrew began.

"Wait!" Bayard said, standing knee-deep in the water,

oddly supported by its buoyancy. "The device . . . I am the device!"

"I beg your pardon?" Sir Robert asked, and Bayard Brightblade began to laugh in relief.

"Brandon Rus," he explained softly, the water rising to midthigh, "has still never missed. For the device was no gnomish machinery, but the Scorpion's firm conviction that there was never a Solamnic Knight who could leave well enough alone."

"I beg your pardon?" Sir Andrew interrupted.

"Raphael," Bayard ordered, "look at the target and tell me what you see."

The lad squinted as he looked out over the waters.

"The same as before, sir. It is still shifting. Almost looks alive."

"It is alive indeed," Bayard replied, wading back toward his comrades, the water to his waist.

"I beg your pardon?" Enid and Raphael asked in unison, and the lord of Castle di Caela laughed again, this time more heartily.

"The fabled 'device,' " he explained, "was no mechanism, but a simple plot. The Scorpion knew that if we found the eye of the worm, which for all the world, I gather, resembles an archer's target, we would do our Solamnic best to strike its center, thereby waking the monster with furious and maddening pain. The only machinery planted on the castle grounds was the parchment geared to draw me to this very spot."

"This rapidly *submerging* spot," Brandon Rus said somewhat urgently, offering his hand to Bayard Brightblade, who breasted the water in front of him.

"But what of the dale worm?" Sirs Robert and Andrew shouted simultaneously.

"It'll die and make you a hero, Robert," Bayard announced. "Looks to me like you've drowned the damned thing!"

"And us in the bargain," Enid added, "unless we get out of here—now!"

Sputtering, coughing water like a beached swimmer, Bayard climbed out of the brimming pool, sidestepping the jetting warm streams from the great well. Again Brandon lifted the older Knight to his shoulder, and as swiftly as his youth could enable and his burden allow, he waded up the corridor, water rising in the tunnel behind him. He stumbled, his strength failing, and called out to those following. And all of them—Enid, Andrew, Robert, and Raphael, gasping at the steam and sliding rock—hauled Bayard and his rescuer back up the corridor. When they reached breathable air, they stopped for a moment and leaned against rock or collapsed altogether on the floor of the tunnel.

"Well, it has happened," Sir Andrew coughed. "We have reached the very foundations of Castle di Caela, and we have seen something there and kept it from wakening, maybe for good. It is over. But I shall be damned if I understood a lick of it."

He smiled, hearing before them the shouts and the pick-axes of the engineers.

It was only a matter of minutes until the hole in the rock and rubble was wide enough for all of them to pass through.

Bradley lifted Sir Bayard through the hole, supported him against the rush of water that entered the tunnel behind him, stumbled for a minute in the onslaught of wave and river-borne rubble, then gained solid footing and strode toward the surface. Around him, the others milled and followed, well-spattered and muddy, battered by rock and daunted by darkness.

Surprisingly old Gileandos lifted his voice in the old song of courage.

> "Even the night must fail,
> For light sleeps in the eyes
> And dark becomes dark on dark
> Until the darkness dies."

Jubilant, the others joined in.

> "Soon the eye resolves
> Complexities of night
> Into stillness, where the heart
> Falls into fabled light."

So singing, they emerge from the fissure into the cellar of the Great Tower, waterlogged and bedraggled but whole.

* * * * *

In the heart of the Abyss, the dark god frowned and turned on a gust of stagnant air. Defeated, he shrugged, smiled ruefully.

"Damn them," he said flatly, and the void shook around him. "And damn the Namer especially, who is now useless."

Then he yawned and, reclining in hot, dry infinities of nothingness, he closed his fathomless eyes and slept away a century.

* * * * *

Whether indeed it was understood or whether it passed understanding, something had changed in the world under Castle di Caela. The gray mist in the crevasse vanished, leaving behind it a dark that was only the absence of light, that hid nothing more than stone and shadow and occasional creeping things, all in all as harmless as what a curious child might find in the earth beneath an overturned rock.

Far above, two pages sat alone at a table in the Great Hall, where they had sat for hours debating how many places to set for dinner. They broke off their arguments and listened, of all things, to a sudden quiet in the rooms and corridors around them.

It was the first time either had listened in months.

Nor was it unrewarded, for they both started to listen right near the turn of the hour, as noon approached and the castle guests filed in for a luncheon that would taste far better today for some reason.

As the incredible smells of roast pork and apples filtered into the hall, first one boy smiled, then the other.

They did not know why they were smiling. It was something, though, about the smells in the air and the curious light in the room. Something about the silliness of having whiled away the morning in the fine points of etiquette, when there were smells and noises to investigate and a meal of roast pork and potatoes to enjoy.

As the noontide clocks struck in Castle di Caela, the air was filled with a chorus of metallic bird cries. For the first time since Aunt Evania and Sir Robert began this collection of offensive machinery, all of the castle cuckoos sang together, marking the passing hour.

* * * * *

Up in the Vingaard Mountains, a high sun washed the vallenwoods and oaks and maples in a brilliant white light. The leaves turned and silvered in the light breeze from the east, and Longwalker stopped on his way through the wooded foothills. He cocked his head, as if somewhere east of him he had heard something shift, some slight but important movement in the fabric of things.

"Now," he said to the Plainsmen about him. "Old Tellus is at rest. The time is back. It will not be long before they all can return, can go back to words and memory."

It was obscure to them, what Longwalker said. The younger Que-Nara looked at one another, then nodded as though they understood their leader.

Someday, Longwalker thought. Someday you will understand all of this. How those in the hearts of the opal are always only a step from you. That as thin as the line is between breathing and translation, it is just as thin when you come back the other way. You will understand this.

Two strix owls took wing out of the dark branches of a blue aeterna. Shocked by the daylight and the Plainsmen around them, they wheeled quickly in the air and swooped into a stand of golden oak not twenty yards away. The children started, then quickly recovered their calm and implacable faces.

Longwalker frowned privately, lost in his thoughts.

"I do not know what this will bring the Solamnics," he confided to his people, "but there is a grove where the plains meet the foothills, where vallenwood and pine and aeterna mix with the lesser trees. There, if their guiding is done and the Que-Tana have followed, we shall find the others, and stone will link with stone, and cousins will clasp hands in friendship and reunion."

He walked away from his camp on the plains with its lean-tos of hide and light wood, the smell of smoke and roast venison. The earth stilled beneath him as the dale worm settled back into long sleep, but even its slightest shiftings stirred the mountains.

Chapter XXIV

The last of the settings remained stoneless, un-adorned. For a moment, the Namer held the thirteenth stone above it.

"This is the One Stone," he said quietly. "Always present in its absence."

He handed the One Stone to the man seated beside him, who in turn handed it to another. And as the stone passed from Plainsman to Plainsman, the Namer brought the story full circle.

*   *   *   *   *

There was no doubting that the surface was near, for now the air smelled fresher, greener in the part of the passage around me. Upward I moved, the borrowed sword in my right hand, my left hand grappling for purchase amid loose and tumbling rock.

The deciding was over.

In a rush, I took off up the corridor toward the light. All around me the vast network of tunnel and chamber was crumbling, shaking. It seemed that everything momentous that had ever happened to me centered around an earthquake, and I recalled thinking, If this is the last thing, then there is something just and fitting in it. Then, with an unsettling lurch, the ground I had just crossed split open not ten yards behind me.

I passed through one cloud of red dust, then a corridor branching to my right, which collapsed with a rolling crash that doubled my speed, if doubling was possible. The air was growing thick and powdery, difficult to breathe.

I pulled my cloak up over my mouth and rose. It was a time for opals, that was certain.

A trio of tenebrals rushed by me, chittering. I followed, and I heard someone or something cry out in front of me the instant before I turned a corner.

My momentum propelling me, I turned nonetheless and saw Firebrand ahead, out of reach and practically past recall, scrambling into a gray steady light as the dust passed in waves behind him.

I heard the shriek and the popping as the tenebrals fluttered into the sunlight. With a prayer to whatever god looked after headstrong fools, I rushed to the surface, too, sword at the ready, toward the sunlight and the sound of Firebrand's chanting.

I burst into the Bright Lands with a gasp, with relief, for whatever awaited me, however dangerous, was a change from the gloom and the damp and the stagnant corridors.

I did not know that standing there in confusing light, armed with a long dagger and a shield, my greatest adversary awaited, who made the dark magic of the Scorpion and of Firebrand look like child's play.

It was Galen Pathwarden, the Weasel, oily and mean, crouched on an outcropping of granite. He looked years younger than I remembered myself, and decades younger han I felt.

I remembered his face when it was *my* face, years and adventures ago, when I had stared at myself hatefully in the one looking glass Father kept in the moathouse. The beady brown eyes, the matted red hair, the rodent's twitch and squint.

What was it Firebrand had said? *Those that your memory summons in a night of bad dreams. And the choices you make, as always, will be wrong.*

Firebrand stood apart from us, laughing wickedly beneath the drooping branches of a vallenwood. The opals glittered in his silver crown, and his eye blazed like the darkest and most powerful stone of all.

"Here's the deal," Weasel whined, slipping behind his shield until he was scarcely visible. "We've come so far together, you and I, to where our differences are just about to bring us to grief. . . ."

I turned my sword in my hand. I could not figure out what to do about this. Somewhere in the corner of my vision, I saw Firebrand move, heard his laughter. Beneath me, the ground rumbled in reply, as though it, too, was laughing.

"So I suggest we just . . . call things off," Weasel urged. "We depart, whether separately or together, leaving this Firebrand fellow to his own sorry devices."

He raised his head from behind the shield and gave me a knowing wink.

It was the moment I had been waiting for.

Three strides carried me across the clearing. Weasel dropped the shield and backed away, cringing and groveling like some shifty, disgusting vermin. I gripped my sword tightly, took one last step toward Weasel, and drove the blade halfway into his chest.

He looked into my eyes and shrieked.

I looked away, unable to return his gaze. A pain wrenched hot in my chest. *And the choices you make, as always, will be wrong*, I heard once again. I saw Firebrand gliding through the shade of the trees at the edge of the clearing, circling me like a large, scavenging bird.

I felt Weasel climbing up the sword, pulling himself toward me, driving the blade deeper and deeper into his chest as he moved. Finally he clutched my sword hand in his thin, leathery grasp and pulled me toward him.

"The deal is this is this is this," he chattered, his fingers groping for my throat. I felt heavy, leaden and slow, as though I, not he, was the one who was conjured from stone.

Behind me, the sound of footsteps approached.

"You're a liar, Firebrand!" I shouted and hung on.

I remember thinking, swiftly and in some recess where words could not reach, as I wrestled myself in the clearing. Thinking that Firebrand could summon figure after figure from my brief but disreputable past. However, he could not make me heed them.

And no doubt Weasel was the worst he could do.

I heaved, straddled my slithering opponent.

There was something of a game in this. And despite my discomfort when the past came to call, I could weasel a game with the best of them, matching trivial strategy with trivial strategy until my opponent collapsed with exhaustion.

I recall smiling at the prospect. My laughter, too, rose out of that tangle of limbs, out of the bright clearing where the villains walked, and when he heard it, Firebrand hushed and the air about us became suddenly tense and sober. Beneath me, the earth stilled.

Then the Weasel in my clutches began to change shape.

Into a snake, its notched head waving above me like the tail of a scorpion . . .

Which he became next, the snake head narrowing into the poised spike of a verminous tail, and the tail descending, descending . . .

But never wounding me, never striking home.

I took courage from this and held tighter as the scorpion beneath me grew and branched and bristled, its chitinous back sprouting white leathery wings and coarse, matted fur . . .

And beneath me twisted a vespertile, perhaps the same one who had folded itself over poor little Oliver . . .

And still I held on, something in the holding becoming adventure, a challenge, a game . . .

Until the great earth roiled and shook beneath me, and to

my right, in the grove, I heard the dry, ripping sound of a vallenwood uprooting.

And it was Tellus the dale worm I was riding, and through all this I kept telling myself, It is approaching, approaching; soon the bastards will run out of changing shapes and we shall see what happens then . . .

And Weasel was water, was light on a sword, was tunnel on tunnel, was nothing . . .

And my grip did not relax, and I was laughing more loudly than ever, thinking, This is the worst you can do? This is all, Firebrand?

And the landscape tilted one disastrous last tilt and waver, and there was a boy beneath me with beady brown eyes, matted red hair, a rodent's twitch and squint.

But a boy who was afraid. Who was only a boy, his bluster and weaseling all he knew of courage in a country prone to shift and explosion, where brothers bludgeoned and tutors ignited, and the whole world rankled at the whim of a self-righteous Order.

He looked away from me and shivered. I felt the sword pass though my heart, too. The wrestle became an embrace as I wrapped my arms around the poor little fellow.

Where before there was a wound, there was now peace.

And as suddenly as he had appeared, Weasel was gone. I lay on the ground for a long, forgetful moment, savoring the peace and the stillness and the air and the light.

Then the ground beneath me murmured again, and somewhere behind and above me Firebrand cursed and fell silent. I rose slowly and turned to face him, the sword in my hand light and familiar.

He held his staff in front of him, and for the first time I noticed it was iron, edged with a glinting blade.

"It is down to the two of us, Solamnic," Firebrand hissed. "It is strange, is it not, that all magics come down to a hand-to-hand fight in a clearing?"

He was already beaten. I moved toward him, waving the sword like a scythe, and we closed in a clatter of metal.

Three times we locked weapons, three times stared at one another over the wrestling blades. He was a strong man, and larger than I, but there was something to all my training, all the thumps and lectures under the tutelage of Bayard Bright-blade that had taught me balance, taught me to shift, to vary my footing and place my weight so that even the most formidable opponent was forced to stretch and stagger.

At that moment, I could have taken on the troll. On the third parry, I felt Firebrand give a little, felt him buckle under the twisting and locking of weaponry. With an agile turn, he leapt back, brushing against a blue aeterna bush, sending cones and needles flying.

"But magic is inexhaustible, Solamnic," he intoned. "And it rises when you expect it the least. . . ."

His staff began to glow, first red, then yellow, then white. I could feel the heat from where I stood. Firebrand stepped forward, brought the weapon whistling down through the air, and I blocked it with my sword, but the heat passed through the metal and became unbearable.

I staggered backward, my sword ringing harmlessly as it tumbled onto the rocks at Firebrand's feet. Defiantly he kicked it away and walked toward me, glowing staff in his hand.

Again the godseyes on his brow began to flicker. His eye half closed ecstatically, and again the earth rumbled.

"The power of life and death!" he gloated. "All of their memories are mine! They would have none of me, but now I have their past and future!"

"*You* killed my brother, you bastard!" I snapped, reaching into my tunic and drawing forth those ragged leather gloves. Quickly I slipped them on, having scarcely the time to raise my hands before the glowing staff descended.

I felt the blade strike leather and metal, felt the old gloves hold with a strength and resilience that was not metal and leather alone, but the years of weathering and sun and rugged use. The staff turned red again, and yellow, and white, and I felt the heat next to me and dropped to my knees at its force . . .

And the ground shook, hurtling the both of us, crown over backside over gloves over staff, halfway across the clearing.

He was to his feet by the time I had picked up my sword and closed with him. Without his eye patch, which had fallen off in the tremor and tumble, he looked vulnerable, weak. The empty socket opened into a darkness blacker than the caverns and the heart of the godseye, and for a moment, I pitied him.

The crown, too, lay in the white dust beside him, fragmented, the light in its stones fading.

Then, with an outraged cry, Firebrand raised the staff to strike. I rocked back on my heels, my blade flashed swiftly through the smoky air . . .

And found the soft home of his neck.

I have heard there is indignity in such a thing—that the Nerakans, for one, punish their worst with ritual beheading.

Father has spoken of the time when the Order itself beheaded the most heinous offenders.

And yet there was a quiet that surrounded us afterward. His one good eye was closed, and the body stood there for a moment, as though it was trying to remember something.

As though the moment of its passing had not been reckoned.

Then it fell, also quietly, and I felt a hand touch my shoulder.

Brithelm stood beside me.

"It may have vanished," he said quietly. "The troll, I mean." He smiled at me sadly. "You will understand," he added, "that I did not tarry to find out."

And the earth wrenched and buckled.

They say that unnatural things began an hour beforehand, before the rumbling and tumult from deep underground.

A traveler, a spice merchant from Kalaman traveling inland to deliver the last of his cargo, who later visited Castle di Caela, watched as panic-stricken tenebrals hurtled into the sunlit air, contracting and crumpling within yards of the caves out of which they issued, striking the earth with that ghastly popping sound and the smell of burnt hair.

It was only in waiting, in standing by the mouth of the highland cavern, that the merchant noticed the ground begin to move.

The quaking was general all over Solamnia, peasants'

ses collapsing in rains of dried mud and thatch, the sta-
filling up with shrieks and movement as the horses felt
tremors and recalled that movements such as these
disaster.

Disaster was what we were courting, there in the rock-
strewn mountains, yet my thoughts were below those
rocks, with Shardos and Ramiro.

They're still under there, Brithelm," I said, my eyes on
the silver circlet at my feet. "Shardos and Ramiro and the
Que-Tana. Perhaps . . ."

I looked a long time at the godseyes, thinking of the
power of life and death and what it might mean to those
trapped under miles of cavern and rock.

I thought also of what that power had done to Firebrand.

Yes, when I picked up the circlet there was the nearly unmanageable urge to put it on.

And, yes, for a moment, there passed through my darkest
imaginings a kingdom where I sat upon a throne and governed.

Omnipotent, yes, but kindly.

"I know," Brithelm said, his arm slipping over my shoulder.
He smelled of dust and the caverns and, to be honest, of not
having washed in too long a time. "I know. Perhaps they escaped by the other passage, the one Shardos told stories
about. That's what you were about to say, wasn't it, Galen?"

I nodded. Whatever else came to pass, I had returned
with the brother I set out to find. Let history and heroics rest
in the hands of others.

I handed the crown to Brithelm, and beneath us the world
kicked and bucked, knocking us off our feet.

The trees about us shook and bent and swayed as though
caught in the midst of a windstorm, and the rumbling sound
that had swelled through our last minutes in the tunnels began to roar, as rock beat against rock deep in the bowels of
the mountains.

Out of the swirling dust came a Que-Tana warrior, shielding his eyes against unfamiliar light. Then Shardos, who
pointed out our vantage point uncannily, sightlessly. He
shouted something and seized a small Que-Tana child by the
arm, dragging her toward us.

Ramiro came next. He stopped in the swirling dust and looked back into the darkness. He, too, shouted something, but I could hear no voice in all the rumble and crash of the tunnels caving in upon themselves. For a frightening moment, the big Knight lost his footing and toppled heavily, the ground tilting underneath him as though he were being funneled into the crevasse that was opening beneath him.

But he leapt to his feet, no doubt the first time since childhood that Ramiro of the Maw had made any movement one might take to be a jump or a scramble. And he had joined us within a matter of seconds, behind him a dozen more of the Plainsmen, then more after that and still more.

There must have been five hundred in all. Squinting, shielding their eyes, their pale skin scalding in even the muffled sunlight, they covered themselves with robes and hides and blankets as their home caved in behind them.

Together we made for the foothills. All around us and above us, the faces of the mountains were collapsing. We moved unsteadily, clutching one another and carrying the children into a safer darkness of leafshade and overhanging branches, where we collapsed, exhausted, as the landscape behind us fell in on itself, like a loaf or cake in the hands of a negligent baker.

A silly image, I am sure, but I do not doubt that even the Cataclysm evoked such foolishness from its witnesses.

To this day, I have sworn off baked goods. They smack too much of catastrophe.

There we sat until it was over. There was a final rumble somewhere off to the north of us, then an incredible stillness, out of which arose an even more incredible birdsong, as a nearby nightingale, duped by the smoke and the dust in the air, warbled in the ruins.

For a while, Brithelm wept for them all—for the Que-Tana who had not escaped, and even for Firebrand. It is safe to say that none of the rest of us could weep for the Namer, and yet each of us stood quietly a moment as the air and the landscape settled.

And I realized that, despite my great misgivings, there was something of history in this.

Chapter XXV

As the voices choired and swelled in the ancient Que-Tana Song of Firebrand, the one man worthy of the name lifted the Namer's crown. Maimed by fire, and an unlikely hero because of his maiming, he had nonetheless led a people into the light.

Unlike the pretender to his name and his crown, this new Firebrand would treat his calling and the stones with reverence and care. Quietly he placed the crown upon his own head. Now he sang the names of the heroes, and the Plainsmen chanted back a refrain as a thousand voices joined in committing those names to memory.

*　*　*　*　*

Going home was a long road, as it always is.

There's some philosophy in that, but lengthening the miles for my little company was the simple fact that our horses were gone. We couldn't have brought them with us underground, where the narrow passages and delicate footing would have jammed them in the rocks, no doubt, or brought a thousand equine pounds down upon one of us.

Still, you couldn't help but regret their absence when the prospect of walking doubled the length of your journey—a journey that had to be long, it turned out, to contain all that I learned.

The dust that the quake had raised did not settle until evening came, until all of us had reached an even thicker cluster of trees at the base of the foothills, spread over a cluster of towering rocks.

From the top of the largest rock, through the parted branches when the moon and the stars emerged, you could see down and east into the foothills and the plains of Solamnia beyond. When the lights winked on in the westmost villages of my adopted country, I was watching with my brother Brithelm, the two of us wrapped in a blanket against weather and wind and night.

"I suppose that one of us will have to tell Father," I observed after a silence. "I mean, about Alfric."

My brother nodded, his eyes still fixed on the country below him. His red hand slipped from under the blanket, its index finger glowing, as he traced aimless designs on the surface of the rock.

"I just imagine him down there among the rocks," I continued. "Him and Marigold, of course. Beginning some ghostly dance in eternity."

"That's almost poetic, Galen," Brithelm said with a sad smile, "until you remember what kind of dancers they were while alive and breathing."

"It's as though everything came together in misfortune down there, Brithelm," I said and paused.

"Brithelm, I have a confession."

My brother looked at me solemnly.

"I saw Weasel back in those caverns. Not me, but the one I was years ago when all this adventuring began. And I came to the conclusion that I'm not all that different from what I was then about . . . about this whole knighthood business. I've been lying, Brithelm. Lying to almost everyone about my courage and my principles and the Measure and the Oath, until now and again I almost believe my own stories.

"It's frightening. I've been thinking it's like one of Gileandos's proverbs coming alive, where 'the liar gets trapped in his own stitchery' or some such self-righteous nonsense. Somehow it got us free, though. Got us all out of Firebrand's clutches and here, back on the road to Castle di Caela and home."

Brithelm nodded. "And why are you telling me this?" he asked.

"Oh . . . I'm not sure. Perhaps I've decided never to lie again."

"I do not think you have decided that," Brithelm replied. Then solemnly he looked back out over Solamnia.

"I am afraid I have a confession, too," he whispered. "You know when I dawdled the time with Firebrand asking him all those questions about tenebrals? You heard the story from the Que-Tana."

"I remember, Brother. What did you learn about tenebrals?"

"Nothing," Brithelm replied. "Can't say as I care, either. Filthy little animals, tenebrals are. Never liked them to begin with."

I stifled a laugh. "Don't tell me *you* were lying, too?"

"Not *lying* as much as . . . being a good guest, Galen," Brithelm replied soberly, his finger still tracing luminous circles by his feet.

"A good guest?"

I said nothing, hid my smile in the blanket.

"But I feel . . . well, *guilty* now," Brithelm said, head bowed. "As if I guided poor Firebrand to misfortune and doom simply by feigning an interest in his surroundings."

"Nonsense, brother," I remarked. "Look at the simple mathematics of the situation. Firebrand had wrestled you down there, was more than willing to put an end to you once he had the opals, and brought me to the caverns of the Que-Tana with all kinds of lies and subterfuge. It all adds up, Brithelm, and your little courtesy does not compare to his malice and weakness and greed."

I discovered I was good at this. Having spent nigh on twenty years in explaining away my own misdeeds, I could explain for others with the skill of a surgeon.

Brithelm relaxed beside me, rose to his feet. All the lights that were to shine in western Solamnia that evening were shining by now.

* * * * *

Five days it took us to get back to Castle di Caela. For the most part, Ramiro served as our guide, the only one among us who had any idea as to the way back.

He had practiced his leadership until it had become almost glamorous. After all, he had guided forth the hundreds of squinting, cowering Que-Tana, many of whom were seeing the moons and the stars for the first time in their benighted lives, into that shadowy grove in the foothills, where they stayed until Longwalker joined them late that evening. There, as the camp fires of the Que-Tana glowed warmly, Ramiro, Brithelm, and I took to the plains, leaving behind us a wandering family reunited, a rudderless people brought to a strong and kindly guidance.

A guidance not only Longwalker's. For Shardos had stayed with the Que-Tana, for reasons we did not yet understand. Brithelm wept openly to say good-bye to the old juggler, and Ramiro and I, though trained to be starched, stone-faced models of Solamnic restraint, left with a catch in our throats as the old man sang a song at our parting, its melody cascading down the hillside after us. From Wayreth Forest it was supposed to have come, and Shardos claimed he had pieced it together from the song of the birds there. I do not remember it all, but I remember one part—"Here there is quiet," it went,

"Here there is quiet, where music turns in upon silence
Here at the world's imagined edge, where clarity
Completes the senses, at long last where we behold
Ripe fruit never falling, streams still and transparent

"Where the tears are dried from our faces, or settle,
Still as a stream in accomplished countries of peace,
And the traveler opens, permitting the voyage of light
As air, as the heart in repose this lasting day."

The very next afternoon we saw them, on a rise behind us, in the distance at the feet of the mountains.

The tall form that walked at the head of the column was no doubt Longwalker's. Silhouetted against the western sky, against the rapidly fading sunlight behind him, he waved at us, lonely and elegant on the horizon's edge.

There, after a moment, a short squat form joined him. Dressed in motley it was, and as it waved to us also, a series of bright lights dappled with all imaginable colors issued from its uplifted hands.

"Bottles!" Brithelm breathed beside me. "Incomparable, brightly colored bottles!"

And suddenly the Plainsmen were gone, vanished in the distance and the falling night.

As we neared home, we traveled further and further into the night, and on occasion, when he was on high ground and you were following below him, you could look up and see Sir Ramiro of the Maw blotting out half the stars on the eastern horizon with his sheer bulk and presence.

My dealings with the big Knight softened considerably on the road home. I guess, as usual, it took an earthquake for him to think kind thoughts about me, but if that was what it took, I would gladly accept it. After all, his guidance was somehow heartening in the highlands and onto the soggy plains, for I remembered trolls and raiding Que-Tana and even more horrible things from the years back.

Under Ramiro's care, the last leg of the journey passed rapidly, almost eventlessly. I learned the Solamnic countryside in better detail than I had ever imagined or hoped I would. Each day we walked as far as our leisure would take us—for after all, our guide Ramiro set the pace of the journey.

The first thing you see of home from the west is the banner that flies atop the Cat Tower.

It was welcome, that banner, even with my dread of how

to break the news of Alfric to my father.

But those dreads were lost, or postponed awhile, in the excitement of reunions, for it seemed that Castle di Caela had news of its own to tell.

We rode through the western gate to the sound of trumpet and drum. Raphael had spotted us in the distance during a stroll on the walls, and with his general efficiency and good will had arranged a Solamnic welcome by the time we arrived at the castle.

Things seemed in disarray all over. The vending carts that usually milled in the bailey were scattered and broken, evidence that the quake we felt in the Vingaards had reached this far into Solamnia. Indeed, a most forgiving Raphael told me that the first quake had left an enormous fissure underneath the foundation of the castle—I was not to hear the adventure surrounding it until later—and that the second quake, arising from nowhere little more than a week ago, had closed it again altogether.

It seemed like farfetched geology to me, but I had seen stranger things to the west and was inclined to believe him.

Brandon Rus had been preparing to leave eastward on a pilgrimage to the Blood Sea of Istar. Indeed, he had packed for the next morning, but he postponed his departure another night and day so that he could hear the adventures that had befallen us. It was from his account that I began to piece together what had happened underneath the castle while we were away. I went to Enid and to Bayard later for the rest of the story, and got more than I bargained for.

You see, not only did they grace me with the account of the pendant and the cats and the dangerous dreams and Marigold's shipwrecked hair, but they had exciting news that surpassed even the joy of restoring the castle.

For it seems that on one of those evenings a month or so before I was made Knight in the Great Hall of Castle di Caela, things more quiet and far more momentous were taking place in the upstairs chambers.

It seems as though I was disinherited, or at least pushed a ways down the line of succession.

For the heir of both branches, di Caela and Brightblade, would be welcomed to the world sometime in the early spring. Enid was not altogether as radiant as the mythology surrounding expectant mothers said that she should be. She was sick of a morning and craved pastry all through the day, but to Bayard she was the splendid bright creature he saw from the battlements years ago, and she was more now, here at the start of their greatest adventure together.

Speaking of pastry, Marigold remained a nocturnal factor in the chambers of Castle di Caela. At night, it seemed, her specter haunted the quarters of Sir Robert di Caela, who, having flooded the caverns below the foundation and thereby saved the castle and, by chance, the surrounding continent, was all prepared to dine on the story for years until the ghost took his appetite away. He looked . . . haunted now, and he jumped at the chance to sleep in the open air again when a band of us gathered to accept Longwalker's invitation to attend the Plainsman Night of Telling in the early fall.

* * * * *

But before the larger and more joyous Telling, there was a telling of my own to go through.

It was the evening after we arrived when I told Father about Alfric.

Of course he knew already. After all, Alfric hadn't returned with us, and when the tale of attack and ambush and underground cave-in unfolded, Sir Andrew concluded the worst. He was resigned when Brithelm and I came to him.

Resigned and expectant.

"I shall save you boys the reliving of this," he said as we entered his chamber, pushing himself away from the desk where, by lamplight, he had been crouched, quill in hand, over a large piece of parchment.

"The simple questions, according to the Measure, will suffice."

Brithelm and I looked at one another.

How like the old man to fall into the arms of the Order when he could not put word or thought around his grief. For there he sat in front of us, eyes brimming. I had never seen my father weep, but come to think of it, I had never seen him with a pen in hand, either.

It was the depths that the armor covered.

"One," he began, his old back rigid. He started to stand, steadying his right leg, injured in a long-past boar hunt. "One. Where did the boy fall?"

"In the heart of the Vingaard Mountains, sir. Into the breast of Huma," I replied, hoping I had the formula right.

"And when did he fall?"

"Elev—ten nights passing, sir. Into the breast of Huma."

And we said it together—that prayer I have heard on solemn occasions, before and since, over old Knights who passed on peacefully in their sleep and over young ones killed by adventure or accident. Over a centaur friend of mine, once in the mountains. And over my brother, who lay beneath those mountains, asleep in the heart of the planet.

> "Receive this one to Huma's breast
> Beyond the wild, impartial skies;
> Grant to him a warrior's rest
> And set the last spark of his eyes
> Free from the smothering clouds of wars
> Upon the torches of the stars.
>
> "Let the last surge of his breath
> Take refuge in the cradling air
> Above the dreams of ravens, where
> Only the hawk remembers death.
> Then let his shade to Huma rise
> Beyond the wild, impartial skies."

The prayer over, the tears shed, the old man looked up at me.

"And tell me one more thing, Galen," he began.

"He fell most bravely, Father," I said. "His last thoughts were heroic."

Brithelm looked at me briefly, but he added nothing, of course. And he always claimed, quite truthfully, that he did not see his eldest brother fall.

* * * * *

But our story must not end without a week in middle autumn, when briskness rode on the wind and the horses' breath misted the air for the first time that season.

We rode together, Brithelm and Danelle and I, along with a mess of Knights and retainers—from Raphael and Bradley all the way to the dog, Birgis—out from Castle di Caela and south, past the Thelgaard Keep and, keeping the Garnet Mountains to our left, into the sacred Telling Ground that Longwalker and Wanderer, the Namer of the Que-Shu, had marked off for the ceremonies at hand.

I would imagine there were ten thousand Plainsmen camped around us, the air filled with smoke and chanting and the smell of leather and grain and memory.

Memory was the richest of those smells. On the first night, we seated ourselves in the immense mile-wide circle that linked tribe to tribe. The ceremonial spears stood anchored in the ground, atop them the tribal totems—the pelts of leopard and bear and fox, the feathers of eagles, and the antlers of the springbok.

We sat beneath the sign of the antelope, totem of the Que-Nara. Longwalker greeted us and with quiet ceremony draped the hides of antelopes over my shoulders and those of Brithelm. A third, smaller hide, well tanned and softened and white and gray like the peaks of the Vingaards, had been saved for the Lady Dannelle.

They smelled of the plains to the south, those hides—of the clean, unchangeable grasslands and the sudden, crisp, metallic smell in the air when winter snows approach. I nestled into the warmth of the fur and watched the smoke rise from the fire that practical Bradley built in an instant before us.

The smoke, caught up in a strong October breeze, eddied toward the southwest, over Coastlund and out to the Newsea beyond it. It curled and surged like a river, and it circled twice over the large central fire of the Telling before gathering itself into a larger, higher current of smoke and bending away over the horizon.

Longwalker sat down in front of me, and the Telling began.

Wanderer spoke first. His tales told of a country to the

outh, of a people nomadic and tireless, haunted by shifts in
he weather and gaps in their memories. Mournfully the
oung Que-Shu Namer began one telling, then paused, then
old another story he seemed to join in midstride, because at
he heart of each story was the melancholy phrase, "And
his we do not remember. . . ."

He spoke through the first night, and we slept until noon-
ime restlessly. Longwalker woke me when the sun was
igh, his voice encouraging, a strange gleam in his eyes.

"Take off the mantles of sorrow, Solamnic," he said, his
yes fixed on the central fire, "for tonight you will see the
elling brought out of the darkness. You will see the time re-
leemed."

And I confess that the smell in the air was lighter, that
omething arose in the midst of us promising joy and his-
ory, and the second night was rollicksome until the new
Que-Nara Namer began to speak.

First, it was a night of reunion. Ramiro, it seemed, had
nade the long journey westward across Goodlund and Bali-
or and the green lands closer to home, a journey so long
hat I wondered if he had housed himself under his own roof
or more than a night before setting off again. He reclined
»eneath the autumn sky, staring on high at the stars in the
Harp of Branchala. A glass of Thorbardin Eagle rested atop
is ample stomach, and his huge head, its long black curly
ocks spread like a fan, rested in the lap of a Plainswoman I
lad never seen before, all paint and nose rings and torrid at-
ention.

He was in good hands, it seemed, though hands that
night threaten his heart with their energies.

I had spoken to the big Knight and was returning to our
:ampfire when the Que-Nara Namer took his place at the
:entral fire and began his telling. The voice sounded famil-
ar, and at once I stopped and squinted toward the great
nonumental blaze.

The Que-Nara Namer was a black man dressed in motley,
and a long, barrel-chested dog squatted beside him.

"Shardos!" I whispered. Of course it was Shardos. It surprised me how I had missed it all along.

The juggler crouched before the fire as he told of the first days of our adventure. From his patchwork robe, he took some glittering tools and began to speak of Longwalker.

I felt a hand on my shoulder and looked up to see the big Plainsman standing beside me.

"Here," he said, handing me a thin band of silver. "Take this to the central fire. The juggler has need of it."

At the moment I stepped into the light of the Namer's fire, Shardos's hand was extended. He smiled as I set the silver in his hand, and he began to tell *my* part of the story as all of the peoples—the Que-Shu, the Que-Kiri, the Que-Nara—listened exultantly.

As my old friend spoke, all the events were set in place, from the banishment of Firebrand in the centuries past down to the Night of Telling and the Namer who seated himself before us. The old man told the stories in the present tense, his hands busy over the fire, twisting yet another piece of silver, which Longwalker himself had brought forth, onto the one I had given him. The Plainsmen nodded around him, their eyes closed as the things he told happened for the first time in their brilliant imaginings.

Shardos brought something from his pockets, and for the first time, I knew fully of what had occurred beneath Castle di Caela, knew of the dark god's plotting and how the thirteenth stone in the crown had shut its wearer in the past, where no voice, human or divine, could reach him through the stones.

But the end of the tale was the best part, for Shardos stood, holding aloft a silver circlet—the restored Crown of the Namer, adorned with twelve opals. Around him, the Que-Tana, robed against the light of the moons and stars, began the Song of Firebrand, the words of which made sense now. For, no longer twisted by that villain beneath the mountain, they found their fitting and proper hero there at the heart of the Telling.

> *"In the country of the blind,*
> *Where the one-eyed man is king*
> *And the stones are eyes of gods*
> *And pathways to remembering,*

"There three centuries of gloom
Pass under rending, drought, and wars,
Until the Firebrand comes to us,
Upon his brow a dozen stars.

Out of his wound the stones will speak,
Will lead us from the groves of night
And with the power of life and death
Restore us to forgotten light."

As he stood amid his newfound and singing people, the juggler held aloft the thirteenth godseye, then handed it to Longwalker beside him, who passed it to Wanderer, who passed it to yet another Plainsman elder.

As the stone approached me from hand to hand, Shardos sang the names of the heroes, and the Plainsmen chanted back a refrain, as a thousand voices joined in committing those names to memory:

"First Bayard Brightblade I give you,
Who rules over Castle di Caela . . ."
"We remember Bayard Brightblade . . ."

"And Ramiro of the Maw,
Enormous in yearning and battle . . ."
"We remember Ramiro of the Maw . . ."

On he went, through Brithelm and Dannelle and Oliver and my own lost brother, but my eyes lost focus and my heart was peaceful as my own name was reconciled with a new and awaited meaning.

"And Sir Galen, keeper of the one stone,
Whose name in our language means 'healer' . . ."
"We remember Galen Pathwarden . . ."

I turned, looking around me as though the celebration would be joined by all my friends and acquaintances, as though they all would be staring straight at me with looks of wonderment and suddenly discovered respect. But all eyes were on the Namer Shardos, who slowly slipped the crown onto his head.

All eyes except for those of Bradley, the young engineer, who was trying his skills on the intricate harnesswork that clothed a young Plainswoman about his age.

There was reconciliation all around me that night.

* * * * *

It spread all over the campsite and lasted the week. I remember the third night, remember Dannelle calling to me as Brithelm replaced me on the watch in early morning. I went to her, expecting that she had remembered at last some other thing she needed to scold me for, but it was not the case at all.

Instead, hers were the suggestions I had pondered making myself those many nights before on the crest of the Vingaards, before we all descended to the dark and the Que-Tana and my captive brother.

Dannelle said she had found the best of spots to bed down, safe but out of sight of the celebrants. That the spot was warm indeed, and surprisingly spacious.

Room enough for two, as she had calculated.

I believed her calculations were correct.

As we joined hands and slipped between brush and high grass to the place and circumstances she had in mind, she whispered to me words that told me the deeds I had dreamt of were preparing to come to pass.

"If you breathe a word of this, to anyone, I'll kill you."

* * * * *

My story ends back at the castle, on a winter night in my firelit chambers.

Tomorrow some of my companions head west, Brithelm back to the mountains, where he will search for his scattered followers—for meteorological old women and insomniac captains and the beautiful night visitors. Together they will raise his abbey yet again and lure down the birds for omens.

Of all things, Father will join his middle son in the life

contemplative. The clerical robe seems ill-fitting, ridiculous upon him. But then, my armor looked so on me not a month ago.

Father seeks monastic life, having left the moathouse to Gileandos, of all people. It seems there was an oath that the old man uttered somewhere beneath the foundations of Castle di Caela—something about gladly giving up all his holdings to see Gileandos again. Whatever the circumstances, the old scholar departed two nights ago for the moathouse, intent on returning to his library and his alembic, both of which smell of juniper and must.

I hear he was having trouble sitting in the saddle.

Something, no doubt, that took place underground.

As for me, I shall stay here at Castle di Caela for a while. Bayard is still confined by his injuries, and the Lady Enid will soon be confined under more delicate circumstances. Brandon Rus is gone on his pilgrimage, strangely lighter of heart, and Ramiro is packing his belongings (and the energetic Plainswoman) for a trip back to his castle in the Maw.

Someone will have to run this place in all the absences.

Sir Robert and I have a plan, you see, regarding horse races in the huge bailey yard. There is room for dogs in the restored grounds, and the servants have been put to work gathering up mechanical birds from storage.

Given a couple of months in which nothing dire happens, we will have this place back in order—a proper place in which the heir of Bayard Brightblade and Enid di Caela can grow into his or her inheritance.

Or so I think tonight, as the winter wind swirls around the castle like water or the Namer's smoke, and I prepare to continue what started at the Telling on the Plains of Southlund. It is time, you see, for my nightly journey, swaddled in blankets and desire, into candlelight and perfume and endearments and the presence of the incomparable Dannelle di Caela.

An adventure not without its own wonders and dangers.

The Elven Nations Trilogy is back in print in all-new editions!

FIRSTBORN
Volume One

Paul B. Thompson & Tonya C. Cook

In moments, the fate of two leaders is decided. Sithas, firstborn son of the elf monarch Sithel, is destined to inherit the crown and kingdom from his father. His twin brother Kith-Kanan, born just a few heartbeats later, must make his own destiny. Together—and apart—the princes will see their world torn asunder for the sake of power, freedom, and love.

New edition in October 2004

THE KINSLAYER WAR
Volume Two

Douglas Niles

Timeless and elegant, the elven realm seems unchanging. But when the dynamic human nation of Ergoth presses on the frontiers of the Silvanesti realm, the elves must awaken—and unite—to turn back the tide of human conquest. Prince Kith- Kanan, returned from exile, holds the key to victory.

New edition in November 2004

THE QUALINESTI
Volume Three

Paul B. Thompson & Tonya C. Cook

Wars done, the weary nations of Krynn turn to rebuilding their exhausted lands. In the mountains, a city devoted to peace, Pax Tharkas, is carved from living stone by elf and dwarf hands. In the new nation of Qualinesti, corruption seeks to undermine this new beginning. A new generation of elves and humans must band together if the noble experiment of Kith-Kanan is to be preserved.

New edition in December 2004

The Ergoth Trilogy

Paul B. Thompson & Tonya C. Cook

Explore the history of the ancient DRAGONLANCE® world!

THE WIZARD'S FATE
Volume Two

The old Emperor is dead, sending shock
waves throughout the Ergoth Empire. Dark
forces gather as two brothers vie bitterly for the
throne. Key to the struggle for succession are
the rogue sorcerer Mandes and peasant general
Lord Tolandruth—sworn enemies of one
another—and the noble lady Tol loves, whose
first loyalty is to her husband, the Crown Prince.

A HERO'S JUSTICE
Volume Three

The Ergoth Empire has been invaded on two
fronts, and the teeming horde streaming across
the plain is no human army. As the warriors
of Ergoth reel back, defeated and broken, the
cry goes up far and wide, "Where is Lord
Tolandruth?!" Banished by Emperor Ackal V, no
one had seen Tol in more than six years. To save
Ergoth, Egrin Raemel's son rides forth to find Tol
and forge an alliance between a kender queen,
an aging beauty, and a lost and brilliant general.

December 2004

A WARRIOR'S JOURNEY
Volume One
Available Now

Strife and warfare tear at the land of Ansalon

FLIGHT OF THE FALLEN
The Linsha Trilogy, Volume Two
Mary H. Herbert

As the Plains of Dust are torn asunder by invading barbarian forces, Rose Knight Linsha Majere is torn between two vows— her pledge to the Knighthood, and her pledge to guard the eggs of the dragon overlord Iyesta. To keep her honor, Linsha will have to make the ultimate sacrifice.

CITY OF THE LOST
The Linsha Trilogy, Volume One
Available Now!

LORD OF THE ROSE
Rise of Solamnia, Volume One
Douglas Niles

In the wake of the War of Souls, the realms of Solamnia are wracked by strife and internecine warfare, and dire external threats lurk on its borders. A young lord, marked by courage and fateful flaws, emerges from the hinterlands. His vow: he will unite the fractious reaches of the ancient knighthood— or die in the attempt.

November 2004